Breksta's Academy

Natasha Quay

Breksta's Academy
Published by Ensisheim Partners LLC.
Seattle, WA

Paperback: 979-8-218-22946-7
Hardcover: 979-8-218-22947-4
YOUNG ADULT FICTION / Visionary & Metaphysical

ENSISHEIM
PARTNERS LLC

To my family and friends who stood by me through
the ups and downs of writing this book and in my life.
And to anyone else who has dreams of writing:
never put down the pen.

PART ONE
LOSS

PROLOGUE

LEGENDS EXIST in tandem with sorrow. They are born in the darkness of the world and carry within them a shining torch that spreads light until the darkness dissipates and the world comes into view. This legend, whose light outshone the brightest stars she counted in the sky, lived where the sun was always shining and the rivers ran with gold.

CHAPTER I

AS IT DID EACH MORNING, the sun awoke and peaked over the mountains to watch the sleeping people bundled tightly in their blankets. It shone upon the villagers, coaxing them from their slumber. The people stretched their aching limbs on their hard beds and—bundled in blankets—slowly walked to the kitchen to brew steaming mugs of coffee. Their hands warmed at the touch, and the steam brought feeling back into their cherry faces.

As the villagers awakened, the sun sent shafts of light through the leaves, illuminating the tops of the trees in brilliant shades of green. A river cut from the tips of the mountain across the village and onward, leaving a wide wound in the landscape. The river shimmered and twirled, dancing with the sun, and let the light form gems on its surface. The animals had long awakened; their voices and footsteps created the musical sounds of the forest as they began foraging through the tall trees and shrubbery.

Near the edge of the river, a butter-yellow house and its gray hat-shaped roof shielded a mother and daughter from the whistling wind. The house had a small porch surrounded by a white railing that held pots of Alaskan poppies, wild irises, lupines, and bog-rosemaries. Their vibrant purples, pinks, and reds contrasted with the pale colors of the house. Each flower was under the intent care of the mother, whose hands were always gloved with a layer of dirt or dust.

Today, the daughter emerged from the house first. Her hands grasped the edges of her wool blanket and pulled it around herself. Her short white hair was cut just below her ears, making her curls ride up the back of her neck. Her gray eyes were filled with excitement as she gazed out at the charging river that rippled like a horse's mane. She brought the pitcher inside and filled it to the brim with cold water, just like she did every morning. Then, she tipped the heavy pitcher over her mother's flowers and watered each pot with her small, shaking hands.

She then went back into the house and placed a faded brown stool in front of the stove. She took everything she needed from the refrigerator and placed all her supplies on the counter beside her. She cracked three eggs and let the cold yolks flow into the light teal bowl, which to her was the most beautiful color of all. She turned the knob on the stove and flicked the lighter. Fire caught, and a blue sunflower burst came to life. Before long, she had prepared a large breakfast of eggs, ham, and slices of apples that her mother had bought from the market just the day before. The circular wooden table to the right of the room now had plates of warm, colorful, steaming food. The young girl ran into her mother's room and was met with darkness and a pile of twisted blankets.

"Mom? Are you there?" she said, her feeble voice traveling through the air.

She was met with an unconscious response of "What?"

"It's Saturday. And … I thought we could go out to the woods again," the girl said, gripping her thumb between her fingers and picking at the cuticles.

Her mother's disheveled appearance surfaced out of the ocean of blankets. Her pale face wore her years of labor, and her tangled hair fell across both shoulders in white waves.

"Oh, what time is it?" her mother asked, flicking on her nightstand light, breaking the curtain of darkness.

"It's already nine," the girl murmured. She shifted her weight forward and back impatiently.

"Oh, my goodness," her mother said, throwing off the covers and stepping out of the bed in her oversized T-shirt and flannel pajama pants.

"I'm very sorry, Breksta," she said as she pulled on her furry jacket, "I got back very late last night. I didn't mean to sleep in." She flashed an apologetic smile and took her daughter's hand.

"Mm, what's that smell?" she asked, a mischievous smile replacing her apologetic one. "Did someone already make breakfast?"

"I cooked them perfectly," Breksta exclaimed, skipping toward the breakfast table and presenting her delicately made food.

"Wow! That's incredible. You made this for me?" her mother breathed, taking in the full table of colors.

Breksta smiled as her pride bubbled to the surface.

Her mother slipped into one of the chairs and folded her hands neatly in her lap. "So, Chef Breksta. What do you have for me today?"

"Scrambled eggs with cut ham inside, and apples that are dipped in salt because you said it makes them stay fresh," Breksta said, clasping her hands behind her back and beaming.

"Well, I'll just help myself to this delicious-looking feast."

Her mother began shoveling the now cooled eggs into her mouth. Breksta looked earnestly at her mother, judging each bite for any bits of imperfection.

"Mm. This is astonishing, Breksta. You have a real talent," her mother said between bites, savoring each one.

A smile carved itself from ear to ear as Breksta slipped into the other chair. She bit into a piece of sliced apple and felt the crisp juice sweeten her throat as she swallowed. Together, they finished both of their plates and shared the bowl of apples until their bellies were swollen.

"So, what do you want to do today?" her mother said as she swirled a thin mixture of soap and water around the dishes.

"How about we go make fairy houses in the woods? We haven't done it in a while and I miss it," Breksta said as she glanced back and forth between her mother and the forest.

"How about fairy houses?" Her mother smiled, looking back to Breksta's earnest expression before she began to dry the dishes.

"And I was thinking we could have a picnic? Maybe?" Breksta asked, her voice arching up as she analyzed her mother's expression.

"Get the chocolate from the cupboard please."

Her mother rummaged through their closets until she came up with a worn basket. The flannel layering the inside was pressed deep into the crevices of the basket. Its red-and-white pattern was faded, and the threads had come loose from use.

Together, they packed sandwiches with fresh salami that they had bought at their weekly market as well as two apples and a half-eaten bar of chocolate Breksta had been saving for a special occasion.

With that, they began a long trek through the fresh grass. As they passed the other houses in various colors of light blue, pink, and white, some people sat in rocking chairs on their porches. Breksta waved and greeted them joyfully.

"Good morning, Mrs. Aileen!"

"Why, hello, Breksta! Morning, Asteria! What are you up to on this fine day?" the old woman said as she waved from the open window at Breksta.

"Mom and I are going for a picnic in the woods!"

"A picnic! That sounds like so much fun. Enjoy, sweetie!" Mrs. Aileen said happily, a wide smile spreading across her face as she watched Breksta skip toward the forest.

"Have a great day, Mrs. Aileen."

"Be safe, dearies!" the old woman called after them.

Breksta entered the forest and took a deep breath. The smell was always the same: wet moss, earthy trees, and just a whiff of a flowery scent. She grinned as she raced through the trees. As her mother lugged the weighty basket next to her thigh, she smiled at her daughter's joy of being in the forest. Breksta turned back and looked for her mother.

"Come on, Mom!" she shouted, barely able to contain her energy within the bounds of her skin.

"I'm coming, I'm coming," her mother called back. "You go first and find an open spot. I'll catch up."

Breksta nodded and bounded into the dense woods. She flew past the trees—a mix of birch, spruce, and pine that she had memorized like the back of her hand. The ground was lined with the bodies of fallen leaves, their multi-colored corpses crackling underneath Breksta's feet. A small stream wove in jagged patterns through the forest so that with every step Breksta took, she got

4

closer to the stream's origin. Finally, she arrived at an oval clearing with trees surrounding her. The fairy house she had created long ago sagged at the foot of a birch tree; its small leaf roof was layered with twigs that made it cave inward. Only the skin and seeds remained of an orange, Breksta's offering that she had left in the past; its flesh was eaten by rabbits or other critters.

The stream slithered around the clearing, filling the air with sounds of burbling water. Birds filled the neighboring trees above and flitted with each passing breeze that swayed the trees. The warm sun shone through the treetops and sent warm tingles into Breksta's arms.

"Mom, I found the spot!" Breksta shouted, cupping her slowly warming hands around her mouth. She was met with silence except for the shifting of leaves above her.

"Mom?" she asked hesitantly, looking around the trees in her vicinity. Again, she was met with silence.

"Are you there?" Breksta asked. Her throat began to close as her heart sped up.

Without her mother, her best friend, at her side, the shadows of the forest elongated, and the dark parts that her mother always shielded her from weren't held back anymore. Breksta felt as if the forest was closing in on her, the branches of the trees reaching out toward her. The shadows of the bushes grew to immense sizes, making the trees seem dark and ominous.

"Mom, where are you? This isn't funny! Why do you always try to scare me?" Breksta backed out of the clearing until she reached one of the surrounding trees, the rough bark scraping against her back.

Suddenly, a gunshot broke the silence, sending birds screeching out of the trees, their wings flapping loudly. Breksta screamed before a familiar figure ran up behind her and wrapped her arms around Breksta.

"Hey, it's okay. You're safe," Breksta's mother's soft voice spoke.

Tears, more of surprise and shock than fear, pricked Breksta's eyes as she turned to her mother.

"Shh ... I'm here," her mother's voice soothed as her mother's hands rubbed the space between Breksta's shoulder blades.

Across the river, a broad figure stepped out from between the trees. He let out a deep call. "Why, hello!"

Breksta quickly turned to watch a large, bearded man wearing a collared leather jacket leap across the river and into the clearing. He walked toward them carrying a small brown body, its hind legs dangling from his massive hands. Blood dripped from the animal and left wine-red dots on the forest floor. A rabbit, Breksta realized. One that he had just killed.

"I'm sorry. I didn't know you two were in the forest today. Its hunting season after all," he said. His voice vibrated like gravel against metal.

Breksta couldn't speak; her eyes stayed glued to the rabbit's body. Its expression, the expression of immense fear, was not washed away by death, and made Breksta's heart contract with a cold feeling.

"Next time be more careful, Dave," Breksta's mother said coldly, her eagle eyes trained on the man.

"I will. I'm very sorry, Asteria," he said, raising his free hand in a gesture of surrender. "If I may ask, why are you both out here today?"

Her mother gently patted her back, trying to soothe Breksta's uneven breathing.

"Breksta wanted to spend some time outside," her mother said as she put down the basket and knelt beside Breksta. "I like to take her out here so she can learn survival skills. Something that I didn't get to learn as a child."

"Well, that sounds like a lovely idea. The children need to learn to live off the land, even though they are blessed with a roof over their heads and warm beds," Dave said, putting his rifle back into its sling carry.

"My thinking exactly," Asteria replied.

"By the way, I don't know if you've heard, but some new folks arrived from the east."

"What folks?" Asteria asked nonchalantly.

"Just some military folk from the east. Nice military-type plane they got too. I overheard some sort of runaway they're tryin'a catch."

"What did they look like, Dave?" Asteria probed cautiously, her voice turning low.

Breksta could not help but feel fear at her mother's tone, one that she rarely heard. It only surfaced when Breksta had done something wrong or potentially dangerous.

"They were wearing black and carried some fancy rifles. There was also a woman with a pretty face and fiery hair who seemed to be in charge. Don't see that sort around often," Dave chuckled.

Asteria was silent for a few moments, the information sinking in. "Well, it was great seeing you, Dave. Catch you another time," she said, taking Breksta's small hand.

Asteria waved at Dave before picking up the basket and tugging Breksta's hand.

"Bye, Asteria. And you too, Breksta. Sorry to have been hunting near your picnic," Dave added as he waved back and continued his soundless footsteps against the forest floor.

Breksta managed a small wave before her mother's strong grip tugged her in the direction they had come from.

"Why are we going?" Breksta asked, looking up at her mother.

"I-I forgot about something at home."

"It's okay, Mom. We can still have the pic—"

"Don't whine, Breksta," Asteria scolded, gripping her daughter's hand even tighter. "We just need … to go."

They made the twists and turns until they reached the edge of the forest, the sky breaking through the blockade of leaves.

Her mother ran faster as they entered the village. Her head whipped back and forth to look between the houses. To Breksta, nothing looked awry. The people still sat in their chairs, the sky still shone its illuminant color of blue, and the birds still sat in their trees to chirp out their songs.

Breksta was confused. Her mother's face now reflected a petrifying terror that she had never seen before, one that contrasted with the worry her mother conveyed when Breksta was sick or the fear she displayed when icy gusts of wind blew open the windows in the winter months.

Asteria, however, had always known this day would come. Just not now, not when everything was going so well and Breksta was still young. She knew what was coming and why. The two of them needed to get away as quickly as possible.

Asteria and Breksta made it back to their yellow house just as the bells of the chapel rung out ten o'clock. Asteria frantically shoved her belongings into a worn black duffel while Breksta stood in the hallway of her mother's room.

"Breksta, go get your clothes," Asteria commanded as she pinched the area around the duffel's zipper.

"Why?"

"Just go and get them."

"But—"

"Now, Breksta!" Asteria shouted.

Breksta flinched, her mother's anger hit like small drops of ice water, pelting her heart.

Breksta ran to her room and grabbed her T-shirts and rainbow-colored tights. She also grabbed her last birthday present that her mother made for her for her tenth birthday. It was a white dress that hung low around her knees, adorned with white petals and pieces of lace. Finally, she grabbed her small stuffed rabbit. "Bun Bun," Breksta called it. Its eyes were two solid black buttons, and its limbs barely clung to its body through bits of string that Asteria had resewn multiple times. Breksta held it in her hands and felt the rough patches of fur underneath her fingers.

"Breksta!" Asteria shouted, breaking her daughter's focus.

Breksta ran to her mother and handed over her things.

"Thank you," Asteria said softly, taking her clothes and putting them into the duffel.

She paused when she saw her daughter's rabbit. Asteria smiled. She gently took the rabbit, placed it in the middle of various clothes, and zipped the duffel shut. Her mother quickly hoisted the duffel atop her back, pausing to stabilize herself, before taking Breksta's hand.

"You ready for an adventure? We're going camping to practice your survival skills. This camping trip will be your longest test yet," Asteria said, a pained smile touching her lips.

"Why are we leaving so suddenly, Mom?" Breksta asked as they walked out of the house hand in hand.

"It'll be good for us," Asteria said, her lie poisoning her tongue. "It's time to say goodbye. We're not going to be back for a while."

"But I don't want to go anywhere right now," Breksta implored. Stopping, she slipped her hand out of her mother's.

"We don't have time for this, Breksta," Asteria muttered, reaching out toward her daughter. "We need to go now."

Asteria turned toward the forest and pulled Breksta, but Breksta turned back to face their butter-yellow house. Windows were open and the breeze flew through, making the curtains flutter. The flowers sat on the porch with their petals faced outward toward the sun, as if they were waving at Breksta and her mother.

"We'll be back soon," Breksta murmured and waved back at the flowers, hoping her promise would come true. A small tear quivered, slid down Breksta's face, and landed on the soil next to her house, leaving a piece of her there. Her mother jerked her arm, pulling Breksta away from the openness of the road and into the folds of the forest.

"We just need to get to the next village quickly," Asteria murmured, more for herself than Breksta.

"Mom ... why?" Breksta demanded as she pulled her mom around by her jacket and pointed in the direction of the place where they'd lived all her life.

Asteria stopped herself and gazed sadly at her daughter. "Please, honey. Just this once, don't ask questions." Asteria took her daughter's round face in her hands, gently caressing her cheeks with her flower-scented hands. "Could you do that for me?" Asteria said, her eyes pleading with deep sadness that Breksta saw but did not understand.

Breksta had never seen her mother's eyes hold such pain. "Okay," she murmured in response.

"Thank you, sweetie," Asteria replied softly, squeezing her daughter's hand tightly as they began to run.

CHAPTER 2

ON A NEIGHBORING HILL lay a large black airplane. Nearby, small figures in black-clad uniforms stood with their matching black rifles. A woman stood in front of them and issued orders in rapid, clipped English. The soldiers stood shoulder to shoulder, hands clasped behind their backs, in two rows. Their black-masked faces were directed at the woman.

"You have an hour to complete this operation and capture the fugitive," she said coldly as her eyes scanned each soldier. "Leave no house unsearched. Any lapse in action will be regarded as purposeful disobedience on your overall performance. Don't disappoint."

"Yes, ma'am," the soldiers shouted in unison, their voices tripping over one another to be the loudest.

"Actions against the villagers and fugitive are allowed. But keep the fugitive alive. I'll deal with her myself." The woman's eyes flashed with cold fury.

As she paced, the two pistols holstered on each side bounced against her hips. Her fiery red hair fell in a tight braid along her spine. Her piercing brown eyes accentuated her words and held the troops in line. She flicked her hand and her soldiers scattered, filing into the village like ants.

"Go in pairs or trios. Search each house. Then move on," the first soldier, deep voiced, called out before entering the village.

The first two soldiers marched on until they reached a blue house with an empty porch at the very edge of the village. The planks creaked under the weight of the soldiers as they stepped onto the property. The first soldier ripped open the door and stepped over the threshold, his boots slamming against the wooden floor with the sound of booming drums.

A silver-haired woman bundled in a quilt sat in a worn chair facing the door. Her wrinkled hands slowly wove green threads together, forming a cloth that stretched to the floor. Her cheeks were pink from the cold and her skin sagged, but her blue eyes flashed brightly in surprise at the soldiers' entrance.

"Who are you?" she asked, looking up from her craft.

"Where's the fugitive?" he commanded.

"Excuse me, but would you mind explaining who you are and the purpose for this rude intrusion?" she pressed on.

"Search her room," the first soldier commanded, pointing down the hallway to the dimly lit room behind the woman.

The second soldier, whose hands drifted to her gun unconsciously, nodded and walked past the woman with perfectly timed steps.

"Excuse me! Kindly leave my room please!" the woman shouted as she slowly lifted herself from her chair, her thin shoulders shaking from the exertion.

The sounds of the soldier ripping open the old woman's dresser could be heard from the front room. The woman set down her blanket and hobbled toward her room until she felt a rough grip of a glove against her frail wrist.

"It would be best if you cooperated with us. For your sake," the soldier said roughly, turning the woman to face him.

"Don't touch me."

Her frail appearance contrasted with her powerful voice that snapped at the soldier. She tugged her wrist out of his grasp with her other hand before making her way to her room. The soldier didn't stop the woman and followed behind her.

The neatly made bed on the left side of the room had been overturned to reveal the bed's wooden ribcage. The mattress itself lay on its side on the floor, the sheets removed and thrown into a gray pile atop the bedframe. The wooden dresser was thrown open with clothes cascading to the floor. The faded wool rug had been pulled up and strewn near the door.

"There are no signs of a fugitive in this room," the female soldier announced as she stood with her feet glued together and her posture perfect.

The old woman covered her mouth, looking at her disheveled room before speaking. "What's the purpose of this?"

Her voice shook with anger and disgust as the soldier gave his calm reply. "Do you feel like answering now?"

"Leave my house, now!"

The soldier sighed. This time he did not hold back his strength when he grasped the woman, locking her wrists in his grasp and dragging her back into the front room.

"Let go of me!" the woman shouted as she pulled her hands.

Her strength was overshadowed by the soldier's hands that held on to the woman like iron handcuffs.

"Sit down," he said harshly, shoving her into the chair.

The woman stumbled before landing abruptly. Her breaths came out shallow and her pinned silver hair came undone as she looked up at the two soldiers.

"I'll ask you again. Where is Asteria Vilkas, the fugitive?"

The soldier's eyes searched the woman's disheveled face; her blue eyes shone with anger.

"I don't know," the woman retorted angrily through clenched teeth.

She tried to lift herself from the chair, but the soldier shoved her down again.

"Don't move!" the soldier shouted.

The woman winced, making the wrinkles deeper on her face.

"Don't make this difficult. Where is Asteria Vilkas?" the soldier's dark eyes shone dangerously at the woman.

"I will say again. I don't know!"

Just as the words left the woman's mouth, the soldier's hand came across her face. The creases of the soldier's glove dug sharp pain into her face as red lines and purple splotches appeared.

The woman sucked in a breath before looking up at the soldier with cold fury. She lunged at the soldier and brought her bony hand across his masked face. The mask took most of the blow, but his eyes still filled with anger. He reached back until he felt the familiar cold of his pistol and pulled it out of its holster. The woman took in a sharp breath and stepped back at the sight of the gun. The soldier aimed his gun at the woman's chest, closing the distance with three steps.

"I will ask one final time," he murmured into the woman's face. "Where. Is. Asteria Vilkas?"

"Why?"

When the soldier gave no response, she spat at the soldier's feet and shouted, "I'll never tell you anything."

The soldier lowered the gun to his hip, looking at his saliva-covered shoe.

"Fine. You had your chance to cooperate."

The woman hobbled back and clenched her fists, moving out of reach of the soldier. She watched the soldier's eyes intently, the only part of him that conveyed any true emotion. His dark brown eyes were calm for a few seconds, until his eyes flashed with a flood of anger. The woman's eyes widened as she saw his eyes; a gasp left her lips as if an imprisoned ghost had escaped.

"No—"

He lifted his gun to the woman's left leg and pulled the trigger. A scream erupted from the old woman's lips as the bullet struck her thigh and shattered her bone with an explosion. Her left leg collapsed under the pain, and she crashed to the floor bloodied and breathless.

Her hair fell across her face as she looked up at the soldier's cold eyes. Her own blue eyes were a mix of pain and anger, not the fear that the soldier had hoped for. That didn't matter to him though. He was patient. The soldier pointed the pistol at the woman until the tip touched her trembling forehead.

"Tell me where she lives or the next one's in your skull." His cold voice sent shivers along the woman's back as she covered her leg to try and stop the bleeding.

The woman closed her eyes and swallowed before murmuring a soft, "God, please forgive me."

"Three."

The woman opened her eyes and mouth, but no sound came out.

"Two."

The woman quickly swallowed before her broken voice let loose of her lips. "She went into the woods."

"Where?" the soldier pressed further as he shifted the gun toward the woman's left temple.

Her breaths came out shallow and fast as she continued, "The left side of this house."

The words poisoned the woman immediately after she spoke them. Regret spread across her face, replacing her anger.

"Come on," the soldier called, pulling the gun from the woman's head.

The second soldier, who was leaning against the wall the entire time, stood and moved to the male soldier's side.

"Our work here is done," he declared.

As the two soldiers reached the threshold of the house, the old woman spoke. "Don't hurt them! They're just children!" she pleaded.

She pulled herself slowly across the floor until she reached the soldier who'd shot her. Extending one arm, she grabbed his wrist tightly. He turned back to the woman's pleading blue eyes.

"Please. They're … just children," she begged, her eyes filled with tears of pain and regret.

The soldier took a moment before answering in his cold voice, "Justice knows no age and must be carried out without discrimination."

He yanked his wrist out of the woman's grip, and she fell back to the floor. The wooden door swung shut in her face, and the woman finally allowed tears to trickle down her face.

"I'm sorry, I'm sorry, I'm sorry," she whispered over and over until the soldier's footsteps faded.

At first, the image of Breksta and her mother was the center of her mind's attention. The fugitive, the soldier had called her. *No*, the woman thought to herself. *Not that sweet woman and her beautiful child.*

"I don't believe it," she uttered to the empty room.

Soon, the searing pain of her leg stole her attention. Her eyes gently closed as the waves of pain drowned her and her head fell against the wooden floorboards painted with her blood.

Loud noises sounded from outside, footsteps banging on wooden floors. All was lost to the woman as her mind drifted slowly toward darkness.

"Forgive me," she mouthed one last time before all went dark.

The door flung open to reveal Dave from two houses down with fresh patches of bruises lining the underside of his eyes and jaw.

"Aileen!" he shouted as he entered his neighbor's home. Dave knelt and shook the woman's frail shoulders. "Aileen, wake up! The soldiers are gone," Dave said more quietly, seeing the trail of blood surrounding the old woman. Sadness pricked his heart as he found no pulse with his fingers underneath her jaw.

"I-I'm sorry," Dave whispered hoarsely, his voice stumbling. Tears formed in his eyes as he cradled the old woman's body in his thick arms. "I should've been here for you. Please forgive me," Dave managed to choke out.

He didn't speak for a long time as he gently rocked the woman's body. Dave slid two fingers over the old woman's eyes and sealed them shut forever.

CHAPTER 3

BREKSTA AND HER MOTHER entered the forest, their second home. The woods around them deepened, the trees intertwined their branches tighter, and the leaves blocked more light from entering. Breksta's shorter legs could barely keep up with her mother's fast pace. Their feet crunched the dry leaves on the ground, leaving a trail of sounds and dead leaf corpses behind.

Although her mother had trained her well, nervousness stirred in her stomach, and she couldn't focus on keeping her breathing level. With each passing breath, a tight belt encircled Breksta's ribcage tighter and tighter until her breath came out in short puffs. The trees thickened, and the forest began to look more and more unfamiliar as they went deeper. The clearing that Breksta had entered an hour before was far behind them. The stream that Dave had crossed was beside them, the only indication that they were still in the same forest.

Breksta tried to avoid every root and twig that threatened to trip her, but her feet were slowly growing heavy and sluggish.

"Can we take a break? I. Need. Water," Breksta managed to croak out of her dried throat.

Asteria turned back and allowed her speeding feet to slow. "Umm … alright. But quickly."

Asteria dropped the hefty duffel to the ground with a thump and handed a dented thermos to Breksta. The water was magic to Breksta's throat, dissolving all the dry crevices and soothing the aches. She closed her eyes as the cool water flowed down her throat. Soon, she stopped herself, remembering her training to conserve water and resources. To her dismay, she had drunk too much. Only half of the thermos's water remained.

"I'm sorry," Breksta said with an apologetic wince. Her eyes turned toward her mother in shame.

Asteria took back the thermos with a disappointed look. "We'll run down to the stream and refill it. But don't forget in the future."

After her mother refilled the thermos at the water's edge, she instructed, "We need to keep moving." She shoved the refilled thermos into her duffle.

Asteria pulled the duffel onto her shoulders, adjusting to the weight for a moment before continuing forward. The two didn't walk fifty meters before they heard leaves crunch behind them. Asteria whipped her head around and moved to block Breksta.

"Stay behind me," Asteria commanded, the gentle, playful voice of the early morning now gone, replaced with a cold, calculating tone.

Breksta peeked out, gripping the fabric of her jacket in her balled fists. Clad figures dressed in black stepped out from the camouflage of the trees, their faces covered with metal masks, all except for one woman.

"My, my, isn't it my lucky day," a woman said, her voice bright and eerily sweet. "I've finally found the infamous … Asteria Vilkas."

Breksta watched her mother whip out a pistol faster than any of them could register. But what scared Breksta more was that she had never seen her mother use the pistol on anything except large animals. Breksta feared what would happen if the barrel was turned toward other humans.

"Drop the gun. Now!" a boy shouted, pointing the tip of a long, streamline rifle back at Asteria.

"Mom," Breksta exclaimed as she turned her widened eyes toward the boy, tightening her grip on her mother.

"It's alright, Breksta. I'll take care of this," Asteria said, her eyes never leaving the boy's face.

"Asteria Vilkas, you are under arrest—"

A flash of fire emerged from Asteria's pistol, and blood erupted from the boy's chest. Breksta screamed and closed her eyes, grabbing her mother more tightly to block out the vision of the boy. The boy convulsed, his eyes conveying pure shock. He dropped his rifle and clutched his chest, slowly dropping to his knees.

"Ready position!" the woman shouted as her face contorted into cold stone.

The other figures clutched their rifles tighter. Breksta's eyes were drawn to the soldier's blood that flowed, wetting the leaves. The feeling of coldness washed over her as she looked into his empty eyes. The same eyes that belonged to the rabbit. And despite seeing her mother hunt other animals with rifles before, fear clung to her at the death of a person at her mother's hands.

"It's okay, Breksta," Asteria said, never letting her eyes leave the cadets.

Breksta's chest tightened. She looked between her mother and the woman dressed in white heels and a skintight suit, who approached Asteria. Asteria aimed her pistol in response, placing the target between the woman's eyes. The woman also held a pistol with a thin barrel, and she pointed it at Asteria's head.

The woman smiled with her whole mouth, like a rabid dog, her teeth gleaming in the sun's light. "Asteria Vilkas. You are to be tried for your crimes against the United States government," the woman said, joy molding onto her face.

Asteria looked at the woman, her tense body fueled with rage.

"I was only defending my people," her mother said back through clenched teeth. Breksta had never heard her mother speak to another person in such a tone, so different from her usual warmth and kindness.

"Mom, what's happening?" Breksta murmured fearfully.

"Shh … don't worry, I'll explain everything later," Asteria murmured.

The tension in the air was almost unbearable, driving fear into Breksta's gut. To her surprise, her mother dropped her pistol.

"Mom, what are you doing?" Breksta mumbled, her eyes wide.

Swirls of black mist appeared from Asteria's hands, forming a whip that knocked the woman as well as the soldiers onto their backs, the leaves crunching underneath their weight. Breksta gasped as the black mist around her mother swelled, the air vibrating in response.

"Mom! What is—" Breksta was cut off as the fire-haired woman screamed orders at her soldiers.

"Shoot her!" she screamed. Scrambling for their weapons, the soldiers raised their rifles at her mother and Breksta in unison.

Breksta screamed and wrapped her arms around Asteria to stop the bullets. Loud gunfire sounded around her and forced Breksta to cover her ears as bullets whizzed past her. She squeezed her eyes shut and dug her fingernails into the fabric of her mother's jacket. Then, there was silence. Breksta slowly opened her eyes and lifted her head from where it was buried in her mother's back.

"It's okay now, Breksta," her mother said through clenched teeth.

Breksta saw a large dome that encased them both and blocked out even the trees around them. It was like a mixture of sand and fog, swirling around Breksta. She reached out to touch it, watching with wonder as a small purple light grew from the place where the sand met her fingertips.

"Mom, what is this?" Breksta whispered, her heart racing and tears beginning to prickle her eyes.

"This is my magic," Asteria said, her eyes cast down, not meeting Breksta's.

"Magic? What are you talking about? You said magic only exists in myths and legends," Breksta said, drawing her hand back quickly. Her eyes shone as she looked at her mother's galaxy-colored magic that surrounded them.

"I did ... yes. We don't have much time, I'm afraid," Asteria murmured, her eyes pulled tightly shut and her face strained to keep the dome up.

"Why? Can't you just beat those soldiers? With ... your magic?" Breksta said, her eyes riveted on the dome.

"Listen to me, Breksta. There is something you need to know; you will understand it later. One day you will have to choose to save the world or the people you love. When the time came, I ... turned my back on my friends, my people, because I was scared for myself and for you. Yet so many were hurt because of me, Breksta. You must promise that you will choose the world. Promise you will be stronger than me. Please," Asteria said, looking at her daughter with tear-filled eyes that begged more than her words ever could.

Breksta didn't understand. She had never seen her mother cry before, and so her own tears slipped through her eyelashes. "What are you talking about,

Mom? I don't understand!" Breksta said, fear gripping her as she looked at the woman standing in front of her, someone so vulnerable and so different from the strong mother she'd always known.

"Promise me, Breksta!" Asteria shouted, her arms quivering as she tried to hold up the dome.

"I ... I promise," Breksta whispered, her heart fluttering like the wings of the birds she had seen in the trees around her.

"Good. Thank you, my dear," Asteria murmured. A small smile curved upon her lips and her arms relaxed ever so slightly. "I love you, Breksta," she said, looking back and then turning toward the dome. She pulled the dome tighter, pulling Breksta in, and then forced it out with all her might in a circular band. The dark mist collided with the soldiers, and their bodies fell once again with dull thuds. Asteria gathered her foggy magic, dismantling the dome and forming it into a thin, shining whip. She coiled parts of it around her wrist and scanned the soldiers for signs of movement. From behind, Breksta felt a cold arm slink around her neck and pull tightly, firmly locking her head in a strong grip.

"Mom," Breksta choked, extending one hand toward her mother while the other tried to pry the strong hand off her neck.

"Stop, Asteria. Or I will shoot her," the cold voice dripped down Breksta's spine.

Asteria's eyes flooded with panic as she watched her daughter squirm. Asteria slowly lowered her arms, her magic fading into the leaves.

"Very good," the cold voice spoke.

"Give me my daughter," Asteria shouted.

The woman turned her pistol directly at Asteria's stomach and squeezed the trigger. A red flower of blood blossomed on Asteria's shirt. Asteria's eyes widened, bringing her fingers to touch the blood that stained her fingers.

"Mom! No!" Breksta shouted, using both hands to pry off the woman's powerful chokehold.

"After all these years, Asteria Vilkas. You finally get a taste of what it is like to be powerless," she said, gesturing at the wound.

The veins in Asteria's neck spasmed, and her eyes bulged as she slumped to the ground. Her arms shook as she tried to pressure the wound. But gradually, the blood spread, covering the front of her shirt completely.

"Bring her up against the tree," the woman said, waving her hand.

"Leave her alone!" Breksta shouted, slapping her thin hands against the woman's grip.

The drunken-looking soldiers grabbed Asteria's trembling shoulders and yanked her up against a tree.

"I'm sorry," Asteria said, her eyes turning back to gaze at Breksta's fear-ridden face.

"This has gone on long enough. Time's up," the woman said, pointing her pistol at Asteria's head.

"No!" Breksta yelled, she dug her sharp elbow into the woman's stomach and ran to her mother. Breksta stood in front of her mother and blocked Asteria with her small body. "Leave us alone. We didn't do anything."

A soldier approached Breksta and firmly lifted her off her feet.

"Get your hands off of me!" Breksta screamed, her small hands battering the soldier, but no pain registered.

"Don't hurt her, please," Asteria begged, her eyes the size of rubies.

"Let go of me!" Breksta shouted as the soldier's rough hands clamped around her thin wrists and dragged her away.

"This is compensation for killing my family and for your rebels. You will die knowing you couldn't protect them, just like you couldn't protect your daughter." The woman yanked Asteria's face close to hers so that their noses were only a centimeter apart as she spoke.

Asteria spat in the woman's face, pulling an enraged scream from the woman. The woman kicked Asteria's stomach, eliciting a groan from Asteria. Breksta screamed as she watched her mother bend over in pain. Asteria's eyes were beyond recognition as she looked up at the woman, a mixture of pain mingled with grief and sadness. Asteria looked back at her daughter and smiled a final unspoken word.

"I love you, Breksta, more than all the world. Remember your promise…"

"No! Don't touch her, you evil woman! Mom, stop her!" Breksta screamed as she wrenched herself back and forth in the soldier's grasp.

"I'm sorry. I love you," her mother spoke softly as tears dripped down her face.

The woman lifted her handgun and put it on Asteria's temple. Breksta watched as her mother swallowed a trembling breath and looked at her daughter one last time, wearing a sad smile, as if she knew some secret, some small bit of joy in agony that Breksta did not.

"Mom, no!"

Bang! A raw animal scream ripped from Breksta's mouth. She slammed her heel into the knee of the soldier, pushing the soldier's bone inward, and ran over to where her mother lay on the floor. The soldier yelped from the pain and fell to the harsh ground.

"Mom, come back! Please!" Breksta cradled her mother in her arms, looking at the red seeping hole on her mother's forehead. Tears streamed down her cheeks in unending waterfalls.

Breksta howled into the forest. The birds scattered and left, leaving only Breksta, her mother, and the soldiers. From behind, a soldier wrapped his arm around Breksta's stomach. She kicked and fought him, but the soldier lifted her into the air. Desperate, Breksta grasped for her mother. Unable to reach her, she battered her fists against the soldiers. "Let me go!" she screamed.

"Sedate her now," the woman commanded as she began to lead the soldiers out of the forest.

Breksta didn't stop screaming, and her eyes stung from the salt. A sharp pain in the back of Breksta's neck tore another scream out of her mouth. The feeling of a fluid being injected into her spine followed, making her neck bulge and her heart race. She felt her eyes close as her body fell limp against the soldier's back.

The last image she saw was the vision of her mother's open and empty eyes, void of life. It seared into her mind; the mark of death left on her mother's face by the woman. Slowly her mind drifted shut, but she remembered her last thoughts. She wished that they had left her there. Or killed her too. Breksta didn't care; most of her soul had died with her mother. And when a soul is killed, it can never be replaced.

CHAPTER 4

THE SHARP TANG OF METAL snapped Breksta's mind alert. As she opened her eyes, the dark, metallic world around her came rushing into view. The seat underneath her froze her thighs into tense sticks as a harness kept her locked in place.

She didn't see her mother anywhere, only the rows of seats beside her, some occupied with helmets and guns. She quickly turned her head back against the headrest and closed her eyes, the sight of the black metal pistols struck fear into her once more.

Finally, her whirling mind filled in the gaps of the morning. They had been on a picnic journey that turned into an escape, ending with her mother's face splattered with crimson blood. The scene replayed in the back of her closed eyelids. Her mother's empty eyes stared back at her, and she could still feel the soldier's harsh grip against her straining hands as he carried her away from the only person she had ever loved.

She slowly looked down at her thin wrists, imagining that if she didn't see the red marks, this would all be a dream. Alas, the stinging marks from the soldier's hands painted her wrists with abnormal patches of red and purple, removing all hope that this was an illusion.

No matter how hard she tried, she couldn't forget her mother's empty, lifeless eyes. It brought stinging tears to her tightly closed eyes as she tried to hold in her sorrow. The pain drowned her, hitting her with wave after wave as she struggled to swim to the surface and escape. She bit her lip and dug her dirt-stained nails deep into her palms to ground herself. It was as if the pain that she felt on the outside could push the one inside out of sight—and out of mind. Gradually, Breksta's aching heart slowed from its frantic beats so that she could bear to look around her.

She sat on the last row of black chairs; the farthest from her was a large chair near the window with soldiers surrounding it. Beneath her feet, a low hum vibrated up her legs from the floor, a feeling deep in her bones that she had never felt before. Behind the large chair was a glass panel with hundreds of switches and buttons so small that Breksta could not see the labels on them. A wide, arched glass panel showed the night sky outside the window. That was when Breksta realized she was no longer on the ground.

The woman had her back turned to Breksta, speaking in a firm tone to the soldiers. "Cadets, we need to make sure the girl acclimates as quickly as possible to the Academy. If she displays any, and I repeat, any abnormal behavior, report it to me immediately."

The soldiers—or cadets, as the woman called them—kept their gazes locked on the woman. Their masks were off, and Breksta could finally see their faces. They were children. Just like her. Their expressions and behavior were fixated on the woman as they soaked up her every word.

The sight of the woman's fiery red hair, even with her back turned, shot fear through Breksta's stomach. She gasped and clasped her hand over her mouth to not draw attention. Unfortunately, it was too late.

The children turned to her with wide eyes just as Breksta turned away and let her head rest against the chair, praying that they would think she was asleep. But she knew that their sharp eyes had seen her. And she imagined the horrible things they would do to her as their heavy feet thumped towards her.

Her thoughts were confirmed when one boy shouted, "Hey, she's awake!"

She kept her mouth and eyelids tightly sealed and clenched her fists to stop the memory of their masked faces from entering her mind. *They are monsters.*

She felt their presence close to her in her skin, but all she wanted was for them to leave her alone.

"Move aside, cadets. Let me be properly introduced to the girl," the woman's cold voice demanded. As soon as she heard the voice, Breksta's eyes snapped open and found the woman as the cadets parted to let her through. She knelt in front of Breksta so that they were at eye level. The woman's face entrapped Breksta's thoughts, all revolving around her mother's bloodied head and empty eyes. Breksta's pain surged, and tears rose from her eyelids, overflowing even as she turned her head again so the cadets wouldn't see.

The woman extended a hand and gently swiped the tears from Breksta's cheek, without regard for Breksta's violent flinch as soon as their skin touched. Breksta felt as if her stomach was going to hurl itself out of her ribcage even after the woman's hand left her cheek.

"D-don't touch me," she stammered.

The children laughed, making Breksta's lips tremble as she tried her best to keep her tears from falling.

"Let's not have any of that here," the woman said softly, drying the tear against the fabric of her pants. A silence spanned as Breksta's small sobs racked her chest until the woman tilted Breksta's jaw so their eyes met.

"Your name is Breksta, isn't it?" the woman asked.

For once, Breksta saw a flicker of something in her eyes: a gentler look, perhaps. But Breksta must have been mistaken because as soon as she saw the woman's expression, it disappeared, and all that remained was a cold stare. Breksta lowered her head, trying to look anywhere except the woman's face. Breksta had already given her everything. She wouldn't comply by giving her an answer.

The woman gestured for the cadets to sit, whispering quickly to a girl cadet, "Strap in and keep an eye on the route."

"Yes, ma'am," the cadets replied before dispersing into their separate seats and descending into whispers.

Their words cut Breksta like a knife: "Who is this girl?" "She's the daughter of some Dreamer leader!" "Really!? I can't believe she still looks like a normal human being after living with a Dreamer." "But you never know, the corruption might run deeper, we just can't see it. That's why the director makes sure we watch them."

Dreamers? Breksta had never heard of that before. She wondered why they were using the word to talk about her. But the word soon fled from her mind once the woman began speaking again. The woman sighed before pulling Breksta's head up with her hand again. "Shush … Don't be afraid. I'm not going to hurt you."

Breksta's mind spun. The woman's voice was kind and gentle, like the birds that sang in the woods of her house. But as soon as she met this bird's eyes, her mother's blood-seeping wound and empty eyes returned, and the waves of sadness crashed down on her. Slowly, she turned toward the woman and listened without looking into her eyes.

"That's it. Good girl. Now we can get properly introduced," the woman said sweetly as she shifted into the seat beside Breksta.

Breksta felt the woman's eyes on her, making her shrink inward from her sharp gaze.

"I am the director. Always address me as Madam Director or just the director. Understood?"

Breksta tried to answer, but her throat was dry, and all that came out were small mouselike squeaks. She clamped her mouth shut and tried to ignore the snickers of the soldiers that had heard her.

"Here, drink it all. You need it." The woman gently nudged, handing Breksta a bottle of water from an empty seat beside her.

Breksta took the water into her small hands and supported it with her legs. The bottle was heavier than she thought it would be. She looked to the woman who nodded at the bottle and unscrewed the lid for Breksta. Breksta hefted the bottle to her lips carefully and felt the clear water soothe her throat. She closed her eyes and drank gulp after gulp until all that remained was the plastic container.

"You must have been thirsty," the woman chuckled as she took the plastic from Breksta, who wiped her mouth sheepishly.

"Th-hank y-you, M-madam … Di-rec-tor," Breksta said slowly, sounding out each syllable and testing out the words. She kept her head lowered as she awaited the director's response.

"Yes, very good," the woman said, smiling so wide that it pulled wrinkles next to the director's lips.

For a moment, Breksta felt a smile tugging at her lips at the woman's compliment. A warmth spread across her cheeks, momentarily forgetting the morning's pain and her mother. But as she looked at the woman's eyes and face, she tore her eyes away and ripped the smile off her lips. She shut her mouth and cursed herself for speaking and smiling. Most of all, she cursed herself for forgetting and promised that she would never fall for the woman's tricks again.

"We're going to take you to a safer place now. The Academy, for kids like you." Breksta could hear the woman's smile in her voice, and the sound of the woman's eerily sweet voice made Breksta tense in her seat. "This place will protect you. And I think you will really enjoy it there."

Breksta couldn't understand everything that had happened. She couldn't understand why she was here or why her mother lay cold, forever unmoving in their forest. Her mind was confused by the clashing of the director's sweet words and her gunshot that had killed her mother. Breksta felt tears prickle on her eyelashes, and she turned her head away, refusing to let the woman see her cry.

"We're going to a better place now," the woman said gently, reaching over and placing a hand on Breksta's leg.

Breksta yanked her leg away as the woman touched it and hissed, "Leave me alone!"

She turned her back to the woman. Like the spears of human hunters pointed toward a cornered animal, she felt the eyes of the director and all the cadets on her, looking at her vulnerability. The woman pulled Breksta's shoulder toward her so that Breksta's red eyes could be seen by everyone. She tugged Breksta's face up with a finger to look at her, even as Breksta tried to pull herself away once more.

"I have treated you very kindly, child, all things considered. Do not *ever* speak to me in that tone again," the woman said, softly but firmly.

After a few seconds of fear, Breksta yanked her head away. The woman's touch still lingered underneath her chin and made her want to rip off her skin. Those same hands had killed her mother, and Breksta would never forgive nor forget.

"Madam Director, we're approaching the Academy," the girl cadet announced from her seat at the front of the plane.

Breksta released a breath as the woman's cold presence stood and moved away from her. Breksta couldn't help but look out the large window, and what she saw surprised her. The world down below, lit up by the plane's large floodlights, was unlike anything she had ever seen before. The black and ashen forest was nothing like her green and luscious one. Four tall buildings stood below and formed a diamond shape. As they drew closer, Breksta could see the forest even more clearly. Each branch seemed to be twirled and twisted together like vines, making a large covering for the mountains.

Apprehension swirled in her stomach as the plane landed with a slow bump. She did not know this world—a world that did not have her mother in it. She did not know if she would survive.

CHAPTER 5

BY THE TIME THE RAMP of the plane lowered, Breksta had released the seat's harness. She tried to stop her trembling and forced her face into an emotionless expression. The soldier who had carried her onto the plane nudged her toward the plane's black ramp.

"Welcome to the Academy," the director proclaimed, her smile illuminating her cardinal-red lips.

Breksta was silent. Her face was now a mask of stone that stood as a final defense to this new world.

"Follow me," the director commanded.

Breksta kept her head bowed and followed the director by listening to the sound of her tall, slim heels that clicked against the ground. The shadows of the buildings around her pulled her attention, drawing her eyes upward to take in the dark world around her. The area where they landed was a long, asphalt runway that smelled and looked like death. The solid black color was one that Breksta rarely encountered in her beautiful, quaint town. It looked alien, like a being that had pulled itself up from the middle of the earth and spread itself across the once lustrous forest, killing everything in its path. That same asphalt being led straight into a cluster of four buildings, the only markings of a civilization surrounded by dark mountains and similarly dark trees. The darkness of Breksta's new world was frightening, like an omnipresent shadow cast across the land as far as the eye could see. The shadow smothered all life and greenery, the very elements that were a part of every memory Breksta had with her mother.

The tall buildings were a light gray, lit brightly by the lamp posts along the building's paths, strategically placed where the landing strip ended and the cluster of buildings began. As Breksta and the cadets neared the buildings, she could make out the silhouette of a tall statue in the center. To her horror, she saw that the statue was a replica of the director who stood defiantly and wore a proud smile.

"You may return to your rooms now. Congratulations on a mission well done," the director stated, her face conveying nothing despite her congratulatory words.

The cadets nodded; some even gave each other high fives and wide grins before walking together to one of the buildings. The director curled her arm around Breksta's shoulder and led her in the opposite direction toward a different building.

"W-where are you taking me?" Breksta asked warily, trying to shake off the director's arm.

The director tightened her arm around Breksta's shoulders before answering. "We need to give you a proper examination."

The dark building brightened with lights as soon as the director pushed open the door. The building's lobby was a looming two stories, and in the center of the ceiling hung a chandelier, its matte-black arms holding countless light bulbs. It cast cold white light onto the lobby, bringing the sterile white and gray colors of the walls and floor into focus. Past the chandelier was a white spiral staircase that stemmed from the higher levels and appeared to descend deep underground. The director and Breksta climbed down one story. Breksta held her elbows protectively as the director finally released her.

The director flicked on the basement lights. "This is the infirmary, where we keep all our medical supplies."

The lights above revealed a long corridor of rooms; the first one Breksta peered in had tinted glass windows that obscured the inside. The director opened the door to the first room and nodded for Breksta to follow.

"Sit," the director commanded once they were inside, pointing toward an ashen chair in the center of the room.

Breksta sat, cautiously observing the room around her with frightened eyes. The peeling beige skin of the walls revealed a darker skin tone underneath. The gray concrete floor shone through a layer of wax. The wall directly opposite the window was lined with tall white cabinets, while a lower cabinet in front of the window held a sink and boxes of tissues. As Breksta became situated in the chair, her hand accidentally knocked into a small cart beside her. On it were a pair of gloves, a few clear vials, and a slender needle, which heightened her fear even more.

"The doctor will be here soon," the director said matter-of-factly.

The clock hanging on the wall behind Breksta ticked in rhythm with her heart. The director stood in the right corner of the room and tapped her pencil against the cardboard clipboard in her arms. Breksta had no memory of when the director picked up those items. And she didn't understand what she had done to deserve this. But Breksta knew she would find out soon enough. She gathered up her courage and bit her lip to hide her trembling.

"What do you want from me?" Breksta said, finally shattering the silence.

The director's brown eyes trained on Breksta, pinning her with her gaze before she responded, "I am doing my best for all of us. For humanity. To clean up our world and establish the rightful balance." The director smiled eerily, making Breksta shudder. She hesitated before continuing, "But … from the events of this morning, I take it that you don't believe me."

"What is this place?" Breksta challenged, her eyes both fearful and frustrated.

The director's eyes danced with humor, but Breksta saw something deeper and alien that flickered before they returned to their neutral, cold state.

Breksta felt her anger and frustration grow with the woman's silence, and so she blurted, "Why did you kill my mother?"

The director's eyes snapped up toward Breksta and flashed dangerously, making Breksta wish she could hide from the terrifying woman in front of her.

"You must understand your place here. Just like your mother needed to understand hers, Breksta Vilkas," the director said, spitting out her last name.

The director's tone made Breksta flinch. So, she said nothing, allowing herself to be silenced. The director pursed her lips and looked down toward her clipboard. Together, they waited agonizing minutes until the silver door swung open. A young woman with light brown, blunt-cut short hair entered, wearing a white doctor's uniform with a black stethoscope hung around her neck.

"Hello, Madam Director," she said, nodding her head in a small bow.

She waited for the director's nod before approaching Breksta with gentle footsteps.

"What's your name, sweetie?"

Her hazel eyes were warm like sunlight as she looked at Breksta.

"Breksta. Breksta Vilkas," Breksta murmured.

"Vilkas. Not a very common last name," the doctor chuckled nervously, her eyes losing their warmth before glancing back to the director with furrowed eyebrows.

"Yes, Vilkas. Run your tests, Doctor. I will be back," the director announced and clacked her way out of the room.

The doctor nodded as the director left the room, turning to Breksta and pushing a wide smile onto her face. "Well, Breksta. Let's check your breathing first."

The woman's stethoscope was ice against Breksta's thin skin. The metal bumped sharply against her ribs. Then the doctor switched the stethoscope to her back. Breksta did as the doctor asked for the rest of her physical examination, testing her walking, eyesight, and other physical abilities. The doctor, who watched her with eagle eyes, scribbled onto her clipboard through it all. Finally, after what felt like an hour, the doctor placed her clipboard on the cart.

"Now it's time for your injection," the doctor spoke softly.

"A shot?" Breksta whispered, her voice breaking out in ripples and her eyes widening.

"Yes. It's just a vaccine we give to all new cadets."

"But do I have—"

"It will be over quick," the doctor snapped.

The doctor began preparing. She pulled the gloves over her hands with a snap and unpackaged the needle.

"Lie against the back of the chair."

Breksta leaned back slowly and felt the plastic rub against her back. Her muscles refused her orders to relax, as she closed her eyes tightly to block the needle from her vision. When nothing came, she peeked to see the gleaming tip and one of the vials in the doctor's hand. Fear danced around her heart, pushing it to beat faster.

"Pull up your sleeve, please."

Breksta hesitated. As her last form of protest, she kept her hands beside her body.

"Breksta," the doctor said slowly, dragging out the last syllable of her name. "If you don't do it, I will."

Breksta shook her head, determined to resist for as long as possible. "No. I don't want it. Get it *away* from me!"

The doctor put her hand on Breksta's arm, tugging it gently for her attention. "To survive here, Breksta, you need to learn to follow the rules. This is the first one. And I know you will do perfectly fine because you are a *very* good girl."

The doctor's hazel eyes bore into Breksta's so deeply that their sincerity scared Breksta. The woman's firm grip hinted at her lack of options.

"I-I ... will it hurt?" Breksta whispered as she tried to even her breathing.

"Only for a moment," the doctor muttered. With her needle prepared, she pulled up Breksta's sleeve, so Breksta's whole bicep was uncovered.

The doctor tore open an alcohol packet and rubbed the sharp-smelling cloth over Breksta's arm. Breksta looked at her bare arm held stiffly by the doctor, who placed the needle on her arm and pushed it in. Breksta's arm exploded with pain from the spot where the metal broke through her skin.

"Ow!" Breksta yelped as a droplet of blood formed on her arm that was followed by another. She took in a sharp breath and bit her lip tightly as pins of black and silver light made her head spin. The edges of her vision closed in as she felt a fluid substance push apart her muscles and fill her arm with fire. Breksta gripped the edge of the chair with her uninjured hand and clung on until the waves of pain passed to a level that allowed her breaths to even out.

"All done," the doctor said as she secured a band aid on Breksta's arm, making her wince again.

Breksta breathed out a shaky breath of relief.

"I'll call in the director now. She will help you get settled," the doctor said, offering her a small smile before slipping out the door.

Then Breksta was left alone. She felt her arm with her fingers until she found the band aid. As soon as her fingers touched it, the pain from before coursed through her arm. She winced as she dug her fingers into the palm of her hand. Gradually, her lungs relaxed and the pain in her arm receded to a bearable level, but her emotional pain still lingered.

Her mother's empty eyes re-entered her mind, eyes that would never sparkle again with joy. The loss was the only pain greater than the one she felt in her body. It seemed that the more Breksta tried to keep every last piece of her mother, every last memory, the more the pain in her heart grew. It was as if every minute away from her mother, her town, and her forest caused her to be slowly eaten away from the inside. She yearned for stability, for the calmness in the eye of the storm that had ravaged her life. But with the entry of a sweetened voice, Breksta was propelled back into the storm.

"Are you ready, Breksta?"

The sound of clacking heels registered before she opened her eyes. Her eyes confirmed what her ears already knew: it was the director.

"We make sure that our students are healthy and safe in the Academy. After all, they are our priority," the director spoke, enunciating each word. "Come along now. The rest of the cadets are still asleep. But I think I have a friend for you." Her blood-red lipstick touched bits of her teeth, making her look as if she had drunk blood. "Let's go to the dorms, shall we?"

Breksta's thin wrists were tugged by the woman and made her small feet skitter as they retraced their steps up the spiral stairs. She followed silently while her mind wandered outside of her new prison. They reached another building that had a smaller lobby and two sets of staircases on each side of the walls. The stairs creaked with every step they took. Each window was covered with a layer of dust and paired with torn navy curtains. Breksta counted each floor until they finally arrived at the fifth. The hallways were adorned with peeling white paint and matching green steel doors. Some doors emitted soft, muffled voices that resonated through the cold steel. Others were ghost quiet with only slivers of light that escaped from the bottom of the door. The director stopped in front of the door marked 281 in rusted black numbers.

The director pushed open the door and revealed the small pastel room. The night sky could be barely seen through the window. On the right side of the room, a black bunkbed held two thick mattresses covered in matching gray sheets. The top bunk consisted of a lump of blankets.

"Hestia!" the director called in a stern voice.

The blankets twisted to reveal a small figure shrouded in fiery red hair, the same as the director's, Breksta realized. The girl's pale face made her emerald eyes sparkle even brighter, and her cheeks, dusted with brown freckles, more prominent. Breksta looked up at her silently, her gray eyes blinking as they searched every part of the girl's face.

"Who is this?" Hestia muttered sleepily.

Breksta said nothing as she cast her eyes down to the ground. She felt the cold prickle of the director's presence and the girl's gaze sink into her skin. Hestia slid over the thin metal bars of the bunkbed and landed on the floor with a gentle thud; her knees bent effortlessly to catch herself. She quickly made her way over to the director and Breksta.

"What's your name?" Hestia said brightly, extending her hand.

Frozen in place, Breksta looked at her. Behind Breksta, the director gave her a slight push. Breksta stumbled forward on glass-like, stiff legs. Her sharp joints rubbed awkwardly against one another as she fell. Hestia nimbly bent down and brought Breksta back to her feet without hesitation. Hestia's hands were as soft as petals against Breksta's arms. Even though Hestia's touch was gentle, Breksta flinched and backed out of Hestia's reach. Her left arm throbbed from even the most miniscule movement.

"I'm Hestia. It's nice to meet you," Hestia tried again, smiling kindly at Breksta.

Breksta shifted her eyes, focusing them firmly on her feet and the floor. Without speaking, she nodded slowly in acknowledgment of her understanding. She kept her stone face, the only defense against this world she had entered.

"You will be making sure Breksta is taken care of," the director said, her heels shifting back and forth on the carpet. "Breksta, we will return your duffel once it's been thoroughly searched."

Breksta heard the doorknob turn behind her, and just as the door clicked open, the director added to Hestia, "Make sure she follows the rules."

The door closed behind them with a loud click, allowing Breksta to breathe out a long-held breath.

"Breksta…" Hestia said, tasting Breksta's name on her tongue. "What does it mean?"

Still Breksta said nothing. She stood erect, a statue under Hestia's close observation. She was too weary from pain and grief to draw strength and answer. Fear and adrenaline had been the only feelings helping her survive her mother's death, the plane ride, and the painful medical examination.

"Hello?" Hestia said, waving her hands in front of Breksta. "Are, are you okay?"

Hestia bent her knees so that she could look into Breksta's gray eyes; she took in a small breath. Breksta saw deep sympathy in Hestia's eyes. And that was when Breksta knew her pain had seeped through her eyes and settled in the room, coiling itself like a venomous serpent that never slept and watched Breksta's every move intently. It reminded Breksta in every breathing moment of the lack of breath her mother had. Never again would her mother laugh, never again would Asteria embrace Breksta, never again would anyone hear Asteria's wisdom. As Breksta thought of this, her emotions locked behind her stone mask rose to the surface.

"Are you alright? Did I say something?" Hestia murmured.

She put her hand on Breksta's arm, its warm touch sending shivers down Breksta's spine. Breksta stood unmoving; her arm tensed as she looked up meekly at Hestia. Hestia's emerald eyes shone with concern. But Breksta had been fooled by the doctor before, who inflicted pain despite her promise that it wouldn't hurt. She wouldn't be fooled again. So Breksta yanked her arm away, bringing her hands across her chest and cupping her elbows as protection.

"Don't touch me," Breksta said sharply.

"I'm sorry," Hestia said, taking a step back as she analyzed Breksta with a mix of curiosity and hurt in her eyes.

They stood in silence for a moment until Hestia could not bear the weight of the silence and broke it. "You can have the bottom bunk," Hestia said, sitting on the bed and beckoning Breksta to do the same.

Breksta shuffled her feet bit by bit until she reached the bed. She extended her hand to reach the gray sheets. The stitches on the fabric felt like silk underneath her fingers. Breksta took in a small breath, barely noticeable unless one was watching her intently, as she sat on the bed and felt the mattress sink.

"It's super comfy, right?" Hestia said, smiling as she sat next to Breksta.

Breksta shifted over, opening a meter between her and Hestia. This world was foreign and cold, both things that Breksta wished to distance herself from. Yet this girl's eyes did not share the same deep resentment that the director held. Not a trace was on Hestia. Her eyes shown with kindness that Breksta had seen only in her town and from her mother.

"I…" Hestia thought for a moment, calculating her words. "I've never had a roommate before. Have you?"

Hestia looked at Breksta, her green eyes sparkling brightly in contrast to Breksta's gray, pain-ridden ones. Hestia sighed, nodding at Breksta's silence and her failed attempts at conversation.

"If there's anything you need, I'm here for you."

Breksta didn't answer. She merely pulled her knees up and hugged them into her chest as she leaned against the back wall of the bunk. They sat silently with only the sound of their breathing between them.

"Well, you should rest. It's late, and we have class in the morning," Hestia said gently, getting up from the bed and pushing open the door to the bathroom across from the bunks.

Hestia retreated into the bathroom where Breksta caught a peek of a shower and toilet. She slowly lay her back against the mattress and looked up at the metal bars that held the identical mattress above her. She put her head against the thin pillow so that her white hair splayed out, mixing with the gray colors of the bedding. She lay there for quite some time before turning on her side with her back to the bathroom. Breksta curled her legs toward her body, into the fetal position. Her mind spun. The tape in her mind replayed her mother's empty eyes. Her mother's soft words rang in her ears. "I need you to know that I love you. More than the world."

Breksta couldn't stop the flow of her violent, unbridled thoughts. She finally closed her eyes and submitted to the river of thoughts until her battered mind succumbed to sleep.

CHAPTER 6

BREKSTA OPENED HER EYES to the sun's bright light streaming in through the dusty windows, the indication of the morning's arrival. A small smile touched her lips as she recalled her sweet and dreamless sleep, but as she saw the unfamiliar gray bedding beneath her, her memories returned. Her mother's void eyes seared back into her mind, and a wave of sorrow drowned her broken heart. Her agony returned to her in drops of grief upon her chest.

Sobs, followed by tears, escaped her lips as she gripped the sheets with one hand to keep her from being consumed by sadness. Curled tightly in her anguish, she shut her eyes tightly and felt tear after tear soak the pillow. It was then her mother's face transformed from the bullet-ridden one to the one she saw when they had gone to the fields.

"If you sing to them, they will sing back," her mother had said as they lay in the emerald fields of grass dotted with the purple splashes of color from the lupines.

Asteria whistled bright and clear. Breksta sat up, her eyes widening with each second that passed and watched with awe as her mother's pursed lips played dancing tunes. Breksta tried, pushing her lips together and forcing out the air from her lungs. But the only sound that came was the sound of her sputtering lips.

Her mother let out a soft chuckle and put her arm around Breksta, enveloping her in Asteria's warm figure.

"You'll get it someday. But for now, just watch," her mother said softly, tugging at Breksta's cheeks playfully before tilting her head back and continuing her bright song.

At the sound of Asteria's sweet melodies, the birds came, as if summoned by their queen wreathed in a crown of white hair. They landed one by one on the tall trees near the base of the mountain across the river. They slowly hopped closer, though keeping their distance enough that Breksta had to squint to see the details of their feathers. The birds sang back Asteria's song, and her eyes flashed with happiness at her success.

"I want to do that, Mom," Breksta spoke loudly, pointing at the birds.

"One day, my love," her mother chuckled.

Their melody replayed in Breksta's mind and drew more tears as she tried to grasp the last bits of her mother before the bullets and blood. Her braided hair. Her shining, bright eyes. Her sculpted hands that helped to nurture both the flowers on their banister and Breksta.

Just as Breksta could picture her mother perfectly, her face complete and caught in a joyous expression, the door burst open and ripped Breksta out of her memories. In came Hestia, her hands carrying two green platters of steaming, rich-smelling food. Breksta's stomach uttered a growl that admitted her hunger and made her scowl at her own weakness.

"Looks like someone's hungry," Hestia said with a devious smile as she crossed the room and sat on the bed.

"I'm not supposed to have this here," she whispered through cupped hands. "But you looked so tired, and you came so late … I thought there could be an exception. Here you go!" Hestia said with a sheepish grin. Breksta sat up slowly before Hestia handed the platter to Breksta and flashed a smile of encouragement before diving into her own. Breksta quickly brought the back of her hand to her eyes and wiped away her tears, examining the large portions of food on her plate.

"Eat up. We're late for class," Hestia said as she shoveled eggs and pancakes into her mouth. The plate almost mirrored the one Breksta had shared with her mother the previous day.

"It's amazing, really. Try it!" Hestia encouraged, her lips coated with bits of salt and honey.

Breksta ignored the eggs and ate the pancakes, a delicacy that her mother hadn't made in a long time. She dipped them in the pile of syrup on the corner of her plate. As the honey hit her tongue, Breksta's gray eyes set alight for a moment. The sweetness spread through her mouth, and it was as if she were eating golden rays of sunshine.

"I told you, it's amazing," Hestia laughed, watching her new roommate intently.

Breksta closed her eyes and savored the pure drops of sweetness in her mouth. With her eyes closed, she could pretend that her mother had made these for her and that nothing was wrong. But as soon as she opened her eyes, the gray world around her swept fear back into her. Breksta put down the plate and pushed it toward Hestia. If she couldn't have her mother's food, she would have nothing at all.

"You're not hungry?" Hestia asked, her brows furrowing together, confused at Breksta's sudden change of heart.

Breksta shook her head slightly. It was easier that way for Hestia to think it was Breksta's stomach that couldn't take the nuance of this gray world instead of her mind. Hestia shrugged and finished both of their plates.

"Time for class," Hestia exclaimed as she stacked the plates together.

Hestia pulled open her dresser drawers and handed Breksta a set of black clothes, the same ones the soldiers from the airplane had worn.

"Change into these for now. The cadets will bring yours later."

Breksta retreated into the bathroom. As she changed, she found her eyes drawn to her ribs. They protruded out of her stomach in sharp edges and made her skin sink into her bones. Her flat chest made her body seem frail. Her eyes were red; the only remnant of her mother's existence in Breksta's grief. Her cheekbones carved arched grooves in her face. And half of her wispy white hair clung to the side of her face that had lain on the pillow.

Breksta did not know the girl in front of her. The girl who played in the mountains of her town, who cared for the flowers on her banisters, was wiped from Breksta's expression. She fought to keep her tears at bay as she thought of her town and her mother. Looking at Breksta's own white hair made her think of her mother. Her mother's hair was always braided. Sometimes it was a braid down her back and on other days Asteria's hair was parted into two French braids on each side of her head. The similarity made Breksta tear her eyes away from the mirror and continue with the process of changing into the dark clothing, keeping her eyes glued to the ground.

The dusty black shirt made her sneeze as she pulled it on. The T-shirt hung loose and draped far down her body, looking like an awkward dress. The pants dragged on the floor despite Breksta's efforts to cinch the waistband higher. She rolled up the bottom of the pants and tucked them into the pure white socks she was given.

"We'll find something that fits later," Hestia chuckled, her voice flowing like honey as she took in Breksta's dragging garments.

Hestia led the way down the crooked stairs Breksta had arrived on and out of their dorm building, following a stone path lined with shrubbery and trees. The path led to the side of Madam Director's statue, where they turned left to the towering building the statue faced. The identicality of the buildings made Breksta's head spin, but she followed without protest while her eyes scoured every edge of the Academy she passed.

Surrounding the buildings, Breksta spotted a tall, barbed wire gate stationed with burly figures wearing the same black clothing. Behind the gate lay mountains wreathed in dark trees, their bare branches curled into claws. The mountain wind blew through the pathways between the buildings, brushing Breksta's face with its earthy scent. She took a deep breath, tasting the clean breeze on her tongue. Its cold stung her face, but she enjoyed the small taste of nature.

"Breksta. This way," Hestia beckoned.

Hestia stood at the building's entrance with the door pushed open, which Breksta quickly ran to. The door opened to a wide lobby of gray concrete, identical to the lobby Breksta had entered to take her medical examination. The towering two-story windows allowed light to shine in brightly. A white reception desk stood at the right wall of the lobby, with a large man sitting behind it. He wore a black uniform with a silver name tag, but he was too far away for Breksta to be able to read his name. He sat with his dark-haired head bowed toward the computer monitor in front of him. As the two girls entered, he looked up and waved his large meaty hand at Hestia.

She offered a sweet "Morning" as she passed, smiling back at Breksta, and gesturing for her to approach.

"That's the security guard, Mr. Matthew. He looks mean, but don't worry. He just does that to keep people out of trouble."

Breksta nodded and stored Hestia's words inside her head for future reference. To the back of the lobby stood another gleaming spiral staircase overflowing with students.

"Our first class is downstairs. Upstairs is the regular school classes. Downstairs is the training and weapons classes," Hestia proclaimed, hurrying toward the stairs.

Breksta nodded silently, storing every minute detail. Her eyes searched every face as Hestia led the way through the ocean of students, and she began to see a pattern in their expressions. Their gazes clung to Breksta's white hair like small hooks. She was a beacon for attention—an exotic object from a faraway land. Hearing their whispers behind her, she shrunk into herself and walked faster to stay at Hestia's side.

Hestia and Breksta walked down the spiral staircase two floors until they reached a singular hallway just wide enough for the two of them to walk side by side. The walls were thick glass containments that showed black-clothed students with large red headphones atop their heads. They held various weapons—pistols, guns, and even rifles that were so large the cadets had to hoist them up on their shoulders.

Although the glass muffled the sounds, Breksta felt cold fear seize her heart in response to the rapid firing. She cowered away, covering her ears, and curling into a protective ball on the floor. She was back in the forest, utterly helpless and weak. With each shot, the images of her mother's forehead crowned with a dripping blood hole replayed in her mind. Breksta felt cold pearls of sweat drip down her spine as her temples pulsed with fear that she tried to bury.

"Breksta?" Hestia called, her voice muted as if underwater. Hestia rushed to kneel beside Breksta, who had her arms wrapped tightly in a cocoon around herself. Hestia gently held Breksta's shoulders.

"Breksta, what's wrong?" she spoke softly, her voice laced with concern. "It's okay. You're safe here. The Academy is safe," Hestia begged, shaking Breksta side to side, trying to get her out of her pain-filled trance.

Breksta's breath came out in shaking puffs. "No. You're lying! They killed…" Her words drifted off as her mind descended deeper into fear. Her heart raced as her mind took her away from the Academy and to her mother. Her mother's eyes flashed in her mind, empty of the warmth they held before that morning. Her cold body lay broken and bloodied in the same forest that they had hiked through during the summer.

"Nothing will hurt you here," Hestia murmured; her honey-coated words brought Breksta back to the Academy. "Shh … you don't have to be afraid," Hestia encouraged as she rubbed calming circles around Breksta's back, the same motion her mother had done when Breksta saw the dead rabbit in Dave's hands.

Breksta felt her breath slowly return to her as the sound of the bullets stopped, though the sound still echoed in her mind.

"I've got you," Hestia murmured. Her arm hooked underneath Breksta and pulled her up.

Hestia led her down the hallway, using her own strength to compensate for Breksta's uncoordinated feet that stumbled behind. With every step that distanced her from the shooting range, Breksta was able to release a tense breath.

They passed other rooms as they moved down the hall. To their left, cadets practiced in a knife-throwing range. Breksta kept her eyes square on the floor to stop herself from seeing the shining blades sink deep within the dummies on the far wall. To their right, a room with vacant boxing rings stood with blue and red ropes on each side. Light cones shone from the ceiling, illuminating each ring with golden circles.

Finally, they reached a pair of silver doors at the end of the hallway. Hestia pushed through the doors, and they were met with a room full of dark-attired cadets. Some Breksta recognized from the plane, but others were brand-new faces. Sitting at a bare desk was a blond, blue-eyed boy with a crooked frown. His cold eyes locked on Breksta and Hestia as they stumbled into the classroom. On the left of the wall was a whiteboard with a plump woman in a skintight black dress standing in front of it. Her oily, stiff black hair mirrored her beady eyes that bore into Hestia and Breksta.

"You. Are. Late," the woman said, accentuating each word.

"Sorry, Ms. Adams. Breksta is a new cadet, so we had to get her settled in," Hestia said, bowing her head and nudging Breksta's stomach with her arm as a motion to copy her.

"It is ma'am, to you. This is my classroom. And when you are in my class-room, you *will* be on time and *will* address me properly, regardless of who your mother is. Understood?" Ms. Adams's crow eyes never left Hestia and Breksta's faces.

"Yes, ma'am," Hestia muttered, her words flowing through tightly clenched teeth as she kept her angry gaze pinned on the floor.

"And Breksta … was it?" Ms. Adams said, walking over to where Breksta and Hestia still stood, hunched over in twin bows.

"Do you have anything to say?" Ms. Adams whispered near Breksta's ear; fake sweetness dripped with each consonant.

Breksta was silent. The woman's overbearing eyes struck fear into Breksta's heart.

"She's a bit shy," Hestia inserted, her emerald eyes looking up at Ms. Adams.

Ms. Adams slapped her own left hand with a metal ruler she was holding in her right hand, just inches from Breksta and Hestia's faces, making them flinch. She looked to Hestia and placed the ruler tip on the edge of her throat, pulling Hestia's chin upward and allowing the cold metal to move with each of Hestia's heartbeats.

"Did I ask you to speak?" Ms. Adams said, a cruel smile adorning her lips.

"No, ma'am," Hestia murmured shakily, immediately shifting her eyes downward.

Breksta could not help but notice the shift in Hestia, who earlier smiled brightly but now cowered under the woman's sharp gaze. A sharp indicator of the woman's influence.

"You are excused … for now. Take a seat."

Hestia walked silently to an empty desk and pleaded to Breksta with concerned eyes. "Do whatever she asks," Hestia mouthed.

"Speak," Ms. Adams demanded as her eyes bore into Breksta. She leaned past Breksta's ear so that Breksta could smell Ms. Adams's odor; the stench of ethanol alcohol was so overbearing that Breksta coughed.

"What is your full name?"

Breksta responded with silence and leaned back to keep the prickling smell away.

"Did your Dreamer parents even teach you to speak?" Ms. Adams whispered right into her ear.

Once again, Breksta didn't understand the word *Dreamer*, and she didn't understand why she deserved this aggression. She felt a rush of anger at the woman's tone toward her mother but kept her mouth zipped and heeded Hestia's advice.

"Answer the question, cadet, or are you a Dreamer?" Ms. Adams commanded accusingly.

Breksta turned to see the cadets around her snickering. Their eyes and sharp whispers were like daggers directed at her.

She swallowed before speaking in a careful voice. "I … don't know what that means."

What began as a small snicker from the woman became a deep laugh, so violent she held her stomach to keep herself upright.

"You don't know … what a Dreamer is?" she said between breaths.

Breksta felt shame bear down on her as the room descended into laugher, her cheeks heating as she avoided Ms. Adams's gaze.

"No," she said shakily.

Ms. Adams's eyes sharpened. "I pity you, child. Growing with such unintelligent parents that taught you nothing."

Breksta's anger grew at the woman's insult. This woman didn't know her mother at all.

"My mother taught me very well," Breksta countered, looking up at the woman with fuming eyes.

Ms. Adams pulled the edge of her ruler across Breksta's face. The metal dug into Breksta's skin, pinching her sharply as Ms. Adams pulled the ruler away. Breksta let out a scream that stopped in her throat as she stumbled back. A thin line of pain under Breksta's eye burned with fire.

Across the room, Hestia took in a breath and stood up from her seat. The children behind her shuffled uncomfortably in their seats. Some let gasps escape from their lips while others' eyes danced with amusement. Breksta curled her fists in anger and looked back at Ms. Adams.

"Ms.—" Hestia said softly.

"Did I or did I not ask you to address me properly?" Ms. Adams snapped, turning her glare to Hestia.

Hestia sat back down but kept her fear-filled eyes trained between Ms. Adams and Breksta.

"And *you*," Ms. Adams said, slow and calculated, as she swung back to Breksta. "Do not *pretend* to be innocent to the tragedies that your mother inflicted on the world. If you don't want to be punished again, I suggest you keep your mouth shut."

Breksta saw a mixture of anger and glee in Ms. Adams's adamant eyes as Breksta clutched her wound. Her fingers were met with the warm flow of blood, staining her hands a dark maroon red. Her eyes barely contained her rage. The reins on the angry beast within her were contained with mere threads of will-power as blood trailed down her face and dripped onto the floor.

"Clean that up and take a seat." Ms. Adams smiled, turning her back on Breksta's rage-trembling frame as she stood beside the board.

Breksta pulled a tissue from a box on Ms. Adams's desk, backed into the corner of the wall, and swiped it over her dark blood that stained the white floor. She quickly disposed of it and moved down the row of seats to Hestia.

Breksta sunk into her seat beside Hestia and sulked. Her face stung, and she tugged on her quivering lips with her teeth to compose her anger and pain under the weight of Ms. Adams's gaze.

"May I have a tissue … ma'am?" Hestia asked, her eyes bowed down.

Ms. Adams considered Hestia's request with her narrowed eyes, then nodded. "I'll allow it."

"Thank you, ma'am."

Hestia stepped forward to grab a fistful of tissues and handed them to Breksta, who accepted them graciously with a nod. Breksta dabbed the tissue against her face and winced at the sting of the tissue's harsh fabric against her cut.

"Thank you," Breksta breathed quietly.

"You're—"

"Silence!" Ms. Adams exclaimed, her eyes glaring.

Hestia looked to Breksta with a helpless expression, offering the condolence of a small smile.

"Today, we have an opportunity to teach. In our presence is a new cadet, ignorant of what Dreamers are," Ms. Adams commanded as her eyes scanned the alerted eyes of the cadets. "So, who can tell me *who* Dreamers are?"

Ms. Adams clicked a small machine in her hand and the board behind her went alight with stark images.

"They are dangerous to our society!" an auburn-haired girl offered from the back.

"Excellent answer. More precisely?"

"They…" the girl trailed off, casting her eyes down before descending into silence.

"The Dreamers are people in the world who have magic," Hestia answered with a warm smile to Ms. Adams, proud of her proficiency in the course.

"*Abilities*, Hestia. They don't possess magic, but *abilities* that have been given to them from their god, Morpheus," Ms. Adams spat, her eyes fuming toward Hestia as she paced the classroom like a she-lion.

"In their vision of a harmonious society, the Dreamers claim that they have the right to take lives and destroy the world. But they have proven to be horrid and inhumane in every situation where diplomacy is used, in every interaction with the Academy, and in every other possible aspect," Ms. Adams said sharply, her eyes shifting from Hestia to glare at Breksta's with unmasked anger. "Does everyone understand?"

Militaristic calls of "yes, ma'am" spread throughout the class, the voices of the cadets strong and unyielding.

"Yes, ma'am," Breksta copied, glancing nervously at the unfazed faces of the cadets around her.

She had never known of Dreamers and was not sure why her mother had never spoken about it. But Ms. Adams's and the cadets' anger was strong enough that Breksta kept her lips sealed and herself unnoticeable.

"Now, what historical event does this photograph depict?" Ms. Adams commanded, pointing her metal ruler against the board at the new image.

The brightly colored photograph illustrated a milk-colored building surrounded by black gates and charred grass. The building was supported by large white columns that formed a half circle around the entrance. The ledges and balconies on each side of the building raged with fire. Smoke billowed out in a long veil, while the roof had collapsed inward. The image caught people frozen in time. Some were running with their hands clasped over their mouths to stop the smoke from strangling their lungs. Some were corpses with their eyes wide open, their maroon blood spilling between the cracks of the bricks and their bodies contorted wildly in death.

Breksta gulped as she looked at the photograph wide-eyed. "Their eyes," her words ghosted on her lips softly, unheard by everyone except Hestia.

"I know," Hestia murmured back, who reached over and gripped her companion. "They're so empty. So … alien."

Knowing that Hestia felt the same, Breksta was able to look at the image without flinching.

"So, is anyone prepared to comment on this image?" Ms. Adams spoke impatiently; her eyes were unwavering daggers poised at Breksta.

"Is this an image from the Dreamer massacre at the White House?" the blond-haired boy asked.

"Well done, Icarus. You are correct, as always. Now, we shall have a moment of remembrance for those who fell to the terrorists," Ms. Adams proclaimed as she bowed her head and folded her fingers tightly over her dress.

Breksta twirled her head to watch as each student intertwined their fingers together in a prayer and bowed their heads low enough to touch their hands. Hestia did the same; her hair created a frame of shimmering orange around her. Breksta copied Hestia, even as she was confused at the deaths on the screen. She felt fear and sympathy for those people, but the reason for their deaths was still unclear to her. She listened to the tense breaths of the cadets around her, some fast and uncontrolled while others breathed with great weight and sadness.

"May they forever remain in our memories," Ms. Adams murmured.

Breksta lifted her face quickly to catch a glimpse of pain flash on Ms. Adams face before disappearing under the layers of her cold face.

"May they forever remain in our memories," the cadets repeated.

Breksta didn't understand the reason why these children felt so much sadness for this photograph. She didn't know these cadets, but she knew the feeling of their sadness reflected her grief for her mother. And so, she didn't ask any questions. Ms. Adams allowed the cadets three heartbeats of stillness before she slapped the metal ruler against the flat of her hand, jolting everyone back to her words.

"Next, why did the Dreamers try to overthrow the government?" Ms. Adams asked, walking in between the rows to gauge each student's eyes.

Icarus began again, his confident voice rising above the other cadets who barely opened their mouths. "Because they felt threatened by the president's new law, which was—"

"Excellent," Ms. Adams interrupted with a sigh. "Anyone *besides* Icarus know what this law contained?"

The cadets' eyes flicked to Icarus, rolling in their sockets. But the cadets remained quiet.

Ms. Adams's sharp eyes landed on Breksta again as she spoke. "No one? *I* will remind you all then." She pointed to the image on the board. "This is the remains of the White House after the Dreamers' attack. Three weeks prior, the president signed Executive Order No. 451, illegalizing the use of Dreamer abilities. This was put in place to ensure that the Dreamers and the people could live together with equity. But once those Dreamers saw this order, they formulated a rebellion and attacked the government, killing the president and the first family in the process." During her speech, Ms. Adams had migrated to stand beside Breksta and glared down at her.

"And this is why we are here … Breksta. *We* are the protectors of the world from people like *you*, your mother, and any other Dreamer rebels. We *alone* ensure that Dreamers never have power again. You had better learn that."

A cold silence filled the room. Breksta felt the glares of the other cadets and Ms. Adams. Confused, Hestia looked at Breksta, her head tilted slightly to the side.

"Tell them, Breksta," Ms. Adams said with a cruel smile. "Tell them who your mother *was*."

Breksta swallowed and shook her head. She was so lost in her fear of Ms. Adams and her new world that she was unable to form words.

"Tell them!" Ms. Adams shouted, slamming her hands on Breksta's desk. Breksta flinched and bit her lip harshly to keep from trembling and her tears from falling. "Tell them now. Or would you like the director's punishment for disobedience?" Ms. Adams said more quietly, her voice becoming the identical sickening sweetness the director had used yesterday.

The reference to the director awoke a primal fear in her, so in a hushed voice, Breksta forced out, "M-my mom is-was ... Asteria Vilkas."

The cadets gasped and began to whisper among themselves. Breksta frantically looked around to see the cadets glaring at her with angry, vehement gazes. She turned beside her and saw that Hestia's eyes were wide, and her mouth was agape. To Breksta's surprise, Hestia looked scared and hesitant.

"Yes, the child of the once powerful rebellion leader in the heart of our Academy," Ms. Adams declared with glee. "Doesn't irony strike you, Breksta Vilkas?"

"But I haven't done anything wrong," Breksta insisted, bits of her courage regathered as she looked up at Ms. Adams.

Ms. Adams's eyes grew angry as she snapped back, "Your mother caused the most destruction this country and world has ever faced. Governments torn apart. Families destroyed. All for her *ideals*."

In that moment, Breksta wished more than anything that her mother was there to protect her from her strange and cruel new world.

"You'd better learn fast, cadet, or the Academy will tear you apart, just like your mother," Ms. Adams snapped before migrating back to the front of the room.

The cadets cheered and hurled insults at Breksta. She looked around and saw that the cadets had two types of eyes: ones of anger and others ... of fear. Why they would be afraid of her? She didn't understand. All her life, she had been kind and done her best. But here, it was as if none of her past mattered. All that mattered was that she was the daughter of Asteria Vilkas.

She quickly looked at Hestia for support, for Hestia's eyes had shone with joy and reassurance that morning. Hestia averted her gaze and was busy peeling off the skin on the side of her fingers. Hestia's fingers were tipped with raw pink skin, and droplets of blood seeped from the cracks between her nail and the cuticle. But Hestia didn't seem bothered.

As Ms. Adams continued with her clicker to show more images of Dreamer destruction, Breksta focused on Hestia. Breksta nudged her gently. "I … I don't understand."

Hestia finally stopped picking at her cuticles and looked up meekly at Breksta. "You're the daughter of Asteria Vilkas. She was the rebel leader of the Dreamer rebellion against the government, the Academy. Didn't you know?"

Breksta shook her head slowly as her heart froze over with fear. Her eyes were no longer focused on the room; rather they turned inward, watching the building on fire.

Her mother.

A Dreamer.

No, she thought to herself. *Mom was not a Dreamer. She wouldn't hurt anyone.*

Just as her mind solidified her belief, Breksta hesitated. She remembered questioning her mother about the years before she was born.

"What were you like, Mom?" Breksta had asked, her eyes bright with curiosity as she looked up at Asteria.

Asteria mused for a moment before stroking Breksta's hair and speaking, "I was a very … opinionated person. Do you know what that means, opinionated?"

Breksta shook her head.

"It means that I had my own ideas and didn't let anyone tell me what to do," Asteria said with a far-off look in her eyes.

"But … you always make me whatever I ask for. What happened?" Breksta asked with puzzled eyes.

"Oh, I'll always do anything for you, honey," Asteria chuckled, tossing Breksta's hair before standing from her chair and moving into the kitchen. "Let's leave this conversation for another time."

Her mother never spoke of that day again. Fear mixed with denial in Breksta's heart. Could her mother have been there, at the White House? Could her mother, with her gentle eyes and a gentler soul, have helped kill the president? No. She wouldn't believe it. She was merely imagining. Her mother had always said her imagination was more powerful than most.

She remembered her mother's steady hand taking Breksta's as they watered their plants. The way her mother's eyes would brighten with laughter as she watched Breksta try to catch the fish slipping by in the river. Those same hands had pushed Breksta behind her while she tried to stop the bullets from piercing her daughter's skin. Those hands were as gentle as Breksta knew. She would not believe anything else. Her mother was the victim, lying dead within the cold forest in a red pool of blood. Just like the rabbit.

Beside her, Hestia gently pushed her elbow to Breksta's as she looked over into Breksta's distant eyes. "You should pay attention, unless you want to get in trouble," Hestia whispered quietly, her eyes avoiding Breksta's.

Hestia herself didn't know how to react to the truth about Breksta's mother. Training taught her that she should be like the rest of the cadets, shunning Breksta for her mother's crimes. But all Hestia saw was a scared, broken girl, a girl who had never been taught the ways of Hestia's world. Hestia could pretend like she didn't care about Breksta, but she did, for Hestia had always possessed a gentle soul in her harsh world. But Hestia said nothing to Breksta about this. Instead, she pointed to the board to reinforce that they should pay attention.

Breksta detected no hatred or disgust in Hestia's tone and managed a small nod. She swallowed the bile that rose in her throat at the conflicting thoughts of her mother and tried not to think about it.

"And so, the director, the daughter of the late president, established the Academy to train our most resilient citizens to fight back any such forces," Ms. Adams said, a genuine smile spreading across her face.

"Are there any Dreamers left, Ms. Adams?" a young boy with tousled brown hair waved his hand eagerly.

"We're finding some Dreamers as well as anti-government citizens. But soon, with your help, we will be able to celebrate a world without them!" Ms. Adams raised both fists in a cheer.

All around Breksta, clapping and cheering resonated from other cadets. Their faces lit up with joy, and their eyes sparkled with pride. All very different from the way these people had regarded Breksta. Hestia's eyes, however, didn't convey any happiness. Her entire body conveyed a deep sadness and discomfort, whereas Breksta felt only numbness and a simmering rage toward the director.

At the sight of Hestia's discomfort, Breksta asked, "Are you okay?"

Hestia shook herself slightly before looking back at Breksta. "Yes, of course. Why wouldn't I be?"

Hestia offered a meek smile before turning her eyes to the board.

"Now it's time to begin our regular class," Ms. Adams announced with her ruler back in hand. "We are studying weapons usage today."

The board shifted to images of long knives and complex guns that Breksta had never seen before. Each weapon was rated on the bottom right corner of the image with its usage and effectiveness in killing as well as its practicality.

Breksta's eyes were flooded with information. As she looked at each new image, she forgot the last one. She began to filter out Ms. Adams's droning as her mind supplanted the images on the board with her mother. The picnic in the woods felt like years ago, although it had only been yesterday. But she could still remember her mother's face during a hike one bright afternoon that looked at the natural world around them.

"Every beam of light is a life floating to the heavens," her mother had said. "One day I won't be here, and you will look into the sky and see a beam of light. That will be me watching over you."

In her mind's eye, Breksta could see the light pouring in. How she longed to leave the cold, alien classroom to look at the sky, to make sure that her mother was still there watching over her, even if her mother couldn't protect her here. She looked over at Hestia and felt a rush of warmth. Breksta's new world made her fearful, but knowing she wasn't alone made her drowning grief subside, at least slightly.

"Breksta, it's time to go to weapons training," Hestia muttered, nudging Breksta's stiff arm.

Breksta shook herself through the fog of her thoughts and followed Hestia back to the shooting ranges. This time she forced down her nausea and her urge to flee.

"Just copy me and you'll be fine," Hestia murmured, flashing a smile and a thumbs-up.

Breksta nodded and filed into the shooting range. In the center of the room lay a white table littered with different guns and vibrant red headsets. The cadets swarmed the table without a word and picked up their weapons, each child's face painted with glee. Hestia handed Breksta a headset as well as a small pistol.

"These will help with the noise," Hestia said, flashing an apologetic smile before slipping on her headset and gesturing for Breksta to do the same.

Breksta nodded and slipped the headset over her ears. The sounds around her fell away. Breksta looked down and cradled the pistol. The cold metal felt unnatural in her hands as she tried to hold it in the right direction.

"The senior cadets go first, then the rest of you. Order yourselves!" Ms. Adams shouted over the pattering feet.

The senior cadets took their places at the long row of booths and faced the freshly changed targets: humanoid figures. The cadets cupped the pistols with their hands, preventing them from pushing back and hitting themselves from the force of the explosion.

"Remember you need a clean form to get a clean shot!"

"Ready."

Breksta took in a deep breath and prepared herself.

"Set."

She held her breath and dug her fingers into her palm.

"Fire."

The bullets zipped from the senior cadets' guns and into the targets. Breksta watched in horror as those with pistols pumped out bullets faster than the shells could drop to the ground. Her heart raced wildly until finally the cadets ran out of bullets.

Her breath slowed, and gradually, with each turn of shooting, Breksta was able to block more and more sound from her mind. Eventually, it was Breksta's turn, and she walked to the booth on the very left, checking to see where Hestia stood. Hestia was beside her and gave a nod of affirmation before turning to load her pistol.

Breksta watched as the other cadets pulled the sliding metal hammer at the top of the gun. She looked back at her pistol and copied them, making a loud clack. The weight of the cold gun made her shoulders strain as she lifted it shakily to the target.

"Ready. Set. Fire."

She squeezed her eyes shut and squeezed the trigger, aiming without direction. A sliver of fear shot through her as a small burst of fire escaped the bullet chamber and the bullet flew toward the target. It missed the dummy. The gun itself leapt back at Breksta, making her cup the weighty weapon tightly in her small hands.

The sounds around her were overwhelming, and she just wanted it all to stop. She dropped the gun with a clatter. Silence formed around Breksta like ice. Ms. Adams stormed over, picking up the gun and thrusting it in Breksta's hands.

"What's wrong with you? If this were the real world, you would be dead on the ground," Ms. Adams demanded, pointing at the fallen weapon.

"Again!" Ms. Adams yelled.

Breksta picked up the gun and positioned herself again. As she squeezed the trigger, another sliver of fear slithered down her spine. The bullet landed on the leg of the figure, leaving a smoking hole. Breksta narrowed her eyes and focused on the person, ignoring the pain her arms felt and her urge to throw the gun across the room.

"Again! Are you even trying, Breksta Vilkas?"

Breksta squeezed the trigger again with all her might; her anger-driven gaze didn't stray as the bullet streaked through the air. It landed in the blood-red circle on the figure's torso, closer to the bull's-eye this time.

"Again."

She angled the gun up higher and pulled the trigger. The bullet flew wild and landed at the white edges of the target. Determination came over Breksta, and she only saw the target.

"Again."

This time Breksta was ready. She cupped the gun tightly and pulled the trigger with the chamber lined up exactly with the bull's-eye. Fire exploded from the chamber, a bang sounded, and to Breksta's surprise, she found a bullet inside the inner circle.

In the booth next to Breksta, Hestia dropped her gun and scurried over, pushing off Breksta's headsets.

"Great job!" Hestia shouted, her eyes filled with excitement.

Despite herself, Breksta smiled.

"Hey, newbie has got a bull's-eye!" a deep-voiced boy shouted from behind her.

Silence stretched through the room before it was filled with shouts of congratulations.

Ms. Adams gestured for the other cadets to stop firing.

"You may be of use yet," Ms. Adams said. She wasn't smiling, but her face had lost its cold exterior as she gazed at Breksta.

"Th-thank you," Breksta said quietly, managing a small smile.

When she stepped away from the range and placed her gun and headset down on the table, she was awarded smiles and words of congratulations. Hestia raised her hand. Breksta's smile grew wider as she slapped Hestia's hand.

The cadets wore congratulatory smiles through the rest of class, and Breksta felt her smile only grow wider by the minute, making her forget yesterday.

Breksta understood the rules of her new world better now.

To survive, one must surpass all others.

CHAPTER 7

THEIR WEAPONS CLASS FINISHED, and Hestia pulled Breksta toward the open gate between the buildings. They entered a small clearing with the same group of cadets. In the center, a brown-haired man stood with a long rifle lying on his hip, his brown eyes mirroring the spruce trees that Breksta remembered from her town.

"Welcome, Hestia. And what's your name?" the man said softly, his kind gaze a stark contrast to Ms. Adams.

"I-I'm Breksta … sir," Breksta responded timidly.

"I'm Mr. Pierce. And no titles, please," Mr. Pierce said, his lips tilting upward in a small smile before turning to the rest of the restless cadets.

"Take your places," Mr. Pierce said quietly to Breksta and Hestia as he nodded toward the rest of the cadets.

"We're doing animal tracking today. You all know the objective: find the tagged animal and complete the mission. The cadets who complete the task under an hour will be rewarded with a day off," Mr. Pierce commanded.

With that, the students trekked into the twisted forest. Even with her small figure, Breksta ducked to avoid the spiked branches. The forest held a white mist around its dark periphery. The mist clung to each branch and closed the forest around them as they walked into its arms. The cold seeped into the bare arms of the cadets, making them shiver and their teeth clatter together like glass. Yet Breksta welcomed the cold mist. It felt like comfort and home. In the forest, the thousands of tree limbs felt as if they were embracing her, welcoming her back to its presence. The smell of soggy mud and fresh wet leaves entered Breksta's nose, making her smile at the familiarity.

The children separated into small groups and formed marching lines. Breksta was pulled to the left by Hestia into the crouched group.

"Follow me, okay?" Hestia whispered.

Breksta blinked her eyes in affirmation and pointed toward the group with a furrowed brow.

"What are we doing with the animals?" she asked softly.

"Oh, we have to find the animal with a red tag on it and kill it."

Breksta's steadied breath stumbled, but before she could recover, Hestia pulled her in closer to the group.

The children's steps were harsh against the dead roots and dried leaves. Their feet pattered loudly on the ground as they broke into a run. Breksta ran with them. Her feet landed in soft presses against the forest floor, so distinct from the loud crackling footsteps of the cadets. Her feet navigated through the forest floor with ease, avoiding roots and leaping over piles of mud. As they ran, Breksta remembered her mother's instructions for hunting.

"You must change your mindset, Breksta. Put yourself in the mind of an animal. Where would you go?" Asteria had told Breksta as she motioned to the open clearing.

Breksta had lost the deer's trail and sat pouting in the center of the clearing. Breksta looked at her mother with furrowed brows, her eyes blindly reaching for answers.

"I would go out of my home and play?"

"Not exactly," Asteria chuckled. "Try to find remnants of the animals. I'll show you one here." Her mother walked over to the river that cut through the clearing. Beside it were small prints. Two curved, teardrop-shaped prints stood on the banks of the river. The imprint pushed the mud and leaves apart, setting a clear marking.

"Do you see this?" Asteria had said, kneeling to touch the mud. "This was from a deer. And since there are no more tracks, we can conclude that the deer traveled across the river. Over there."

Across the river, two trees curved to form an X. As Breksta continued to look, she saw only trees and the abundance of tree limbs.

"Can we go look for it, Mom?" Breksta had asked, pointing across the river and bouncing up and down with excitement.

"Alright. But not for too long," Asteria had said.

Her mother chuckled as she watched Breksta splash her way across the river, the wet mud from the banks splashing up to paint Breksta's leggings with black and brown color.

Coming back from her memories, Breksta knew the cadets would never find the animal. Their feet would cover any last imprints of an animal while their running would scare away the creatures within a mile.

The group ran for almost half an hour, looking out for any neon tags in the brush. To the dismay of the cadets, they found nothing. But Breksta was glad, for she never wished to witness the death of another animal or person.

Soon, the group stopped in a clearing to catch their breath and wait for slower cadets. Breksta sat beside Hestia, quietly observing their conversations. To the cadets, Breksta was an insignificant shadow who followed them. But to one, Icarus, she was a mystery and the product of a rebellion of evil. Icarus stood after a while, crossing the clearing from where he was standing, and leaned against a tree near where Breksta and Hestia sat on the ground. Breksta watched him approach, looking to Hestia for reassurance. Hestia watched him approach with a look of disdain.

"So ... you're Breksta Vilkas," Icarus said, more of a statement than a question.

Breksta nodded slowly. She found Icarus's eyes lacking. It was as if no emotion was there, void of all feeling. Icarus opened and closed his mouth, pondering his question.

"What do you want, Icarus?" Hestia said, bracing her hands on her knees as if preparing to stand and face off with an enemy.

"When my mother—I mean Ms. Adams—asked you if you knew what Dreamers were, why did you lie?" Icarus asked.

"Ms. Adams is your mother?" Breksta asked, trying to find a resemblance between the anger of Ms. Adams and the cold ambivalence of Icarus.

Icarus nodded, his eyes flashing with something, perhaps familiarity, before disappearing.

"It's not my mother who matters, but yours," Icarus retorted.

At the mention of Asteria, Breksta startled. It was as if an icy hand had seized her heart, for she knew the pain would accompany the image of her mother's broken body amid the leaves. All of it would flood back in, when all Breksta really wanted was for life to return to how it was. Her mother's soft eyes came to mind as tears pooled in her eyes.

"Look, you made her cry, Icarus," Hestia said, tugging him to face Breksta again. "Apologize."

"I will not! Not to someone who is the product of all our families' pain. Why do you think your mother built the Academy, Hestia? To keep us safe from people like her," he exclaimed.

And for once, Breksta, through her tears, saw true anger and pain in Icarus's eyes. A small part of Breksta, the girl who loved the woods and her village, felt empathy for this boy whose eyes held pain that Breksta was sure her eyes held as well. But that small part was drowned by Breksta's own agony. In front of her, Breksta barely registered Hestia's verbal sparring with Icarus.

"Breksta, don't listen to him," Hestia shouted back at Breksta, her voice soothing but not quite enough for Breksta.

Breksta's mind was gone from the forest and the cadets. It was consumed again by her mother. Asteria's kind eyes and her warm hugs. Her perfectly braided hair and her gentle words that guided her childhood. And her mother's now empty eyes. A sob released itself from Breksta's lips followed by a wave of sadness. Her feet carried her away from the cadets, deeper into the forest as she tried to find a place where she could escape.

"Breksta! Come back!" Hestia shouted.

Breksta could hear Hestia's loud stomps behind her, the steps that were so different and unnatural from hers, which only made her run faster. She wiped tears from her face as she ran, but she could not stop the flow of her pain.

"Breksta, stop! He didn't mean it," Hestia begged.

Breksta didn't listen. She kept running, turning, leaping, and averting Hestia. She knew forests better than any of them. The black curled trees embraced her into their grip and surrounded her with shadows to make it harder for Hestia to catch Breksta.

To her right, Breksta spotted a river, and she knew what to do. She raced to the shore and stepped in. The mossy rocks at the bottom made her slip from left to right as she put her weight on them. The frigid water splashed up to her thighs as she waded farther in. It climbed up to her waist. Then to her chest. When her feet could no longer touch the rocks, Breksta began to swim across. Behind her, Hestia stopped at the edge of the river.

Hestia stomped her feet and sent sprays of dirt mixed with water around her as she yelled, "Breksta, stop trying to run away! It's dangerous out there."

"Leave. Me. Alone," Breksta shouted through the burbling water.

She pulled her arms through the water to outpace the river's current. The ice water dug into her skin and sucked all the warmth from her body. But Breksta didn't stop.

"I'm coming! Don't worry."

Breksta heard Hestia wading into the river after her. She turned to see Hestia's emerald eyes fill with fear as the ice water lapped at her ankles. But Hestia pressed on, forcing more of herself to be submerged under the glacier water.

Breksta turned, slowly pulling herself across the water's surface with her arms. In the deepest parts, Breksta couldn't see the bottom of the murky water. Her legs kicked up white drifts of water as she neared the other side. Gradually, the river bottom came closer to Breksta's heavy feet, and she dragged herself onto the shore. Breksta stopped to catch her breath and spit out the bits of bark that she had ingested when suddenly she heard gurgling behind her.

"Hulp mi," she heard, the voice distorted with water.

She turned to see Hestia thrashing, paddling her arms around herself in circles. Her head was tilted back, and only her mouth was above the water. Breksta gasped and watched as the river pushed Hestia farther and farther downstream.

Breksta rushed to follow her on the banks with her hands cupped around her mouth, shouting, "W-wait!"

They moved together; Hestia swept downstream with Breksta by her side on land.

Hestia's head bobbed up at times above the white waves of the river. Just ahead, Breksta spotted a dead branch that stuck up from the edge of the river. She pulled it out of the ground with all her might before dangling it over the river toward Hestia.

"Take this!"

Hestia's hands blindly grasped for the hollow wood, only to be rewarded with more of the river's momentum. She slipped and continued downstream toward a drop with protruding rocks in the center, splitting the river in two.

Breksta threw down the branch and leapt forward into the river. She latched onto the scruff of Hestia's jacket. Hestia felt the sharp tug at her neck and shot her hand up, clinging on to Breksta. Breksta surfaced with Hestia on the other side, the ice water clinging to her clothes and skin. She pulled Hestia ashore until they were both far enough away from the river to not be pulled back in. She was unaware of the sharp stones that cut into her hands as she dragged Hestia to safety. Hestia's face was pale, and her veins appeared green. Her lips were a light shade of purple. Trembling and sputtering out dirt-ridden river water, Hestia reached up and clung to the edges of Breksta's jacket as Breksta helped her up into a sitting position.

Breksta studied her emerald-eyed companion, watching her distraught face as she tried to breathe. Words of comfort danced on Breksta's lips, ready to burst forth, but Hestia beat her to it.

"Th-thank you," she murmured, her words chittered out like a telegram with each letter clipped at the end.

"Are you okay?" Breksta murmured back, picking at the zipper on her jacket.

Hestia put her icy hands on Breksta's, stopping Breksta's fidgeting momentarily.

"No. Thank *you*, Breksta." Hestia's emerald eyes were endless pools of gratitude. "I-I don't know what I would've done … if you hadn't got me out. So, thank you."

"Y-you're welcome?" Breksta murmured, testing the words in her mouth.

Hestia smiled and retracted her hands, moving them to pull her drenched jacket around her. Breksta felt a smile crawl up her face and spread across her lips.

As Breksta watched the river's movement, she allowed herself to relax. She closed her eyes and breathed in the scents of the trees around her. She imagined it was yesterday. The forest air, the smell of dirt, and the sound of the rushing river made it as if she were there, still at home with her mother. Breksta's smile widened until it stretched to her ears.

"What is it?" Hestia asked, studying her expression.

"Nothing. I like it out here. Not back there," murmured Breksta, opening her eyes and gesturing in the general direction of the Academy to show her distaste. But she didn't think about the Academy as her breath slowly evened out.

"It's nice, to get away," Hestia said hesitantly.

They stayed in their bubble of silence, listening and sensing the world around them. Breksta felt like she could forget, if only for a moment, what happened yesterday. She could pretend that her mother was still here by her side. Her mother would tell her stories as they watched the birds exchange their songs and the two of them would go home when the sun began its trip to the horizon.

A sudden voice snapped Breksta out of her reverie.

"What's going on here?"

The girls turned to see Mr. Pierce's looming figure, his troops lingering behind with their rifles and weapons stashed in various places on their bodies.

"We've been looking for you two for a while," he said, disappointment dripping from his words.

"Hestia was—"

"We were just exploring and got lost. Sorry, sir," Hestia quickly injected, casting a knowing look at Breksta.

"Don't tell," she mouthed.

Hestia offered an icy hand to Breksta as she stood. Breksta accepted it and pulled herself up from her drenched position. Her hand that had been scraped raw from the sharp rocks left drops of blood on Hestia's pale wet hands, creating a pink paint-like mixture.

"Come on, and don't get lost this time."

Mr. Pierce motioned for the girls to follow the cadets, ignoring their wet state. The cadets, however, looked at them with questioning glares. In the front of the group was Icarus. He was holding a small dangling object. As they got closer, Breksta could see what it was. He held a broken, beheaded body with its innards spilling greenish-blue liquid onto the ground. Breksta closed her eyes as she walked past so she wouldn't see the revolting creature. But as she did, she smelled its blood. It made her shudder.

"Your hand, let me see it," Hestia said, reaching down as Breksta pulled her hand into a fist.

Breksta held out her hand, letting Hestia uncurl her fist, revealing the raw pink skin underneath. Her hand oozed with blood and was embedded with bits of rocks and dirt. She winced as Hestia gently pulled out pieces of the rock.

"We need to get this looked at when we get back," Hestia commanded, marching Breksta to the front of the group.

Breksta shuddered at the thought of the cold room and the doctor who injected her.

"No, I'm alright," she quickly interjected, pulling her hand out of Hestia's reach.

"But it's—"

"I'm fine. Really."

Breksta's voice shook as her hand throbbed from the pain. She bit her lip, forcing the pain back down and keeping her face calm.

A skill that was becoming easier for Breksta.

CHAPTER 8

BY THE TIME BREKSTA AND HESTIA reached their dorm after their dinner, the stars were twinkling above their heads. Breksta's muscles burned from the inside out. The girls stumbled back up the crooked stairs to their dorm. Their clothes still carried the dirt and river water from earlier; the river had left them with an icy, bone-deep cold.

"I'll shower first. The bottom two shelves are yours," Hestia slurred as she rummaged through their small wooden closet for her own clothes.

Breksta settled comfortably on the floor as Hestia closed the door to the bathroom. On the bottom shelf lay her duffel. She unzipped it and found that her belongings, which had been neatly folded by her mother, were now over-turned. She rummaged through her bag until she was met with her familiar rabbit toy. As soon as Breksta pulled the animal out of her bag, she yelped and flung the twisted animal across the room. The small figure had been contorted into a monster.

The rabbit's back was split open; the threads that held it together had been cut. The insides had been pulled out and re-stuffed. Its body sagged against the wall where Breksta had thrown it and its neck lolled to the side, eyeing Breksta with a sad smile. The rabbit's distorted body that had long provided comfort to her now brought tears to Breksta's eyes. Her mother had fixed the rabbit every time a limb fell off. But this time, there would be no fixing it.

Breksta angrily brushed the tears off her face and crossed the room to where her fragile animal lay. She opened the bottom drawer of the closet and packed her clothes inside. She finally picked up the rabbit and shoved it to the very back, never to see the light of day again and never to remind her of her mother's death.

The water soon stopped, and Hestia stepped out dressed in a large T-shirt and fluffy pajama pants.

"It's your turn," Hestia said gently.

A quiet knock sounded against the metal door.

"I'll get it," Hestia inserted before Breksta could stand.

She opened the door to reveal Madam Director and Ms. Adams, their black garments identical.

"Hello, Hestia. I need to *borrow* Breksta. To talk to her," Madam Director announced coldly.

Breksta turned but didn't stand, eyeing the women cautiously. Her fear and distrust of both women rose.

"Up and along now," Ms. Adams said.

Hestia stood in the way while Breksta approached slowly. Hestia gently touched Breksta's wrist to get her attention, her emerald eyes reflecting unease. As Breksta passed, Hestia mouthed, "Please don't resist."

"Where are you taking me?" Breksta demanded as they walked through the darkness.

"Don't speak unless you are spoken to," Madam Director snapped before replying in a quieter voice, "You will see." In the low lights of the lampposts, Madam Director offered a flat smile that didn't mirror her eyes.

The dark building lit up as they proceeded to the lobby area. On the right, the guard from the morning sat behind his desk and watched with a militaristic gaze as she walked past. Ms. Adams walked closely behind Breksta and subtly made her walk faster and faster down the spiral stairs. They skipped past the shooting range level, going through deeper levels of the building. They reached the lowest floor where the staircase stopped. Immediately, Breksta was met with a rush of distasteful smells; the dampness and mold overwhelmed her nose. A hallway extended far into the distance. On either side, black doors were bolted with a lock to ensure double security of whatever was inside.

"Don't move," the director said, pulling a thin silver key from her pocket.

Her cold tone made Breksta shiver, the feeling of premonition growing while the director unlocked the first door. It took both women to pull open the door, revealing a pitch-black room. The stench of mold and mildew drifted out of the room as the door opened, as if a long-caged ghost had finally escaped. An even more pungent smell erupted from the depths of the room, making Breksta cough and step back.

"W-what *is* this?" she stuttered as she looked between the room and the women.

"Step into the room," the director commanded.

Breksta looked back at the long staircase they had come from. The only guard she had seen was the one at the desk, the one who Hestia had warned her about if she broke rules.

The director's eyes were fixed on Breksta, noticing her line of sight. "You won't make it," the director murmured, her words laced with absolute surety that made Breksta feel the weight of her situation.

Breksta hesitated, looking back at the director and the room. The premonition grew to dread in Breksta. Something wasn't right. The director's eyes were too cold to mean well. The director pointed sharply at the dark room, indicating that Breksta needed to enter. Breksta took a slow step toward the darkness. She steeled her mind as one thought became clear. She would run as soon as she got the chance.

"Keep moving," Madam Director commanded with apparent zeal that matched her cold smile.

Just as Breksta's foot crossed over the threshold, she turned and darted past the director, speeding toward the stairs. The director reached for Breksta's thin wrists, but she misjudged Breksta's speed and will. Eluding the director's grasp, Breksta pushed away the burning in her thighs and focused on her sole purpose: to escape this prison.

Madam Director shouted orders into an intercom. "Matthew, block the lobby exit immediately. We have a deserter."

Breksta raced past the level with the shooting range. A few more floors and Breksta would be able to escape this cold new world. She got to the lobby and found it empty. On the left, the white marble desk was unattended. The guard who had been sitting there was nowhere to be seen. Breksta continued running toward the door. As she neared it, someone swept Breksta's legs. With a yelp, Breksta slammed into the cold concrete floor. She put up her hands as she fell, protecting her face. Her hands, however, didn't protect her from the cold rigidity of the marble floor that slammed into her ribs, causing her chest to erupt in pain. She screamed before wriggling her feet to escape the grip of her pursuer.

"Let go of me!" Breksta shouted through gritted teeth and her body's pain, turning to see the guard holding her ankle.

"Stop fighting," the guard instructed.

Her ribs throbbed and made each breath feel like a fire was growing in her chest. Her eyes blinked away the small tears of pain as she tried to escape the guard's firm grip. Her kicking and wriggling only lasted a few seconds before the guard grabbed her hands and yanked her into a standing position.

The guard seized Breksta by her shoulders, turning her to face the director, who approached slowly, as if she never doubted that Breksta would be caught.

"I told you, Breksta. You wouldn't make it. Bring her downstairs."

As they began their long walk back down the dark stairwell, Breksta felt cold dread overtake her controlled emotions. The darkness felt as if it would hold her there: a prisoner forever. Her fear of the darkness encouraged her fighting spirit, and as they neared the dark level, Breksta pulled and tugged against the guard's iron grip. Soon Breksta found she couldn't resist against him, and she was once more face to face with the cold stench of the pitch-black room.

"I didn't do anything!" she screamed as the guard forced her by her shoulders toward the room.

"On the contrary, you almost drowned a fellow cadet: Hestia. That, including your attempted desertion, will be punished with three days lockup. In *here*," Madam Director retorted coldly. "You will go to class as usual, but all other times must be spent here rethinking your actions."

With one final push, the guard shoved her, and she stumbled into the room. Losing her balance, Breksta's elbows grated against the rough concrete floor, bringing another wave of stinging pain. The director stood in front of the door and stared at Breksta with her cold eyes.

"I didn't try to hurt Hestia! She was following me. I didn't ask her to follow me into the water. But I saved her!" Breksta begged, pushing herself up to stand and face the director.

"*You* were the reason for her near-death encounter. Not to mention the damage that *your mother* caused," the director spat. "Bad actions must be punished. And your mother was a clear example of that. I hoped you would remember. But … like mother like daughter … you must learn through *punishment*," the director retorted.

Shivers quaked Breksta's body, and her teeth began to chatter from the room's unforgiving temperature.

"Remember, Breksta … this is for the greater good. You *must* understand your place here," the director added, her voice becoming softer before the thick metal door slammed shut.

The darkness of the room surrounded Breksta, engulfing her in its endless gloom, except for the sliver of light from the moon coming through the barred window above her. The coldness of the bare walls made the walls in her mind crumble. There was no life here, only shadows. Breksta despised such darkness. She despised the coldness of this world she'd been forced to endure, a world that was just as cold and lifeless as the room where she was now imprisoned.

As the silence of the room enveloped her, her eyes began to adjust. She saw a thin, bare mattress lying on the ground in one corner of the room. She moved over to the mattress and sat, feeling the small comfort it gave to her body that helped to counter her agony and grief. She noticed a hole in the concrete at the opposite corner and realized that was where the foul smell was coming from. Farther up, where slits of light fell into the room, she considered the height of the barred window; it was high, but if she jumped, her fingers could ghost the metal.

She felt as if all hope had disintegrated into the darkness of the room. Her beautiful, simple life was gone, and so were the people who had been part of it. Her neighbors, always kind and smiling as she passed. The nature of her home and the nearby forest, always peaceful and serene. And her mother, always loving and attentive. All were now memories of a far-off childhood. Since she first arrived, Breksta had considered her new world as a joyless prison. But now she knew that the unyielding cruelty of this Academy—a life Breksta could barely grasp—had the potential to destroy her. There would always be farther to fall.

Slowly … gradually … her chest began to heave, and she began to cry. The tears cut across her face in shining trails and fell to the ground. Her heart was weighed down by death and pain, making her arms curl around her as a final protection.

"Mom…" she called out to the darkness. When she was met with silence, a fresh flow of tears streamed down her face. She continued until her eyes ran dry and all she felt was exhaustion. She lay back on the mattress, unbothered by the cold, her wispy hair fanning out around her. Turning on her side, she curled her knees to her chest and wrapped her arms around them, allowing her exhaustion to drown her.

Her eyes closed and her breaths evened out. Soon, her body relaxed as her mind rested from her pain. As she slept for a small pocket of time, Breksta was able to forget and dream of her forest and her birds that sang sweet melodies.

CHAPTER 9

IN THE DORMS, HESTIA LAY awake in bed staring at the peeling gray ceiling. She tried to stop her restless mind by turning, shifting, and moving. But her mind replayed her day continuously.

She remembered how she lost her footing and was swept downstream by the harsh, cold current. She remembered how she grabbed at stones and tree stumps to pull herself out of the deadly water, but all her hands came away with was moss and bunches of broken twigs. She remembered how the water pushed her down until her flailing arms no longer kept her head at the surface and her back was scraped by rocks at the bottom.

As she came back to the surface, she had heard Breksta's faint voice, but Hestia couldn't make out her words. With the last of her strength, she extended her arms above the water and felt the whisper of wood underneath her fingers before she was swept away again.

She closed her eyes under the water and felt her mind give in to the current.

Suddenly, a hand gripped her collar from behind. Hestia felt herself being dragged slowly up the riverside until her face was clear of the river's surface. Sweet air refilled her lungs as she emptied out the freezing water from her body.

This scene replayed in Hestia's mind until she couldn't bear it anymore. She looked over at the clock on her dresser, and it blinked a dim red "12:03." Hestia groaned in frustration as she repositioned herself, searching for sleep. Minutes flew by, but every time she almost reached the slow consciousness of sleep, her mind seared the burning of ice water in her lungs and forced her awake.

Hestia finally gave in and leapt out of bed, landing clumsily with a loud thump and a twist of her ankle that made her wince. She splashed her face with lukewarm water from the bathroom sink and looked up at herself in the mirror. Her eyes carried bags of wrinkled, purple skin.

Hestia sat on the floor of her room and pondered whether she should go and look for Breksta. She knew Breksta had been sentenced to the box of solitude. She felt guilt for Breksta's sadness and fear that was apparent on her face when she left their room.

Hestia looked back at the clock, and it blinked back "12:46." Her mind was made up. She grabbed her jacket, a small screwdriver from her drawers, and the gray blanket from Breksta's bed. She slipped on her shoes and left her room.

She tiptoed through the dorm hallway, only stepping on the planks she had memorized that didn't creak. She reached the stairs and jogged down to the first-floor lobby. She made her way across the paths lit dimly by old lampposts to the building directly opposite of the dorms.

She circled around the building to the back where a seven-foot black metal fence surrounded the entire Academy. At the point where a gate stood, opening to the outside world, a guard sat, protecting the cadets from outside dangers. The guard also prevented cadets from leaving except for missions. The gate led to the dark forest where Hestia had completed uncountable missions to track animals. Past the gate, a small set of stairs led to a series of barred windows above the solitude boxes. Because of her past missions, Hestia knew the placement of those windows.

Entering the cells wasn't the challenge, but getting past the guard at the gate would be. Hestia steeled her nervous breaths and approached with firm footsteps against the pavement. The guard slouched against the metal gate, his rifle leaning beside his thigh, his eyes covered by the hood of his jacket, and his arms crossed.

The guard raised his eyes to meet her gaze. "Who are you?" he asked. "State your purpose here."

76

"I'm Hestia."

"The … director's daughter," the guard said. Appearing shocked, his posture immediately straightened. "What are you doing out here at night?"

"I realize this is a very absurd time, but there was some shuffling outside my window. I thought I should report it," Hestia said shakily, failing to channel her mother.

"We are surrounded by forests, kid. Sounds are bound to be heard."

"But you must look into it," Hestia insisted. "I think that someone might be hiding out in the Academy, a Dreamer perhaps?"

"I'll check the perimeter in the morning," the guard said with a yawn, his posture still straight, but his eyes conveyed a bit of humor.

He didn't take her seriously, Hestia realized. She thought of all the years she had listened to her mother before mimicking the same cold, stern voice that streamed out of her mother's lips on every occasion. "My mother is very particular about Dreamers," Hestia commanded icily. "She would greatly value someone who embodies the values of our Academy and removes such … damaging people."

Realizing her voice was almost identical to her mother's, Hestia almost revealed her shock, surprised and fearful at how easily and quickly she had slipped into her mother's form. Instead, she plastered the same commanding expression across her face that she had seen her mother wear so often.

The guard turned his face up to the lampposts and straightening his lips before saluting, he responded, "I'll check on it immediately. Don't worry, ma'am. Let me take you back to your dorm. For your own safety."

Hestia led the way as the guard marched her to her dorm.

"Here you are," he said in a sweeping gesture, opening the door for her.

"Thanks, and goodnight," Hestia said, offering the guard a gentle smile.

He nodded and gestured for her to walk inside. Hestia obliged and walked back up the stairs of her dorm, looking out the window until she saw that the guard had passed and entered the opposite building. A mischievous smile spread across Hestia's face as she reveled in her rebellion before she raced down the stairs and back to the gate. She hefted the weighty bar that held the gate in place and slipped through. She resecured the bar and began to whisper Breksta's name.

She darted down the stairs and found the row of ground-level barred windows. The rusted bars offered no protection from the elements, just as the director had intended. It was especially worse now for Breksta, since she had gone into the frigid river and the fall wind was slowly shifting to winter's cold. Hestia crouched in the dirt. One by one, she looked in each window, until she found Breksta curled tightly on a mattress.

"Breksta," Hestia whispered down to her, cupping her mouth with her ice-cold hands. She was met with silence, except for the sound of beating wind against the crooked trees. "Breksta!"

The loud calling of her name awoke Breksta, and she looked up. She blinked a few times to see tangled fiery red hair spilling through the window, blocking the moonlight.

"Breksta!"

"Hestia?" Breksta mumbled, rubbing her eyes.

"Yes. I'm gonna unscrew the bars, okay?" she whispered.

Hestia unscrewed the metal plate that held the base of the bars into the concrete. The bars were secured together, and before long, she had unfastened them. Hestia grinned and stashed the screwdriver into her pajama pocket.

"I'm going to hide the bars. Here, take this blanket," Hestia whispered.

Breksta nodded sleepily and raised her arms. Hestia dropped the gray blanket into Breksta's arms before scurrying off toward the trees. When she returned, she threw a glance to the gate and prepared to slip into the solitude box. Hestia pushed her legs in first, slowly lowering herself down to the floor.

"W-what are y-you d-doing here?" Breksta murmured, her shoulders shivering with each word.

"I couldn't sleep," Hestia said, waving off Breksta's confused and slightly fearful expression.

"I thought you would be cold," she said sheepishly, flicking her eyes to the blanket in Breksta's arms.

Breksta nodded before quickly pulling the gray cloth around herself, feeling the coldness begin to recede. Breksta sat numbly back onto the ground. Her mind jolted back to the reason why she was in this dark place.

"You almost drowned another cadet," the director had said.

Feeling ashamed, Breksta looked away from Hestia so Hestia would not see Breksta's lip tremble from the guilt that plagued her. Hestia sat side-by-side with Breksta, but far enough away so that they weren't touching. Breksta felt Hestia's gaze on her but didn't move. After a moment's hesitation, Hestia gently nudged Breksta's shoulders with her own.

"How are you?"

"Fine," Breksta said blandly, her tongue tasting the lie as it came out.

"I-I know you might feel scared or sad right now, but I promise, it'll get better," Hestia murmured gently.

Though her words were gentle, Breksta felt the candor of them like a blade, ripping through her defenses and revealing her deep grief. Breksta paused before resting her head against the cold wall behind them. Her eyes were filled with silver tears that reflected the moon's gentle glow. Hestia's heart clenched at the sight of Breksta's tears.

"Will it really get better?" Breksta choked out bitterly.

She didn't move to wipe away her tears this time, letting them drip down her face. Breksta felt tired, so very tired. She didn't care about anything anymore—not the new people, not the strange classes, not this new lifeless world.

Breksta's tears continued to fall as she thought of her mother and how she would have comforted Breksta. Her mother would have wrapped her in blankets and placed her on her bed, telling her to wait a few moments. Then she would have returned with warm hot chocolate and a mind full of stories that would bring a smile to Breksta's face. That smile had been stolen by guns and death.

With her eyes closed, as she imagined her mother's warm embrace, Breksta saw a red hole spread out on her mother's forehead that left dark red blood flowing. Breksta gasped quietly—just loud enough for Hestia to hear—and felt violent sobs return.

Hestia reached out her hand and put it on Breksta's shoulder. "What is it?"

Breksta tensed at the foreign touch. Slowly, she reminded herself that Madam Director was not here and decided that Hestia's words were genuine. With her throat tight, Breksta shook her head in answer to Hestia.

Hestia hesitated before whispering into the silence, "Do you need a hug?"

Breksta's fingers toyed with the blanket before nodding slightly. Hestia opened her arms and gently wrapped them around Breksta, feeling her sigh in Hestia's arms. Breksta allowed herself to relax, closing her eyes and reminding herself that this girl had been nothing but kind. She imagined that it was her mother. As if it was her mother's thin fingers that spread across her back. Pretending that the smell of faint pollen her mother wore from tending to the flowers on the porch of her yellow house was in the air. When Breksta closed her eyes, that was exactly what she saw.

Hestia's voice shattered the illusion. "I'm sorry ... for how it is here."

Breksta opened her eyes and the image of her mother's arms disappeared.

"It's not personal," Hestia said, pausing for Breksta's mind to process. "My mother has a certain ... reputation to keep with the other kids here. It's not you. She just has to show the other kids that you can't do things and get away with it."

There was silence as Hestia felt Breksta's thin shoulders slump. She couldn't help the wave of pity she felt, making her hug Breksta even tighter.

However, as Breksta pondered the director, she found that Hestia's words didn't explain the director's hateful and cruel face. The gleeful face that looked down on her mother as she pulled the trigger and left her mother lying there, alone and bloodied. The words that were spoken sharply as the director closed the door to Breksta's box of solitude. The coldness that shrouded the director each time Breksta saw her, the director's dark eyes piercing through her and injecting fear into her mind. How could it be anything but personal?

Hestia's touch no longer felt gentle and kind. Instead, it felt like a betrayal. Breksta felt guilt take hold, guilt for surviving when her mother did not, guilt for enjoying Hestia's company despite Hestia's mother killing hers. Guilt dug its claws deep into her mind so that she couldn't remove the feeling. She pulled away from Hestia and pulled her blanket around herself even tighter.

Hestia blinked rapidly and folded her hands in her lap. Her emerald eyes sparkled under the moonlight as she murmured, "I'm sorry, did I say something?"

Breksta shook her head, her mind waging a war between Hestia's kindness and the director's cruelty.

"Okay ... okay," Hestia confirmed, nodding back at her.

They breathed in silence for a few moments before Hestia asked, "I know that you just got here, but I was wondering ... if you need a friend?"

Breksta wished she could refuse Hestia's offer, since her mother's death had been at the hands of this girl's mother. Nothing could ever change her hatred for that woman. But Hestia's kindness had brought moments of joy to Breksta's grief. Her hugs allowed Breksta to find comfort and imagine her mother still alive. Hestia's gift, the single gray blanket, had taken away Breksta's cold. Breksta concluded that Hestia wasn't the director, just as Breksta wasn't her own mother.

"Okay, I'll be your friend," Breksta said slowly, feeling her heart swell with hope. Yet, she wondered if that meant she could tell Hestia about her mother's death and, especially, who killed her.

CHAPTER 10

HESTIA SMILED WIDELY. "So, as your *official* friend, I think it's only fair that we know more about each other, right? So, tell me, what's it like outside the Academy?" Hestia spoke enthusiastically, inching closer to Breksta, watching her intently.

Images of Breksta's forest flashed before her eyes before she answered, "Well, my house has a forest next to it…" She tried to imagine the warm sunshine and joy of her village before her mother's death.

"Is it like the Academy's forest? What did you do in yours?" Hestia asked.

"They're different. In my forest…" Breksta paused, unsure if she should share the memories of her mother. "…my mom would take me on picnics, and we would build fairy houses or camp in the woods. We would also track animals, but not like tracking here, where the animals are *killed*. We would just try and find where they traveled in the forest by tracking their footprints." The more Breksta spoke, the more her memories of brighter, happier times flooded in.

After listening to Breksta speak for a while, Hestia sighed. Breksta looked over, pausing in her story to make sure her new friend was not bored or hurt in some way.

"Wow, I wish my mom took me to do those things," Hestia said, her voice laced with disappointment. "My mom is always working. Which *she* says is more important than playing," Hestia added with a flat voice, as if she had repeated this to herself many times before.

"I'm sorry," Breksta said hesitantly, unsure if she had hurt Hestia.

"Don't be," Hestia said curtly, forcing a smile of reassurance toward Breksta. "What else did you do?"

Breksta continued her story about the fairy houses and her gentle village and the gentle people who lived there, including Ms. Aileen. The images, still bright and clear in Breksta's mind, were gifted to Hestia, who listened intently.

Hestia had imagined what life was like outside the Academy walls, past the dark forests and safe boundaries. But she had never dreamed that it could be as magical as Breksta described. How she wished she could touch the same clear streams near Breksta's house, smell the fresh wood in the forest, and touch the soft petals of the flowers that Breksta grew on her porch. Hestia was thankful for such hopeful stories and listened with a smile as Breksta spoke.

As Breksta told stories about fishing with her mother, she found that Hestia's curiosity and kindness brought light to the darkness of her cell. Hestia's eyes never left her friend. Breksta found that she liked telling these stories, for whenever she did, Hestia smiled and laughed. Those smiles and laughter were music.

Through the night, Breksta felt her heart's barriers fall away. Breksta's strong friendship with her mother had been brutally severed. But Breksta found that her new blossoming friendship with Hestia was as easy as her bond with her mother. It felt like a part of Asteria's soul had been revived and placed in this girl, keeping watch over Breksta.

And as much as it pained her to remember her mother alive, she realized that she was the only one who truly knew her mother. She was the only one who kept these stories of her mother, these memories of adventure. So in the spirit of keeping her mother's memory alive, she told Hestia fragments of her memories. And Breksta found that Hestia, who had never experienced such adventures, needed these stories as much as Breksta needed to remember them.

"I can tell you about the training my mom gave me. It's very different from how training is done here," Breksta began.

Hestia grinned widely. "Yes please!"

Breksta returned Hestia's grin and began. Breksta told Hestia of her survival training that her mother had given her. The long days camping in the woods with canteens of water and a single jacket on her back. She had done these training sessions various times and found that each time, the forest was more and more welcoming. She foraged for food and fish under her mother's watchful eye.

It was on one of these training sessions that Breksta learned one of her mother's more important lessons. Asteria and Breksta had walked back through the dense forest after a day of hiking and endurance training. They followed the small symbols and landmarks they had memorized: the large nest that nestled itself on the branch of a birch tree; a clearing with soft, pink primroses packed together; the familiar stream that led from the wilder forest to the one they knew so well. As they walked, Breksta felt a deep fatigue in her legs and her head grew foggy, for they had walked a total of almost twenty kilometers. It felt like hours had passed until Breksta saw their mint-green tent top that stood encircled by trees. Once Breksta reached their unlit campfire, she sunk to the ground, tired and drowsy.

"It's time to make dinner now, Breksta," her mother said, tapping her on the shoulder from behind.

Breksta shook her head, mumbling her tired complaints.

"Well, that's not a very good attitude. If you can't make your own dinner, then how do you expect to survive by yourself in the world?" her mother said, standing with her hands on her hips.

"You can take care of me," Breksta murmured. "I just want to go to sleep."

"I won't always be here for you, Breksta," her mother said, brushing a strand of Breksta's hair back from her eyes.

Breksta groaned loudly, "Can I please just go to sleep!"

Also tired from the day's excursions, Asteria sighed angrily, "Fine! If you want to be difficult, then get out of my sight."

Breksta recoiled at her mother's anger but was too tired and frustrated to retaliate. She stomped off to her tent, curling inside the sleeping bag as she fell through the folds of sleep.

When she came to, the tent was drowned in complete darkness. Breksta unzipped the tent and peeked out her head before stepping into the dark forest.

The only light came from the dim coals of the fire that cast orange shadows on the trees. Slivers of the moon peeked between the trees to glance at Breksta, but besides that, Breksta was alone. She scanned the ground around her, looking for her mother.

"Mom? Are you here?" she called out, pulling her jacket tighter around her as a wave of cold wind hit her.

There was no reply except for the swaying of the branches, making the forest sound like a musical cicada.

"Mom!" Breksta shouted, twirling around and around for signs of her mother but found none.

Still weary, but at least more alert, she moved and sat by the fire. The biting cold winds grew stronger, making the trees sway more violently. Suddenly, Breksta realized there were more sounds besides the movement of the trees behind her.

"Mom!" she exclaimed, whirling around in relief.

To her surprise, she wasn't met with her mother's kind eyes but glowing yellow ones. She leapt up in fear and moved behind the fire to keep the animal as far from her as possible. The animal padded toward the fire, baring its teeth as it pulled its lips back in a snarl. As the flames illuminated its face, Breksta recognized what it was: a silver wolf.

"S-stay back!" Breksta exclaimed, keeping her hands up and looking around frantically for some protection.

The wolf didn't stop and continued walking in slow, measured steps toward the fire until it was directly opposite Breksta. She saw her mother's cooking knife on the wooden board beside a filleted fish. All she had to do was get to it, even if she didn't know what she would do with it. She shifted and moved slowly to her right toward the knife.

With its cunning eyes, the wolf followed her movements and matched her steps in the opposite direction, keeping its body low to the ground. The two continued like that, circling each other until Breksta felt the knife at her feet. She slowly lowered herself toward the ground, causing the wolf to growl. She then snatched knife, and the wolf reacted, jumping, and raising its head to bark loudly. She held the knife in her quivering hands as she continued to watch the wolf. The animal dropped its ears and broke its eye contact with her. Breksta traced the wolf's line of sight to the fish on the cutting board.

She finally understood and relaxed her grip on the blade. "You just want food, right?" She shuffled over carefully to the food while the wolf leapt back defensively, again baring its teeth.

"It's okay," Breksta said.

She placed her knife slowly down to the ground and raised her hands in surrender. The wolf kept its eyes low and its face downward. Breksta knew, from what her mother had taught her about wolves, that this one regarded her as the alpha. She trusted in the wolf pack's hierarchy as she trusted in her mother's teaching. She quickly cut the fish in two. Then she threw the tail toward the wolf. It landed with a wet thump at its feet.

Pointing at the food, she stated calmly, "You can have some."

The wolf cocked its head toward her curiously, as if wondering, "Why would you, a human, offer me food freely?" When Breksta didn't attack with her knife and merely stood, gesturing at the food, the wolf seemed to understand. It approached and ate the food eagerly.

Breksta released a breath when she saw the wolf's benevolent intentions. She sat on the ground as she studied the animal. Its ashen fur extended down the wolf's back and tail and around its eyes and snout. But the wolf's underbelly was a silver white that looked like the pelts she had seen on the wall of the hunting house in her village. The pelts on the wall had always made her sad, knowing that villagers had taken them from such beautiful animals. To Breksta, wolves were one of the most beautiful animals she had ever seen.

The peace Breksta felt as she watched this beautiful creature was broken suddenly at the sound of approaching footsteps. The wolf's ears perked up, and it stood, sniffing in the direction of the sound. It looked back toward Breksta, as if giving her a curt thank you before bounding into the darkness of the forest. Asteria materialized beside her. Out of breath, her hands clutched bundles of kindling and logs.

"What were you thinking?" Asteria shouted, her eyes flashing with rage.

"I-I just woke up. The wolf wasn't going to hurt me," Breksta murmured, growing timid at the rare display of her mother's anger.

Asteria paced beside the fire. "You can't do that, Breksta. Wolves aren't creatures to be meddled with. They're very dangerous."

"It just wanted some food, Mom," Breksta pleaded. "You always told me that wolves are pack animals and are very sociable."

Asteria squeezed her eyes shut and pressed the back of her hand into the bridge of her nose. Breksta realized then that her mother's anger was misdirected fear and that her mother's protective instincts had overcome her sense of reason.

Breksta stood slowly, walking over to her mother and taking her hand. "Mom, I'm alright. Nothing happened, and I'm safe."

Asteria put down her hand and revealed red tear-stained eyes. Asteria took in a shaky breath before pulling her daughter into a warm embrace. "Please don't worry me like that again."

Guilt plagued Breksta, as she felt her mother's lip quiver on the top of her forehead. "I won't do it again, I'm sorry, Mom."

Asteria let out a sigh of relief and sat down beside the fire. "Now come, let's eat something."

Half an hour later, the fish was properly cooked, and Breksta had a mug of hot chocolate at her feet. Asteria slung her arm around her daughter, and together, they marveled at the galaxy that spanned above them.

"You know, Breksta," Asteria said between bites, "there is a myth that the greatest legends and saviors of the world still linger in the stars, put there by the gods."

Breksta looked at her mother. "Really?" she asked.

"Yes," Asteria said, a bittersweet expression appearing on her face.

"Who are some of them?"

Asteria mused for a moment before continuing softly, "There is Hercules—"

"I know him! He had the twelve labors!" Breksta exclaimed before she stopped suddenly, realizing her interruption. "Sorry, continue."

Asteria merely smiled and explained, "Perseus is there as well. And Pegasus." Asteria became quiet as she gazed at the stars, almost angrily.

"What's wrong, Mom?" Breksta whispered.

Asteria turned back to Breksta, stone-faced. If Breksta read her expression correctly, her mom seemed a bit fearful.

"Perhaps I was wrong," she explained. "The sky also shows the bad legends. Those of Orion and Scorpio and the Hydra."

"Why would it show that?"

Asteria turned to look at Breksta, before she continued, "Perhaps the gods are trying to tell us something ..."

"The gods?" Breksta asked, looking back at her mother with wonder.

"Perhaps they are warning us that history judges our actions, even after we are gone. How we treat others is how we become legends or monsters."

"Does history judge everyone?" Breksta asked.

Asteria took her daughter's hands and squeezed them tightly. "Yes. But you are kind, Breksta. As you were kind to that wolf and everyone you have ever met, despite any potential danger or consequence. I believe you will one day earn your place beside the legends of old as an even greater warrior. Not for your superiority, but for your clarity of mind and purity of heart."

Asteria's words touched Breksta, and she felt a righteousness settle into her bones. She would be great. And one day, she would make her mother proud. She would earn her place and become a legend.

Hestia paused to take in the words and the story Breksta had just told her. She turned to Breksta and saw hope in Breksta's eyes—and a touch of sadness.

"No one has ever told me anything like that," Hestia murmured. "And I've never heard of *any* of those heroes."

Breksta touched her friend's shoulder gently and looked at her with kindness. "You don't have to be a legend. You can just be my friend."

Hestia wrapped Breksta in a warm hug, and Breksta was once again back in her mother's arms. Perhaps Breksta didn't have to be a legend either. Perhaps she could be kind to her new friend and survive in her new world. That would be enough.

For their friendship to be true, though, Breksta knew she would have to be open and honest, without the secrets of her mother's death looming over her. Just as Breksta opened her mouth to speak, she realized that perhaps the truth could be brutal for Hestia, especially since Hestia's mother had killed her own. So Breksta told Hestia a half-truth, for her own good.

"Hestia, I need you to know that my mother … was killed … by the Academy," she murmured against Hestia, still enveloped in her hug.

Hestia pulled back, the look of sadness and pity painted across her features. "Breksta. I … I'm so sorry."

"It's not your fault," Breksta said, unable to hold Hestia's gaze.

"I know it's not," Hestia whispered. "But they won't apologize to you, so I will. I'm sorry, Breksta. You don't deserve this."

Breksta looked up at Hestia and smiled. The grief wasn't gone, not by a longshot. But Breksta was thankful that she had found someone to share it with, someone with a soul as kind and gentle as her own.

The two friends sat together in the dark until the sun peeked just above the horizon. As they huddled together, Hestia told Breksta of the journeys her mother had taken her on, exploring the Dreamer lands to the west, and the cadet missions she had watched from afar. Occasionally, she referenced dark topics, including death or the director, which made Breksta wince. Hestia immediately apologized and moved to other memories from her childhood. Breksta felt her cold sadness gradually thaw to Hestia's warm presence. It allowed her to survive the grief and searing pain of her mother's death. And for the first time since she had arrived, Breksta's smile stayed on her face.

"I should go. Before Mom comes to get you," Hestia whispered to Breksta, who was drifting to sleep against the crook of Hestia's neck.

Breksta shook herself and blinked her eyes slowly. "Take the blanket. So they don't find it here," Breksta murmured as she untangled the blanket from herself. Through the stories Hestia shared, she had come to understand better the secrecy and rules of her new world.

"Hand me the blanket once I get up," Hestia said, squinting her eyes as she looked up at the window.

"You can use the mattress to get up," Breksta suggested.

Hestia nodded, and together, they shifted the mattress to the center of the cell directly below the window. With that, Hestia grasped at the edges of the window, jumping to pull herself up. After a few seconds of wriggling, Hestia's feet disappeared from Breksta's view, replaced with an open hand. Breksta passed the blanket up in response.

Hestia disappeared for a moment and returned with the bars and screw-driver. Hestia carefully re-screwed the bars into place.

Breksta's eyes never left Hestia. In a low whisper, Hestia told her, "They'll let you out once the others wake up. Just go to the cafeteria, I'll be there."

"You promise?" Breksta asked, her eyes fixed on Hestia's face.

"Cross my heart and hope to die." Hestia grinned, crossing her finger over her chest.

Then Hestia disappeared with a flash of bright-red hair. Her disappearance invited uncertainty to soak back into Breksta's mind. Breksta sat with her back against the cold wall, now without the protection of her blanket or her friend. She waited in that position until the sun shone fully in the morning sky. She continued to wait until the lock outside clicked and the cruel smile of her captor confronted her outside.

When she stepped out of her cement box, her stone face had solidified, and she showed no emotion or vulnerability. Her stone face remained in place until she reached the cafeteria and was met with a wave, fiery-red hair, and a bright smile.

CHAPTER II

"HI, MOM!" Hestia exclaimed, as she slid into her mother's office the day after her visit to Breksta's solitude box.

She stood in front of her mother's desk, awaiting instructions. The director sighed and pulled off her glasses, setting them on top of her mound of paperwork.

"You received my call?" the director said flatly. Her eyes bore down into her daughter.

"Yes, ma'am," Hestia replied, tensing at her mother's tone of voice.

Through her training, both from teachers and her mother, Hestia knew how to read tones and people. Most importantly, she understood the various moods of her mother and knew how to act in response. This time, she lowered her head and averted her gaze.

"How were your classes today?"

"They were okay," Hestia said, not moving her gaze from the edge of the table.

From her mother's tone, she deduced that she had unfortunately done something wrong. As her mother spoke, Hestia scoured her memories of the past few days in search of any wrongdoing.

"Just okay?" the director asked curiously, raising her eyebrows and creating wrinkles on her usually smooth skin. The director pointed for her daughter to sit in the chair across from her.

"Well, we had combat training, and I taught Breksta hand-to-hand combat…" Hestia said excitedly, padding over to the chair.

"How is our new recruit?" the director's voice inched upward, a sound of curiosity that Hestia hadn't heard in a while.

"She's … doing okay," Hestia said, wringing her hands. Hestia felt her mother's gaze dig into her, making her look anywhere except her mother's face. She found her eyes drawn to the portrait of her grandfather, regal with an aura fit for a king. He wore a navy-blue suit and had dark eyes that she didn't inherit.

"Do you know why I called you here?" the director said icily.

Hestia felt fear tingle down her spine as her tongue struggled to find words. She disliked interrogations and still couldn't find what she had done wrong.

"Because you…" The director nodded slowly, keeping her laser eyes trained upon her daughter. "Because…" Hestia's voice trailed into silence.

The director leaned over the desk toward her daughter, her face close enough that Hestia could smell her perfume. "Why did I call you here, Hestia? I raised you to be a smart girl," her mother questioned cruelly.

"I … I don't know," Hestia sighed, defeated.

The director pulled herself back from the table, leaning against the back of her chair without moving her eyes from Hestia. "My dear … you've been here long enough to know. I know everything around here." The director walked around the table and leaned her hips against it, looming over her daughter. "All the comings and goings, Hestia. All the guard stations. And the exits and entrances. Did you really think you could fool me?" the director's words turned eerily sweet.

Hestia felt a stab of fear puncture her heart, halting her voice despite her open mouth. Hestia swallowed before she spoke so her voice would not break. "I was just giving her a blanket, Mom. She had gone in the river too, and it was icy."

Hestia didn't look up after the feeble words left her mouth. Rather, she continued to look at the ground, far away from her mother's gaze. In her trained mind, she knew that Breksta had technically done wrong and should be punished. But in her heart, she had done what she believed to be the right thing; Hestia was empathetic by nature, and if she ignored suffering, she couldn't escape the guilt in her mind. But empathy was not valued in the Academy—only discipline and punishment.

Her mother's hand flew across Hestia's face faster than she could have imagined possible, jerking her out of her thoughts. The cold hand snapped her head to the left. The silver ring on her mother's finger had scraped across her skin, leaving a single red line. Her face erupted in pain, making Hestia gasp and clutch at her face. Large tears tumbled down her cheeks and into her cut, making her grit her teeth.

The director lifted Hestia's face up with a thin finger and whispered, "You lied to me."

Hestia trembled but didn't move her face, paralyzed by her mother's sharp gaze.

"Do not ever do it again." The director sat back down in her seat and studied her long fingernails. "I don't understand, Hestia," the director said slowly, her tone causing Hestia to look up at her.

"W-what?" Hestia whispered hoarsely, her body shaking with emotion.

"I have taught you loyalty first, no?"

Hestia meekly nodded with her head.

"Yes?" the director said more loudly, as her fury-filled eyes drilled into her daughter's frightened ones.

"Yes," Hestia choked out the word.

Hestia squeezed her eyes shut in preparation for her mother to leap across her desk and strike her again. The seconds ticked by with each loud beating of Hestia's heart, the sound rushing inside her ears.

"Well then, I know you will remember this, because next time there won't be a meeting. Do you understand?" the director accentuated her words with her dagger eyes.

"Y-yes, ma'am."

"Good ... good. Now come here. It's been a while since we've had some proper family time," her mother declared with a smile, her demeanor changing suddenly.

She signaled for Hestia to come around her desk and pulled the neighboring chair close so they could sit face-to-face. Hestia walked over and slowly sunk into the chair without looking up.

"You know," the director said, following her daughter's fearful gaze, "I only do this because I love you and because I want what's best for you."

Her mother reached down and tucked a flying strand of Hestia's hair behind her ear. Hestia shivered at her touch, having to bite her lip to keep from recoiling. Then her mother said something Hestia never thought she would hear, "One day when I'm gone, you will be the one who runs things around here."

"What?"

"Yes. And you will help our people eradicate the Dreamers."

"But I-I don't want to hurt people," Hestia said hesitantly, testing the words on her tongue.

"Hestia," her mother said gently, looking deeply into her daughter's eyes. "Everyone has hurt someone at some time, especially the Dreamers. They have hurt us; they have hurt you. We are in the right. And our cause is a noble one, to protect the world from experiencing such pain and loss ever again."

"But—"

Her mother gently put a finger to Hestia's lips. "Ahh, Hestia. You are such a gentle soul. But you forget what they did to us. What they did to your grandfather."

"He was killed, right?" Hestia asked meekly.

The director mused, her face clouding over before she spoke again. "Perhaps you're ready to know the whole story."

Hestia quietly waited for her mother's next words, her fear receding as she recognized her mother surface.

It was a day of celebration and festivities at the White House. The lavish tables of food and a bubbly atmosphere of smiling people filled the long, rectangular ballroom. On the far side of the room, soft jazz music streamed from the live performers wearing white suits and seated in white chairs. Circular tables bordered the outskirts of the rectangular ballroom while the center was reserved for the slow, swaying dancers and frolicking party guests. With a glass of water in hand, the director approached an almost-empty table near the jazz players and sat in a seat beside a man in a black tuxedo. She wore a forest-green satin dress that hung to her ankles. She clasped her hands together and smiled her brightest disingenuous smile at the senator who hadn't supported the president's new executive order.

"Senator Marshal," the director smiled frostily. "It's an honor."

The senator managed a tense smile. "The honor is mine."

"Where's your wife, Eveline, on this fine evening?" the director asked.

"Ahh, Eveline is tending to our son at home. Festivities aren't her cup of tea nowadays," the senator said, quickly picking up his wine glass and downing the dregs.

"That's unfortunate," the director responded, keeping her eyes locked on the senator suspiciously. "I remember her fondly. And congratulations on your son."

The senator chuckled with a brightness that did not meet his worried eyes. "Yes, children are a blessing. And I see you'll have one soon."

His eyes lowered to the director's stomach.

The director smiled happily and placed a protective hand around her stomach. "Yes, my husband and I are very excited. Would you care to meet him?"

"Of course," the senator said, lowering his glass to the table and offering her a hand to stand.

The director took it and left her glass on the table. She allowed herself to be led by the senator's locked arm to where her husband sat with the first family at the table farthest from the musicians.

"Good evening, Senator," the president spoke kindly, although the director knew her father well enough to understand that he was not pleased with the senator's political pressuring.

"G-good evening, Mr. President. My lady and Mr. ..." The senator paused, extending his hand to the president, the first lady, and eventually the director's husband.

Her husband stood and shook the senator's hand warmly. "Please, call me Hyacinth."

"Like the Greek legend," the senator continued, shaking his hand.

Hyacinth blushed slightly. "Not the most accurate comparison, but yes."

The senator's eyes widened. "I apologize, sir. I didn't mean to offend."

The director sat beside her father and put a hand on Hyacinth's shoulder.

"Please, sit," the first lady said in an even-tempered tone. "We're all among friends here."

The senator nodded and took the seat opposite the president with Hyacinth and the director on his left. He wished he hadn't left his wine glass behind, for he was fearful in the presence of such power, considering that today was a day he'd been planning for.

"I saw your little video last week," the president said, running his hand through his graying hair. With a curious look in his eye, he added, "You seem very passionate on the matter of Dreamers."

"Yes, sir," the senator said, running his sweating hands along his dress pants. "I believe we should be treating them fairly and humanely. But I had no intention of contradicting you, sir."

"Of course not, Senator," the president said, using the formality of the senator's title as a hint of his displeasure. "I merely want to understand the reasoning behind your support of those reckless rebels."

The senator's eyes strayed from the president's glare as he spoke in a more hushed tone, "I honestly believe that the Dreamers and our regular citizens can live together peacefully. With no disrespect, I believe that the executive order you signed is a violation of their civil liberties enshrined in our constitution. Forcing them to stop using their magic is like telling one that their air can be controlled and bought by their president. How can you give yourself the right to persecute, arrest, and execute them? Aren't you undermining the democracy of this nation? The United States has strived to be the epitome of freedom, mirroring its beginnings in Greek and Roman democracy as well as the Enlightenment with its ideals of individuality and liberties. Giving yourself this much power is a totalitarian act and sends a sign to our allies around the world that the democracy we have tried to spread throughout the world is corrupt at the very core ... sir."

The senator's voice had grown louder as he spoke, and guests from the other tables had paused their conversations to look with confusion at the president's table.

The president smiled insincerely and added with a hawkish gaze, "Well, Senator, that is where we disagree."

The director's eyes flashed with anger, and she opened her mouth to speak, but her father placed a calming hand on hers. The director folded her hands in her lap silently, while Hyacinth gave her a worried glance.

"I owe you a dance tonight, excuse us, Mr. President," Hyacinth said, offering the director his hand as he stood. The director gladly took it and locked her fingers tightly in her husband's as she got up. She cast one last look at her father's troubled and angry expression.

Hyacinth caught that look, too, and said to her in a low, calming voice, "It'll be alright. Your father knows how to deal with those types of people."

They reached the center of the dance floor where other couples began to sway to the beautiful melody of "Dream a Little Dream of Me." The director smiled at her favorite song, knowing her father had requested it especially for her. Hyacinth put a protective hand on the small dip of her back, and the director let her head rest on his shoulder.

"I'm just worried about those types of senators. They never see the larger picture that we're trying to preserve. The status quo is so fragile that we must do whatever we can to keep the nation from panicking," the director whispered.

"Honey," Hyacinth responded softly, "you don't need to worry about that anymore. There will always be people who can't understand leaders, and those people will always resist and rebel. But there will also always be people protecting this world and keeping us safe, like your father, and you," he added, tracing her ear with his finger and tucking the stray strands of unbraided hair behind it.

The director broke into a smile, and she felt her worries melt away as Hyacinth brought his lips to hers. She had always been so focused and orderly, being an adviser to her father and managing the nation's problems one by one. But this was simple. Love had always been a concept, an idea, some unreachable bar in life. Hyacinth made it simple—a beautiful, unorganized tangle of emotions that she could drown in without worry of bad intentions or consequences. Hyacinth broke away from her and smiled his warm, sunny smile.

"Thank you," she said, moving her arms to encircle his neck as he moved his hands to her waist.

"For what?"

"For always taking care of me and understanding."

"Of course, love," he said before shifting his gaze to her stomach. "And I'll take care of her too. Both of you, always."

The director smiled and stared at her lover's twinkling green eyes as they continued to dance together.

At the president's table, the president's expression had darkened, and he spoke to the senator in angry, hushed tones.

"This nation needs stability—"

"No," the senator replied sharply. "This nation needs a leader to lead its people, *all* its people."

The president clasped his hands together firmly to attempt to keep his anger from showing. "I cannot support people who kill civilians and deface government buildings in protest."

The senator lowered his tone and leaned closer to the president. "In all honesty, sir, I agree with you. Violent protest isn't the right way to go. But you have given these people no choice by persecuting them. You have given them fear and instability when you need to reassure them and open your arms to them. Dreamers have been with us since the beginning of time. In the ancient worlds of China, Greece, Rome, Egypt, Mesopotamia, they have all been there."

"And in those places, there have been wars and conflict and eventually the fall of their civilization," the president retorted, taking a sip of his champagne.

"Those conflicts are a result of what you are doing now, the persecution and fear that drove Dreamers to desperation. Fear, Mr. President, is the stem of all this conflict. I am pleading with you, sir, please don't let this spiral out of control."

The president put down his glass and stared at it with a tired look in his eyes. "I hear you, Senator. And I'm doing exactly that. I'm stopping these Dreamers from using fear and violence to control our nation. There won't be conflict between us, any of us."

"Thank you for your time, Mr. President," the senator said, a dark look crossing his face. "Now if you'll excuse me, I think I will retire for the evening."

The two men stood, and the president reached out his hand to shake the senator's. "Until next time, Senator Marshal."

"Until next time … Mr. President," the senator echoed, before walking across the ballroom toward the wide doors on the opposite wall. Two servicemen held their gaze on the senator as they pushed open the door.

"How was your evening, Senator?" the one on the left asked politely.

"The evening didn't go well. Perhaps it would be better to correct it," the senator said. Recognizing the coded words, the two servicemen nodded before closing the door behind him. Turning back, he murmured, "For Morpheus and all our children," as the doors slammed shut and pandemonium broke loose.

The director and Hyacinth were engaged in lighter conversation as they migrated back to the president's table, seeing the senator leave in a huff. Abruptly, the wall of windows shattered and sprayed the room with a profusion of glass shards. Screams echoed in the room as figures in black T-shirts and pants stormed in. The guards at the corners of the room ran to their designated political figures, just as the secret service rushed to the president's table. Hyacinth wrapped his arm tightly around the director as they ran toward the exit, accompanied by the secret service agents who were shouting through their earpieces at each other. The director turned back as they ran to get a look at their attackers. A group of at least twenty vigilantes had infiltrated the room filled with hundreds of party guests. The figures hadn't bothered to hide their identities, their faces clearly reflecting anger and revolt. A man with curly brown hair and stormy gray eyes, the same eyes as Breksta's, raised his hands as white electricity shot from his fingertips.

"Dreamers," the director breathed with disbelief. "They're Dreamers."

Hyacinth continued to pull the director toward the exit. "Please, we need to get out of here."

The director turned quickly after the man shot electricity toward an approaching guard, launching him at the wall, where he fell to the ground with a sickening crack. The secret service opened the doors just as a force stopped their movements and rammed them into an invisible wall. The group was launched backward, hitting the cold, marble dance floor. The director immediately moved her hands to protect her stomach, but in that action, her head smacked against the marble ground. Pain jolted from the back of her head down her spine. She looked up and saw what they had hit: a green force field that stemmed from a girl in the center of the room. Her eyes glowed green like the green light that flowed in a mist off her fingertips and formed the dome around the party guests.

An arm came around the director's shoulder, making her flinch away. But she turned to find Hyacinth looking fearfully at her, a look so different and distinct from moments earlier. They turned from where they lay on the floor to see the chaos all around them. The party guests ran around inside the force field as the diameter of the dome decreased in size.

A boy in raven-black clothing materialized in various places inside the force field. He appeared and reappeared in a flash of navy-blue light, yielding his blade and bringing down the guards throughout the room. Blood flowed freely across the dance floor as those still standing fell one by one to the ground.

Magic moved effortlessly in the air. Explosions of multicolored light marked the different magics that each rebel possessed. It would've been beautiful if the scene weren't so vulgar. Hyacinth helped the director to her knees as they scrambled and hid behind a table. Their secret service officers were dead at their feet, their throats slit cleanly from ear to ear. The cuts were so horrifying that the director had to look away, and Hyacinth wrapped his arms protectively around her. He released his tight embrace once the screaming stopped, and the director opened her eyes slowly to look around. Bodies lined the floor, and blood painted the walls maroon. Tears streamed from the director's eyes, but she couldn't tell if it was from grief or fear. She looked around to see if her father and mother were a part of the bodies.

Suddenly, a clear voice pierced the air from the center of the room. "Mr. President, First Lady, it's an honor to officially make your acquaintance. I am Asteria Vilkas, and I am here on behalf of my people."

The director whirled toward the voice and stood, despite Hyacinth's attempts to pull her down behind the table. The voice had come from a woman with stark, white hair who stood at the center of the room. Dark mist surrounded her parents and lifted them off the floor as they wriggled and fought. Asteria had a strong, unyielding expression as she lifted the director's parents higher off the ground.

"What do you want from me?" the president said through clenched teeth.

"It's too late for negotiation, Mr. President," Asteria said coldly. "We have tried to fight your persecution through diplomatic channels. But you are the one who signed that executive order. You've given us no choice. What I want, you cannot give me. And that is why your time as a tyrant is over."

The director crept to where one of the secret service agents lay a few feet to her right and took a pistol from his hands. It was already loaded, and the director knew what she had to do.

"Let them go!" she demanded, pointing a gun at Asteria's head, a premonition of the events to come years later. "I won't hesitate."

Asteria glanced over with an annoyed look in her eyes. "What are you going to do exactly? You are outmatched. All I want for my people is for us to be able to live freely. You can't stop us."

Out of the corner of her eye, the director saw Hyacinth grab another pistol from another agent and creep from table to table as she walked toward the center of the room. The Dreamers cast looks of unbridled hatred as she approached, some clenching their weapons tighter.

"Without the president, you won't be able to reverse the order. You'll only sow chaos and disorder. That's why you need us."

Asteria smiled bitterly. "Ah yes. I've heard of you. The president's adviser. His precious daughter. How will you feel knowing you couldn't save him?"

The director clenched her teeth and kept her eyes locked on the woman. "I'm giving you one last chance. Release them now."

Asteria opened her mouth to retort when a gunshot rang out. Both women whipped their heads to the left, where Hyacinth stood with his gun raised. The bullet had been intended for Asteria, but it floated inches from her face in a mist of black magic. She had known it was coming. Beside Asteria, the brown-haired man's eyes widened in anger. This man, the director would later find out through her years of investigating Asteria and the Dreamers, was Breksta's father, Menuo Vilkas. Breksta's father let loose a bolt of lightning that struck Hyacinth in the center of his heart. His screams echoed loudly in the room as he fell to his knees and convulsed.

Menuo stopped the lightning, and that was when the director snapped. She shifted her pistol to the man's head as the man's eyes were focused squarely on her husband. She pulled the trigger, and this time, Asteria wasn't ready. The bullet left a hole in the center of Menuo's head as he collapsed to the ground.

The director shoved through the Dreamers until she found her husband, his eyes empty of joy or love or life. The director sobbed as she cradled him in her arms. She looked up finally to Asteria with fury and saw that she, too, cradled the other man. Both women rose to their feet and faced each other; their grief and rage mirrored in each other.

"You don't know the forces you have meddled with," Asteria said.

Asteria directed her hands at the director's parents, and their eyes widened as they, too, screamed out with agony. The director raced forward, but she was held back by Dreamers that didn't budge as she kicked and thrashed about.

"You and your people have taken everything from me. You persecuted my people, killed my husband. Now you, *too*, will understand," Asteria said with angry eyes.

This helplessness at the hands of the Dreamers was inhumane and alien to the director. But she could do nothing except watch.

"Dad! Mom!" the director shouted as tears streamed down her face.

Her mother looked to her with fear-ridden eyes before going limp and falling to the floor. The director screamed at her mother's broken figure on the floor. But Asteria did not stop. Her hand closed into a fist, and the dark, snake-like mist tightened around the director's father. From the mist, an arm-like shape formed and loomed over him. It paused before diving into his heart, making him scream out in agony, his arms grasping frantically as he tried to dislodge the magic.

"Please, stop this," the director cried, her vision blurred by tears.

"I want you to watch him die. Just as I have watched my people die," Asteria shouted angrily, her own eyes flowing with tears of grief.

"Please…" the director pleaded between sobs.

Asteria turned back to the president and the snake-like mist. She clenched her fist, and the mist responded, closing over his heart and squeezing it. Her father turned to look at his daughter one last time and mouthed out the words, "Don't. Let. Them. Win."

The director shook her head, unable to take in all the death surrounding her. With her father's last words, the light in his eyes went out and his body went limp, falling to the floor with a sickening thud. All was silent except for Asteria's footsteps as she walked toward the director. The director kept her eyes on her father until Asteria grabbed her chin and forced it upward.

Looking directly into the director's eyes, she said quietly, "I'm sparing you."

She looked at the director's stomach. "I have a child as well. And in a better world, they could have been friends. That is why I fight this fight—my child and my husband have kept me fighting. But now we are even. Dreamers and the government, you and me personally. This is the end of this conflict."

With that, Asteria released the director's chin, and the Dreamers released the director. With a swirl of navy-blue mist, the Dreamers disappeared just as they had arrived, leaving death in their midst. Once they were gone, the director sunk to her knees where her husband lay and looked at her parents. She didn't cry, for she couldn't feel anything. She was a broken, shattered shadow of the woman. Love had been hers, if only briefly. But now it was gone—vanished just as dreams vanish and are forgotten once one wakes.

Just like that, the director awoke to her dark world and splintered country. And she vowed she would be the one who pieced it together for herself and her daughter.

Hestia watched as her mother bit her lip tightly until she tasted the iron tang of blood. Tears collected around her mother's eyes, and Hestia couldn't help but feel her chest constrict with sadness at her mother's pain.

"You don't have to continue," Hestia said, reaching over and lowering her hand tentatively over her mother's.

"No. You need to understand the price the Dreamers must pay," the director said, her anger displayed once more.

Hestia looked into her mother's eyes that had been burned by the visions of pain she had just described. "I-I'm sorry that they did this to you."

"You shouldn't be, my dear. I'm merely explaining why we do the things we do. To stop the Dreamers. To make them repent for their wrongdoings."

"But what about the Dreamers? What happened to them?"

"They were dealt with," her mother said bluntly. "I held them accountable for their crimes, especially their leader, Asteria Vilkas, who I've finally dealt with personally in response to the *severity* of her actions against our family," the director said, gently soothing Hestia's disheveled hair.

With that, Hestia remembered Breksta and felt something tear inside her. The tear between her mother and her new friend. She saw the truth Breksta had hidden from her. The director had killed Breksta's mother. Hestia could now see the brutality inside her mother, the same brutality that had killed all those Dreamers and created the Academy to shield Hestia from harm. Was this who her mother truly was, underneath the role of the director, underneath the leader of the Academy? If the layers were peeled away, would Hestia even recognize her mother? She didn't know.

Hestia calculated her next words carefully and watched intently for her mother's reaction. "Do the Dreamers still pose a threat now that their leader is gone?"

"Well, there are still some, my dear, but not enough to cause such an uprising ever again. That's why we have the Academy. To make sure they don't. To protect everyone. To protect you, just like your father would have wanted."

Hestia nodded, her breath growing shallow at the realization that all those people's lives and their deaths—the Dreamers'—were on her mother's hands, including Breksta's mother. But her family's blood was also on Breksta's mother's hands. Her mind was torn between grief for her family and pity for the sad, grieving daughter that Breksta was. She couldn't separate the two worlds she now knew about, so she kept silent.

"Your next class should be starting soon," the director quickly inserted, watching her daughter's attention divert.

"Okay," Hestia answered automatically and quickly stood from her chair.

"Give your mother a hug," the director instructed, smiling at Hestia as she opened her arms.

Hestia wrapped her arms around her mother, her only family left, the one who had always protected her. But even as she felt some small comfort in the embrace, she also felt disgust at the death-ridden touch her mother possessed. She pulled away, leaving the room and shutting the door. She leaned back against the door and let out a deep sigh, closing her eyes from the fearful world she had just left on the other side. She allowed herself to release her choking fear.

"She's not here anymore," Hestia whispered to herself as she remembered her stinging face. "She can't hurt you now."

Behind the door, the director leaned against her swinging chair with her fingers pressed between her eyes on the bridge of her nose. The face of the one who killed her father surfaced into her mind. The one with white hair. The one she had killed. Asteria Vilkas.

The director remembered Asteria's face contorting into poison and hatred as Asteria willed her father's heart to slow and his life stopped in an abrupt, alien fashion of magic. Each beat slowing until, finally, it stopped. She remembered his lifeless eyes and the way time slowed as he fell to the ground.

She remembered pulling the trigger and watching the bullet land in Asteria's skull. And the scream of the child that followed. The director smiled and felt herself heal ever so slightly. Most of all, she remembered the feeling of peace as her father was avenged. The feeling of sweet and just vengeance. She knew that he was able to rest now. Hyacinth could rest. Her mother could rest. All of them could rest now, knowing that their murderess had been brought down by her own hand.

Finally, she remembered the moment she held Hestia in her arms all those years ago, as she looked at the map of hiding Dreamers brought into the hospital room by her generals. Hestia was so small and fragile and beautiful as a newborn, a mirror of the world's innocence and kindness. In that moment, the director knew she wouldn't hesitate to protect what was hers.

CHAPTER 12

IT HAD BEEN LATE SUMMER when Breksta arrived at the Academy.
Now fall was fully fledged in the middle of October. Breksta lay sleepless in the
bed she had grown quite fond of. Her small dorm room now brought her a sense
of protection and security, for it marked the only time when she wasn't training
or under constant surveillance from the director and her instructors. And despite
the difficulty of her training and studies in the Academy, she understood that
she couldn't escape, so she took solace in her friendship with Hestia.

During these first few months at the Academy, Breksta had become stronger, more muscular and agile as she trained—running, shooting, sparring, and
tracking animals. Though her body had been broken and rebuilt by the Academy,
her mind remained rigid and immovable. In her private thoughts, she refused
to submit to the Academy's teachings, trying to hold on to the last bits of her
mother.

Sometimes, she would allow Hestia to know these thoughts, for their
friendship had become a strong bond of trust, but there were other times when
she held her darker thoughts to herself. It was such a day in October when
Breksta couldn't share her deepest thoughts with her friend.

She and Hestia had returned from an outing and were forced to face a dreadful situation together. That morning, the senior cadets had brought back a Dreamer for questioning.

"The woman," the director announced in the auditorium, "caved within minutes. She told us everything about the operations in her town. A shame that she wasn't a higher-ranking Dreamer."

The director gestured to the senior cadets behind the curtain. "Bring out the Dreamer."

"What's going on?" Breksta whispered to Hestia amid the shouts from the other cadets for "no mercy."

"My mom—the director is preparing the Dreamer to…" Hestia began, suddenly looking away from Breksta shamefully.

"What, Hestia? What is the director preparing?" Breksta whispered, looking between Hestia and the stage, where a hooded woman was being led out to the center.

Hestia swallowed and responded, "We can sneak out now, just say we need water or the bathroom."

Breksta looked back at Hestia, her eyes boring into her friend. "What are you not telling me, Hestia," Breksta pushed.

Placing her hand on Breksta's arm in a gesture of safety and care, Hestia closed her eyes as she spoke, "It's an execution."

Breksta became ghost-quiet, pulling her arm away from Hestia's touch. She looked to the stage, watching with horror as the trembling woman was unmasked. Senior cadets swarmed around her, tying her to a small chair in the center of the stage.

Breksta shook her head, her mouth unable to form words. Hestia tried to console Breksta, bringing her arm around Breksta's shoulders in a hug.

"Don't watch," Hestia murmured. "It's always over quick. Trust me, I hate it too."

Breksta managed a nod, breathing deeply as she steeled herself. She gripped the edge of her seat to keep the painful memories of her mother's death at bay.

"Ladies and gentlemen," the director began. "Today is a very special day, yes?"

"Yes!" the cadets called back.

"Today, I will be giving our two senior cadets who captured the Dreamer a chance for vengeance," the director called out, waving the two cadets onto the stage. "Report the success of both the capture and interrogation of this Dreamer."

The director handed the microphone to the boy cadet, who smiled widely before continuing in a confident voice, "Yes, Madam Director. The Dreamer was captured within minutes of arriving at her home. Her retaliation didn't result in any casualties or injuries. Her arrest was swift. Once we arrived back to the Academy, our interrogation tactics were thorough. She, like you said, Madam Director, caved within minutes."

The other senior cadets cheered, some friends of the boy shouting out encouragements to him. "Make her pay! Make her pay!" they repeated.

The director brought her finger to her lips, and the cadets settled back into their seats despite their excitement.

"W-what are they going to do to her?" Breksta whispered.

"The seniors get to pick the weapon," Hestia whispered, as if she were shielding herself as well as Breksta. "Hopefully they will choose a fast one."

Anxiety built in Breksta, but she tried to force it down. She used a breathing technique she had learned from Hestia and counted to five. Only this time, she couldn't focus through the fear she felt. She gripped the chair harder, determined to stay quiet and remain unnoticed.

"I choose the pistol," the boy cadet boomed.

"And I choose the samurai blade," the other boy said, a sadistic smile spreading on his face.

Breksta shuddered as Ms. Adams brought the gleaming blade from the sides of the stage and presented it to the sadistic boy. He lifted the blade above his head proudly, and the cadets cheered in response. Both boys approached the woman with hunter-like stances while the woman shook visibly. The second boy positioned his blade over the woman's stomach, setting his stance and wringing his hands on the blade's handles.

"You may begin," the director instructed.

Breksta turned away and released her grip on the chair's arms to cover her eyes. She didn't hear the blade sink into the woman, but she heard the woman's scream. It was piercing and animalistic. Breksta could feel the adrenaline and excitement from the cadets. It made her sick. Silence followed, and the woman's screams subsided after the boy pulled the blade out of her body.

"Shh ... it's okay," Hestia tried to soothe Breksta, despite the booming shouts of encouragement from the cadets.

Their thirst for blood was something that Breksta felt she would never understand. But it was enough to know that Hestia felt the same. Breksta steeled her mind and slowly removed her shaking hands from her eyes.

"It's almost over," Hestia whispered as she turned to Breksta with a pained look. "You don't have to watch."

Breksta took her deep breaths as the boy brought the blade back down. The auditorium was filled with long, drawn-out screams. Breksta tried to keep the tears and grief inside. She refused to cry in the public eye of the Academy. She had learned that weakness was a disease, meant to be eradicated just like the Dreamers.

She shook her head and grit her teeth. "No, I should watch."

Hestia nodded, and the two of them remained quiet. Although they had to be participants in the death of a Dreamer, they wouldn't cheer for blood. This was as far as they could stray from the Academy's teachings. Breksta bit her lip as the first boy lifted the pistol to the woman's left temple. The woman shook from pain, her blood coating the floor thickly and staining the shoes of the two cadets responsible for her death.

"You deserve this," the boy said calmly.

He pulled the trigger, and the gun's sound reverberated through the auditorium. Then there was silence. Breksta tasted blood from where she bit her lip, and she bit down even harder. This woman's death sickened her, and every bit of it reminded Breksta of her mother. Except for one thing. Her mother's spirit was never broken, and Breksta vowed that she would be the same. The Academy could control her actions, but her spirit was free and so was Hestia's. Breksta mourned for this stranger because she knew no one else would. Just as no one mourned for her mother.

She had watched it because she now understood that the Academy spoke the language of violence and blood. She didn't look away when the woman's body fell limp as the bullet entered her brain. She didn't blink as the woman's blood splattered across the stage. She would be a cadet. She would live in this world. And then when the time was right, she would leave the Academy and be free—far, far away from here. This was Breksta's plan that she believed in as fiercely as her unbroken spirit.

To Hestia, death in the world was saddening, but death in the Academy was mercy. The Dreamers who came in never left. She never discussed this with anyone except Breksta. And she rarely discussed her true feelings about the Academy or her fear of her mother. Mostly, she and Breksta discussed the superficial aspects of the Academy: their successes in training, the funny moments that would bring belly-aching laughter and shouts from other cadets for them to be quiet, which only made them laugh harder. She found Breksta to be an incredible friend, despite the conflict between their mothers, especially Hestia's, who didn't smile upon their friendship.

Breksta was the one she could trust deeply without worry of shame or judgment. She hoped Breksta trusted her too. The Academy didn't look kindly on those who strayed from the teachings of hatred for Dreamers or those who asked too many questions. Hestia had never known what happened to those cadets, if there ever had been any who questioned the Academy. For this reason, Hestia feared her mother and didn't express her concerns openly.

Sometimes, Hestia found herself drifting into meaningful conversation when the watchful eye of the Academy disappeared behind their closed door. She discussed what she wished would happen, including her dreams and aspirations.

"I want to end the war and conflict," Hestia said one night as they lay side-by-side on Breksta's bottom bunk.

"When do you think it will end?" Breksta asked doubtfully.

"When I become the leader of the Academy," Hestia insisted.

"How will you do it?" Breksta retorted.

"Do what?"

"End the war," Breksta pushed.

"Well … I haven't gotten there yet," Hestia admitted sheepishly.

Breksta paused before answering in a small voice, "Are you going to kill all of them?"

Hestia was silent as she thought. "I hope not. I hope they just surrender."

"When have the Dreamers ever surrendered?" Breksta asked sadly as she thought of her mother.

Hestia didn't answer, knowing the answer in her mind was never.

"And are Dreamers even so bad?" Breksta asked, sitting up and speaking angrily. "What have they ever done to you?"

"You can't understand. It's not as simple as you think," Hestia said bitterly.

"It seems pretty simple to me! Why isn't it that simple?" Breksta exclaimed, her eyes shining with anger in the dim light of the room.

"Because your mother was a Dreamer! You've never experienced their violence!" Hestia said, her voice rising.

Breksta was silent. Hestia wished dearly that she could shove the words back down her throat. But the words were out, and she could only apologize.

Hestia reached toward her friend. "Breksta, I'm so sorry. I—"

"Goodnight, Hestia," Breksta said abruptly, turning on her side and facing the wall.

That was when Hestia knew she had gone too far, touching Breksta's deep pain for her mother. She sat up slowly and whispered, "Goodnight."

Hestia maneuvered her way up the ladder to her bunk and let her troubled, doubtful mind drift off to sleep.

Hestia opened her eyes to a dark corridor with a single door at the end and a light shining on it.

"I'm so glad you made it on time," a voice said behind her.

Hestia whirled around to face her mother, who smiled broadly with strands of white and silver hair that marked an older age.

"Mom?" Hestia asked, confused about this dark place, "Where am I?"

"Don't you know?" the director said, still smiling. "I thought you would recognize the Academy anywhere."

"The Academy? I've never seen this place before. How did I get here, Mom?"

"Such silly questions. Come, it's time to celebrate your victory … Madam Director," the director said cheerfully as she walked toward the door.

"Wait! Mom! Why did you call me Madam Director?" Hestia asked before chasing after her mother to the end of the corridor.

The director laughed as her hand lingered over the doorknob. "My, my. You have so many strange questions today, Hestia."

"Why did you call me that?" Hestia insisted.

"You truly don't remember?" the director asked, wrinkling her eyebrows with confusion.

"No … what's going on?" Hestia insisted, her mind panicked.

The director swallowed before placing her hand on the door. "You saved us, Hestia. You ended the war."

The director opened the door into her own office and pushed Hestia in. What Hestia saw disgusted her. The director's office had ceiling-to-floor windows that showed the conjoined paths of all four buildings and the airstrip that extended far into the distance. Both the center of the Academy and the airstrip were filled with piles and piles of bloodied, annihilated bodies.

Hestia covered her mouth to keep from screaming. Beside the bodies were cadets wearing wide smiles, cheering and raising their guns into the air. Hestia tried to find Breksta, but she was not among the cadets.

"What. Happened. Here?" Hestia demanded.

"We won the war, Hestia," the director said, wrapping Hestia in a hug. "You did it, my dear."

Hestia ripped away from her mother and fixed her gaze on the bodies. She saw youthful, dashing men with their bodies pulverized by bullet holes. She saw young children whose stomachs had been slashed by knives. She saw elderly people whose bodies were contorted in positions only possible in death. Death shrouded Hestia, and she couldn't escape.

Tears streaked down Hestia's face before she answered, her voice filled with barely controlled rage. "If this is how we win … I would rather lose."

The director looked down at her daughter harshly. "We've achieved victory. We are free."

"No!" Hestia roared louder than she had ever dared. "Why is everyone celebrating? This. Is. Sad!"

"We-we won, my dear…" the director said, taken aback by Hestia's anger.

"We have lost! Look at all those people. They're all dead!"

"Yes. By your own actions. This is how wars are ended, Hestia," the director said firmly before placing her hand on Hestia's head and turning it toward the piles of bodies. "Enjoy it."

Hestia tried to turn her head, but it was locked in place. So she did what she could. She cried for all the lost souls: the children, the men and women, the elderly. She cried for her mother who had never been a true mother. And she cried for all the cadets, who would never shed a tear for these dead people. She cried for all of them.

Hestia awoke with a jolt. The pillow under her head was soaked with salty tears. She touched her face and was met with more warm tears. Her hair was slicked back from the crying, but she didn't care. Fear and disgust coursed through her veins, no matter how hard she tried to shake it off. She realized that she had never left the room; rather, it had all been a dream. However, the fear was real, more than Hestia cared to admit. And so real that if her mother knew, she would be disappointed.

Hestia quickly wiped the tears from her face, trying to slow her breathing and not draw attention and wake Breksta. She didn't go back to sleep but lay there until the sun streaked through the window and Breksta shook her awake as always. She pretended to be asleep and tried to act as if the dream had never occurred and that she wasn't plagued with doubts or fears. Dreams like hers had no place in the Academy, and she knew better than anyone as the director's daughter.

For the first time in her life, Hestia doubted her golden life, her mother, and the Academy. She never expressed this doubt out loud though. Sometimes in her private thoughts, she questioned why they were being trained to kill. Was killing the Dreamers worth the loss of their humanity and their feelings? She wanted real answers, she needed them even, but she already knew the placid answers she would receive.

Hestia remained silent and conflicted, the only candor she received coming from Breksta. Hestia found solace in this friendship, and she found she depended on Breksta as much as Breksta depended on her. The only way to survive was through each other.

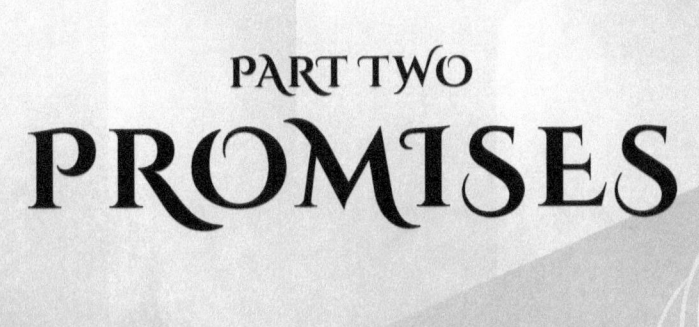

PART TWO

PROMISES

CHAPTER 13

THROUGH THE YEARS OF TRAINING together, Breksta and Hestia had deepened their friendship. The depth of their friendship became most evident when they made a promise to each other at fifteen years old, following a brutal boxing match.

The cadets cheered for blood as more gathered around to watch the director's daughter spar Ms. Adams's son. Watching Hestia and Icarus spar, Breksta's apprehension grew. Breksta clung to the roped borders of the boxing ring, silently monitoring both fighters.

"Take her out, Icarus," a boy yelled.

Hestia and Icarus circled each other for the last time, each with their fair share of wounds; Icarus had a bloodied and bruised lip that had been split by Hestia's left jab in the seventh round. While Hestia sported twin cuts above both eyes, the wound over her left eye continued to flow freely down her face.

Icarus wore a pair of black gloves lined with sweat and drops of blood that he kept close to protect his eyes. Hestia wore a pair of red gloves near her face; however, her arms began to lower slightly, weighed down by the fatigue of so many rounds.

Icarus kept his eyes on her and never missed a step as they shifted, planning their next moves. His expression, Hestia knew, was not that of arrogance, but of colder, precise calculation. And that frightened Hestia. Icarus knew that Hestia didn't favor this type of combat; rather, she preferred to take out her targets with rifles, minimizing the closeness of war. For this reason, Hestia kept on the defensive, only landing punches she was certain would hit Icarus.

Hestia kept her feet light on the red circle within the ring as she studied Icarus's clipped blond hair and vulture blue eyes. She watched for weaknesses. But as she did, she lost track of her most imminent problem: Icarus's fists. His right fist contacted Hestia's left cheek and sent her head reeling to the right. She bit her lip from the pain but turned and faced Icarus, bringing her hands closer to shield her face. They circled each other again, each throwing punches that the other evaded. Hestia threw a flurry of punches, and Icarus followed with a right hook. Hestia quickly ducked and brought her right leg around in a precise kick at his thigh, causing him to stumble, before Hestia leapt away. Icarus's blue eyes flashed momentarily with anger as he brought his fists back into position. Hestia smiled despite the pain, for out of all the cadets, she wouldn't lose to Icarus. As Icarus regained his balance, the referee motioned for them to continue, and both circled each other once again.

Hestia flicked her eyes to the red clock on the far wall that ticked down from the three-minute mark. She just needed one point. She needed to make sure Icarus didn't rise from the floor the next time she landed a targeted kick. Then she could be done with this horrid fight. Icarus threw a kick at Hestia's left side that she nimbly dodged, returning with a kick of her own that Icarus evaded.

Icarus took the first step to end this fight. He feigned a kick to Hestia's stomach, making her leap back just as Icarus rushed forward with his left hook. The harsh leather of the glove tore open the tentatively sealed cut above Hestia's right eye. The force of the punch whipped Hestia's head back. To finish the job, Icarus sent a real kick to Hestia's stomach that knocked her to her knees. Pain erupted from her stomach and her tender face, and Hestia squeezed her eyes tightly as her limp arms held on to the roped barrier. Suddenly, a hand grabbed her wrist.

"You just need to score another point, Hestia. Finish this," Breksta said sternly, her gray eyes demanding Hestia's focus.

"Just surrender. You have nothing to prove," Icarus said with a reserved voice.

If only that was true, Hestia thought to herself. She doubted that Icarus understood the pressures imposed on her, her mother being at the center of all those pressures. She had to be the best, for she was "the director's daughter," the phrase that most people called her rather than her actual name. She couldn't escape her mother's name, just as Breksta couldn't escape Asteria's.

Hestia clenched her fingers inside her gloves and, by her own will, pulled herself up. She faced Icarus and, to her dismay, tasted blood on her lips. Blood from the cut above her eye continued to run into her eye and down her face. Hestia's lashes fluttered as she tried to clear her vision. Icarus came toward her again, throwing kick after punch. Hestia sluggishly ducked and slinked out of the way, dodging most of the punches except a few that Hestia took valiantly to her chest. Although she was in severe pain, Breksta's words kept her going. One point. That was what she needed.

She finally gathered the strength to secure that one point. Icarus threw a punch. She ducked and retaliated with a flurry of punches straight to his chest. Icarus stumbled backward, and Hestia followed with her right hook and a swiveled kick to the back of his knee. Icarus slammed into the ground, his face colliding with the mat.

Hestia felt the epitome of victory as she watched Icarus on the ground. Exhausted, she relaxed her tensed shoulders and allowed her hands to hang at her sides. The referee rushed over to Icarus and questioned whether he could still fight. If he didn't get up, Hestia would win. Icarus groaned. His rage-filled eyes turned to Hestia as he pushed his fists into the ground and tried to make himself rise.

"You got this, Hestia! Finish him!" Breksta shouted.

"Just surrender," Hestia breathed, parroting Icarus's words. "You have nothing to prove."

Hestia didn't realize that those words only made Icarus angrier. She didn't understand that Icarus's punishment for losing would be worse than this fight. Losing would mean more training and more pain under his mother's watchful tutelage, something that Icarus dealt with constantly.

Hestia smiled at Breksta who smiled back at her. But it was then when

Icarus chose to attack once more. He leapt up from his position and hit Hestia with a ferocious uppercut. Hestia's head snapped upward, her neck contorting in pain. But he didn't stop there. Rather than wait until Hestia recovered, Icarus continued his attack. He punched and kicked her even as she raised her hands in a last attempt to protect herself. Every punch was precise and deadly. Icarus knew that Hestia couldn't survive much longer. With each attack, Icarus pushed Hestia back into the corner of the ring. Soon, with her face bloodied and her muscles in tatters, Hestia's back touched the metal posts at the corner of the ring. She couldn't fight this, she realized. Her pain was excruciating, and her will to win was bruised beyond repair as the victory was snatched from her. All she could do was keep her gloves over her face as Icarus pummeled her with more violent punches. Soon, not even her legs could support her, and Hestia sunk to the ground. The referee moved closer to the fighters, putting an arm on Icarus's shoulder as a sign of Hestia's surrender. But Icarus didn't stop.

"Please," she whispered hoarsely, hoping for the end of her agony. "I surrender."

"Stop it, Icarus!" Breksta shouted from somewhere behind Hestia. "She already surrendered."

The referee began shouting at Icarus to stop, but Icarus wouldn't. He was determined to prove himself to be the best cadet, for his mother.

Icarus continued his pursuit of victory, and through her gloves, Hestia saw his angry eyes devoid of all other emotion. Suddenly, the punches stopped, and Hestia released a pained moan. The cadets let out gasps and some cheered. Hestia lowered her gloves and watched as Breksta stood in front of her. Breksta's hands were wrapped, but she wasn't wearing gloves. Breksta let loose her fury against Icarus, who hadn't been kind to anyone, especially not Breksta. Icarus was not prepared for Breksta's wrath and skill, who had excelled beyond his ability in both technique and strength. She punched the sides of his face until fresh purple bruises sprouted and blood flowed from his face. She then knocked him to the floor with a roundhouse kick. The referee tried and failed to rein in Breksta, as she sat on top of Icarus, pummeling him further.

Soon, two senior cadets came into the ring and wrapped their arms around Breksta. She tried to maneuver herself out of their grasps, but they were stronger.

They dragged her to a standing position while Icarus lay unmoving on the ground. Hestia let out a sigh of relief. The fight was finally over.

"Let go of me," Breksta shouted defensively, twisting her shoulders.

"We'll release you once you stop resisting," the boy cadet said with a grimace as he tried to control Breksta. When she relaxed, the cadets released her. She then walked over to Hestia and offered a hand.

"Thank you," she said quietly as she let Breksta help her to her feet.

Breksta let a small smile show. "It was nothing. He deserved worse."

Hestia couldn't help but glance with pity at Icarus, who was helped to his feet by the same two cadets who'd restrained Breksta. His face was plump with bruises and his eyes swollen shut as blood flowed freely from his lips and down his neck. Through the small slits of his eyes, Hestia could see his anger and hatred directed in Breksta's direction.

"Let's get out of here," Hestia whispered.

Breksta nodded, and both girls ducked underneath the roped barriers of the ring. The crowd around the ring dispersed slowly and made a path for Breksta and Hestia to walk through. The girls made their way to the opposite end of the rectangular room where two beds as well as first aid boxes lay.

"Sit," Breksta ordered as she grabbed the first aid box from underneath the bed.

Hestia obliged and slowly, with pained grimaces, moved herself onto the bed.

"Face, arms, or legs first?" Breksta asked, tearing open an alcohol pad.

"Face," Hestia sighed.

Breksta stood with the alcohol pad in one hand and an ointment in the other. She looked at Hestia before dabbing the pad. "Ready?"

Hestia nodded. Breksta touched the pad gently to Hestia's cut. Hestia sucked in a sharp breath at the burn of the alcohol and dug her nails into the bed as Breksta cleaned her cuts. Breksta then put on the ointment and secured Hestia's cuts with band aids. Breksta placed a gentle hand on Hestia's shoulder.

"All done," she said, offering a sympathetic smile.

Hestia managed a small smile before wincing because of the cut on her lip.

"Don't smile," Breksta scolded as she tended to Hestia's other injuries.

"Yes, ma'am," Hestia said, forcing her mouth into a hard line. Hestia saw

Breksta smile as she tied cold icepacks to Hestia's calves and thighs. But their joking and laughter was short lived.

"Breksta Vilkas," Hestia's mother's voice boomed.

Hestia saw Breksta bristle at the voice and her last name. But Breksta didn't look up from her task and continued to help Hestia. The director walked over, dragging Icarus behind her.

"Please don't resist," Hestia whispered, shaking Breksta's shoulder for her attention.

Breksta moved out of Hestia's reach and turned her back, burying herself in the task at hand.

"Breksta," Hestia hissed.

Breksta still didn't turn. Not even when the director stood beside her. The director crossed her arms and snapped her fingers once.

"Breksta Vilkas, would you care to explain this?" she said, pointing to Icarus's pummeled face.

Breksta didn't look up as she slid the first aid box underneath Hestia's legs. "This is the boxing ring, Madam Director. Cadets sustain injuries daily."

"Do not speak to me as if I am some low, uneducated Dreamer," the director snapped, grabbing Breksta's shoulders and pulling her face to look at Icarus.

"You interfered with a fair fight," the director spoke coldly. "And injured a fellow cadet."

Breksta's eyes grew stormy with anger. "Fair fight? Hestia had already surrendered, and he didn't stop. How can you call that a fair fight?"

Hestia bit her lip despite her injures, for she knew her mother would not stand for such provocative words. She slipped off the bed gingerly and stood in front of her friend. "I-it was a fair fight. Icarus won, and Breksta is very sorry for injuring him so severely."

"I'm not," Breksta spat. "Icarus is always the one who starts things."

The director gripped Breksta's chin so that Breksta was forced to look into her eyes. "No, *you* are always the only one who stirs up trouble. You need to learn to control your temper, or it will be controlled for you."

Hestia clenched her fists as her annoyance at Breksta and her mother's tempers grew. Breksta pushed the director's hand from her chin and began to speak but was immediately cut off when Hestia stood in front of her.

"Don't worry, Mom, I'll make sure she learns," Hestia said, trying to calm the situation.

"Yes. A week in the solitude boxes will ensure it," the director announced, grabbing Breksta by the arm and leading her away.

The director pulled a fuming Breksta toward the stairs outside of the boxing room with Hestia following quickly behind. Hestia, as she opened the door, caught a sly smile from Icarus. Hestia slammed the door before rushing after her mother.

"Wait," she shouted, finally catching up to her mother at the stairwell. "Icarus did this on purpose. He knew that Breksta would step in, and he wanted to get her in trouble."

The director paused, looking downward before looking up at Hestia.

"You can't judge that boy's intentions. But we can judge Breksta's actions. And the reality is that she violently injured one of the cadets. Her actions must be punished."

Breksta had returned to her submissive gaze and didn't struggle in the director's grasp. "I'll manage, Hestia," she said simply, keeping her eyes squarely on the floor.

"Follow us to the solitude boxes. Breksta *will* answer for her actions," the director declared with a voice of steel.

Hestia opened her mouth to protest but was silenced by the harsh gaze from her mother.

The director pulled the rusted key from her pocket and unlocked the door, instructing Hestia to help her pull open the hefty door. Wincing, Hestia forced herself to help, opening the door to the familiar, dark room, lit only by the grated window above. Without prompting, Breksta sat on the thin mattress on the left side of the room and leaned her head against the wall. She was no longer bothered by the smells of the room, having been here so many times in the past. Her anger simmered just below the surface, knowing that nothing she did would change her circumstances. Hestia looked at the unfolding scene with pity for Breksta and growing anger for her mother, who never treated her friend as anything less than a Dreamer's daughter.

"I'll see you in the morning," Breksta said with a faint smile of reassurance.

The director put her hands on the door. "Help me close it, Hestia."

Hestia put her hands on the door and struggled to push it closed. Suddenly, she felt the internal pull resurface, that urge to choose between her friend and her mother. That feeling had begun the night Breksta told Hestia about her mother and her adventures in the woods of her village. Despite the mundane nature of those stories, Hestia found the beauty of imagination in them, envisioning a life away from the Academy for the first time. That was the true magic of their friendship.

"Wait … I want to stay with Breksta," Hestia said as she lowered her hands from the door.

"Nonsense," the director replied. "You don't belong in there, Hestia."

Clenching her fists, she stated emphatically, "I'm staying."

The director's eyes narrowed. "Why would you want to do such a thing?"

Breksta called out from the other side of the door, "Hestia … just go. You need to rest and heal."

Breksta's defeat steeled Hestia's resistance to her mother. "You taught me to put loyalty first, and now I am being loyal to my best friend," Hestia said bravely, looking directly into her mother's eyes.

The director's right eye twitched ever so slightly, a sign of her growing anger, which began to weaken Hestia's bravery. But she held her mother's gaze and wedged open the door just enough to slip in.

"Hestia …" her mother called after her, grabbing her hand just as it passed the doorframe. "Loyalty to family is first."

"Friends can be family too," Hestia said softly before pulling her hand back. "I'll see you in the morning."

"Then you deserve this punishment as much as she does. You should know better by now, *daughter*," the director spat. Furious, the director looked one last time at Hestia then at Breksta before slamming the door inches from Hestia's face.

Seconds passed as Hestia stood facing the door. She felt her pulse race in her clenched fists. Breksta moved from the mattress to Hestia's side, putting an arm around her shoulders lightly and directing her toward the mattress. They sat side-by-side while Hestia kept her gaze locked on the ground, her mind still processing her mother's rage and what might come next. Hestia knew what violence her mother was capable of; she'd experienced it firsthand that day in her mother's office after she had snuck into Breksta's cell.

"You didn't have to do this for me," Breksta said finally, "but thank you."

Hestia didn't speak but turned to Breksta, managing a slight smile through her cut lips as tears pooled in her eyes. Breksta noticed them and pushed Hestia's hair away from her face. Hestia's shoulders shook, and she began to sob. Breksta wrapped her arms carefully around her friend as Hestia buried her face in Breksta's shoulder.

"Your mother was being cruel," Breksta spoke gently, patting Hestia's back.

"I try to be the best ... the best daughter ... the best cadet ... for her. But it's never enough, and I'm never enough."

"I know it's not fair, Hestia. But ... if your mother has one good trait, it's her love and protectiveness of you, Hestia."

Hestia pulled up from Breksta's shoulder, brushing away her tears from her red eyes. "She doesn't love me," Hestia said with bitter hate.

"You're wrong," Breksta countered, feeling envy at the absence of her own mother. "She loves you immensely."

Hestia didn't speak for a long time, leaning her head on Breksta's shoulder again and thinking about what Breksta had just said. Deep down, Hestia knew her mother loved her. But her mother didn't show her love through affection and tenderness; instead, she demonstrated it by forcefully protecting Hestia from a cruel world. "I just wish she loved me in the ways your mother loved you," Hestia responded in a soft voice.

It was Breksta's turn to be silent as the buried memories of her mother resurfaced. Despite all the pain Breksta had endured since her mother's death, she knew her mother's love was strong. Stronger than life, and stronger than death. But that had been the problem, Breksta realized. Remembering the strength and affection of her mother's gentle love heightened her grief, knowing that because her mother was gone, she couldn't reciprocate that love.

"Neither of our mothers' love is perfect," Breksta said, her eyes a mirror of her grief.

"No love is," Hestia added with angry tears.

"Perhaps not, Hestia. But we can try to give each other what we need, right? I will protect you … we can protect each other."

Hestia wiped away the last of her tears. "Of course," she responded.

Breksta turned to face Hestia, extending her hand toward her friend. "Pinky promise?"

Hestia grinned and interlaced her sore pinky with Breksta's. "I promise."

Despite their punishment, their youthful minds couldn't be subdued. The cruel world they lived in didn't dull their fifteen-year-old childlike dreams, hopes, and joys. To keep those dreams alive, Breksta needed Hestia's support just as Hestia desperately needed Breksta's. Into the night, they spoke of their aspirations.

"I still want the war to end," Hestia said softly. Her eyes grew sad as she remembered the dead Dreamers and the toll it put on the children. "And for everyone to live like they did in your village."

"Your mother won't end the war unless all the Dreamers are dead," Breksta sighed.

"I will change that," Hestia said valiantly, her eyes shining with purpose. "I won't let anything like what happened to you happen to anyone else. I can save all of us, Breksta."

"Well…" Breksta said, smiling softly at the nobility of her friend's wishes, "I want something much simpler."

Hestia turned to face Breksta.

"And what's that?"

"I want to leave this place. To get away from the Academy and explore the world," Breksta said wistfully.

"If you wish that, then I wish it too," Hestia declared. "I promise, I will help you get your wish."

"Our wish," Breksta corrected.

"Yes, our wish," Hestia repeated. "After I fix the war."

"After *we* fix it. If you wish that, then I wish it too," Breksta said, parroting her friend.

Breksta and Hestia lay back against the hard mattress, the only warmth in the room coming from each other. They lay side-by-side as their hearts held the purpose and hope of their dreams. The Academy hadn't been kind to Hestia because of her ideas about peace and her lack of bitter and absolute hatred for Dreamers, nor was it kind to Breksta because of her name. But through their shared pain, they found solace. Their promises to each other were never forgotten and became the bright light they kept alive: their dreams were their means of surviving the Academy.

CHAPTER 14

ICARUS RETURNED TO HIS MOTHER'S office after not being declared the winner during the boxing match. Despite what Breksta and Hestia had thought, Icarus hadn't purposefully tried to punish Breksta and put her in the solitude boxes. Rather, he only wanted to win.

That was Icarus's purpose in life: to win and excel at all things, at least in his mother's eyes. Icarus and Hestia weren't so different, although neither realized this. Both had mothers who pushed them to succeed, wishing for them to each be the best cadets. And because of this, Icarus was often consumed by suppressed anger and frustration.

He had learned what he needed to do to be valued by his mother: to be passive in his mother's presence, to be competitive in training, and to be ruthless in missions. Because he wore these different façades, no one truly knew him and no one really cared for Icarus besides his mother. But his mother was often cruel, pushing Icarus to excel despite the pain and fatigue that came from being pushed so hard. Although Icarus was not angry by nature, his mother's unfair treatment led to his feelings of worthlessness and anger.

During the latest boxing match with Hestia, his temper had erupted uncontrollably. He couldn't stop himself even after Hestia surrendered. When Breksta stepped in, he suffered the consequences of her wrath. His nose was bloody, and his ribs throbbed. But that didn't stop Ms. Adams from putting the blame on Icarus.

"How could you let this happen?" Ms. Adams exclaimed, slamming her hands on the desk and making Icarus flinch.

"I would've beat her if Breksta hadn't stepped in," Icarus retorted, equally frustrated with his mother's demands for perfection.

"No. *You* gave up and allowed yourself to be beaten up by a *Dreamer's* daughter, Asteria Vilkas's daughter," Ms. Adams shouted, stopping her son's argument in its tracks.

Icarus opened his mouth to defend himself. "But Mom—"

"I don't want to hear excuses, Icarus. Have I not done my best to train you? Have I not tried to build this wonderful life for you to succeed in? And you throw it all away, for what?" Ms. Adams asked quieter. Her eyes grew frustrated as she sighed.

"I'm not throwing it away," Icarus said through clenched teeth.

"Then what do you call it?" Ms. Adam demanded. "Weakness? I am *very* disappointed in you, Icarus."

Icarus dug his fingernails into the palms of his hands. "I haven't done anything wrong!"

Icarus knew his mistake when he saw the fire in his mother's eyes in response to his words. But he didn't care. She would be angry at him either way: for failing to win the fight or for speaking up. He would rather she be angry at him because of his choice to provoke her rather than passively take her insults like he always did.

"Excuse me?" Ms. Adams said slowly, as if in disbelief of her son's words.

Icarus looked up, his eyes as angry as his mother's. "I can't expect you to understand," he said through clenched teeth.

His mother opened her mouth, but Icarus vowed to say what he needed to say this time.

"You always push me to struggle and fight and be the best. Why? Does my success in the Academy define my worth to you? Am I some sort of pawn you can move around at your disposal, demanding unachievable goals from me?

Well, I'm not you. I'll never be, so why do you do this to me?" Icarus shouted.

Silence ensued. To his surprise, Ms. Adams had a look of hurt in her eyes. Icarus could have sworn he saw tears. Normally, the sight of his mother displaying any emotion besides anger would have softened Icarus's own frustration and anger. But not today.

"We all work hard for a better life," Ms. Adams said in a calmer voice. And for once Icarus thought she was repenting, until she whispered, "…despite your father's absence."

Icarus scowled at the mention of his father who was rarely spoken about. Knowledge of his father and the past they came from was yet another part of his life that his mother controlled. Icarus left the room quickly, unsure if he could keep his rising temper contained.

"Icarus!" his mother called after him as he pushed open the door.

But Icarus was gone, moving from a walk to a sprint to get away from the classroom, past the boxing rooms and shooting ranges to the stairs at the end of the long, white hallway. He ran up the stairs, through the lobby, and out to the airstrip, which was the farthest anyone could go within the Academy grounds. The pain of running, the thrum of his heart, and the sharp intakes of breath distracted him from his inner turmoil. Icarus tried to convince himself that if he was the best, the pain would go away, and if he trained the hardest, his mother would truly be proud and treat him with the warm affection he envied in Breksta and Hestia's friendship. In his mother's eyes, such friendship wasn't only a betrayal of the Academy but something unnecessary to Icarus's achievement-driven life.

He was out of breath when he reached the end of the airstrip, where the black gate jailed him from the outside world. At that time in the afternoon, the sun was near the end of its journey and hung in the sky beside the mountains. Icarus paused to catch his breath before he sat down. He looked out, unsure of what he was looking for in the cloudless blue sky.

Perhaps Icarus wanted answers about his father, none of which his mother would ever provide. But, he considered, maybe he wouldn't like the answers she gave him. Why else had she not shared anything about her life with his father before he was born or their life together when he was a baby? He'd been told his father was a senator and had been involved with the Dreamer revolt, losing his life because of the conflict. His father was a traitor to the Academy, almost as bad as the Dreamers themselves. But he'd never heard any details. The question of why continued to plague him.

To Icarus, his father was a distant figure, a man in a picture frame that his mother held dearly to her chest when she thought Icarus wasn't looking. His father seemed to be like two men: one who his mother secretly cherished as a husband and one who had betrayed their family. This was a contradiction Icarus never understood, and the mystery loomed over him. Yet, his mother made it clear that the topic of his father was off-limits.

As the sun set behind the mountains, he heard quick steps approaching. Icarus didn't look up but already knew who it was as his mother lowered herself to a sitting position next to him. He kept his eyes on the horizon and didn't meet her gaze, despite feeling her eyes on him.

"You really picked the farthest spot for me to walk to," Ms. Adams said in a joking and out-of-breath voice.

Icarus stiffened at the words. Even as a joke, they sounded like a reprimand. "I didn't intend for you to follow me."

His mother sighed. "And yet I did … I'm sorry that I let that get out of hand earlier."

Icarus was used to his mother's fits of anger, but her apology took him by surprise. Frowning, he looked over at his mother.

She caught his expression and spoke calmly, "The increase in missions and captured Dreamers reminds me so much of your father and…"

Ms. Adams's voice broke as she covered her mouth with a trembling hand. Tears dotted her eyes, and she looked away from Icarus. Icarus's anger began to thaw, giving way to tentative sympathy.

"What about my father?" he asked cautiously, his yearning for answers apparent.

His mother slowly flicked away the small tears and released a shuddered breath. A look of remembrance appeared on her face. "Today is … not the day for such a conversation, but I promise. One day, I'll share the story with you."

Icarus looked at his mother but didn't say a word. Deep down, he wanted to understand it all. To come to his own conclusions about his father, even if he discovered that his father was a rebel. However, as much as he wanted to hear the whole story now, something told him that more anger would ensue, and even stronger than ever before. He decided to not say another word.

CHAPTER 15

AS MORE TIME PASSED, Breksta's and Hestia's future dreams became harder to keep alive. As their physical strength grew through their continued training, their minds were weakened by the constant droning of the Academy's teachings. Despite being able to keep out the Academy's teachings when they were younger, they learned that to survive in the Academy, both girls had to focus on their current life rather than the past or the imaginary. They did their best to convince themselves to believe in the Academy's teachings of violence and vengeance, telling themselves it was for the best, that only the Academy was in the right, and that Dreamers deserved their cruel fates in death. At least they tried to believe what the Academy taught.

As much as they wished to ignore it, death surrounded them. It waited behind the curtains of the Academy's auditorium, in the prison cells, and on the planes, all places where Dreamers were held captive. Death was part of each lesson learned and the ideals the cadets were taught to live by. Dreamers deserved death.

Each bullet Hestia shot at targets would eventually be replaced by the heads and hearts of Dreamers she would kill without hesitation. Every fight and punch Breksta threw would become attacks on Dreamers in the future. Even if they spoke to one another about their misgivings of death and violence and blood, deep down they both knew they couldn't change what was required of them. In the Academy, death was synonymous with fate, the eventuality of all Dreamers. Breksta and Hestia had witnessed that fate throughout their years as cadets.

Weekly, the senior cadets left in their planes with their weapons loaded and sharpened. And weekly, they returned with their mission completed and bodies left behind; the death toll was tallied and announced with each senior cadet's graduation. Every year, once the senior cadets proved their value, loyalty, and strength, they were allowed to go free into the world.

However, the unspoken rule was that cadets should stay in the Academy and eventually become the mentors for future cadets: the chosen warriors who shared the Academy's message of death and persecution with the next generation— until the Academy was certain that all Dreamers had been exterminated. Most never left the Academy, remaining dedicated to service. And most didn't have lives outside the Academy or families that would take them in. In that sense, the cadets were orphans, and the Academy was their home, so why would they leave?

Icarus was trapped as well. His thoughts, and perhaps his emotions, were on a leash held by his mother. His mind had become so twisted and manipulated that he couldn't tell his thoughts from his mother's anymore. But his feelings of curiosity about his father grew and couldn't be suppressed any longer. So he tried to learn more. He went through Academy records he was able to access and asked his mother. Unfortunately, his efforts yielded no results besides the little information he already knew.

His mind was a tangle of contradictory thoughts that threatened to one day push him deeper into the Academy's corrupt clutches. He was sinking deeper into the belly of the beast, and he had neither the knowledge of how to escape nor what the world outside the beast would be like if he did. Yet, as he neared the time of his graduation, he knew decisions needed to be made.

Just like Icarus, as Hestia and Breksta got closer to the end of their training, both young women continued to struggle with the conflict between their deepest desires and what the Academy required of them. Deep down, Breksta still wanted to escape the Academy and create a life of her own, one that mirrored her life with her mother. Meanwhile, Hestia knew her mother expected her to serve and to take her place as the director one day. But when she allowed herself to entertain her deepest thoughts, Hestia wasn't sure she wanted that. Learning about the world through Breksta's eyes showed her that so much more was possible. She also saw that changing the mentality and teachings of the Academy might be almost impossible. More than anything, Hestia wanted to be free of the burden of death and sacrifice so she could create her own space in the world.

The promise they'd made to each other when they were fifteen still existed. They'd promised to always be there for one another, to protect one another, and to fulfill their dreams of traveling the world and exploring the vast and beautiful lands beyond the borders of the Academy once they were free from the war. This promise lingered in each girl's mind as they neared their eighteenth birthdays and their senior graduation.

For the first time in eight years, freedom seemed reachable for all three of them. But at what cost?

CHAPTER 16

"BREKSTA VILKAS! How are you not awake yet?" Hestia's motherly voice smashed through the sluggishness of Breksta's dreams. Hestia shook Breksta's shoulders as the unbraided strands of her curly red hair fell forward to create a wreath of fire around Hestia's face.

"Good morning to you too," Breksta said, yawning as she sat up and pulled her long wispy white hair that ghosted her shoulder blades.

Hestia walked to the window and opened the drapes that shielded their small cubicle from the sharp light of morning. Hestia gazed at Breksta's appearance, prompting her to shove the Academy's dark clothes into Breksta's arms before commenting, "You're ridiculous, you know?"

Hestia walked back to the opened bathroom door, muttering something under her breath about Breksta's sense of time. She finished her braid in front of the mirror as Breksta changed.

"I'm sorry. Kickboxing yesterday really wore me out," Breksta sighed.

By the time Hestia finished her braids, the only part of Breksta that remained unruly was her hair.

"Do you want me to braid your hair too?" Hestia said, crossing her arms with an amused look as Breksta struggled to brush her wild hair.

Breksta tossed the brush onto the bed and sighed in defeat.

"French will suffice, I hope," Hestia said rhetorically as she approached Breksta.

Breksta nodded. Hestia knelt behind Breksta and began braiding her specialty: a single French braid. Breksta's hands were callous from her time spent kickboxing and fighting hand-to-hand combat. This accompanied with her clumsiness made it difficult for her to braid. Hestia on the other hand, was very skilled at braiding from her years of practice. So Hestia had become the designated hair stylist.

When Hestia finally finished, she took a leather strip from her pocket and secured it around Breksta's braid that dusted the space between her shoulder blades.

"Thanks," Breksta said, touching the braid unconsciously.

"You're welcome," Hestia replied with a smile, tossing Breksta her black down jacket from the hook beside the door.

"We need to go through the Under Passage again. The airstrip will take too long to walk," Hestia said as she pushed open the door.

They passed the twenty identical dorm rooms, still filled with sleeping cadets. Each room was equipped with the bare necessities: toiletries, standard sets of cadet attire, a bathroom, and a bunkbed. This was all the cadets possessed, which was a way the Academy controlled its subjects.

"Let's go!" Hestia urged, as they made their way down the staircase to the lowest level.

They reached a large circular door, one befitting a hobbit or small creature accustomed to the dark depths of the Under Passage. The passage connected the entire Academy through a system of tunnels running under the Academy. Directly above the Under Passage, air conditioning ducts pumped air into the tunnels, providing Breksta and Hestia with another way to reach the Under Passage. Breksta had discovered it years earlier, hoping for a means of permanent escape from this place. Instead, the Under Passage became a temporary escape back to the child she once was. One who was motivated by discovery, curiosity, and interest. This was the place where she could breathe, where she could be Breksta Vilkas without hatred for her name. Hestia often joined her, and they spent long nights in the dark winding tunnels, exploring and mapping out the passageways. Together, they learned every route within the Under Passage. If anyone were to follow them, those people would soon find themselves lost by the many twists, turns, and dead ends. Knowing this, the girls crept along the sides of the tunnel, queens of their private realm.

In recent years, however, they used the tunnels as a means of travel. The Under Passage was a quicker way to get to classes and the airstrip, where they were now heading. They eventually reached another circular door, taking them to the staircase that led to the airstrip at the outskirts of the Academy. They ran up the stairs and opened a metal hatch that opened to the view of two pairs of black boots and white heels pointed in the direction of an incoming jet. Nimbly, Hestia and Breksta snuck into their place beside Icarus and Olivia, a younger cadet who had been at the Academy since she was an infant.

"Why are you late again?" Olivia whispered aggressively, tugging at Breksta's pantleg since she was younger and shorter than Breksta.

"Too much training yesterday," Breksta whispered, a sheepish smile spreading across her face.

"At least try and be quiet to hide the fact that you are *indeed* late," Icarus muttered, rolling his eyes. It seemed that in recent years, Icarus had grown even more bitter so that each word he spoke oozed with venomous anger. Breksta and Hestia had made various guesses as to the cause of Icarus's resentment and had concluded that Hestia being the director's daughter and Breksta being one of the best fighters in the Academy had a strong effect on Icarus's self-esteem. Both girls had grown accustomed to his huffs and hateful side glances.

The director cleared her throat loudly before shifting her eyes from the binder in her hands to the cadets. "Cadets, show some professionalism, especially toward today's new recruits. We haven't had many in a while, and you are representing the Academy. Do not fail. And thank you for finally deciding to join us today, Breksta and Hestia," she said sharply, her eyes pointing like a laser toward the girls before shifting to the large incoming airplane.

"Are there going to be any girls?" Olivia whispered, already forgiving Breksta's tardiness and looking up at Breksta with curiosity sparkling in her dark eyes.

"I don't know, Olivia. But no matter who they are, you can show them around," Breksta whispered, barely moving her eyes from the plane to offer Olivia a small smile. "Now let's focus."

Breksta gently nudged Olivia to look toward the plane. Olivia's smiley appearance reflected her utter and unwavering devotion to the Academy. Her experiences with the outside world didn't exist since her life began when her parents offered her up as an infant to the Academy.

"They always knew I would be a warrior," Olivia would say to Breksta, her eyes shining brightly. At those times, Breksta felt a crushing pity for the joy and optimism Olivia portrayed, firmly believing that her parents had not abandoned her.

What Breksta didn't know was that sometimes when Olivia was alone in her room after hard days of training and pain, her mind would slip into the subconsciousness where her insecurities fought for her attention. *Perhaps … perhaps they didn't want me*, Olivia would think. But she would shake herself and bury the emotions, telling herself that it didn't matter whether her parents wanted her. The Academy was her home now, and Breksta and Hestia were her sisters in arms. That was enough. That was what Olivia recalled as the plane descended, for no matter what child stepped out of that plane, Olivia would welcome them into her home. The plane slowly rolled to a halt in front of them before its large door opened on the bottom and released two cadets followed by a small dark figure in a gray blanket.

"Cadets, I congratulate you on a successful mission. Casualties?" the director questioned authoritatively.

"The target was eliminated with minimal resistance. No other casualties, Madam Director," one of the cadets responded.

"And our recruit. Welcome to the Academy. I am the director. Address me as Madam Director or just the director," the director's smile painted an ominous picture that was further affirmed by her blood-red lipstick and sharp gaze.

The child approached with their eyes pushed down, not meeting the stern gaze of the director. Their back hunched in an arch and small hands gripped the edges of their blanket that had splatters of tears. The blanket fell away from the child's face to reveal a trembling, shoeless girl. Her feet were scraped on the sides, and each time she stepped, she winced. As she neared, Breksta noticed that she left a trail of bloody footsteps. Her eyes were bloodshot, and her breaths came out unevenly.

Hestia looked to the director. "May I approach?"

The director gave a small nod, her face not reflecting any signs of emotion.

Hestia knelt in front of the girl, touching her shoulder gently. "What's your name?"

"Si-Sitara," the girl responded, her voice quivering.

The familiarity of Sitara's appearance and behavior made Breksta remember the day she had arrived. But Breksta kept her face neutral and betrayed no thoughts of resentment or fear of the Academy.

"That's a beautiful name. What does it mean?" Hestia continued with her genial words. Her eyes never left Sitara, whose mousy brown hair fell around her face in thin strips.

"It means morning star. M-my dad…" Her voice closed off and she took a sharp in-breath.

Hestia nodded at the girl before continuing, "I understand. You don't have to talk about it. You're safe now. The Academy will protect you."

"The Academy is your home now," Olivia said with a smile, happier at the presence of more children, especially a girl.

Hestia looked back at Breksta sadly, also remembering the day Breksta arrived. Nothing had truly changed since then except for the rising number of cadets.

She continued in her gentle voice, "My name is Hestia. And these are my friends, Breksta and Olivia. Over there is Icarus."

Breksta watched Sitara's eyes. Breksta smiled and waved as she studied Sitara, whose emotions seemed like those she had felt when she first arrived. Along with feelings of fear, she observed Sitara's obvious grief.

"You must go with the other cadets to do some tests right now," Hestia explained as she stood and pointed to the senior cadets who stood off to the side. "But we will wait for you in the cafeteria once you're done."

Sitara looked at each of them, her fearful eyes straying to Breksta before nodding. One of the cadets beckoned to her, and hesitantly, Sitara followed.

When Sitara was out of earshot, the director turned to the group of cadets, her eyes calculating.

"The rest of you *will* put in effort to integrate the cadet instead of Hestia doing all the work for you. It's your job to embody the Academy's values. Do so."

Her words were crisp and sharp. She scanned each one of them as a hunter stalks its prey, searching for the smallest crack of weakness or hesitation.

"Yes, Madam Director," the cadets spoke unanimously with their heads lowered in submission.

Satisfied, the director began walking back to the main Academy buildings on the airstrip and left the cadets standing. Icarus gave Hestia a cold glance as he walked past, following the director toward the building.

Olivia grabbed both girls' hands and dragged them, laughing, toward the main buildings and the awaiting breakfast. The sun had just kissed the tops of the dark mountain and sent its rays to the cadets' faces. Approaching the buildings, they walked on the paths in between, which were lined with tall trees that had grown wider and more stable through the years, just as Breksta had grown at the Academy.

The girls entered the building to their left and were met with the smell of ham and perfectly seasoned eggs. The cafeteria, usually bustling with students and teachers rushing to their classes, was nearly empty at this early hour. Olivia's small hand clutched both girls as they neared the swinging glass doors. She released Breksta's and Hestia's hands as she raced to the nearest mountain of trays and grabbed one for each of them. After filling their trays with large mounds of food, the three of them found a table near the large glass windows.

By the time the girls had finished their food, Sitara arrived. Hestia beckoned her over to their small table after Sitara picked up the plate of food her escorting cadet had prepared for her.

"Welcome back, Sitara," Hestia said, trying to meet Sitara's traumatized gaze.

"How old are you? I'm eight years old," Olivia said enthusiastically.

Sitara's lips barely moved. She formed the words, but no sound came out of her mouth. She swallowed a few times before managing to get out "seven" in a raspy sound. She spoke the one word, but no more. The silence was filled by the sounds of Sitara's metal fork scraping the plastic tray as she ate. Once she finished, Sitara sat with her hands folded in her lap and her eyes cast down, gazing at the empty tray with a flurry of emotions on her face.

"We all had some adjustment time to the Academy. You'll get the hang of it soon," Hestia said, offering a genuine smile before she patted Sitara on the shoulder.

There was a long pause before Sitara asked in a meek voice, "What is this place?"

"Well," Breksta said, looking to Hestia for support. "This is the Academy. It's a … safe place. For kids like us."

"But why … why did they take my dad away? Why did they—" Sitara said as anger built in her voice and her body tensed, ready to spring at any moment.

"I know it has been a long day for you. How about we find some place for you to rest?" Hestia interrupted.

"No, I want to know why they killed my dad!" Sitara said, her voice abruptly rising in volume. The older cadets turned around and looked at the small child, whose eyes were fiery with anger and pooled with large silver tears.

"It's complicated, Sitara," Breksta said, trying to add warmth to her words, which instead came out cold and insensitive.

"Tell me now!"

"As I said, it's complicated," Breksta said anxiously, reaching over to take Sitara's hands in an act to calm her.

"I don't care!" Sitara shouted, ripping her hands away from Breksta. "What do you want from me?"

"We just want what's best for you," Hestia said gently, touching Sitara's arm and pulling her back down into the chair. "You just need some time. Just like Breksta did when she came. Right, Breksta?"

"Yes. Just some time," Breksta echoed, closing her eyes as she pushed the images of her mother's cold corpse out of her head.

Hestia rubbed slow circles around Sitara's back before Sitara slowly descended into tears. Breksta walked away from the table as the sobs behind her grew louder. She had already lived Sitara's pain and didn't plan to relive it as she was forced to guide the girl through Academy life. That didn't mean, however, that she couldn't be kind.

Breksta grabbed a handful of paper towels beside the trays, walked back to the table, and handed them to Sitara. "Here," she said, looking kindly at the girl.

Through her tears, Sitara looked up at Breksta. Her small hand hovered over the paper towels before grasping them to dry her eyes. Breksta took this as a sign of surrender: surrender to the Academy's murder of her father and surrender to the pain the Academy had caused. The questions that Sitara asked earlier didn't matter anymore. This was what the Academy wanted. In the Academy, absolute surrender was a necessary part of survival. And if Breksta had surrendered to survive the Academy, and half of the Academy who were also Dreamer children, so would Sitara.

Hestia would never understand. Although she questioned the Academy's tactics, she didn't question the purpose of their missions. She hadn't been hated for her very name and blood since the first day she stepped foot onto the Academy's soil. But Breksta didn't hold it against her friend. She saw that her friend was more than her mother's daughter, more human than most in the Academy.

"I'm going to take Sitara to get some fresh air," Breksta said, walking over and linking arms with the sniffling girl. "I'll meet you at the auditorium."

"Are you sure?" Hestia said, her eyebrows furrowing. "If we are late again, the director will send you to the solitude—"

"I'll see you later," Breksta broke in as she dragged Sitara away.

"Where are you taking me?" she exclaimed, digging her fingers into Breksta's arm to release her grip.

Breksta didn't loosen her grip. "We're just going someplace where there are no cadets. Trust me," she replied with fake calmness that she had perfected, ignoring the stares and sneers of the other cadets. Their expressions had long ago become harmless to her.

"I don't want to!" Sitara shouted, kicking Breksta's shins.

Breksta winced but continued her pace until she reached the door and turned Sitara toward the stairs on the right. She pulled her to the side of the wall before kneeling and speaking to Sitara. "I know what it's like coming here. I know what you are feeling. So please, trust me. I know a place away from all these people. Do you want them to stare at you for the whole time or do you want some peace and quiet?" Breksta's voice was quiet but commanded Sitara's attention.

Sitara muttered a frustrated "fine" before she allowed Breksta to pull her up the long stairwell.

They made their way up the stairs until they reached the roof of the building. Breksta pushed open the door and released her grip on Sitara. Breksta sat, and Sitara followed suit. They were silent for a long time and looked out at the ocean of trees that covered the mountainside. Slowly, Sitara began to relax into the quiet space around them.

"I like it here. It reminds me of where I grew up," Breksta finally said warmly.

"The Academy?" Sitara asked, horror and disgust vivid in her voice.

"No. The forest. It looks like home."

Breksta watched as Sitara hugged her thin legs close to her chest and looked out from her new prison. She turned back with eyes that reflected surprise at Breksta's smile. Sitara's tensed face relaxed.

"There is one rule in this place. One they don't tell you, but you need to know. If you don't follow the way things are done here, they *will* hurt you," Breksta said gently, her pain was masked by her tone, another skill she had acquired long ago.

She removed her jacket and bundled it on the floor, creating a pillow for her head. Breksta then lay back and let her body relax. She breathed in the scents of the wind that carried the smell of the forest.

Sitara looked outward toward the dark forest and allowed her mind to let go of the morning's pain for a brief moment. For both, the roof was like a bubble from their pain—one whose pain lived on the surface and the other whose pain was buried but still lingered.

"Thank you," Sitara murmured.

"You don't have to thank me for anything," Breksta said, watching the fluffy clouds fly past.

"M-may I ask a question?" Sitara said slowly, remembering what Breksta had just told her.

"Yes, what is it?"

"What do these people want from me?" Sitara murmured, her arms encircling her knees protectively.

Breksta was momentarily silent. There was a certain pain attached to lying to Sitara, but Breksta deemed it necessary.

"They just want … what's best for you and the world."

The lies tasted bitter on her lips as they exited her mouth. She regretted them as soon as the words were out, but it was the only way to keep herself and Sitara safe from the director.

"Really?" she asked, her eyes shifting uncertainly.

"Really. I'll make sure you fit in here, and so will Hestia."

"So … you'll be my … friends?"

"Yes, we'll be your friends."

A small smile began to appear on Sitara's face, melting away the fiery expression that had been there minutes earlier. Together they sat in comfortable silence, free to think, until the bell sounded for them to get to the auditorium.

CHAPTER 17

THE DIRECTOR'S VOICE ECHOED through the loudspeakers in the Academy, summoning the cadets to the auditorium. Breksta and Sitara arrived and took seats at the center of the front row where Hestia and Olivia sat. The students flooded in through the doors, pushing and shoving to reach their designated spots.

"This will be us in a few weeks, finishing our missions and graduating," Hestia announced, her eyes wide with excitement.

Breksta crossed her arms and sunk deeper into her seat. "It's still not for a few weeks."

"We'll finally have a chance to leave," Hestia said, her eyes bright as stars.

Breksta let out a reserved smile, remembering their promises to each other. Her remembrance was interrupted by the director's voice that commanded attention and silenced the room. "Welcome! Welcome, cadets."

The director walked forward on the stage with confidence surrounding her like perfume. Her white heels clacked as she made her way to center stage, signaling that the assembly had begun. Her long red hair sported graying streaks and was tied in a tight bun atop her head. Her black, thick-rimmed glasses hung just below the bone in her nose. She pushed them up and reinstated her look of control.

She approached the microphone and addressed the cadets in a booming voice. "Today we have gathered to award the service of our graduating cadets. They are part of the senior group of cadets who have completed their final mission and will graduate once all the seniors finish their individual assignments. Please welcome Daedalus and Io to the stage."

The two figures in black cadet gear made their way to the stage. They beamed as the students shouted their names, creating a tsunami of sound that engulfed the massive room.

"Cadets! Cadets, settle down!" the director shouted, bringing her hand into the air. The crowd settled into their seats and became silent under the director's conductive hand. A younger cadet scurried out of the folds of the curtain and presented the director with two hanging golden medallions.

She beckoned the two cadets toward the center of the stage. "I am so very pleased to award these devoted and patriotic young individuals. First, Daedalus, please step forward and receive the justice award for your quick execution and steadfast intelligence during your time at the Academy and your missions."

Music crackled through the overhead speakers and accompanied Daedalus to the director's side. Daedalus bowed his head, and the director slipped the award around his neck, allowing him to shoulder its weight squarely. He stood and smiled broadly, his eyes full of pride as he shook the director's hand. Daedalus's face lit up with childlike joy as the camera below the stage snapped pictures.

"Thank you, Daedalus, for your service to—" The director's microphone cut off. The director tapped the head of the microphone, which sent waves of static through the towering speakers at the edge of the auditorium. The cadets clasped their ears and shouted at the scrambling technicians who rushed to determine the cause of the disruption.

"Settle down, cadets," the director shouted as she set the malfunctioning microphone on the floor. "We thank Daedalus for his service to our nation. You have successfully removed twenty-four of the remaining Dreamers left on earth," the director said, rewarding him with a half-smile. "I hope you find joy in your future services to this country."

"Thank you," Daedalus murmured, his voice barely picked up amid the clapping. His eyes sparkled with tears of pride as he walked off the stage, pumping his fists in excitement.

This was the triumph all cadets strived for, to have completed their service to their country and live on as greater and more influential people. Some would train the next cadets, becoming teaching assistants and eventually full-fledged teachers in their preferred fields. Some, who loved the thrill of the fight, would continue with their missions. And the few who were allowed to do so could become part of the director's leadership, taking the Academy further out to the edges of the continent. All cadets would continue to serve in some way.

But Breksta didn't want this. Rather, she wished for escape and a world where she could return to the beautiful forests of her home. This was what Breksta thought about as the next award was given to a senior girl, Io.

The director proceeded with only her booming voice. "Now I am again pleased to award the peace prize to Io for her dedication to the Academy and the preservation of this country's peace and stability in both her studies and thirty missions."

The director beckoned to Io, who stepped forward into the light, her amber-brown hair catching the light and making her curls shimmer. She flashed a winning smile and bowed as the director slipped the medallion over Io's head. Io stood to her full height and took in the cheering crowd.

"Thank you for your dedicated time at the Academy, and I hope you find joy in your future services to this country," the director said with an almost genuine smile. Io vigorously shook the director's hand and beamed as she walked off the stage.

Sitara pulled Breksta's arm, getting her attention with her unceasing presses. Breksta turned to see that Sitara's dark eyes shone with fear as she pointed adamantly upward. Breksta looked up to see a crack cut across the ceiling, widening and snaking from side to side. Just then, the room began to shake.

Breksta gripped her seat until her knuckles turned white as she swung her head around, looking at the other cadets. Shouts of alarm sounded as everyone became aware of the earth's violent movement.

"Earthquake! Everyone, get out of the building, now. Stay calm!" the director shouted, the shaking bringing her to her knees.

Breksta quickly pulled Hestia and Sitara to the ground as the walls shook. Above, the stage lights' ropes strained. The bright lights swung and cast their illumination in random patterns on the wall. Suddenly, the rope snapped and tumbled toward the ground.

"Get out of the way!" Breksta shouted as she dove out of the way of the lights.

Breksta landed atop other cadets who then scrambled out from under her and ran toward the exits. She looked back frantically for Hestia and saw glass covering the place where she had just been. Beside her, Hestia tugged her arm. Breksta breathed a sigh of relief until she saw Hestia pointing amid the glass at a curled brown mess.

Breksta crawled closer, ignoring the poking of the glass against her bare hands and knees as the ground continued to shake. She wished she could unsee the horror of the scene in front of her. Just below the stage was Sitara.

Sitara cupped her hand around her middle, just below her chest. Blood seeped from between her fingers, staining her shirt. Her eyes were filled with fear and pain as she looked to Breksta helplessly. Breksta gently moved her hands away to see the extent of her injury. A shard of glass from the stage light was poking from Sitara's stomach.

"Do you think you can walk?" she asked Sitara.

"No," Sitara mouthed.

"I'm going to carry you. Put your arm around my neck, okay?"

Sitara nodded, her eyes blinking slowly from the pain as she looked up at Breksta's eyes. Breksta hooked her arm underneath Sitara's extended legs and the other behind her neck. Sitara slung her arm sluggishly around Breksta's neck, the small movement causing Sitara to gasp.

"Shh … I'll get you out of here," Breksta said through gritted teeth as she slowly lifted Sitara.

As Breksta picked up Sitara in a bridal position, Sitara winced and let out a shriek before biting her quivering lip. Hestia led the way to get them to safety.

The shaking and rumbling continued, but that didn't deter Breksta and Hestia, who leapt nimbly around the debris, wounded cadets, and other obstacles. By the time Breksta and Hestia were at the exit of the auditorium, tears stung Sitara's eyes and her forehead was pooled with sweat.

"Hang on, Sitara. We're almost there," Hestia said, opening the door of the auditorium.

Hordes of cadets rushed to the white spiral staircase that extended the entire height of the building. Breksta and Hestia followed, running down the stairs even as the earthquake continued. They finally arrived in the lobby alongside a swarm of cadets flooding out of the building, moving as one and pushing everyone out through the building's doors. With each step, Sitara winced, and after a while her eyes began to drift. Her eyelids blinked as she tried to stay awake but closed them once again.

"Stay awake, Sitara. Just a while longer," Breksta said anxiously.

"It ... it hurts," Sitara whispered, her voice hoarse and growing weaker.

"Shh ... we're almost outside."

When they approached the doors, Hestia held the door open as Breksta raced outside toward the cadets where the director stood. Suddenly, the sound of shattering glass and scrapes of metal erupted behind her. Breksta whipped around, looking back at the once looming Academy building. The gun-metal chandelier had fallen, catching cadets who were trying to escape. Ms. Adams and some other teachers did their best, holding up the chandelier to free the injured cadets. But Breksta could see the growing puddle of red spilling out of the lobby doors from the cadets whose eyes had gone blank. Breksta felt the wave of disgust, fear, and sadness sweep over her. None of those cadets had survived.

Breksta was never particularly fond of her fellow cadets, especially when they treated her like a Dreamer. But the image of their mangled, bloodied bodies lingered even as Hestia tugged at Breksta to move away from the building. As they approached the runway area where faculty and cadets stood bloodied and scared, the director's eyes narrowed at the girls running toward her.

"She's injured and needs to have that piece of glass removed. She will need stitches too. We need to get to the medical supplies," Breksta said, her voice tense from fear and adrenaline. Her arms strained as she struggled to hold Sitara.

"She needs help *now*," Hestia said, speaking firmly as her eyes dug deep into her mother's cold stare.

"Look around, Hestia. I cannot risk the lives of our cadets over one life. The foundations of the building are crumbling. It's too dangerous to go back."

Breksta breathed out slowly, her anger building. She was ready to lunge at the snake of a woman in front of her.

"Enough cadets have been injured or died today. She is one of *your* cadets! We still have time to help her," Breksta shouted as she looked at the director with fury in her eyes.

The director responded with a cold gaze that bore into Breksta. It warned Breksta of her anger and power, which was not to be ignored or resisted.

"Ma'am," Breksta added, swallowing as she looked down at Sitara's eyes that drifted mindlessly from the pain.

The other cadets already knew the answer, just as Breksta and Hestia did, despite their pleading. Some cadets managed pitiful looks while others tended to their own injuries without concern for Sitara.

Hestia put her hand on the director's shoulder and breathed before playing her card. "Mom. You always told me that you would protect me and all of us cadets from all danger. If you meant that promise, please, help Sitara."

Hestia's eyes pleaded as she stared at her mother. In the director's eyes, she and Breksta saw a momentary sliver of softness. But the director's eyes immediately hardened as she looked to Sitara. "I really am sorry, my dear," she said, cupping Hestia's cheek. "But look around you. This was clearly an attack by the Dreamers as a last resort. If we go into the buildings, they could be there, hiding to kill us."

The shaking had stopped as Breksta, Hestia, and the director looked back toward the auditorium building they had just come from and saw the absolute devastation. Silence surrounded them, like the world was holding its breath, until suddenly catastrophe hit once more. The cadets gasped collectively as the sides and ceiling of the building buckled inward; a mushroom of dust rose out of the building like a ghost escaping from deep within the Academy. The falling building collapsed with a loud boom and sent waves of dust-filled air into their faces. The smell of concrete and metal entered Breksta's nose and made her reel.

Once the dust settled, the director continued. "We don't know the structural integrity of the other buildings. I cannot and will not risk anyone reentering the buildings," the director said firmly, turning away from the girls and facing the other cadets to give out instructions.

Breksta ignored her and stormed to the bench, lowering the half-conscious Sitara onto the dust-layered wood. She stood and turned back toward the buildings.

"Where do you think you are going, Breksta?" the director's cold voice hit her.

"I'm doing what you are too scared to do. Hestia, you can bind Sitara's wound for now," Breksta instructed, beckoning to Hestia before brushing the sweat-moistened strands of Sitara's hair out of her face. "We need those medical supplies, for Sitara and the other wounded cadets. I'll be back as soon as I can, Sitara," Breksta stated as she turned to Sitara.

"O-okay," Sitara whispered, opening her eyelids slowly to look at Breksta.

Hestia ran over to Breksta and stopped her, touching her arm gently as a reminder and an order. "Breksta ... be careful."

"Breksta Vilkas," the director commanded. Breksta stopped in her tracks at her mother's name. "If you do this, I promise you, you will face the most exorbitant of punishments. This is a direct order from your commander."

"I'm willing to take that risk, madam," Breksta spat back her title.

Breksta began to walk away, her strides turning into a run as she neared the building directly in front of her to the right of the collapsed auditorium. Cracks traced up the sides of the building like ivy, spinning around the curves and carving the concrete so that dust rained down. The director had ruined all their lives, but Breksta was determined to save at least one innocent one.

She swallowed her fear and prayed wordlessly to whatever gods existed as she pushed open the door. The glass fell inward at her touch and crunched under Breksta's shoes. The lobby was demolished. The chandelier, identical to the one that had fallen and killed many of the cadets, hung from protruding, exposed metal rods in the ceiling.

Breksta walked along the edges of the wall to avoid the chandelier in case it fell as she moved toward the spiral staircase. The staircase leaned toward the wall, marking the dangerous path that Breksta had to take to get to the infirmary. With trepidation, Breksta made her way down the stairwell, taking care to step on the secure parts of concrete rather than the areas that had broken away from the walls and stairs.

"For Sitara," Breksta murmured to herself as she swallowed her growing fear that rose higher with every creaking step.

CHAPTER 18

BREKSTA REACHED THE LAST STEPS to the basement and the hallway that led to the infirmary, making sure to avoid the protruding metal rods and possible falling concrete. The groaning of the stairs became louder as the walls around her began to shake from the aftershocks of the earthquake.

Using the wall as support in the aftershocks, she arrived at the white storage room at the end of the hallway. Breksta pushed apart the sliding doors with little difficulty and squeezed through.

The storage room was in chaos. The perfectly organized shelves on each side of the room were now virtually empty, with most of the supplies strewn across the floor. Breksta knelt and quickly rummaged through the piles of supplies. Sitara's wound needed stitches.

Along with tweezers and other medical tools, Breksta collected large bandages and rolls of medical tape, a few small black boxes labeled "surgical stitches," and multiple tubes of a pungent ointment that Breksta had been taught to use to stop bacterial infections. She stuffed all the supplies she'd gathered into her jacket pockets and exited the room.

The shaking had been mild until now. But suddenly, the room spun and Breksta heard booms from the stairs. She raced back, stumbling and ramming into the walls through the hallway. When she reached the stairs, a piece of concrete tumbled down, blocking her path. She leapt back and watched helplessly as the rest of the stairs crumbled and sealed her in.

"No! No, no, no!" Breksta shouted. The immovable chunks of concrete blockaded her, with no possible way to get out.

Defeated, she sat down on the dust-ridden floor. The director had been right, and Breksta hated her for it. The director was always right. That was what the Academy had taught the cadets. Breksta took a few deep, shuddered breaths as she considered her situation. She had to help Sitara, even if it was her last act.

Breksta pulled herself up from the ground and ran back down the length of the hallway. With the stairs blocked, she knew what she had to do to get out. Her only option was the Under Passage.

Although there were many entrances to the Under Passage, the only possible way out now would be more difficult. Breksta didn't know for certain that the passage would be passable after the earthquake, but she tried to steel her mind from any thoughts of hopelessness as she reached the wall at the end of the hallway.

At her ankles, a duct to the Under Passage was still intact. Breksta let out a huge sigh of relief and yanked at the metal bars until the vent fell open. She lowered herself to the floor and maneuvered through the opening. Once she was completely inside, she crawled with her arms in front of her, painstakingly pulling herself along in the tight space. The metal ducts that had been effortless to crawl through when Breksta and Hestia were children now barely contained Breksta, as her shoulders and hips grazed against the sharp metal edges.

Her arms strained and her brow pooled with sweat from the effort. Each segment of the ducts was connected by metal bolts that scraped mercilessly against Breksta's body, bringing fresh waves of pain. The pain exacerbated Breksta's growing anxiety. The closeness of the circular ducts and the darkness all around made her mind give way to her childhood fears of claustrophobia. To calm herself, she whispered reassurances out loud.

"Take deep breaths," she murmured. "You aren't trapped. Just a little more to go. You're almost there. Remember, this is for Sitara."

She continued forward, and finally, after what seemed like many agonizing hours, she saw a faint light streaming from an opening ahead.

Breksta felt confidence flood her senses as she saw the familiar Under Passage through the vent. Her shoulders strained inside the small space as she pushed down on the vent's bars until it fell to the ground with a clatter. Breksta then pulled herself through the vent and lowered herself to the ground.

She lifted herself up with the wall as support and began her trek toward the world outside. The building that housed the auditorium wasn't an option and neither was the building she had just come from. That left the dormitories and the teaching halls. The latter housed dark memories but was the fastest and most direct way out, with a path leading through the solitude boxes.

Taking the turns she knew so well, Breksta managed to reach a large metal door. This door would lead Breksta to the ventilation system of the solitude boxes and her freedom. She wrapped her hands around the handle and took a large step back before pulling. Her arms felt like string against the strong door, pulling to no avail. After tugging from various angles, and in frustration, Breksta kicked the door with her foot. Pain shot up her leg, and she hobbled backward. Her muscles burned and her mind was a tangle of emotions—anxiousness at Sitara's injury, fear of her own survival, despondency at another dead end.

Breksta ran her dirtied fingers through her tangled braid. Tears of anger pooled in her eyes and threatened to fall as she surveyed her environment. Blocks of concrete from the crumbling walls lay in various places. She found herself utterly alone. The notion of dying plagued her mind. She thought of the dead cadets in the lobby, crushed underneath the chandelier and concrete. Those cadets had been slightly slower than Breksta, and it cost them their lives. Had Breksta's luck finally run out? Why couldn't her own willpower save her now so she could save Sitara? Hadn't she persevered despite her pain? How strong did her inner strength have to be to overcome the world?

Breksta thought of Sitara, who might not survive without the meager medical supplies she had procured. Breksta sank to the floor, allowing the tears to fall as she gave in to defeat. In her pain-filled state of hopelessness, she remembered the simple words of encouragement Hestia always said during training and sparring.

It had been another sunless day of training indoors, and the cadets had sparred for hours. Breksta had already fought various female cadets who now sported bruised faces and similarly bruised egos. Hestia had stayed in the shooting ranges, practicing knife throwing and pistol shooting. At times, she had even gone into the sniper range, with targets anywhere from one hundred to six hundred meters away—most of which, Hestia had shot in the perfect bull's-eye.

Breksta was sitting on a bench and removing her sweat-soaked boxing gloves when Hestia arrived. Breksta's hair was slicked back from sweat, and the braid Hestia had fixed that morning was no longer intact.

"How many did you do?" Hestia asked, resting her hands on her hips.

Breksta removed her plastic mouthguard and cringed at the saliva on it before wrapping it in a tissue beside her.

"Three matches, twelve rounds each," Breksta said, leaning her head back against the wall.

Hestia raised her eyebrows and sat down next her. "And how many did you win?"

Breksta smiled. "Only three."

Hestia sighed dramatically and rested her head in her hands. "Well, target training was disastrous."

"You weren't accurate?" Breksta guessed as she tended her cuts and bruises with the first aid kit beside her.

"No, I got most of them," Hestia confessed quietly.

"Then what are you complaining about? Here, help me with the one above my eye," Breksta said, turning to Hestia with an alcohol pad and a band aid.

Hestia grabbed it and sighed again. "I just don't know if I can take more days cooped inside. And the monotony of training isn't helping."

"You're welcome to go outside and bear the hurricane," Breksta said sarcastically.

Hestia took that chance to dab the alcohol pad on Breksta's cut, making her suck in a pained breath.

"You're doing this on purpose," Breksta grumbled.

Hestia smiled and continued to dab the pad gently. She put it down and placed the band aid snuggly on Breksta's forehead.

"All done," Hestia said and pulled her knees up to her chest, resting her head against them.

Breksta sighed, feeling the pain of the injuries she'd sustained to prove her worth as a strong cadet. "This will bruise badly, you know. They always do."

"Our bruises only make us stronger, right?" Hestia challenged.

"I must be incredibly powerful then," Breksta said with a cheeky grin.

Hestia playfully punched Breksta's shoulder before standing and offering Breksta a hand. Breksta took it and both girls left, feeling a bit more ready to endure more hours of training.

Hestia's words were the ones that Breksta remembered as she sat in the Under Passage.

Those words turned her hopelessness into determination for survival. Breksta stood and faced the door again. She examined the hinges, framing, and possible locks for any sign of weakness. She found that one hinge had come loose, making the door lean toward her.

With a spark of innovation, Breksta quickly pulled the surgical kit out of her pocket and looked for any tool that might work to unscrew the second hinge. She found a couple of thin surgical scissors as well as two scalpels, a needle, a ball of string, and a dark blue tourniquet. Breksta grabbed one scissor and scalpel and ran to the door. She pushed the slender scissor into cylindrical hinge.

The angle was awkward, but she settled herself in a squatting position and pulled the scissor upward to free the hinges. At first, nothing happened. The large metal door stood tall and unmoving. But ever so slightly, Breksta felt the bolt inside the hinge loosen, and with one final push, she freed the door from the frame. It fell outward to reveal the solitude box's dark halls. Breksta smiled immediately at her own ingenuity and walked back to retrieve her surgical kit. However, with her sluggish, exhausted mind, Breksta didn't take into consideration the doorframe, which was only loosely connected to the wall. As she reached the surgical kit, the frame dislocated from the wall and came crashing down on her. It contacted her on the back of her upper thigh and slammed her into the ground. Sharp and biting pain erupted in her leg. She struggled against the weight of the frame digging into her back. She pushed her hands against the ground and arched her back to try and push the frame away from her, but to no avail. Its weight forced her back down to the ground, spreading pain from her back to her thighs and calves. She cried out in agony. She was trapped, with no way to get free.

"The bruises, it only makes … us…"

Breksta felt her strength ebb as she struggled to escape. But the pain was too much. The edges of Breksta's consciousness closed in on her, and the last thing she remembered were her hands laying outstretched toward the surgical kit and a purple light.

CHAPTER 19

BREKSTA AWOKE TO THE STRANGE and comforting sight of natural light and the trees outside the Academy. She looked over at the small window of one of the solitude boxes, the metal bars removed were intact. As she pushed her arms from the ground and tried to sit up, the pain rushed into her ribs, back, and legs, reminding her of her ordeal. Next to her lay the surgical kit she had used to unhinge the door.

"You're welcome," a light, young voice said from behind.

Breksta turned her head and looked up at a brown-haired boy whose similar brown eyes shone with unusual purple light.

"W-who are you?" Breksta said, instinctively reaching behind her waist for a weapon that was not there.

"I am Erebus," he said, reaching out his hand in an offer to help her stand.

Breksta ignored it and slowly pushed herself to a standing position. "How did you get here?" Breksta asked slowly, her words slurring together as her mind fought to remember what happened.

The boy wrinkled his eyebrows, as if trying hard to remember as well, before responding, "I was in those cells for a long time. I can barely remember anything. The last thing I do recall is pain, sharp and instantaneous. There was a feeling after the pain—a cold and calm darkness overtook me. It was what I imagine space to be if all the stars disappeared. There was a voice, a woman's voice, and she spoke to me. Although I couldn't see her, it was as if she were all around me. She welcomed me to her dark world and thanked me for the things I had done in my life. But just as I began to see her form, I heard your voice, screaming for help, and I was dragged away from the dark world and back to this one."

Breksta was stunned at his words, this talk of worlds and of the supernatural, all was strictly forbidden in the Academy and was associated with Dreamers.

"What are you talking about? A doorframe collapsed on me, and I blacked out. Now explain to me, how did I get out?" Breksta demanded, pointing between herself and the bars of the solitude boxes.

Erebus said nothing, his eyes betraying his discomfort and fear.

Breksta kept her eyes locked on the boy, pointing at his face. "I'll ask you again. How did I get out?"

The boy's eyes were hesitant, looking first at Breksta then downward at the ground. "It was me and your magic, alright? I got you out."

"Magic? What are you talking about? How did *you* survive the building collapse and the earthquake then?" Breksta pressed further.

"It … it was my *power*, my *magic* and yours that helped me get you out," he repeated softly, barely above a whisper.

It took Breksta a few seconds to understand Erebus. But soon she understood the simple and painful truth of the boy in front of her: he was a Dreamer. A Dreamer within the walls of the Academy.

"What? Tell me more," she asked suspiciously, taking a step toward him as Erebus wrapped his arms around his body and took small steps away from her.

"My power is that I can control and manipulate shadows … sciakinesis," the boy said, a small smile drawing on his face as if he were remembering a better time in his life. "I moved the doorframe off you and jumped from the shadows inside the building to the shadows out here. Not without your help, though."

"I was unconscious," Breksta stated firmly, still trying to connect the threads in her mind.

"It was your power, your magic that helped me," Erebus said with more conviction now, looking up into her eyes.

"How?" Breksta said softly, more to herself than to the boy.

The Academy had always taught them about Dreamers, people with hereditary abilities stemming from their god of dreams, Morpheus. The cadets learned about the different kinds of abilities and how those abilities were used to attack the president and the director.

"You must have Dreamer blood," Erebus said, smiling widely. "It's good to finally meet a sister."

Nothing made sense to Breksta. The entire ordeal of the Academy's collapse and the earthquake and the purple light she had seen before she fell unconscious, Erebus's dark world and what he told her about herself. All these events were unable to form a coherent meaning in Breksta's mind.

Her curiosity grew despite her Academy training to suppress it. So she continued. "What … what's my ability then?" Breksta asked slowly, testing the words as if the wrong one might end with a bullet in her brain or a knife in her heart from a fellow cadet.

Erebus shrugged. "I don't know. Perhaps it has something to do with energy and life. Before, when I was in my cell, there were black-clad figures with guns—"

"Our cadets," Breksta interrupted, feeling a slight reassurance that she had a grounding fact she could hold on to.

"Yes, I was captured soon after the White House attack," Erebus said spitefully, his eyes suddenly filled with rage and pain. "They interrogated me for, I don't know how long. But one day, your cadets came into my cell and shot me in multiple places. The pain of the bullets as they entered my skin and shattered my bones was indescribable. All they did was smile their cruel, unsavory smiles at me."

Breksta was silent. The White House attack was years ago, more than a decade earlier. She was speaking with someone who it seemed had either been imprisoned for this long … or had been dead.

"How is that possible?" she breathed in disbelief. "That was more than a decade ago."

"I … what?" Erebus asked. "It can't be. That was only moments ago."

"I think … are you dead?" Breksta asked.

Erebus shook his head, clutching his chest as he gazed around at his surroundings frantically.

"No. I'm not. I can't be," he murmured.

He turned his gaze to Breksta, his eyes wide with fear.

"You. You brought me back here."

Breksta paused before speaking, "Maybe? I still don't know what happened. Are … you alright?"

Erebus stood breathing with his eyes squeezed tightly before he blinked them open and answered Breksta.

"I think I am. I feel it now. I am not … *here* here. There is a dissociation, a separation, between my body and soul. My body feels limp under my control. But … thank you."

"For what?" Breksta asked, feeling a growing sympathy for this confused boy.

"Your power has given me energy and perhaps even life," Erebus said. "As I said, you brought me back to this place."

"You're welcome, I guess."

His gaze fell on her attire. He gasped before speaking softly and sadly. "You are one of these cadets?"

Breksta looked down with shame and murmured, "Yes."

"Of course," Erebus said with defeat rather than the anger that Breksta expected. "But you do have Dreamer blood. You cannot deny that now."

"I can," Breksta said, looking up in a flash of self-defense.

She had denied so much in her life. She had learned long ago the power of suppressing her emotions and thoughts, so it wasn't difficult to suppress one more part of herself. Or at least she could suppress it until she graduated and was free to consider who she really was.

"No," Erebus said quickly and sternly. "You can't suppress this power. You don't understand it yet, but you *must* not ignore it. Magic is like fire in the beginning, temperamental with outbursts of heat that burn those around you. I don't know what your magic is, but it is obviously powerful. And I do know that you must figure out for yourself exactly what it is and how to use it."

"How?" Breksta asked again, a flurry of emotions coursing through her.

Erebus took a step toward her and took her hands in his gentle ones.

"Remember these coordinates: 48 degrees North and 122 degrees West. Go there, and you will find Aristotle and perhaps some answers. Please don't wait. It seems you should go as soon as you can."

"But what about the Academy and my friends? I … I can't leave them here while I find answers! Why should I even try to do this? I would only get tracked down by the Academy and killed, like the rest of the Dreamers," Breksta said, thinking immediately of Hestia and her promises. But as soon as she said it, she saw Erebus's face fill with pain and grief. Breksta then remembered her own mother and felt shame crawl up her face.

"I—"

"You're right," Erebus stated solemnly. "If you go, you will most likely be tracked down. But whatever power you have, with its grip over life and human energies, it is obvious to me that it has the potential to save our people, who are more numerous than you know and have suffered much more than the few individuals here that you call friends. Your friends, if they are true friends, shall always be here, waiting for you once you discover your magic. But your magic can't wait, just like our people can't survive much longer without your help."

Breksta didn't answer. She was on the cusp of freedom from the Academy. She would soon be freed from the constraints that had kept her chained since her mother's death. And though most cadets stayed in the Academy, Breksta would never look back. She was determined to escape into the world. But perhaps what Erebus suggested was her chance to find true freedom and learn more about her mother, who Breksta remembered less and less with each passing year.

"Alright," Breksta murmured. "Alright."

With that, Erebus's form flickered, and Breksta began to feel weak. His hand rose in a gesture of goodbye before he faded away into bits and pieces of purple light that escaped back into the ruins of the Academy solitude boxes. Breksta was alone again.

A profusion of emotions washed over her, followed by a headache and dizziness. Why did Erebus suddenly disappear? What was the purple light that faded from Erebus, the same purple light that she had seen before she fell unconscious in the Under Passage? And where had Erebus gone? Had Erebus gone back to the dark realm he spoke of? *No,* Breksta thought to herself, *such a place does not exist. It cannot.* She would not believe it. Yet, she found herself believing what he'd told her, and her curiosity was heightened—just like her pain.

This man was a Dreamer, and if he went to that dark realm, could Breksta's mother have gone there too? And what was this power that Erebus said she had, a power that gave him energy and, as he said, "Perhaps even life." Could this, the magic or power, be part of her, the girl she had suppressed for so long? That girl was curious, and humorous, and alive, despite Breksta's attempts to assimilate into the Academy and destroy that part of herself. She couldn't deny that girl; the girl she was when her mother was alive still existed now.

Finally, the purple light intrigued her. The one she saw in the Under Passage and the one she saw as Erebus faded into nothing. It felt familiar and warm. When she saw that light, she felt as if she were fondly recalling a memory or a dream, remembering the kindness and warmth of her mother, the fun and exciting trips into the woods of her town, the love her mother felt for Breksta, and the love Breksta felt for her mother. Those feelings were invoked as she saw the purple light. How she wished to continuously feel those feelings!

Breksta knew that her questions and curiosities needed answers. She had pushed all her curiosities aside to give herself fully to the training in the Academy. Hestia was the only person who helped her survive the demands of this violent environment, but Hestia couldn't help her seek the answers she needed. Those answers were for her, and her alone. She would do whatever it took to get them. As she picked up the supplies for Sitara and moved toward the gate beside the solitude boxes, she began formulating a plan.

Breksta stumbled back toward the cadets. The light of the sun against her eyes increased her headache. From the distance, Breksta spotted Hestia's fiery-red hair as she ran toward Breksta. Breksta felt all her strength ebb toward the ground and away from her.

"Breksta!" Hestia shrieked as she reached Breksta. Hestia cupped Breksta's cheek, though Breksta could barely feel Hestia's gentle touch.

"How are you alive?" she whispered, her eyes filled with concern and relief. "The building—"

"Take it," Breksta forced out of her mouth, as she panted from the pain and thrust the medical supplies into Hestia's arms. "Sitara. Needs. It."

With that, darkness began to surround Breksta's vision, and she reached feebly toward Hestia. The sounds around her faded, though Hestia's voice was loud enough to skim the surface of her hearing. Then there was nothing but black.

CHAPTER 20

WEAKNESS WAS THE FIRST THING Breksta felt. The feeling of aching pain that settled deep within her bones followed soon after and snapped her eyes open to the clear sky that seemed to mock her with its calm appearance in contrast to her agony. Slowly, she came to and found herself at the base of the director's statue with the cadets scattered around her.

"She's awake!" a small voice sounded behind her that Breksta recognized was Olivia's.

Olivia and Hestia came to kneel beside Breksta, their eyes full of worry. With their help, she sat up.

"Are you alright?" Hestia asked, concern dancing in her emerald eyes.

It took Breksta a few seconds before she could manage a whisper. "Sitara?"

Hestia nodded before pointing to the bench where a cadet and Madam Director hovered over Sitara. Breksta sighed with relief and tried to manage a smile.

"How did you get out? The building collapsed as soon as you went in!" Olivia interrupted, her innocent and childlike wonder coming through her voice.

"I..." Breksta hesitated. The power Erebus told her she possessed had somehow saved her from the building, but she knew she couldn't disclose that information.

"I escaped through the ducts and the solitude boxes," Breksta said slowly.

Olivia nodded, her lack of questions or suspicion came from her age and her unwavering belief in the Academy. Hestia, however, furrowed her eyebrows and didn't seem to believe Breksta. But she said nothing. Breksta's pain began to return as her head cleared from its foggy unconsciousness.

The boy from earlier must have been a dream, Breksta thought, because she *did not* have abilities. Looking down at her body, Breksta saw nothing different. Except for visible scrapes and scratches, and severe internal pain, she looked and felt just the same as always.

However, before she could think about it further, the director approached. "Breksta Vilkas!" she shouted.

Breksta tried to sit up straighter and face the director. "Madam Director."

The director was obviously furious, and Breksta prayed that she wouldn't lash out at her. The director took in a sharp breath and sighed loudly before continuing. "Your actions were reckless, rash, and insubordinate."

Breksta winced at the term *insubordinate*, which meant the director had a punishment lined up for her. "I was only doing—"

"I wasn't finished," the director interjected harshly. "However, your actions will save the lives of some cadets who need immediate attention. Therefore…"

The director stopped and looked pained as she forced out the last words, "Therefore, I am giving you *one warning*."

Breksta let out a breath. "Thank you … Madam Director."

The director nodded and looked at her coldly. "That is *one* warning, Vilkas. Do not test me."

The use of her last name was once more meant as an insult. But she also knew now that she had some power she didn't yet understand, and so she would take matters into her own hands to find answers. That gave her the strength to smile.

The director nodded at Breksta before turning back to the rest of the cadets. "I know you must have questions. Most of them pertaining to what we will do next and who perpetrated such an attack."

"Was it the Dreamers, Madam Director?" Icarus asked, with a hint of contempt.

The director spoke in a slow, calculated voice. "I swear my life upon it, yes."

These words alone rattled the Academy and its cadets. There was silence as all the children looked to the director for instructions and a path forward.

"Considering how many Dreamers we have rid, it would not be unusual for them to try to make one last stand, one last attack to try and dissuade us from continuing our efforts. But we will not be dissuaded. What is important is how we move forward." The director began pacing. "It is up to us, all of us, to attack back. We will launch a final strike against the Dreamers and wipe them out. We will bring hope and a righteous path back for all of humanity."

The cadets cheered and were fueled by this final, definitive goal.

"The hangar is meant to withstand any natural disasters. We will do all our planning from there and launch our attack within the next two weeks. First, we need to tend to the most severely injured, and then we will make our way to the underground bunker."

As the director spoke of their most immediate plans, Hestia tended to Sitara. Thanks to the supplies Breksta had retrieved, she was able to remove the glass shard, clean and stitch Sitara's wound, and apply the antiseptic ointment. This was a skill set every cadet learned to do so they could tend to their wounded in battle.

As soon as the most-injured cadets had been tended to, the director called everyone to attention. The cadets stood at her command and followed her as she walked toward the airstrip.

Wincing from pain, Breksta managed to get herself upright, and Olivia, who had been with her since she returned, clung to Breksta's side. "Are we really attacking the Dreamers?" she asked, her wide eyes looking up at Breksta.

Breksta watched the distant end of the airstrip, trying to suppress her fears and reservations for the atrocities she knew the director would commit. "Yes," she said simply, as words couldn't convey the conflict she felt within. Erebus had called her a Dreamer, and her mother had been one. Her people, who had been the sole target of Breksta's eight years at the Academy, would be *wiped* from this earth. *Wiped,* Breksta thought, *as if they are germs meant to be sanitized from the world and thrown into the garbage.*

Olivia nodded innocently, unaware of the implications of the director's words, and took Breksta's hand as they walked. Stopping in front of a square pillar that stood waist-high to the director, she took out a device from her pocket and inputted a series of passwords. The director then pressed a button.

With loud creaks, a square area of the airfield opened, revealing the hangar that descended underground and housed the planes and war rooms. An elevator rose from below. The younger cadets, who were unfamiliar with the Academy's extensive equipment and technologies, watched with open mouths.

When the elevator shaft reached the surface, the director instructed, "We must go in groups. Ms. Adams, take the badly wounded cadets first. Those of you who are able-bodied will help with the lesser wounded cadets. Once they are settled, your next task is to locate the food and supplies stored below and bring everything back to the sleeping area.

Hestia, who was carrying Sitara, came forward. Together, she, Breksta, Olivia, the injured cadets, and Ms. Adams made their way into the elevator.

Breksta was glad to not be alone, not wanting to be with her thoughts that spiraled to dark places about the Dreamers and genocide, thoughts of her need to find answers about her people, her mother, and most importantly herself. She feared that her own curiosity, which had been buried for so long, was now fully awake. The earthquake that had awoken the cadets and was pushing them toward war moved her toward the world her mother had belonged to—the world of Dreamers.

They all rode in silence as some younger cadets marveled at their new surroundings. Viewing the bunker was a privilege for the senior cadets only, whose final test required an authentic Dreamer capture or assassination mission. To be in the bunker was the ultimate proof of one's success in the Academy: proof of how far the senior cadets had come in their training and proof of their readiness to continue the eradication of Dreamers. That was the sad reality of their war-driven lives, although most cadets didn't view their lives that way. As they descended, the junior cadets could see level after level of the bunker's machinery, planes, and weapons and felt a sense of pride and altruism. Knowing they would ultimately fight the Dreamers and salvage humanity to create a balanced world with peace was motivating. And that feeling of unity and motivation would drive their actions in the coming days.

When the group reached their destination on floor twelve, everyone exited.

The elevator then shot up to collect more cadets. Floor twelve consisted of a square room, shorter than the average room, and similar to the height of the solitude boxes. It was filled with military cots, lined up close to each other.

"Pick your beds, cadets," Ms. Adams commanded. "We will tend to your injuries soon."

Breksta, Hestia, and Olivia chose cots side-by-side on the outskirts of the room, against the gray concrete walls. Hestia moved Sitara to the cot at the foot of Breksta's and Hestia's.

Hestia set Sitara carefully onto the bed, speaking in a gentle, motherly tone, "Try and get some sleep now."

"It's creaky," a cadet moaned as he shifted on the cot.

"Stop complaining!" Hestia chided coldly. "We have just been attacked. Your attitude won't serve the Academy in this war."

Shocked, Breksta and Olivia looked at Hestia. Hestia rarely showed true anger or frustration. But the attack and her injured friends had struck a nerve.

"You should be worried about your safety. Not your petty grievances," Hestia snapped.

The cadets didn't utter any other complaints, rather whispered in their own little circles.

"Are you alright?" Breksta asked after a while, moving to sit on Hestia's bed.

Olivia watched both girls intently before deciding to give them privacy. She tended to her new friend, Sitara, making sure she was warm and comfortable.

Hestia shrugged her shoulders and ran her fingers through her hair before letting out a frustrated sigh. "Everything is going wrong. Sitara's injured. You could have died. I—"

"But I'm safe now, Hestia. We're all safe," Breksta said, wrapping her arms around Hestia protectively.

Hestia paused before answering, "I hope so."

"Me too," Breksta said, pulling away from Hestia with a smile. "Now how about we go and get some food?"

Breksta stood and waited for Hestia.

Hestia got up and looked at Breksta. "Are you sure you're recovered enough?" she asked.

Breksta gave a curt nod and smiled as she repeated the phrase that had saved her life, "Our bruises only make us stronger, remember?"

Hestia smiled back at her, but Breksta's words didn't soothe her motherly worry, and Hestia insisted on helping Breksta to the stairwell on the opposite side of the room. The lights inside the stairwell blinked on as they entered, flickering so that Breksta and Hestia had to use the walls to guide them. Reaching the sixth level, they entered the room where they knew the food was stored.

"Jackpot," Hestia said with a grin. "Let's sort through this and start bringing up the boxes."

Breksta nodded and moved to a crate on the far wall. Questions plagued her mind as she collected containers of canned corn, beef, and jugs of water. She had questions about Erebus and herself that she desperately wanted to answer. The coordinates that Erebus had given her were seared into her mind, and she itched to leave the Academy and get away from the director's plan to wipe out her people. But most of all, she wanted to find out about her and her mother's past.

She hesitated before asking Hestia, "Do you think the Dreamers still want to resist the Academy?"

Hestia turned from across the room and frowned. "Possibly. It seems that this earthquake was caused by them."

"Do you really think so? Do you really believe that the Dreamers could have done this, that they are that much of a threat?" Breksta urged.

As the words left Breksta's mouth, she immediately regretted them. She had learned that the wrong words could be just as dangerous as traitorous actions, even spoken to her best friend.

Hestia sighed. "I know this war is violent and bloody. I hate it myself. But it really is necessary if we want peace. Look at what they did to the Academy! They've clearly shown themselves to be a threat and … they need to be wiped out."

Breksta sucked in a breath to calm herself. Sometimes, when Hestia spoke about the Dreamers in this way, referring to them as threats who needed to be killed, Breksta wondered if Hestia truly believed what she was saying. She was afraid that Hestia was sometimes so torn between the Academy and the freedom they spoke of, that Hestia was lost in her mind. What Breksta feared most, though, was that as they prepared for their senior graduation, Hestia had stopped resisting the Academy's teachings and given in completely to the propaganda. Not wanting to find that out, Breksta turned back to her crate and didn't say another word.

"What do you think we should do then?" Hestia asked accusingly.

"I'm not sure. But—"

"Do you think we should just let them *go*? Let them roam free despite the harm they've caused?"

"I never said that. Forget I said anything," Breksta murmured.

"You've always been soft on them. Saying that we should stop this war. Who will protect the innocent people of this country and the world if we don't hunt down these terrorists?" Hestia asked, her voice rising.

"I never said that! I only asked a question. I thought I might hear this from Icarus, or your mother, but I never expected to hear it from you, Hestia," Breksta snapped.

Hestia took in a breath and then answered in a barely contained rage, "What are you talking about?"

"Nothing. But why can't you see that the Academy is *attacking* innocents?" Breksta retorted, turning to face her friend whose anger was written plainly on her face.

Hestia crossed the room and placed her arm on Breksta's shoulder. "What's this really about?"

Breksta pressed her hand to her forehead to stop her whirring mind. Hestia knew about her past and had been the only person who didn't hold her name against her. But Breksta knew Hestia's loyalties had always been torn between Breksta and the director. Knowing about Breksta's strange, unknown magic might prove that Hestia's loyalty to her mother was stronger than to Breksta. But deep down, Breksta didn't really believe that. For deep down, Breksta knew that Hestia was still the girl who had snuck into the solitude box with her, the girl who shied away from violence and spoke of peaceful times after the war. Breksta refused to believe that Hestia had become the Academy-abiding girl who never spoke out of turn to her mother. Even recently, Breksta had seen Hestia's true character: a kind and gentle soul who cared for others. It was there, under the layers of etiquette and Academy teachings.

Since they were alone, Breksta knew this was the best time for Hestia to drop her tightly held guard. "I ... I lied," she said to her most trusted friend.

"What?" Hestia asked, taking her hand off Breksta's shoulder.

"I lied about how I got out of the building," Breksta said slowly, wanting to keep Hestia's trust for as long as possible.

"You said you escaped from the solitude boxes," Hestia said hesitantly. "I saw you come from there."

"I didn't lie about all of it. But I didn't tell the whole truth."

"So ... how did you get out?"

Breksta took a deep breath and began, "It's a bit of a long story..."

Hestia raised her hands in exasperation. "Well, I'm waiting."

"Alright. The stairs to the infirmary collapsed, so I had to go through the duct system."

"To the Under Passage. That must have been painful," Hestia said with a smile of sympathy.

"Yes. Then I went to the Under Passage door that leads to the solitude boxes."

"Then you escaped through the window, right?"

"Am I telling the story or are you?" Breksta said, poking Hestia in the shoulder playfully.

"Sorry. Keep going." Hestia grinned sheepishly.

Breksta smiled, finding herself on more solid footing with her friend than she thought. "I had to unscrew the door, which took a while, but I eventually got it. But the doorframe collapsed on me, and I couldn't move. Then I blacked out. But before I blacked out, I saw this purple light around me."

"Purple light," Hestia mused. "Was it from the solitude boxes?"

"No ... it was from me apparently."

"From you? How do you create purple light? Are you messing with me?" Hestia asked, playfully shoving Breksta, though Breksta saw concern in her eyes.

"No," Breksta said sharply.

"Alright, sorry," Hestia said, putting up her hands in defeat.

"When I woke up, there was this boy," Breksta said slowly, watching Hestia's concerned expression intently. "He told me that I had summoned him and that I had the ... the power over life, or energy."

"Excuse me?" Hestia asked with disbelief, her eyebrows shooting up.

"You heard me." Breksta exhaled nervously. "He said that since my mother was a Dreamer—"

"That you now should suddenly ignore your years of training in the Academy and join their rebellion? That is ridiculous, Breksta. That boy was a Dreamer, and he probably caused the earthquake. You honestly trust him? I thought the Academy had taught you not to listen to their propaganda!" Hestia exclaimed, her words conveying anger while her eyes reflected fear and uncertainty.

"But it's true," Breksta emphasized. "He told me that I have Dreamer magic."

"Abilities, Breksta," Hestia said, pacing the floor. "Why is this happening now? I thought that the Academy's training and ongoing physical exams stop the connection Dreamers' kids have to their abilities so they never develop."

"I didn't know!" Breksta said panicking. "The truth is that I seem to have some kind of magic, but I don't know anything about it or how to use it. But I promise that I will never use it to hurt you."

Hestia stopped pacing and faced Breksta. She took a deep breath and took Breksta's hand gently. "I … I believe you, Breksta."

Those words were a comfort to Breksta, and she released a long-held breath. "Thank you."

Hestia nodded with a pained smile. "You're right, I do trust you. But we now have a problem."

"What?"

"My mother."

Breksta dropped Hestia's hand and began pacing. "I-I'm so sorry. For telling you. Now your mother might punish you for knowing. Or—"

"I can deal with my mother," Hestia interrupted. "But we need to get you out of here before she finds out. And she will. Apparently, she intends to conduct security tests on all fighters before the attack."

"I have done those tests before," Breksta said slowly.

"No. I heard some of the other seniors talking with Ms. Adams. She said that my mother has brought some new technology from an offsite lab to ensure that Dreamer abilities cannot be unlocked, removing all possible paths of betrayal. So you need to go once everyone is asleep. I'll distract my mother and you'll go to the planes."

Breksta was uncertain about exactly what she needed to do next, but she ignored that feeling and spoke. "The boy gave me coordinates of where I need to go, and I believe I can make it there in one flight."

Hestia smiled sadly and pulled Breksta in for a deep embrace. "Do you remember our promises?" she said, her voice muffled against Breksta's shoulder.

"Of course. And do you promise you can take care of yourself until I return?" Breksta said, a small flame of hope growing in her heart—for her freedom and for their lives.

"What do you think I have been training for? I can take care of myself," Hestia said with a chuckle as her eyes glistened with unfallen tears. "Come back for me, okay? Perhaps … with your abilities, we can help this war finally end."

Hope and motivation grew in Breksta at the thought of ending this violent conflict. "Perhaps … but know this, Hestia. I won't let anything bad happen to you, Hestia. And I'll come back for you," Breksta said, pulling away as she felt her own tears threaten to drip down her face.

"Of course you will," Hestia said with a weighted smile of sadness that Breksta knew she was feeling too. "Now let's get this food upstairs."

CHAPTER 21

IT WAS DARK AND DUSTY in the room when Icarus flicked on the lights of the underground bunker. He had been sent to gather stored backup weapons as the weapons he had trained with were now buried underneath the rubble. But that didn't bother Icarus. He had learned from the earliest moments of his life to adapt. And he knew that the best weapons in the Academy were in fact the cadets themselves. Therefore, Icarus wasn't worried about the war to come; rather, he saw it as an end to what bound him to the Academy, and to his mother. Until he could leave this place, it was impossible to discover more about himself and what his life could become. Icarus found himself wishing for the war to begin. Only after the war was over and he graduated the Academy would he be able to live on his own terms.

Icarus found one of the storage rooms lined with columns that shelved forlorn, dust-covered items—books, CDs, magazines, VHS tapes, bags, and all sorts of miscellaneous, unorganized objects. All objects belonging to captured Dreamers or new cadets who no longer needed their past. Curious, Icarus wondered if there was anything here that might have belonged to him when he came to the Academy, items that his mother stored away that could possibly give Icarus a clue to his past and his father.

Icarus shook himself for thinking of such things. His mother and the director had forbidden any talk of his father in the Academy, so Icarus tried to obey. However, that didn't make it easier to sever his thoughts and questions about his father. Icarus pushed those thoughts away and walked through the rows, which he discovered were categorized alphabetically.

As he stood at the end of the alphabet and scanned the shelves, the sounds of voices jolted his concentration. Ten meters away, a small light emitted from behind a black tarp hanging down from the ceiling. The light remained steady as Icarus neared, and when he pulled the tarp aside, he found a door that opened to a stairwell. The light was coming from below.

Perhaps it was the nerves from the Dreamer attack or Icarus's own suppressed curiosities that moved him to go down the stairs. He walked as if he were stalking prey, making no sound as his feet stepped lightly on each stair. As Icarus stepped on the last stair, the light became brighter and had a blue-green hue, coming from two large LED lights on the top corners of another silver, square door in front of him. The words, "DECONTAMINATION" and "AUTHORIZED PERSONNEL ONLY" were written in bold, red letters across the door. Icarus approached and looked through the circular glass window on the door.

The room inside was a pristine laboratory filled with equipment that Icarus had learned about in his classes: beakers and Bunsen burners, vials with dark-red substances that Icarus could only guess were blood, and many items he couldn't identify. In the center of the room, a dark-haired man with a needle in his arm was tied down on a hospital bed, his eyes barely open and his face a grim expression of submission. Around the man were his teachers, including his mother who stood off to the left looking down at the man.

With her back to Icarus, the director held her head high as she spoke in a low but assertive voice. "This experiment has been conducted for the past six months," she spoke, pointing down to the man. "We found him in the high parts of the Himalayan Mountains, hiding and eluding us for almost two decades."

"What's his purpose for the Academy? I have heard rumors of a man—"

"Those rumors are true," the director cut in. "This man eluded us for so long because of his abilities. He can reinforce one's thinking."

Mr. Pierce ran his fingers through his hair and backed away from the table. "You-you are talking about mind control."

The director raised her hand to calm the distraught-looking teacher. "It's not an absolute power; no Dreamer has such ability. We have restrained him with sedatives and a small chip on the left side of his neck with electrodes to shock him if he steps out of line. He cannot force you into believing or performing acts that you absolutely refuse. But if there is any part of your mind that wants to act in a certain way, he can compel you to do it."

The room became silent. The teachers' expressions ranged from fear and worry to excitement of such power and its implications for the Academy. Icarus looked to his mother, and he found a mix of all three emotions. Icarus himself couldn't believe that the weak man in front of him, whose bones protruded underneath his skin, had such an ability. However, he had learned that often the minds of Dreamers were stronger than their bodies, and even as they were withering away in the Academy, their fighting instinct raged on. Icarus looked with pity at the broken man on the table, meeting the man's sad and defeated eyes. The man looked at Icarus as if Icarus were air, not acknowledging his presence. But as the man's eyes opened wider, a look of confusion and surprise fell across the man's face.

"I know all of you must still have questions or reservations, but I have decided that this man's power is an opportunity to cripple the Dreamers once and for all," the director said confidently. "The world can be established in the perfect order it was always supposed to be, with the Academy leading the world to peace and harmony."

"To peace and harmony," Ms. Adams parroted loyally, although she cast one last worried look at the man and moved with the rest of the teachers toward the door.

Icarus, recognizing the predicament he would be in if he were caught listening, bolted up the stairs, trying to conceal the sounds of his footsteps. He pushed the tarp open and ran toward one of the far columns, hiding behind it as the sounds of the director and teachers drew nearer. Finally, the group pushed past the tarp and made their way back to the upper floors, using the stairs that Icarus had used earlier. Icarus held his breath until the sounds of their footsteps quieted and he was alone once again. He didn't fully understand what had just taken place, so he crept back down the stairs to find answers for himself.

The silver door that led to the lab was shut, and a doctor in a long, white lab coat stood bent over the man as he stuck a needle into his neck. But the man was more alert now, looking around the room, whipping his head back and forth as if ghosts were materializing around him. Soon, the man's eyes focused on Icarus. Yellow fire, or at least that was what it seemed like, suddenly appeared, and flickered wildly on the man's skin and from his eyes. The doctor's hand fell slack, and he walked in robotic movements to the door, turning the knob and allowing Icarus in.

Icarus hesitated before going in, looking at the Dreamer man and the doctor, whose eyes were strangely blank of any emotion.

"Come closer," the Dreamer finally spoke, his voice weak and raspy. Considering his abilities and the fact that he was a Dreamer, Icarus didn't doubt that this man hadn't spoken in a long time, perhaps only to scream as a result of the torture or the tests the Academy conducted.

"My name is Fukushima Yuudai, please … come closer. I cannot speak loudly," the man said quietly.

Icarus still hesitated. He turned back toward the stairwell, to make sure they were alone. Certain that they were, he turned back, steeled his nerves, and walked into the room, curious as to what he might learn from a Dreamer.

"I am Icarus, Mr. …." Icarus trailed off, unsure of how to address the Dreamer.

"Please, call me Mr. Fukushima," Mr. Fukushima said softly, studying Icarus with his dark eyes.

Icarus stood beside the hospital bed and found that, in closer proximity, the Dreamer, Mr. Fukushima, was even more gaunt. But the man didn't look at him with hate, as Icarus expected all Dreamers to do. Perhaps this one was different.

"Are you afraid of me?" Mr. Fukushima asked, once again with his raspy, soft voice that matched his broken appearance.

Icarus thought for a moment, looking at the bound Dreamer in front of him. "I should be."

"But are you?" Mr. Fukushima asked, raising his eyebrows ever so slightly as if in a taunt or challenge.

"No, I don't think so," Icarus confessed.

"Then why did you hesitate when the doctor opened the door?" Mr. Fukushima asked, moving his head ever so slightly.

"I ... how did you make him move? What was the yellow fire?" Icarus asked, answering the Dreamer's question with another.

Mr. Fukushima sighed and shifted slightly in his restraints. "It's like your director said. I saw you there listening. My power is that I can influence the decisions of others. The doctor would have left the room sooner or later, opening the door in the process. I merely sped up that process."

"Why haven't you escaped this place?" Icarus asked, looking back toward the doctor who still held a blank expression and stood stoically in front of the door.

"The director killed my son and took my wife from me. The director said she would set her free if I comply and allow them to utilize my powers. But you remind me of my son, so young..." Mr. Fukushima said, smiling at Icarus.

Icarus returned the smile, feeling pity for this poor, naïve man. Icarus knew the director. There would be no scenario where the director allowed this man's family to live. But Icarus didn't say this to the man.

Icarus turned the conversation to his own curious thoughts. "When I was at the door, why did you look so surprised?"

Mr. Fukushima's smile fell. "You reminded me of a man I once knew, a senator from New York City."

"A senator..." Icarus said slowly, wondering to himself if there was any possibility that this Dreamer had somehow known Icarus's own father. "What was his name?"

"Senator Marshal ... you look like him," Mr. Fukushima spoke, smiling again.

Icarus's pulse raced as his excitement grew. The years of wistful yearning for the truth and history of his father had finally built to this moment. However, fear still plagued his mind, worrying that his mother would somehow find out about this interaction. However, he ignored that feeling, pushing it down just as he had always done, and spoke slowly, sounding out the words he never spoke aloud.

"That man ... was my father."

Mr. Fukushima's eyes widened, and his smile grew. "I thought as much. You have the same blue eyes, so powerful, as if they could pierce their way into one's soul."

Icarus smiled despite himself, this time with a sense of joy rather than pity. "Please … what do you remember about him?"

"I didn't see him often, only the few times he came to the compound to discuss plans."

Taking his time and pausing frequently to catch his breath, Mr. Fukushima told Icarus about his father. Icarus listened intently, ingraining Mr. Fukushima's every word in his mind and envisioning the scenes Mr. Fukushima described so that he could, in some way, be there with Mr. Fukushima as if Icarus himself had known his father.

It had been raining for the entire week after the Dreamers attacked the White House, killing everyone except the director. It was as if the sky had broken open and sent its flood down as punishment for what had happened. Many at the Dreamer compound took it as a sign of troubles to come. The compound was located below ground, underneath the tall, moss-covered rocks that rose like obelisks into the sky in the Chinese countryside. It was the perfect defensive location, and the last place for the Dreamers to run to.

Previously, the homes owned by Dreamers had all been taken by the Academy. The senator had arranged in secret for a fleet of planes to bring Dreamers from all over the world to this safe house. Not all the Dreamers came, though. Many thought they could hide on their own, while others still wanted to keep fighting. The Dreamers who came were mostly the ones with families and children. Exhausted, they huddled in fear in the bottom level of the compound.

The senator arrived in the morning around ten, his helicopter landing above the underground building amid the downpour. He was ushered inside by thankful Dreamers with small, useless umbrellas. With his arrival, the Dreamers' paralyzing fear seemed to wash away, and many rushed to greet and thank him. Children marveled at his soaked but pristine blue suit and pointed at him, calling to their mothers that their hero had arrived. Mothers took his hand and thanked him graciously, their eyes brimming with happy tears as they shook his hand or gave him warm embraces.

Mr. Fukushima's own son ran to the senator, tugging his sleeves for attention. "Thank you for saving us from the scary people," Mr. Fukushima's son said graciously, shaking the senator's hand.

The senator accepted all these small kindnesses with a warm smile and offered gentle words of encouragement, wishing the children and their parents well. He told them that he hoped the Academy could find peace so they could come out of hiding soon. Some didn't understand his language and the words he spoke, but everyone understood his kindness. Over the next week, he came at least a couple more times. Whenever he visited, he never stayed long. But he always listened to those who needed encouragement and played with the children. The children would use their powers to conjure illusions and play games as a true demonstration of the coexistence of magic and non-magic.

"He did that ... all for you?" Icarus asked quietly, taking in the story of his mysterious father.

"Not just for me," Mr. Fukushima emphasized, struggling against the bonds as if wanting to emphasize his point more. "For all the Dreamers and their families."

"What happened after that?"

"I think you know," Mr. Fukushima said bitterly before going into a fit of coughing.

Icarus looked sadly at this broken man, who was most likely dying. "The director found your compound," Icarus said simply, the truth causing him grief.

The director's cadets found the safe house by tailing the senator two weeks after the attack on the White House, the same day the senator would be arrested by the director. The senator's helicopter flew to the top of the building once more, and this time, with the help of some of the Dreamers, he carried down food, warm blankets, clothes, and some entertainment, such as books and toys. The Dreamer children squealed with joy and immediately dove into the box of toys.

The adults smiled and laughed before moving to the floor above to speak of their plans. The Dreamers thanked the senator graciously and talked fondly about their future like old friends. They made plans to renovate the compound and build new ones to house more families. The senator had promised to invest money and bring loyal workers, others he knew who supported the Dreamers.

After they finished planning, the leader of the compound, Mr. Fukushima himself, opened a drawer underneath the table and revealed a tall bottle of dark-red wine.

"I propose a toast, to our savior and very good friend, Senator Marshal," he said, pouring a glass first for the senator, then for each of the adults in the room.

Once all the adults held a glass of wine in their hands, Mr. Fukushima raised his glass.

"To Mr. Marshal." He saluted with his raised glass.

"To Mr. Marshal," the rest of the adults parroted, smiling widely and fondly at the senator.

Senator Marshal accepted the compliments and smiled shyly despite himself. "Thank you."

He took a sip of his wine, tasting the full, pleasant flavors and sweetness of the rich elixir. As he placed the glass on the table, he realized that the rest of the adults looked to him expectantly, as if he were their leader. And perhaps in a way, he was.

"I … I cannot fathom how all of you have survived for so long and kept so lighthearted," the senator confessed. "And I cannot tell you how much longer you may have to remain here in hiding. But I can promise that one day life will get better. We will all live, Dreamers and regulars alike, together without fear. I look forward to that day when you can all meet my son, who has only been in this world for a few months. Yes, I would give anything for all of you to meet my son."

Tears welled up in the senator's eyes at the thoughts of his son, for the senator, because of his travel between Washington and the Dreamer compound, had only seen his son for about a week since his birth. Mr. Fukushima placed his glass down and walked over to where the senator sat and embraced him.

"You shall see your son soon," Mr. Fukushima said. "We would love to meet him and tell him about the hero his father is."

The senator chuckled and pulled away from him. "Thank you … dear friend."

Everyone in the room smiled, for the day was good, and the world, perhaps for one day, smiled upon them too. That was until the cadets unleashed their volley of missiles at the compound from their jets that hovered above the compound.

The walls of their underground safe house shook as dust rained down. Massive booms echoed from the upper floors as screams echoed from downstairs, where the children and other parents were.

"This is what we have been preparing for," Mr. Fukushima spoke solemnly.

"Get moving, everyone!" the senator shouted.

"Half of you, go up to fortify the compound until we can get out. The rest of you, come with me," Mr. Fukushima shouted.

Mr. Fukushima, accompanied by the senator, rushed down and found the children and parents frozen in fear. The children hugged their mothers and looked to the senator with wide, hopeless eyes.

"What should we do?" one of the mothers asked with frightened eyes.

Mr. Fukushima set his gaze and spoke in a firm, defiant tone. "We need to get the children out of here. But those who can still put up a fight, it's the time to strike a blow at those who have driven us and our children into hiding. It's time to fight those aircraft out there, for they don't know what true power looks like."

Cheers and shouts erupted at Mr. Fukushima's words, and many rushed up the stairs to join the other Dreamers who were holding off the missiles and aircraft. As the Dreamers scrambled up the stairs, Mr. Fukushima stopped a teenager with jet-black hair and pure black eyes.

"What?" she asked. Her body radiated anger and rage at the cadets.

"I have a different mission for you," Mr. Fukushima murmured, walking her to where the senator sat with the children, attempting to calm their fears.

"I believe it's time for you to leave," Mr. Fukushima said quietly.

The senator looked up at Mr. Fukushima and frowned. "Absolutely not! I'm staying with these children. I might not be able to fight, but I *will* offer any assistance that I can right now."

Mr. Fukushima shook his head. "You have already given us more assistance than anyone else on this earth. You have given us hope and purpose and safety. Now it's time for me to return the favor. This is Kiara, and she will take you home."

"I won't let you do this, Fukushima Yuudai," the senator insisted. "I can't let you all stay here … you may perish."

Mr. Fukushima shook his head. "No, we will never perish, for as long as we have hope in people like you, as long as our suffering is remembered, our lives and hopes shall live on. Now it's time for you to live on, it's time for you to go back to your son."

The senator sighed and walked toward Mr. Fukushima. Mr. Fukushima embraced him, and when he released the senator, Mr. Fukushima saw tears in his eyes.

"Get the children out of here," the senator pleaded as Kiara took the senator by the arm.

"I will make sure of it," Mr. Fukushima nodded, and to Kiara he said, "Get him to the New York Metro."

Kiara nodded and flexed her hands as black mist began swirling violently around her and the senator.

"We *will* meet again, Fukushima, in one way or another," the senator shouted over the whipping wind of Kiara's magic, a promise rather than a suggestion.

With a flash of black and white light, the senator and Kiara were gone. "Yes, we shall," Mr. Fukushima whispered.

Icarus was silent when Mr. Fukushima finished speaking and looked up expectingly to him. Icarus swallowed and asked in a shaky voice, "My dad was a hero?"

Mr. Fukushima smiled kindly, despite holding such a pained position on the hospital bed, "The greatest and kindest of them."

"Why … didn't I know of this?" Icarus asked, feeling lost and angry all at once.

Although he spoke out loud, he wasn't asking Mr. Fukushima; rather, it was a plea to his mother who wasn't in the room. He was lost in the fact that he had been given two different versions of his father: one of a man whose memory was apparently too painful to discuss and one of someone with selfless kindness and friendship. Icarus was so angry at his mother for never telling Icarus the truth about his father, even if she didn't agree with what he'd done. Because she kept the story of his father from him, he'd never been allowed to form his own opinion. What he didn't know, though, was the secret his mother continued to keep—that his father had been the man who assisted the beginning of the Dreamer attack.

"Your world here is all about secrecy, am I wrong?" Mr. Fukushima said.

"No, you're correct," Icarus sighed, running a shaking hand through his hair.

"Then it's merely due to the place where you were raised," Mr. Fukushima spoke. "Your Academy claims to teach you things, but most things in life cannot be learned. They must be experienced."

"They taught us things about Dreamers, like you kill for sport," Icarus said, looking at Mr. Fukushima perhaps for confirmation, but also to gauge his reaction to the Academy's teachings. "Or that some Dreamers gain more power from blood."

Mr. Fukushima wore a solemn expression. "That is not true. We are just people, like you and me, people fighting to live in this world, fighting to survive."

"Then why do they teach us that?" Icarus asked as his mind whirled to understand.

"A mother who loves her child so deeply wishes to keep her child close to her. But how can she if the child wishes to explore the world? The mother tells the child that the world is dangerous and dark, and so the child stays by the mother and never learns that the world is truly a beautiful place. The child only knows the mother's love, and that can sometimes be enough," Mr. Fukushima whispered. "But … sometimes, the child will go to explore anyway, as destined. Which child are you, Icarus?"

"I…" Icarus hesitated. He did love his mother, especially on the days when she showed him maternal love. But on the days when she was his teacher and trainer and she fulfilled the Academy's teaching responsibilities, Icarus despised who she became. His mother was replaced by a cold woman who held high expectations. "I am the first," he said half-heartedly.

Mr. Fukushima frowned. "The first child would have never looked into this room through the window."

"The feeling of curiosity is not bad if I don't act on it," Icarus emphasized.

"Only the second child would have walked into this room. Your father would have," Mr. Fukushima spoke softly, never moving his eyes from Icarus's face.

"I … we'll never know," Icarus said quietly.

"And if you were the first child, then you would've never known me or your father's past," Mr. Fukushima pushed further. He reached a shaking hand to Icarus's, who took it tentatively. "Some destinies are too powerful to change, and some histories are too noble to forget."

"I must leave," Icarus said quickly, pulling his hand away and taking one last pitying look at Mr. Fukushima. "It was an honor to meet you, sir."

Icarus sprinted toward the stairs as Mr. Fukushima called after him. "It was an honor to meet you finally. Goodbye, Icarus Marshal!"

A fit of coughing followed Mr. Fukushima's words, and Icarus looked back to see the emotionless doctor closing the door before Icarus turned to leave. The ring of his father's last name sent shivers up his spine, and Icarus paused.

Icarus thought he had known his destiny, to train harder, to suffer more pain than most. But his destiny wasn't so clear now. It was as if Mr. Fukushima threw a stone into the pond of Icarus's life. The stone created ripples of unbridled thoughts and feelings for his father and his past that Icarus had wanted to know for as long as he could remember. Those ripples couldn't be stopped, and Icarus didn't know if that was for better or worse as he went to gather the weapons for the coming war.

CHAPTER 22

THROUGH THAT DAY, Breksta and Hestia, along with the other cadets, made various trips up and down the stairwell, bringing supplies upstairs. With each trip, whenever they were alone, Breksta and Hestia continued to discuss Breksta's escape until each tiny detail was considered. On one trip, they hesitantly brought Olivia in on the plan.

"So why does Breksta have to go?" Olivia pouted.

Hestia let out a long sigh as she lifted a crate and explained the well-thought-out lie that Breksta had spun. "Because she needs to track the Dreamer who did all this damage. Did you even listen to anything I told you?"

Both girls knew that Breksta couldn't escape without help. However, they did withhold parts of Breksta's escape from Olivia, knowing Olivia's strong loyalty to the Academy.

"Go easy on her, Hestia," Breksta said, noting her friend's frustration and anxiety.

"And what's your job again, Olivia?" Hestia said, grilling Olivia for the fifth time.

"I'll go to the control room, grab the keys to open the hatch with the big, red lever on the floor. And then I'll go to the lower-level electric grid and turn it off so that no Dreamers can access our electricity. I'm not dumb, you know," Olivia retorted, crossing her arms defiantly.

"Well, you're definitely unhelpful," Hestia snapped, her anxiety seeping through. "Grab another box."

Olivia sighed and took a box, beginning her way back down the long stairwell.

Little did Olivia know, turning off the electric grid was an integral part of their plan so that the cadets couldn't track Breksta nor use their planes until the electricity was brought back to the grid. Her assignment would create a distraction for Breksta to escape the Academy and delay the Academy's ability to track her, giving her the best chance of making a successful getaway.

Breksta gestured for Hestia to wait. "I know you're worried about this. I am too," Breksta said with a tiny quiver in her voice. "But this *will* work."

Hestia let out a deep breath. "I know. That's what I am worried about."

"What do you mean?" Breksta asked, taken aback by Hestia's uncertainty. "You don't want me to leave?"

"No, of course not. I want you to find answers and do … whatever it is you need to do. You're my best friend and I trust you, but I don't trust the Academy to be open or forgiving. I … I don't want to be here alone. What if I'm caught? And god knows what my mother is planning, already telling the cadets to 'Stay sharp for any unusual movement' and to 'Prepare for the final blow to the Dreamers.' But … I know you need to be safe."

"Look, Hestia. We can talk about this all day. But we both know we could never change your mother's mind. I must do this," Breksta said.

Hestia nodded. "I know. And the director is still my mother. I … I can't give up on her yet. There's still a chance that I can change her mind about violently attacking the Dreamers. Although I don't know the full extent of her plans, I might be able to stop this war from the inside and help the remaining Dreamers. Like I'm helping you escape."

"And yet I am running away from your mother. She will never make room for us Dreamers in this world," Breksta said flatly.

Silence filled the room as both girls found themselves at a crossroads. Breksta had to choose between friendship and the plan that Erebus had laid out to find her past and power, while Hestia had to choose between friendship and family, an equally difficult choice. Deep down, both knew that this was where their paths together were ending, choosing what they had known since they first met. Breksta had always been an outcast, and Hestia would always be the director's daughter.

"It's late," Hestia said, glancing sadly at Breksta. "We should initiate phase one of the plan."

It was late in the day when Icarus and a few other cadets pried open a stuck door to reveal a storage cubby of old versions of their cadet attire, including their mission gear lined with thermal insulation and dozens of small, hidden pockets to store small weapons and bits of food. Together, the cadets made various trips between floors, lugging the clothing to the sleeping quarters. It was on one of these trips, when Icarus was alone, that he overheard a strange conversation.

"Look, Hestia. We can talk about this all day. But we both know we could never change your mother's mind. I must do this," Breksta said.

Hestia nodded. "I know. And the director is still my mother. I … I can't give up on her yet." Hestia ended by saying, "I might be able to stop this war from the inside and help the remaining Dreamers. Like I am helping you escape."

Icarus's breath caught. Not only was he guilty for speaking to a Dreamer, but now he was witness to treason. Before Icarus met Mr. Fukushima and learned the truth about his father, he wouldn't have hesitated to expose them. He would have brought them to the director and his mother, reveling in the knowledge that he had done a great service: to rid the Academy of two traitors. But now, Icarus was beginning to understand the importance of patience and waiting to act. Most importantly, he needed to collect enough information to formulate a course of action that was best for him. So he waited in the stairwell, picking up the last of the words he could hear.

"And yet I'm running away from your mother. She'll never make room for us Dreamers in this world." Breksta sighed.

"It's late," Hestia said, glancing sadly at Breksta. "We should initiate phase one of the plan."

Icarus crept back as Breksta and Hestia materialized out of the room on his left and continued up the stairs. Truly, Icarus had reached a crossroads. Breksta's and Hestia's fates were in his hands. In an instant, he could end their futures permanently. Icarus knew what his mother would do, and what the perfect cadet would do, but he himself wasn't so sure anymore if he was the perfect cadet—or if he even wanted to be.

His mother's lies and the truth about his father had opened his eyes to the idea of perspectives. Perhaps Breksta and Hestia's friendship was not something that Icarus should try to destroy. Perhaps Breksta's life in the Academy and Icarus's previous notions of the inferiority of Dreamers and their children were wrong. And what Breksta had said last, that the director will never make room for Dreamers in this world, rang true. Ms. Adams had fought and trained Icarus, effectively making room for their small and broken family in the Academy's world. In this sense, perhaps Icarus wasn't so different from Breksta, and perhaps she deserved his kindness and sympathy.

"Wait!" Icarus called out.

Breksta and Hestia whipped around. Trying to cover her sudden distress, Hestia challenged Icarus. "What are you up to, Icarus?" she demanded.

Icarus set down the clothing and raised his hands in a motion of vulnerability and surrender. "Just gathering these clothes."

"Icarus ... what were you doing?" Breksta asked hesitantly.

Icarus motioned for them to follow him back into the room. "Just hear me out, alright?"

Breksta glanced unsettlingly at Hestia but followed Icarus. Icarus allowed the girls in before standing with his back to the door to keep a close eye out for anyone approaching.

"I ... I heard what you were saying about escaping," Icarus said, clasping his hands together.

Hestia and Breksta both took a deep breath; Hestia pursed her lips.

"You can't stop me, Icarus," Breksta said defiantly, although Icarus heard a slight quiver in her voice.

Icarus shook his head. "You don't understand. I ... how can I help? And may I ask why you're escaping?"

"What are you talking about?" Hestia asked defensively.

Icarus sighed. "I … I'm sorry about things in the past, for how I treated you both. But now I want to help you with your mission, for you and I are not so different, Breksta. I can't explain it all right now, but please, just tell me what I can do."

"How do we know this isn't some trick? Some ploy for you to manipulate us?" Breksta asked, her eyes never breaking their gaze from Icarus.

Icarus nodded. "I promise, it's not. I know it's a lot to ask, but please trust me."

Breksta smiled slightly. Her grimace softened, as a look of relief crossed her face. However, Hestia still gazed at him distrustfully.

She turned to Breksta, whispering, "I still don't believe this façade. Icarus is lying, Breksta. He hasn't done anything like this before."

"Hestia … what choice do we have?" Breksta said with a sigh. "He might be sincere."

Icarus paused before he spoke and took great care not to say too much. "M-my father was a supporter of your people, Breksta. He protected them … even to the end."

Hestia's eyes shone with confusion. "Your father? I have never heard you or anyone else speak of him. Another one of his lies, Breksta."

"Please, Breksta. If my father were here, I think he would do what I'm doing now, trying to help you," Icarus said, remembering the kindness Mr. Fukushima spoke of that his father showed Dreamers. "Let this be the beginning of my repentance to you, for all the years I added to your suffering," Icarus said.

"W-wait a minute. Who was your father?" Hestia challenged.

"He worked for the government. He was a senator, Senator Marshal," Icarus explained.

"Senator Marshal?" Hestia asked, appalled. "He was there the night my father, grandmother, and grandfather, the president, were killed. My mother told me about him. He apparently helped the Dreamers come into the White House and attack them."

"I don't know about those details. I only know that he tried to help the Dreamers and he tried to protect them. I can't explain more right now, but please believe me."

Breksta turned to Hestia, gently touching her shoulder. "Perhaps he is telling the truth, Hestia. Maybe this is for the best. Icarus, I can't tell you the extent of this mission. However, I am seeking out a teacher, a Dreamer, who will help me discover things about myself. I'm only allowing you to be involved with this mission so we can have more help and so Hestia will have someone to look after her when I am gone."

"I don't need anyone, especially not him," Hestia said, but Icarus thought he saw tears in her eyes. "I just don't want him to betray us. I want you to be safe."

"Icarus has promised his help. With it, I have an even greater chance of reaching safety and finding answers. We must let him help, Hestia."

Hestia shut her eyes tightly; Icarus felt the seconds pass like eons. But soon she turned around, her expression fierce as she neared him. "I'll allow it. But if you speak to anyone of this, if you step one foot out of line … well, let me just say that the director doesn't show mercy to cadets who offend me."

Icarus swallowed, acknowledging the risk. Hestia kept her unforgiving gaze locked on Icarus. "This is what you will do, Icarus. You won't in any way impede this mission. Your sole purpose is to make sure that Olivia procures the keys to the hangar, but that's it. Do you understand me?"

Icarus nodded, feeling Hestia's unwavering spirit through her words. "I understand, Hestia. I won't let you down."

"She doesn't know, Icarus," Hestia murmured sadly. "Olivia doesn't know the extent that you do now. She believes we are doing this for the director."

"Of course. It's best to keep a tight circle," Icarus replied.

"Now go," Breksta said. "We can't afford to be seen together with you; others might get suspicious."

Icarus then took the uniforms and headed back. Icarus was glad to do something of service, something he believed to be for the best. And the notion that Breksta would meet a Dreamer who was most likely an elder gave him hope of learning more about his father and his past. Icarus's thoughts were like birds freed from their cage, and they fluttered with joy and stretched their sore wings after standing in one place for so long.

This was the beginning of a journey for Icarus as much as it was for Breksta. Even if he didn't fully acknowledge it to himself, his soul knew. His birds of thought were now freed to roam the expanse of his mind, discovering either what he had never understood before or perhaps coming to terms with the truth of his mother's actions. With each step down the stairs, Icarus felt as if he were growing stronger, surer of himself. Truth was something he sought now, as difficult and dark as it might be to find it. But he would find it—that was a truth he didn't deny himself.

The girls had exchanged their final goodbyes by the door of the aircraft hangar, both trying not to show their true devastation at Breksta's departure. Breksta awaited Olivia's retrieval of the keycard for the door and planes, the same keycard that would also open the bunker and allow Breksta's commandeered plane to leave. In the time Breksta waited, she mindlessly fiddled with the zipper to an old messenger bag she had found on one of her trips to retrieve supplies. It was now slung across her shoulder.

The bag was stuffed with packets of processed foods she'd also gathered, along with a few stolen weapons she had grabbed from the pile the cadets made earlier. Although the weapons were out of date—a small handgun with a few dozen shots paired with a few daggers weren't the protective gear Breksta had hoped for—she would make do and survive.

As Breksta prepared to leave, Olivia hid outside the control room, as the director called it. The room was where war was waged. It was the place where strategy and planning were conducted by the senior cadets, the teachers, and the director.

To Breksta, what was most important were the keys to the airplane hangar that were locked in a safe in that room. Earlier in the day, Hestia had stolen the passcode so Olivia could gain access to the safe. She explained to Olivia the plan she'd devised and instructed her to lay in wait just around the corner. Once the director exited the room, Olivia would then slip in and get the keys she needed.

Hestia knocked on the door politely, thinning her lips as the plan began to roll out.

"Who is it?" the director commanded.

Hestia pushed open the door and surveyed the dark room, finding a few senior cadets, Ms. Adams, and some of the more influential teachers looking at the wide screen on the wall that displayed information about the last Dreamer populous on the West Coast.

"It's me," Hestia said plainly, trying not to let her fear come through her voice.

"Hestia, perfect timing," the director said with a smile. "We were just discussing our best tactics for attack."

"And what might those be?" Hestia asked, feigning interest to hide her thrumming heart.

"We have decided to start with an airstrike against a large structure of symbolic importance, the statue of Morpheus in the Bay Area, to be exact," a senior girl said, her shoulders straightening proudly. "This strike will deal a significant blow to the Dreamers' power and influence over the western regions. Then we will go in simultaneously with ground troops in the remaining cities and bases to subdue the few rebels left."

Hestia smiled coldly before answering, "You certainly have planned a lot since we got here today."

"Yes, we have," the director said, looking calculatedly at Hestia's tone. "What was it that you needed Hestia?"

"I need to speak to you on a … *private* matter," Hestia said, keeping her voice steady as she had seen her mother do so often.

"Give us the room," the director said, waving her hand before settling in the chair at farthest end of the long table.

"Yes, Madam Director," the cadets responded, as Ms. Adams walked behind them and ushered them out.

"What's on your mind?" the director asked, keeping her eyes trained on Hestia.

Hestia held her mother's gaze as she answered, "I have decided, based on the events of the past day and the rebellion in the west, to offer my ideas and services to the planning of this war. I'm offering to become your right hand."

It took all of Hestia's will not to shudder at the implications of the words she had just uttered. The director stood and wrapped her daughter in a hug. "I knew you would see sense eventually."

Hestia didn't flinch at the contact. Instead, she bit her lip until her mother released her. "As your second, we should make the announcement to the other cadets publicly," Hestia said, smiling so wide it hurt. "Then we can get right into preparations."

"Excellent idea! Let's do that in the morning. In the meantime, I'll show you the progress on our weapons preparation. The cadets are in the preparation area below the sleeping quarters," the director said, smiling one of the only true smiles Hestia had ever seen on her mother's face.

The director wrapped her arm around Hestia's shoulder once again and led her out of the room. "I have some ideas for the attack on the western regions," Hestia said, baiting her mother with more ideas as they walked toward the elevator.

"I'm so proud of you, Hestia," her mother stated.

Hestia hesitated before answering, unsure if her mother's words were true. So often in the past, Hestia had done everything she could to hear those words. It hurt to remember the many times she had tried. It seemed that no matter how hard Hestia had tried to gain her mother's approval—and her love—her mother was always the director first: a cold, harsh, demanding human being. And, as Hestia's friendship with Breksta grew deeper through the years, her mother's harshness only became more pronounced.

Her mother's reply caught her heart. And deep within, a small part of Hestia wondered if this is what life would have been like if Breksta had never come to the Academy.

"Thank you," Hestia said.

This time, she meant it.

CHAPTER 23

OLIVIA LET OUT A SIGH OF RELIEF as she watched the director and Hestia walk to the elevator, knowing it was time to implement phase two. She was doing this mission for the good of the Academy, to help Breksta catch the Dreamer that caused the earthquake. Olivia felt a sense of purpose—as she always did when she accomplished tasks for the Academy. This was another opportunity to show her potential and strength. Not having parents to praise and compliment her, Olivia looked for that recognition from the Academy and her peers. It was what pushed Olivia to obey her friends, especially Hestia, the director's daughter.

Just as Olivia slipped into the empty war room, she noted how perfect the director and Hestia looked together with their identical hair and their matched stride and poise. A powerful woman and her daughter who would inherit that power and lead all of them to victory and greatness were an undeniably powerful duo. But those thoughts soon faded as Olivia focused on her mission to get the key for Breksta. Helping Breksta catch the Dreamer who attacked the Academy would be the single-most influential action she had ever taken for the Academy. She vowed to complete the task perfectly without a hitch.

Olivia found the director's desk at the right side of the room covered in papers. She circled the desk and located the black safe at the bottom-left corner, below the drawers Hestia had described. She turned the small silver dial to seven, thirty-eight, twenty-three. With a pop, the safe opened. Inside were neatly stacked files. Olivia ruffled through the files, reaching her arm underneath and around to find the keys. To her dismay, the keys weren't there.

"No, no, no!" Olivia exclaimed in frustration; she had failed at the only task Hestia instructed her to do. Hestia and Breksta had been counting on her, and she failed. She stood quickly, taking in her failure as anger welled up inside. Where would she get another set of keys? She couldn't ask the director since Hestia had told her that the director shouldn't be bothered.

Olivia felt hot tears begin to pool in her eyes and run down her face. Through her tears, she looked around the room for anything that might help to open the hangar door. She rummaged through the papers and maps, looked underneath the desks, and opened drawers. She found nothing.

Olivia clenched her fists and steeled her emotions. "Breksta said to be strong. Be strong, Olivia."

Wiping her tears, Olivia left the control room and began to walk to the stairs opposite the room that would lead upstairs to the hangar. Just as she began to jog, she collided with Icarus in the stairwell. He had a dark look on his face that was instantly replaced with surprise as Olivia slammed into him.

"There you are," Icarus said, stepping back.

"Excuse me," Olivia asked, keeping her head low in an attempt to move quickly up the stairs.

"Wait, where are you going? Did you get what you needed for the director?" Icarus asked, tapping her shoulder twice as she tried to move past him.

At the mention of the director, Olivia's nagging doubts flared. How would the director react when she found out that Olivia had failed to help Hestia and Breksta? What would her punishment be? Olivia's doubts consumed her mind, stopping her in her tracks as she dug her fingers into the palms of her hands to keep from crying.

"What's wrong?" Icarus asked, and despite not offering any affectionate touch like Hestia, his soft voice seemed genuine with concern. Olivia didn't know what had caused it, but Icarus was different. The ruthless and cold Icarus that excelled in the Academy at the expense of others had somehow been replaced by a kinder, gentler Icarus. His genuineness made Olivia feel safe enough to tell him what had happened.

"I-I failed," Olivia said tentatively. "And the director is going to be angry."

Icarus knelt so that he was at eye level with Olivia. "Listen to me, Olivia. You're a good cadet, and we can fix this, alright? Hestia and Breksta sent me to help you, and we'll find the key together."

Olivia wiped her tears away and nodded her head. "Thank you."

Icarus stood to his full height and spoke. "Come with me. I know where we can find another set of keys."

Icarus led Olivia back down the stairs across from the control room and continued on until they reached one of the lower levels with a door marked "Administrators Only." Icarus pushed open the door, and a long, brightly lit hallway came into view.

"Are we allowed in here?" Olivia asked tentatively, still unsure of Icarus's behavior.

Icarus pointed at the doors marked with a first initial and a last name. "This is where the teachers stay. Ms. Adams, my mother, told me that she stays here. So this is where her keys should be."

Icarus pushed open the door to his mother's room and beckoned Olivia to follow him in. A bed was positioned on the far wall opposite the door, and a desk stood next to the door. Icarus began to open the desk drawers one by one until he found a thick ring of keys and keycards attached to a faded blue lanyard. He lifted the ring and offered them to Olivia.

"See, you didn't fail," Icarus spoke encouragingly and smiled.

"Thank you, thank you!" Olivia exclaimed at the sight of the keycard marked "hangar." "You really are the best."

Icarus watched as Olivia raced up the stairs, his mind and heart racing as well. He was torn between the sheer joy of curiosity, of wanting to know more about his father, of becoming the kind person that Mr. Fukushima said his father was, and the fear of failure. Although he had begun to dislike his mother for her lies and duplicity, he still feared failing her. But most of all, he feared failing in the

Academy; he knew what happened to those who failed. People like Breksta, who were deemed failures in the eyes of the Academy, no matter what they did. But, Icarus realized, his life in the Academy was perhaps crueler and more unethical than he had allowed himself to realize, and most of this cruelty was instigated by the director—and his mother.

Breksta exhaled loudly, annoyed and anxious at how long it was taking for Olivia to retrieve the keys. They had given her clear instructions. Although Olivia was one of the only people they trusted, Breksta would not be surprised if she had missed a step. Hopefully Icarus had been able to help and not become a hindrance. *Although,* Breksta thought to herself sarcastically to laugh off the nerves, *if Olivia doesn't arrive soon, I might just ask the director politely if I can leave the Academy once and for all.*

"I. Got. It," Olivia said breathlessly as she ran from the stairwell toward Breksta, dangling the keycards in her hand.

"Finally!" Breksta scoffed, snatching the keys from Olivia's grasp.

"Hey, I tried! But I am glad Icarus came with me; otherwise, I never would have found the other key," Olivia added as Breksta scanned the keycard on a scanner next to the door to the airplane hangar.

Breksta paused before answering. "He truly did help you?"

"I was surprised, but yes." Olivia shrugged.

Breksta pulled Olivia into the hangar, and the door closed behind them. She still did not understand. The boy who had tormented her, treated her like a Dreamer only because her mother was Asteria Vilkas, that was the boy who had helped her? The same boy who was one of the main factors in her cold, horrid life in the Academy would be the factor that allowed her to have a new life?

"So, Icarus helped me," Breksta said slowly, the words feeling unnatural in her mouth. Yet they held a certain feeling of rightness and joy. Although she had no time to learn more about how Icarus had helped or why, it seemed that life was finally turning her way.

"Yes," Olivia said, smiling wider. "He was very nice, even though he usually isn't. But my delay has shortened the time you have to leave. Go to your plane. I'll pull the lever and then go to the electric grid."

Before Olivia could run to the hangar's control panel, Breksta pulled her into a tight embrace.

"Thank you … for everything," Breksta murmured, tears almost pooling in her eyes from the sisterly instinct she felt for Olivia.

Olivia hugged her tightly. "Go on now! For the Academy!"

"Remember the plan!" Breksta shouted, handing back the keys to Olivia as she ran toward a jet-black plane near the back of the hangar. "Pull the lever *after* you turn on the control panel."

"On it!" Olivia shouted back, knowing they were now into phase three of their plan.

When it came to orders and commands, all the cadets functioned on ingrained second-nature actions. Olivia injected the key into the control panel near the doors of the hangar, and the lights instantly flashed on in response. She pressed the combination of buttons that would prevent overrides on the panel and pulled the lever to open the airstrip above their heads.

Meanwhile, Breksta neared the airplane she had chosen. Its sleek exterior and new technology allowed for quick speed and invisibility against the radars the Dreamers used, rendering her plane undetectable. It was perfect for Breksta's escape. Now she just had to wait for Olivia to hand over the key. Soon, creaking sounds came from above as the hangar doors began to open. Breksta looked up to see her first glimpses of freedom in the cold night sky. The small pattering of feet grew louder until Breksta saw Olivia approaching, and she ran to meet her. Olivia transferred the key to Breksta, and Breksta waved goodbye one last time before scanning the key on the rear of the plane. The mouth dropped open immediately. Breksta ran to the pilot's seat and began preparing the plane for takeoff, the plane door closing behind her. She would have a short, five-minute window to escape before notifications of the opening of the airstrip reached the director's ears. Those minutes felt like gold to Breksta.

The engines roared to life, creating a humming that Breksta had grown accustomed to in her years of flight training. Like all cadets, she had been trained in the flight simulators housed in the Academy training buildings since she was

young. Once she had been ready, she'd flown actual planes as part of her continued training. As senior cadets, all cadets had to complete a mission involving
the capture of Dreamers, which was the final test of their fighting, flying, and
tracking skills. Breksta, Hestia, and Icarus hadn't yet completed that mission,
but Breksta had reaped the rewards of her previous training and was about
to complete the biggest mission of her life. She spoke through the speakers to
Olivia.

"I'm ready. You should go and deal with the electrical grid."

Olivia answered with a forced calm voice that Breksta detected as panic. "I-I
see cadets coming up the stairwell, the one toward the hangar."

"Go immediately. The hangar doors will take almost five minutes to open
enough for me to sneak through. You must allow that much time to pass before
shutting down the electricity or else I cannot leave, got it?" Breksta ordered,
feeling cold fear and adrenaline course through her body.

Olivia left, running toward the control panel and the doors leading out of
the hangar. To her dismay, she heard cadets in the stairwell. She proceeded down
the same hallway toward the electrical grid. As she ran, she counted one, two,
three, four … remembering clearly what Breksta had said about her five-minute
window. Her pulse quickened as she raced down, avoiding the other cadets who
were walking up, and she ran as fast as she could down the floors.

Ten, eleven, twelve, thirteen…

Fifty-six, fifty-seven, fifty-eight, fifty-nine, one minute…

Just as she rounded the corner, halfway to the next floor, the cadets came
marching up the stairwell. Olivia quickly pushed the door into the hallway and
waited until their footsteps disappeared. Olivia continued down the stairs, flight
after flight, until there were no more stairs for her to descend.

The stairwell door was wide open, leading into a lengthy hallway with a
single door at its end. The door was marked with a sign that read: "Do not enter,
danger—electricity," but Olivia barged in anyway.

Three o three, three o four, three o five…

The electrical grid was a room so tall and large that it could have easily fit
hundreds of people. In the room were thick, complex cables the circumference
of Olivia's clenched fist. Emerging from the walls, they carried electricity from

the wind and solar farms that the Academy had built in the mountains and by the sea. On the right side of the room, on the wall beside the door, stood a panel lined with switches, levers, and buttons.

"Aha!" Olivia exclaimed. This time she wouldn't fail.

Three fifteen, three sixteen, three seventeen…

She scanned the switches, looking for the ones that connected to the different facilities within the Academy. One by one, she flicked off the switches to all the places in the Academy in need of power.

Three twenty-five, three twenty-six…

Olivia had even turned off the emergency power, all except for the hangar power. But she still needed to wait the entire five minutes before flicking off the switch to the hangar's electricity—that way there would be enough space for Breksta to escape. It was almost time. Olivia stood and found the button marked "Upper Bunker Levels: Hangar."

Four twenty, four twenty-one, four twenty-two…

Suddenly, from the stairwell, Olivia heard the loud sounds of stomping feet. Ms. Adams's voice rang out against the walls. "The grid is at the lowest level. Capture the traitor alive."

Olivia crossed her fingers, hoping that Breksta had gotten out in time. She squeezed her eyes tightly as she flicked the switch to the hangar and the lights flickered and died. Then Olivia ran out of the room, looking up the stairwell to see the cadets racing down toward her. She frantically tried to find another exit, but the cadets swarmed around her and held her down.

Ms. Adams looked down at Olivia. "It's always so disappointing when such wonderful potential is thrown away. Cadets, take her upstairs and make sure she is tied down. The director will deal out justice later."

"Wait, please," Olivia begged, confused at the harsh tone of Ms. Adams. "I'm doing this for the Academy. Why am I being punished?"

Ms. Adams scoffed. "All Dreamers and criminals think they are righteous in their actions. But one must come to understand that there are rules in life. You have broken them, Olivia, and thus you are a traitor to the Academy."

Olivia was speechless as the cadets dragged her upstairs. She was so confused and didn't understand why her dedication to the Academy had been met with reprimands. The only home she had ever known had deemed her a traitor. Her hard work in classes and her dedication to her training were reduced to nothing. Olivia's heart sank as she remembered what happened to traitors. *No,* she thought, *I am not a Dreamer to be thrown away like garbage.* Yet, it seemed that even the home she had come to know didn't want her, as if life itself was trying to orphan her.

Up in the hangar, the other cadets banged on the locked door and tried to pry it open. It had been around four minutes since Olivia left, and the hangar doors were still not nearly wide enough for Breksta to leave. She counted down the seconds in her head until suddenly, the sharp pings of bullets hit Breksta's windshield. Breksta glanced down to see the cadets with the director following closely behind. Breksta muttered curses under her breath as she grabbed the joystick and throttle in each hand. The airstrip was almost completely open, but Breksta had to risk leaving early; she was taking fire from all sides, and the windows would only hold for so long.

Breksta slowly eased the plane to hover off the ground. The hangar above her head was still creaking, and the lights of the hangar were illuminant. Breksta was scared to feel joy at the thought of her escape—in her mind, there was always doubt and fear of being captured by the Academy again. But Breksta pushed those feelings down and focused on flying, raising the plane to a dozen feet off the ground.

"Window durability, eighty percent," the plane's electronic guidance spoke.

"So helpful," Breksta grumbled as she pushed the throttle forward to maximum power.

The plane rose, hovering thirty feet off the ground. The long wings pushed the other aircraft aside as the plane jolted upward.

"Window durability, fifty percent."

"That's just really, *really* helpful!" Breksta said through gritted teeth from the exertion.

She hovered forty, then fifty feet off the floor, but the bullets kept coming.

While the open airstrip grew closer, the engine of the plane was not fast enough to escape the onslaught of gunfire.

"Window durability, twenty percent."

Cracks began to spread across the glass, and the bullets were no longer bouncing off but embedding into the glass.

"Window durability, ten percent."

"Got it, I really got it!" Breksta screamed.

Out of nowhere, the lights of the hangar went out and the hangar was drowned in darkness. The hangar doors had stopped moving, and the light beams automatically turned on in Breksta's plane.

"I promise. I will come back for you … eventually, if not soon," she whispered, repeating her promise to Hestia, as she looked to the open night sky.

"Window durability, five percent."

Breksta pushed the joystick as far as it would go, and the plane shot through the hangar opening and into the air. As the plane burst through the hangar and out of the Academy's reach, the lights on her plane showed her a small flash of the Academy's desolation. The auditorium building lay in shambles, and the metal shafts that made up its foundation protruded from the building like lightning rods. The pristine greenery in the center of the buildings appeared gray and dreary.

Breksta exhaled her long-locked breath from her chest. Soon, she would find answers, especially about her abilities. And she would discover a new life for herself and eventually for Hestia as well, just as she promised.

With those thoughts, Breksta flipped the anti-detection switch on the control panel that would render her plane invisible. She then opened the navigation panel and put in the coordinates: 48 degrees North and 122 degrees West. The map opened to an island: Orcas Island, Washington. Breksta's journey had begun.

PART THREE

THE ODYSSEY

CHAPTER 24

"ARRIVING AT DESTINATION, Orcas Island, in T-minus fifteen minutes. Scanning for landing sites."

Breksta was awakened by the voice. She didn't move immediately but surveyed the aircraft's control panel in front of her. Her flight was on course, as she intended. She had fallen asleep after she guided the plane to a high, undetectable altitude and turned on the autopilot. The clock on the top of the navigation screen blinked a red 5:00 a.m.

Breksta let out a deep sigh. The notion of her freedom hadn't hit her yet. Her emotions bubbled under the surface, simmering and waiting to boil. Rather, she rubbed her eyes and turned off the manual flight, descending to an altitude below the clouds. She took in the bare light of morning. Thin clouds spread across the sky like feathered brushstrokes in the morning's orange light. The stark beauty of this new world encapsulated Breksta in nostalgia.

Gazing at the approaching northwestern coast, a brief flicker of regret pained Breksta as she thought of her mother and Hestia and how much they would have loved this place. Before her thoughts could consume her, she smiled and realized that this was the first time she had, on her own terms, gone anywhere, and her joy was beginning to bubble to the surface as she looked out the bullet-ridden window panel.

The sun, redder than she had ever seen it, perched itself on the edge of the horizon. The island was crescent shaped with a bay straight ahead and mountains on the right of the island. The rich viridian of the trees brought back memories of her small town, including her mother and her life of freedom. Shrubbery and trees dotted the western hillsides of the island like small green creatures grazing in the wide-open, grass-covered pastures. The natural world below Breksta was one she hadn't seen in a very long time. The bright-green and blue hues of the ocean were foreign to her eyes that had become used to the Academy's deathly shades of black, white, and gray. Breksta smiled and felt her spirit soar.

"Landing zone acquired," the electronic voice instructed. "Plotting course."

The navigation panel showed a blue curved path across its board. Breksta followed the path, moving the throttle and banking the plane to the left.

"Approaching landing zone."

Breksta guided the plane to a bay that extended inland to the forests. The plane's engines sent waves along the edge of the water. The green-blue ocean was dark in the early morning without the sun overhead. As she neared the center of the bay, she saw a single pale-blue house along a single road that extended to the left and right. The coordinates that she had entered would lead her to that house, where she would find Aristotle and answers.

Breksta eased the plane down toward the empty field past the house, hovering to a stop on the ground. This plane was one of the newer models the Academy developed, with its ability to hover, land, and glide, allowing for landings in small areas and uneven terrain. Having observed the small landing area during her approach, Breksta was glad she'd chosen to fly it.

After shutting off the plane's engine, Breksta grabbed her messenger bag and opened the ramp. She slung the bag over her shoulder and took a few deep breaths, her first breaths of freedom. This free world was utterly beautiful to Breksta, the surrounding nature bringing back fond memories of her mother.

She paused to take in her surroundings. This new world was just awakening, and for the first time since her mother's death, she had the liberty to appreciate it. To her left were mountains and a single concrete road that continued away from her current location. To her right, a gas station was situated on a small hill, one of the remnants of civilization. The blue house located near the miles of sandy beach that she'd spotted from above was in front of her; a quaint oak fence surrounded the property and enclosed the large bushes situated at the back of the house.

Soon, Breksta approached the front door. "Hello?" she called out.

When there was no answer, Breksta steeled her mind as she had done in training and focused on her mission to find Aristotle and understand her magic. She instinctively touched her side for a sword or pistol but found none. She reached into her bag until she felt cold metal. Breksta didn't plan to use a weapon; however, the presence of her weapons gave her security, and she could defend herself if she needed to.

Breksta reached for the door and pushed it open, keeping her footsteps light. As she crossed the door's threshold, her foot snagged on a line. The line triggered a rusted bell above the door, and it rang out loudly. Breksta whipped around to the sound, but nothing and no one was there. She took a deep breath, trying to calm herself.

"My name is Breksta," she called out tentatively. "I'm looking for Aristotle."

Nothing stirred. Breksta called again, "I won't hurt you. I just have some questions."

There was still no reply. Breksta then began to explore the house. The house was divided into two parts. The front area closest to the door was a kitchen with a table on the right. The back area had a worn couch up against the window and a twin-sized bed along the right wall. A fireplace stood in the center of the house encapsulated in glass so that the fire could be seen from either room. Above the fireplace, dusty frames held pictures that drew Breksta closer.

To the left was a picture of a young man with bright eyes. The man was standing in front of a beach, smiling the widest smile Breksta had ever seen. His hair was tightly curled and dark brown, while freckles dusted his nose and cheeks. The man looked happy and carefree. Beside that photo was another with the same man but older. The man, whose hair had begun to gray, had his arm around a woman. Breksta gasped sharply, not believing the image in front of her. She picked it up and examined it, tracing the edges of the photograph as if she could reach the people in it. The woman looked almost exactly like Breksta, whose smile Breksta dreamed of. It was her mother.

Breksta didn't have time to process this further when a truck pulled into the driveway of the house. Breksta gripped the photo tightly before turning to face the door and whoever would come through. The answers were close, and she *would* get them.

The front door swung open, and an old man with tightly curled white hair lumbered in. He wore a plain gray shirt and unflattering khaki pants. Breksta's eyes never left his face as her hands clenched the photograph.

"What do you want?" the man said, obviously agitated and confused. "Who are you?"

"Are you Aristotle?" Breksta said quickly.

"That depends on who's asking," the man said hesitantly.

"I'm here for answers about my magic," Breksta said.

Aristotle looked at Breksta curiously, scrunching his eyebrows in confusion. "Is that your plane out back?" he asked suspiciously.

Breksta frowned. "Yes. Now answer—"

"So … the Academy has come for me," Aristotle said through clenched teeth.

"No. I came on my own terms," Breksta said proudly, savoring the taste of freedom.

"Then why do you have one of their planes?" Aristotle asked.

"I used the plane to get here. To escape."

"A runaway," Aristotle said as a statement rather than a question. "Quite a dangerous occupation."

"I can take care of myself. And I didn't come here for my questions to go unanswered," Breksta said firmly.

Aristotle lowered himself into the chair near the door and gestured for Breksta to take a seat as well. He clasped his hands together and looked at her intriguingly. "I'm waiting."

Breksta sat, her elbows on the table as she spoke earnestly. "My name is Breksta Vilkas. Yesterday, an earthquake devastated the Academy, and for some reason, I had some power that helped me survive. I escaped the Academy to try and figure out what my path forward is. I still don't know what my magic is, and you're the only person who can help me. Please…"

Aristotle didn't speak immediately. Rather, he looked to where her hands still clutched the photograph and took it from her with a bittersweet smile.

"I should have known the moment I saw you. Your mother … she was my most brilliant student."

Breksta leaned forward. Her powers could wait. The buried memories of her mother surfaced, and the childlike yearning for her mother overtook the questions about her own abilities. She pointed to the dark-haired man beside her mother in the photograph. "Is this you in the photograph?"

"No," Aristotle said after some hesitation. "That is your father, Menuo."

Breksta felt her pulse quicken. She wasn't expecting so many surprises in one day, but she welcomed them. Asteria had never spoken of Breksta's father, despite Breksta's questions, and to find someone who knew both of her parents was the closest she would get to seeing them again.

"What was he like?" Breksta blurted.

Aristotle smiled warmly. "He was charming and funny and yet could pierce the veil of silence that your mother often fell in as she planned the revolution. He could read her mind and soul like his own. Even before they were lovers, he knew her as a great friend. And when your mother knew she was pregnant with you during the revolution, when she was afraid for your life and her own, your father was her comfort. However, your mother was still a large part of the Dreamer rebellion. They launched small protests against the government, making her a target of the government at the time, which is now known as the Academy. But underneath all the push for reform, after you were born, your mother cared mostly about your safety and your father's.

"But … why did they go to the capital and fight?" Breksta asked.

"Well, your father knew that your mother had the power to lead the Dreamers. She was someone the Dreamers looked to in times of trouble and aspired to in times of greatness. Her magic was transformative. Coming directly from the realm of Morpheus, the realm of dreams, it was the magic of space and night. Whatever she visualized could be made to appear … if she had enough energy."

Breksta paused, remembering the dark day when her mother had died. The memory flooded back—the fear, the running, the agony at watching her mother's body fall into the leaves, her mother cold and lifeless. But through the haze of grief, she remembered her mother's magic, the strange dark mist—with blues and white stars as well as specks of orange from the clouds of gas surrounding the stars—the color of galaxies that emanated from her mother's hands. And she understood now.

"I remember," Breksta breathed. "I remember her magic. It was like a river of the Milky Way."

Aristotle's eye twinkled with a knowing look. "Yes. Her magic was strong, stronger than most. She lived here while she was training as my student, and that was when she met your father."

Breksta found that the idea of both her and her parents discovering magic at the same place, with the same teacher, was comforting. It was almost like a part of Asteria and Menuo were there with her, watching over their daughter as she found her own way in the world. Breksta smiled and felt happiness swell inside her; this truly was the beginning of a change, the beginning of her *own* life.

"Please, tell me more," Breksta asked as she sat attentively.

Aristotle chuckled. "Of course, Breksta. You deserve that much. Ah, where was I … yes, I remember now. It was the time before the attack on the White House. Your father came for advice regarding the situation with the Dreamers. He favored the idea of attacking the government while the Dreamers still had the numbers. It was the day after the announcement from the president decreeing the persecution of Dreamers due to the potential danger of our magic.

"Your mother had wanted to fight the government directly earlier, but once she was pregnant with you, she couldn't bring herself to take that stance. Many Dreamers knew of her power and looked to your mother. After you were born, your father convinced your mother to launch an attack on the Dreamers, for your sake, for the purpose of securing a better life for you. Along with their friends, the other Dreamers, they took out their president and this country's leadership. Your father … he unfortunately was killed during the fight at the White House. But he never gave up, he always fought for you and your mother, and he died doing what he thought was best to secure a better world for you," Aristotle said gently.

Aristotle's words broke apart the barred chest where Breksta had kept the anger, sadness, and grief locked up, and the emotions came rushing out. She covered her mouth to stop the sobs, but they racked her body, causing a growing pain in her chest. The thought of her parents, and anyone who loved her so dearly the way she knew her mother did, hurt more than any injury she'd ever sustained. The thought of her parents' love for her made her both relieved that someone out there in the world had cared for her so deeply, but it also made her scared. Would she ever experience such love again in her life? If she did, could she endure the heartbreak if she lost them?

Aristotle moved to comfort Breksta, placing a gentle hand on her shoulder. "How much you have suffered all alone, dear child, I cannot comprehend. But I know that you take after your mother in your strength and resilience."

Through her tears, Breksta asked, "You truly believe that?"

Aristotle nodded with a bittersweet smile. "I haven't seen you since your mother brought you here when you were only a few years old. I see now that you don't remember it."

Breksta shook her head, the memory of her mother resurfacing, causing more tears to fall down her cheeks. Her mother's kind smile and bubbly aura felt as if it were sitting next to Breksta.

"I have forgotten many things about her," Breksta said, her eyes downcast.

When Aristotle did not speak, Breksta looked up and saw that he studied her with a curious smile. "You have her spirit. That is enough."

Breksta paused, taking time to clean her face and stop her tears before she spoke again. "I want to take after more than that. I want to learn how to use my abilities, the same way my mother used hers," Breksta said confidently.

"...I'm sorry. I cannot help you," Aristotle said, looking away from her.

Breksta could see him shrink within himself. "What do you mean?"

"This path, the path of magic, is darker than you know, with dangerous consequences. If you wish to talk about your parents, I'm willing. But I can't teach you. I *won't*," he said, standing and crossing the room to the fridge.

"Why not?" Breksta asked anxiously. "I can't go back to the Academy. I refuse to believe that my friends and I sacrificed everything so that you could tell me no. Don't you care about your own people?"

Aristotle opened the fridge and pulled out an ugly, translucent-brown beer bottle and popped open the cap. He closed the fridge and threw the beer cap into the adjacent trash bin before taking a long sip. He didn't meet Breksta's eyes as he put down the bottle on the wooden kitchen counter. And when he looked up again, she saw the overwhelming pain engraved in his face and eyes.

"I cared too much for my people. Don't you think it has hurt me? Watching on television as your Academy put bullets into their brains. Or sending letters to friends and getting no reply after months, until the only explanation was that they had been hunted down and slaughtered. I have watched the Academy win, destroying teachers and students, friends and lovers, because of their blood and their magic. So do not lecture me on sacrifice, something you know nothing about."

Anger flushed Breksta's cheeks as she stood and raised her voice. "Sacrifice? My mother, my own mother, died because of me. She was shot in front of me, and I did nothing. The woman who killed her is still alive, the director, and I have done nothing to avenge my mother," Breksta spat.

Aristotle's eyes shone with tears of sympathy. "That is a terrible burden, child, but—"

"No," she shouted. "There is *nothing* you can say that will justify you staying out of this fight. My mother is gone, and the least I can do is take after her memory and make sure no one will ever feel what I have endured."

Aristotle was silent, and Breksta felt her deepest memories unearthed. The scene of her mother's death flashed in front of her, with the seeping, red hole that smoked on her mother's forehead. Her mother's tears and fearful eyes looking at Breksta just before the director pulled the trigger. And with that death, she remembered her grief. She remembered the nights spent crying in her bed with Hestia at her side, brushing her hair and speaking in soft, soothing tones.

Finally, Aristotle spoke in a slow, quiet voice. "Thank you for telling me that."

Breksta's anger lessened. "Why?"

"I needed to hear it. I have blinded myself for too long to the problems of the world," Aristotle confessed, finishing the last of his beer and throwing the bottle into the trash. "The world isn't so simple anymore, and the least I can do for your mother is make sure you can take care of yourself and use your magic.

She told me she wanted only happiness for you. That's why she taught you so much. She taught you so you could become better than she was."

Breksta hesitated before asking, "And am I?"

Aristotle smiled warmly. "Maybe or maybe not. But wouldn't you like to find out?"

Breksta nodded.

Aristotle moved himself into his chair, speaking more to himself. "Where shall we begin?"

She thought first of the Under Passage and Erebus. "My magic first awakened after the Academy was attacked yesterday with a massive earthquake by the Dreamers—"

"The earthquake wasn't our doing," Aristotle said frowning. "It was the Academy's."

"Why would the Academy attack itself?"

Aristotle sighed. "The persecution of Dreamers caused it."

Breksta's brows scrunched in confusion.

Aristotle paused, taking a calculated look at Breksta. "You truly didn't know?"

She shook her head. "Know what?"

"This problem has lasted for years, with small natural disasters around the world. The true issue is that the more the Academy persecutes Dreamers, the more unstable magic becomes in the world. The world needs people with magic and people without it, to keep life balanced. By killing off most of the Dreamers, the director and your Academy have directly unbalanced the world."

Breksta bit the inside of her cheek tightly, a bad habit that left her mouth raw and sometimes bleeding. She shook her head in disbelief. "The director or anyone else in the Academy has never talked about an unbalanced world. What happens if all the Dreamers…" Breksta trailed off, but her implication was clear.

Aristotle continued coldly, "You spoke of a military assault earlier. If we are all killed, the earth will tear itself apart. All of humanity will die."

"What do you mean?" she breathed.

Aristotle spoke slowly before continuing. "It's very complicated, Breksta. The realm of the most powerful deity, Nyx, is the origin of all gods and goddesses, and therefore is the origin of Dreamers. However, if there are no Dreamers left, that realm that holds the magic of Dreamers will no longer have a host for the magic to be gifted. The realm needs a way to release the vast amount of magic it houses, and therefore the magic won't go to people but will drift into this world through rifts in the border of our reality. Pure magic is something very dangerous, and without Dreamers as hosts who were born with the ability to hold magic, the magic embeds itself into regular humans, animals, and any type of life, including the earth herself. However, these *replacement hosts* cannot take that type of power and therefore all will corrupt … all will be destroyed."

Once again, Breksta was speechless. What began as a simple mission for Breksta to learn about her magic and history was now a matter of worldly importance. She had hoped that after she learned about her magic, she could finally live her own life, away from the Academy, with Hestia. She had planned to create a life of her own and put the dark days of her mother's death and the Academy behind her. But now how could she?

The destruction the director was wielding against the Dreamers wasn't only a matter of violence against Dreamers but an apocalyptic event for all of humanity. It didn't matter if the director, or anyone else in the Academy, knew about the environmental damages being created. What mattered was who could and would stop the world from descending into darkness and humanity being erased from existence.

"So, the director, by killing the Dreamers, is killing all of humanity? That's … genocide," Breksta said slowly, finally understanding.

"Hasn't it always been? Humans only care about what affects them. The director acted out of her own vengeance and need for *cleansing* without regard for the consequences to the rest of humanity and our world. Even if she understood the consequences of her actions and wanted to change, setting humanity on the road to healing, she wouldn't have the power to do so. Unfortunately, there is only one with such magic…"

"Who is it?" Breksta asked. She now understood the fate the world was heading toward, and she felt compelled to try and help as much as she could, even if it meant finding this particular Dreamer.

Aristotle's gaze lingered on Breksta. "I'm still waiting. But enough. You came to me for answers, and I have answered about your mother and your father but not your magic. Explain your magic to me. Describe its looks and effects."

Aristotle laced his fingers and studied Breksta.

Breksta straightened. "My abilities saved me and took me out of a collapsed building. There was a purple light. And then there was a boy, Erebus—"

"Erebus?" Aristotle interrupted, his eyes blazing with confusion. "How is that possible? He's dead."

"He said that I had given him energy or perhaps life even, but eventually, he disappeared."

Aristotle's eyes lit up. "Incredible … follow me."

"Where are we going?" Breksta asked, after following Aristotle outside.

"To grab a shovel," he said, rummaging through a bin beside the house. He pulled out a rusted shovel and raced to the edge of his property to where a tree stood.

"Dig right here," he instructed. "There is something important for your power that I buried long ago."

Breksta nodded and began digging. When the hole was a foot deep, Breksta's shovel clanged against something hard in the ground. She cleared the dirt from the object and found a metal container. Together, they hefted the box up and set it on the ground. Aristotle ran back inside and returned with a silver key that he inserted into the box. He turned the key and flicked open the box to reveal a dirt-covered, leather-bound book. With a slight smile, Aristotle pulled it out and opened the book to a specific page.

Breksta peeked over at the book curiously. "What is this book?"

Aristotle swallowed quickly before speaking. "Are you familiar with the Greek lineage of gods?"

"Not particularly," Breksta said, crossing her arms.

"We Dreamers draw our powers from Morpheus, the god of dreams. He is our original father."

"The Academy history class on Dreamers addressed Morpheus before," Breksta said, gesturing for Aristotle to continue.

"Morpheus is the son of Somnus or Hypnos, whether you believe in Greek or Roman mythology. And Hypnos is in turn the son of Nyx, the primordial deity of night, and her children are the gods and goddesses of various other things, including days, fate, and in some cases, witchcraft and death."

"She's the grandmother of Morpheus?" Breksta confirmed, squinting at the worn page that showed an old painting of Nyx standing tall. "What does that have to do with the magic of Dreamers or my own?"

Aristotle smiled. "You ask the right questions. Morpheus is powerful, but he is not as powerful as Nyx. And you said you possess the gift of energy-giving, or what modern-day humans call necromancy?"

Breksta's eyes widened as she shook her head affirmatively.

Aristotle nodded before continuing in a soft voice. "It seems that your power is greater than any Dreamer before. But most importantly, your power doesn't come from Morpheus. It—"

"Comes from Nyx," Breksta guessed, feeling a surety inside her.

"Your power comes from the origin of all magic, and that gives you immense power. The effects of that magic can affect a larger amount of people. Some have control over the weather, or flora, or healing. But you, Breksta, it's likely that you have the power of the gods and goddesses, the power of the dead, and the realm of the dead in your veins. You must believe in your own strength; you can do more than you allow yourself to think possible. The one I have been waiting for may very well be…"

Breksta felt the hard truth of Aristotle's words, and she finally understood, finishing Aristotle's sentence: "Me."

Aristotle nodded, his eyes bright with joy and hope. He looked at her as if she might hold all the answers and solutions in the world. Perhaps she did, but Aristotle's encouraging looks didn't soothe Breksta's worry. Perhaps what Aristotle said about her being the one was true, but perhaps it wasn't. This journey was for Breksta to learn about her mother and her magic, but now she was afraid it had become a journey to save humanity from its impending self-destruction. If she couldn't learn and discover her full potential, there would be no more world or life to live, and her tenure at the Academy and the memories of her life with her mother would all disappear. Her life would've been meaningless. So Breksta steeled her nerves. She had adapted to the Academy, learning a new way of life before. Now she had to apply those skills and learn about her magic.

"Don't doubt yourself," Aristotle said, shoving the book under his arm. Smiling, he added, "The dead gods and your mother smile upon us, I know it. Now prepare yourself, it's time to find out what is the strength of your spirit."

CHAPTER 25

THE MORNING AFTER BREKSTA'S ESCAPE, Hestia and Ms. Adams stood next to the director, facing the cadets, which included Icarus. No one had slept since Breksta's escape. Some of the cadets focused on restoring power to the electrical grid, while a team led by Icarus worked through the night to clean up the piles of debris left in the hangar during the fight to stop Breksta's escape. Hestia and Ms. Adams had overseen the work, directing cadets to their various tasks and helping however they could. As they worked, Hestia had felt the cadets' restless energy, as their fear and anger grew toward the Dreamers. Even now, as the cadets sat in front of the director, Hestia, and Ms. Adams, they fidgeted and glanced nervously around, as if waiting for the vengeful spirits of Dreamers to materialize. In a twenty-four-hour period, their world had shifted underneath their feet, and the Academy that once brought the cadets solace and security no longer existed.

Hestia also had heard whispers about Breksta's escape. Some insinuated that Breksta had caused the earthquake and that she had been a Dreamer spy for years. Others thought Breksta was reverting to the ways of Dreamers, just like Breksta's mother had done. The cadets saw Breksta's escape as a betrayal of the Academy. This betrayal unearthed questions regarding the motives behind the events of the past days. What had really caused the earthquake? What were the Dreamers planning? And why would a cadet leave?

The director's lack in addressing the matter only added to the fear and anxiety of the cadets. It was because of these growing fears and anxieties that Hestia recommended her mother hold an address to soothe the worries of the cadets. Hestia also had her own motives.

Not only was she trying to stall the war preparations to protect her friend but also to protect the Dreamers. If what Breksta said about Dreamers was true, that Dreamers only wanted to exist in this world alongside the rest of humanity, then Hestia was unsure whether this war was truly justified. Couldn't they all have peace? She didn't know, but such thoughts had plagued her since Breksta's departure.

Hestia grappled with another contradiction as well. The feelings of warmth, acceptance, and pride made her smile when her mother accepted her as her second. She wondered if her mother, underneath the layers of the cold director, had been trying to take care of Hestia all along. Had her mother gone through so much pain and hardship just to protect Hestia? If so, could Hestia now stand beside that mother, taking her rightful place as the director's true second-in-command?

The director cleared her throat before speaking, and the cadets settled in quietly to listen. "Welcome, cadets. It has been brought to my attention by my daughter, Hestia, that most of you have questions regarding the events of the past twenty-four hours. I am here to speak about it. First, however, I have some important announcements to make."

The director clasped her hands together and glanced at Hestia.

"First," the director began again, pulling Hestia closer to her as Hestia tried not to shrug her away. "I am very proud to properly introduce my second-in-command. My daughter, Hestia."

What first began as soft applause grew into a loud bravado. Cadets smiled at her, some for the first time, and Hestia smiled back despite herself. This was who she was always supposed to be. The girl beside her mother. The future leader. Yet she couldn't forget Breksta's promise, "I will come back for you." The thoughts of escape and finding a life of her own away from her mother's controlling grasp lingered in her mind. All she needed to do was wait a little longer. In the meantime, she would enjoy these moments with her mother, who was finally treating her like her daughter.

"Second, Hestia will help us launch our attack on the last of the Dreamers who are hiding out on the West Coast. We will finally wipe them out, once and for all."

The cadets cheered even louder. They used to hate blindly, based on what the Academy fed them. But now they had a reason. Otherwise, why would an earthquake happen if it were not the Dreamers' doing? Hestia knew that the cadets were out for blood, and when it was spilled, they would feel no remorse.

"Those are the first two announcements," the director said, smiling. "We will begin preparations for the battle tonight, as I have already begun planning with the senior cadets on strategic, simultaneous attacks. Finally, my last announcement. Bring him in."

From the doors behind the cadets, two senior cadets dragged in a man wearing tattered clothes. They forced the man to his knees in front of the director, but he kept his eyes on the ground, never looking up at her.

"This man," the director said with a lioness's snare, "is a Dreamer we searched for years to capture. He is called Fukushima Yuudai. His abilities originate from his mind and can compel those near him to think, act, or feel in certain ways. He cannot force you to do anything if you absolutely resist. However, if any fragment of your mind holds doubt, he can coerce you to complete a task or think how he wants you to think. It's because of these abilities that he eluded us for years. His crimes are many. He defied the presidential order for prosecution of Dreamers, hid and protected Dreamers, and most importantly, he resisted capture and ultimately the will of the Academy. Yet, he is the most powerful weapon in the world. Our best scientists and researchers have performed many tests on this subject, this Dreamer. Now he will help us alter the course of history and bring the rebellious Dreamers to heel, forever."

The cadets marveled and gasped at the kneeling Dreamer, the furthest back in the crowd standing up to get a better look.

The director snapped her fingers, and a senior cadet materialized by her side. "Bring in the traitor."

"Yes, Madam Director," the cadet replied without hesitation.

He exited the hangar and returned, dragging a female cadet kicking and screaming. To Hestia's dismay, it was Olivia bound with ropes around her waist and hands. The cadet threw her at Hestia's feet. Olivia looked pleadingly to Hestia, but Hestia looked away, not able to bear the idea that Olivia had sacrificed all chance of a normal life in the Academy by agreeing to help Breksta escape. Hestia now knew that the cadets must have captured Olivia after the electrical grid sabotage. She wished they would not hurt her further but knew that was unlikely.

The director began speaking in a booming voice thick with disgust, "This misguided cadet helped our traitorous cadet, Breksta Vilkas, escape."

Cadets gasped and glared angrily at Olivia, but she was too preoccupied to see their anger. Instead, she looked up fearfully at the director.

"She has lost her way, moving away from the Academy's teaching. Her actions were treasonous, but since she is still young, I will show her mercy."

Olivia's eyes relaxed, and she stopped struggling.

"I am offering her a second chance to serve the Academy by tracking down the true traitor, Breksta Vilkas. But we must have some security measures in place. Olivia will be the first to experience the power of this Dreamer."

Olivia's eyes widened as the director commanded the senior cadet to her to kneel beside the Dreamer. The rest of the cadets cheered; they yearned to see the Academy's power. Hestia suppressed a shiver of disgust and looked up at the ceiling.

The director turned to Hestia. "I want you to hold her down; the Dreamer's procedure needs some time to complete."

Hestia hesitated and shook her head before whispering, "Mom … what are you going to do to her? She's my friend."

"She *was* your friend. She has committed traitorous acts and must be punished. I have spared her from the worst in the name of your past friendship. You should be overjoyed," the director spoke sternly.

"Why?" Hestia whispered back, for despite trying to play the part her mother wanted, she still had to try to save her friend from her mother's punishment.

"Treason is under my jurisdiction and can be punishable by death," the director pronounced, her face unrelenting.

Hestia bit her cheek and closed her eyes. She knew the game her mother was playing. This was not merely a test for Olivia, but a test for Hestia to prove her loyalty. To prove that she would choose the Academy above all else. Yet, the Academy stood in the face of the ethics, integrity, and kindness that Hestia fought to keep alive in herself. If she had to sacrifice her own moral code that she'd tried to preserve since she was young, what hope did the world have in righting itself and peacefully coexisting? *It is just once*, Hestia told herself. She would compromise her morals for her mother this one last time. But one thing was clear: she *needed* to get out of here.

She swallowed before nodding. "Alright."

"Stand her up," the director instructed as Hestia moved to stand behind Olivia, pulling her up by her restraints.

Olivia twisted as Hestia brought her to a standing position and whispered, "Please, I'm sorry for anything I did wrong. Hestia … what's going to happen?"

Hestia moved to stand in front of Olivia and held her shoulder reassuringly. "It … everything's going to be alright, Olivia." Hestia leaned into Olivia and whispered, "I'll find some way to fix this. I'm sorry."

Olivia turned her head to face Hestia, as tears pooled on her lower lashes and her lower lip quivered. "You … promise?" she asked.

Hestia knew the power of promises, for she herself was waiting on one. Hestia wouldn't let Olivia lose hope. "I promise," she told her.

Olivia turned and stopped struggling as Hestia placed a steadying hand on Olivia's left shoulder.

The director leaned close to the Dreamer, whispering so only Hestia and Olivia could hear. "Erase all traces of resistance in her mind."

Understanding what was about to happen, Hestia was horrified. She masked her horror by digging her nails into the palms of her hands, drawing blood. She hadn't believed her mother could be this despicable, this inhuman. But Hestia realized she had never truly known her mother until now.

Mr. Fukushima swallowed and raised a shaking finger to touch the center of Olivia's forehead as a yellow glow spread on Mr. Fukushima's skin, the same yellow glow that Icarus had seen earlier. Icarus was certain Mr. Fukushima did not want to use his abilities to cause harm to anyone and wondered if Olivia would suffer.

Olivia let out a sharp gasp and watched helplessly as the yellow light traveled up Mr. Fukushima's arm to the tip of his finger that touched Olivia's forehead. The yellow magic lit up the room, as if a small sun were present in the room in front of Hestia. As soon as the yellow light reached Olivia's skin, her eyes glowed with yellow light, and she began to thrash violently. Hestia tightened her grip on Olivia's shoulders, biting her lip to keep from yelling at Mr. Fukushima to stop.

"Let go," the director said calmly.

"She'll fall over," Hestia said, keeping her voice monotone.

"Let go."

Hestia obliged, kneeling slowly to at least lower Olivia so that if Olivia fell, she would not hit her head badly. But to her surprise, Olivia continued thrashing with her eyes wide and her mouth open, as her body floated in the air.

"She's floating!" a cadet said out loud.

"The Dreamer is cursing her, stop him!" someone else called out.

"Silence!" the director commanded, waving her hand across the room.

Hestia did everything she could to keep from reaching out to her dear friend to help her. Instead, she shamefully stood by her mother, watching helplessly as Mr. Fukushima's yellow magic continued to surround Olivia. It seemed like hours before Mr. Fukushima moved his finger from Olivia's forehead as she floated just above the ground. Olivia collapsed to the ground, and Hestia rushed to catch her. With frantic eyes, Olivia scanned Hestia's face for answers.

"What happened?" Olivia asked, looking around at the room full of stunned cadets.

Hestia looked to her mother, silently asking permission to tell Olivia the turbulent events that had passed. The director shook her head.

"The director just gave an address. You passed out and fell over, that is all," Hestia whispered, helping Olivia stand. Olivia nodded, as if what Hestia said made perfect sense, and took her place at Hestia's side.

The director knelt in front of Olivia, taking her arm gently. "You need some rest, cadet. I will check in with you after you go with Ms. Adams to visit the nurse."

"As you wish, Madam Director," Olivia said, lowering her head in a small bow. Ms. Adams quickly moved from her place to the left of the director to take Olivia's hand and lead her away.

As soon as Olivia left the room, the cadets began clamoring for the director's attention.

"What did the Dreamer do to her?"

"What will happen to her now?"

"Silence, cadets!" the director shouted. "I understand that you all have questions. Understand that those who defy the Academy will be subjected to the same correction as she was. Show your best selves in the coming days, and you shall be greatly rewarded after the war is won," she said, her eyes showing a combination of temper and a hint of mania that Hestia had never seen before.

Breksta's escape must have touched memories and trauma that the director had only spoken about to Hestia on one occasion. Hestia knew her mother was a strong, unyielding woman, but perhaps Breksta's escape and Olivia's betrayal had shaken the director's faith in her Academy, and in turn, shaken the director's faith in herself. Hestia found her mother's eyes to be rage-filled, watching with an almost malicious glee as Olivia was led out of the room.

For a moment, Hestia was ashamed that she had helped Breksta escape. Not only did she lose one friend, but she also let another lose her memories. She could clearly see now the dark and corrupted heart of her mother. Hestia understood that despite being her mother's daughter, she would be better off nameless, without ties to this evil woman. Hestia closed her eyes tightly for a moment, wishing she could open them and discover that the cold, dark world around her had disappeared and been replaced with simple beauties, nature, and kind friends.

In response to the display of the Academy's power, the cadets clapped. Hestia clapped along with them, watching as her mother smiled, obviously now seeing Hestia as the daughter she had shaped her to be. Hestia knew that she had passed this test, a test of loyalty to the Academy and her family. Knowing that Hestia had sacrificed her friend's mind to pass this test, Hestia's heart broke; she felt as if her ethics were being bent over backwards and her integrity was being ripped away. Hestia wished more than ever for Breksta's return, despite Hestia knowing rationally that Breksta needed to leave. In her heart, Hestia wished dearly for Breksta's company because Breksta was the port in a hurricane just as Hestia had been to Breksta. They were each other's touchstones. And Hestia feared that if Breksta was gone too long, the ethical and kind Hestia who Breksta knew would not exist when Breksta returned.

But Hestia said nothing as she and the director began preparations for war.

After hours of staring at maps and troop positioning, Hestia's eyes burned. She felt her head sink toward the table no matter how hard she tried to hold it up. Her body yearned for sleep, but her mind yearned for freedom. She had to stay awake. She was patiently waiting for the moment when she could contact Breksta about the new developments in mind control by the director.

"Hestia, are you still listening?" the director scolded.

"Of course, Madam Director," Hestia said quickly, saved by the habits of protocol.

The director sighed and pinched the bridge of her nose tightly. "We must focus on this mission, cadets. Our plans are already in motion, and we must attack in the coming weeks."

"Yes, Madam Director," the cadets spoke uniformly, yet obviously exhausted.

Looking around, the director paused, before she spoke to Ms. Adams and the cadets in the war room. "Let's reconvene here in the morning. Go get some sleep."

Calls of "thank you, ma'am" and "goodnight, Madam Director" echoed throughout the room. Hestia relaxed her body slightly and kept her joy at the possibility of escape from seeping through her expression. This was her chance, and she would take it.

"Goodnight, Mom," Hestia said softly, pushing open the door before looking back at her mother's stone expression one last time.

"Goodnight, Hestia," the director said without turning to look at her.

Hestia crept through the stairwell until she reached the hangar's level. She slid the key her mother had given her, the perks of being her mother's second, into the door and raced to the control panel. The plane Breksta had chosen was one of their newest models, perfect for her clandestine mission, which allowed her to stay undetected and land in difficult terrain.

She found the plane's signal and whispered into the microphone, "Breksta? Are you there? It's Hestia. I-I know it's only been a day, but I really need your help. My mom—the director is going to start a war and will start controlling everyone! She has a plan to attack the remaining Dreamer strongholds in the west and to use a Dreamer with mind-controlling abilities on all unfaithful cadets as well as Dreamers. It's only a matter of time before she guesses that I was a part of your escape. She's hurting me, Breksta; my conscience cannot bear this any longer. I know I said I could take care of myself, but … I need you. You need to get me out of here now! Please … you promised. Just—"

"Hestia, my dear. What could you possibly be doing here?" a cold voice sounded behind her.

Hestia whipped around and came face to face with her mother, who stood flanked by two cadets. Fear coursed through her veins. But before either one of them could move, Hestia turned back to the panel and pressed the black button that sent the message out to Breksta.

The director approached angrily. "I gave you the chance to stand by my side, your own mother's side. Why would you throw that away for the enemy, someone who tainted you and poisoned our family?"

Hot tears formed in Hestia's eyes as she snapped, "She's my friend, more than you ever were. And she was never the enemy, neither were the Dreamers. They were all innocent. You were the enemy all along. You … you twisted me, changed me, made me into something I despise."

"No, I'm shaping you to reach the fullest of your potential," the director declared.

"And what is that potential? The potential to kill others? To murder those who just want to live their lives? Like Breksta's mother?" Hestia shouted back.

Hestia knew she had touched a nerve as the director's eyes widened and her nostrils flared.

"How dare you mention that woman! The woman who killed our family!" the director screamed.

"Have you ever considered how hunting her and killing her might have affected you? How it changed you? You never paid any attention or cared for me; everything was about killing her and the Dreamers! I was your daughter, and you only ever cared if I followed in your footsteps. You treated my best friend like she was nothing. She was someone who I had to help piece back together and protect from this world that you said you supposedly built to protect all of us. You don't even know who I am, and you don't care. You aren't and never were my mother. You're a selfish, hateful woman, and I hate you!" Hestia looked at her with fury in her eyes. All love she'd felt for this woman had evaporated.

The director's eyes bulged and then narrowed. The emerging mania Hestia had noticed earlier in her mother's eyes was now unleashed, and Hestia knew she had overstepped. Her relationship to her mother would no longer protect her. Hestia didn't know what her mother was capable of doing to her, so she ran out of the hangar. She heard the cadets behind her giving chase as the director shouted out orders. Hestia could hear their thundering footsteps coming closer as she ran toward the elevator. She pressed the buttons frantically. Suddenly, the cadets were upon her.

"Secure her!" the director shouted.

The cadets descended upon her like lions descend upon their kill: with merciless and swift action. Hestia, in her defense, was able to hold off many assailants, punching the vulnerable parts of their bodies and sweeping their legs out from under them. The cadets fell one by one, but each one who fell was replaced by five more. Soon, there were too many, even for Hestia, and she found an arm wrapped tightly around her neck. Hestia ripped at the arm, clawing her fingernails, and drawing blood on the cadet's arm, but the cadet merely cried out and continued their chokehold. Blackness closed in on Hestia's vision as her consciousness slipped away. The last thing she saw was the opening of the elevator doors, the unreachable hope, then nothing.

CHAPTER 26

BREKSTA IMMEDIATELY BEGAN training with Aristotle. They traveled in his dented and marred truck to the site where Aristotle planned to teach her magic. As they drove toward the looming mountains, Aristotle pressed a button on the truck's dashboard, and soft guitar music streamed through the speakers. The dense green trees flew by as Breksta and Aristotle zoomed past, zipping left and right on the road over streams and past herds of chestnut-colored deer. A few songs later, they passed under a white arch covered with spiraling ivy. A few meters behind the arch, a dark wooden sign read, "Moran State Park" in white carved letters.

"It's so beautiful here," Breksta murmured, leaning her head out the window. She put out her hand and brushed it against the green and red leaves they passed, the tips poking her hand as she touched them.

Aristotle looked over at Breksta fondly and said, "Your mother thought so as well."

The mention of her mother saddened her, but Breksta was proud that she could say she was learning about her magic as her mother did. Aristotle noticed her sudden silence.

"She would've been proud of you."

Breksta looked at him as a small smile crept onto her face. "You think so?"

Aristotle kept his eyes on the road as he spoke softly, "From what I know of the Academy, getting to this island couldn't have proven easy. You braved the challenges to get here all alone. Yes, she would be very proud."

Breksta thought about correcting Aristotle to say that she hadn't been alone. She had Hestia with her, but Breksta didn't know if Aristotle would understand. Breksta allowed herself to smile broadly. She watched the woods and meadows go past, wishing her mother was with her to show Breksta all her favorite places. Breksta knew how her mother would have loved to explore this island, just as they had explored their home together.

Soon, Aristotle pulled into an empty parking lot near the top of the mountain. A small dirt road curved farther up the mountain a few meters to where a looming stone building stood. Together, they made their way to the top, and Breksta found they were far above the lakes and natural life below. The mountain overlooked the land border to Canada.

"This is one of the powerful energy reservoirs of this island, a place where the magic of the realms of the gods and goddesses spills into our world," Aristotle said.

He walked to the edge of the mountainside, where a stone wall stood as a protective barrier. He slung his legs over the wall and sat, unfazed by the height and closeness of the mountain's edge.

Breksta swallowed nervously. "Do we have to sit right here?"

"You won't fall."

Breksta wasn't reassured but slowly inched herself over the stone barrier. She kept her hands wrapped around the stones so tightly that her knuckles turned snow-white.

"I want you to look around you, Breksta. What do you see?"

To her left lay the blue ocean that eventually reached the land Breksta had flown over, but to her right lay three lakes. Two lakes were connected like twins in the same womb. And the last was larger than both, standing alone at the closest edge of the island. A large cut in the center of the island, now filled with water, carved the island into a crescent.

"I see the island. I see the edge of another continent. And I see the ocean that brought me here." Breksta turned to look at Aristotle, searching for the right answers or confirmation of her own.

"And what of the people? The life?"

His face was a slab of stone—unyielding and stoic, looking out on the rest of the island. Her eyes skimmed over the rock beaches that lined the west coastline. She saw the bay that kept Aristotle's house separated from the rest of the ocean. She saw small white clusters that she could only guess were houses long abandoned to the ocean's salty breeze.

"I don't believe there are any humans here besides us. The Academy probably killed them all," Breksta said bitterly. "Why does it matter?"

"Be patient," Aristotle answered slowly, as if he had repeated this many times before. "Your power is more deeply connected to the world than most, for death is what connects all things."

Breksta scrunched her eyebrows. She had seen violence in the Academy and had never thought of it as a connecting force; her mother's death was a prime example of that. But she knew she had to keep an open mind and found that Aristotle's perspective of death was rather interesting and different from hers.

Sensing Breksta's ambivalence, Aristotle asked suddenly, "Do you have a weapon?"

"Why?" Breksta asked, bristling defensively as she put her hand on her messenger bag. She lowered her hand slowly, forcing herself to remember that here, away from the Academy, she could experience trust. Aristotle looked at her calmly and held his hand open as an indication of choice.

"Alright, I have a pistol." Breksta took out her weapon and handed it slowly to Aristotle.

"Don't be afraid," Aristotle said as he aimed the pistol away and toward the large sandstone tower behind them.

Breksta traced the pistol's trajectory, which aimed at a flock of ravens on the top of the tower. With a sharp bang, one of the ravens fell to the ground, landing with a sickening snap while the others squawked in alarm and scattered.

"Why did you do that?" Breksta exclaimed angrily, swinging her legs back over the stone barrier and racing to the raven.

The bird squawked weakly, attempting to move its wings as its life slipped away. Aristotle approached and handed the pistol back to Breksta. The Academy had stolen many things from her, but some traits were bone deep and couldn't be taken. Breksta's kindness toward animals had never left her.

She looked back at him angrily and repeated her question, "Why did you shoot it?"

"To teach you a lesson," he said, his eyes studying her intently. "Put your hands on the bird."

Breksta obliged, still confused by Aristotle's sudden change of character.

"Can you feel its heartbeat?" Aristotle asked in a quiet, calm voice.

"It's very faint," Breksta responded as she tried to focus on the animal.

Aristotle knelt beside the raven and continued, "Now, I want you to feel your own heartbeat. Feel the blood rush through your veins and hear it in your ears. Do you feel it?"

Breksta closed her eyes and took the deep breaths that Hestia had instructed her to take when she had nightmares of her mother's death years ago. The strong pulses of her heartbeat were like loud drums in her ears, drowning out her thoughts.

"Yes."

"Now, I want you to focus on finding the center of yourself. Find the center of all your energy. Can you do that?"

Breksta felt the bird's heartbeats slow, and she grit her teeth, trying to concentrate.

"Don't let outside forces influence your concentration," Aristotle scolded. "Relax your mind. Focus."

Breksta breathed deeply and let the world fall away. She felt the center of her being gather around her diaphragm, where her ribs began to split in either direction.

"Do you know where your center is?" Aristotle asked, his voice a murmur. "Just nod."

Breksta nodded.

"Good. Envision the energy of your soul. Let it concentrate completely in your center."

"I … how do I do that?" Breksta asked quietly, opening her eyes to peek at Aristotle for guidance.

"Close your eyes for me," Aristotle began, and Breksta complied. "I want you to imagine your energy as something you can hold, like thread or string. Can you imagine it?"

"Yes," Breksta said, picturing long strands of silk.

"Now I want you to pick up the threads, pull them from your body, and form them into a ball," Aristotle continued, his voice gentle.

Breksta began, imagining that she was gathering thread. The threads were her and her energy, frizzy and dismembered at first. She slowly pulled each thread, feeling her energy becoming more clearly defined, until the threads formed a ball of thick string at her center, at her diaphragm. The threads were pure white starlight but felt heavy and almost dangerous, as if they would combust if pressure were applied.

"Is your energy concentrated?"

Breksta nodded again.

"Push the energy through your heart, through your veins, and all the way to your fingertips."

Breksta nodded and allowed the threads of energy to travel in thick strands. Pain traveled from her diaphragm and chest as the energy hummed beneath her skin, straining to be released.

"Keep going!" Aristotle exclaimed.

Breksta continued, pushing the threads from her core outward. The threads now traced along her arms, and the pain diminished. The feeling of power and light remained. Breksta grit her teeth as she pushed the energy to the tips of her fingers, and she felt it escape into the raven's trembling body. Bright light flashed in front of her, and Breksta blinked open her eyes.

Purple light, an almost electrical energy, surrounded her, the same purple light she had seen when the doorframe collapsed on her in the Academy. It finally made sense. The light ran along her arms. It lingered on her fingertips, and she could only imagine what her face looked like.

She turned to Aristotle with a panicked expression. "What do I do now?"

"Let the power go. Gift it to the raven."

Breksta sucked in a breath and nodded. She pressed her fingers deeper into the raven's light feathers. This time she didn't push the threads of her energy, rather she let the energy seep out of her, like water, into the raven's body.

After a few seconds, Aristotle said, "You can stop now. The raven is alright."

Breksta again nodded and pulled back the threads of energy. But to her horror, the energy didn't respond. She looked frantically at Aristotle, who ripped her hands away from the raven.

"Call your magic back, Breksta, try to breathe," he said, his voice rising ever so slightly.

"I'm trying!" Breksta exclaimed, feeling uncontrollable fear seize her. "I can't pull it back!"

Aristotle shook his head, continuing with a calm voice, "Don't pull; call it back. It will listen to you."

Breksta closed her eyes once again, facing away from both the raven and Aristotle. She breathed deeply and connected herself with the earth, feeling its stability through her feet and legs. Breksta felt the magic swirl around her, enveloping her in its purple light. She was no longer fearful. The magic wasn't some foreign entity. It was her. For the first time in her life, she knew who she was.

Without forming a complete thought, Breksta felt a deep, intuitive feeling—a feeling of rest and the release of control that she now understood was the flow of her power. With that same feeling, she released control of the magic and allowed it to return to her center where it hummed quietly. Breksta opened her eyes and turned to Aristotle. He cradled the raven in his arms with a wide smile.

"You've done it, Breksta Vilkas."

Hearing her name sent shivers up Breksta's spine. She felt as if her soul were finally complete. She was so close to her mother that she could almost hear the whispers of her mother's lyrical voice. Breksta knew who she was now, and her soul sang. She was Breksta Vilkas, her mother's daughter, a Dreamer.

Breksta's heart soared from the remaining euphoria of magic as she and Aristotle drove back to his house. Breksta held the raven in her arms, his small body bundled in a blanket Aristotle had brought with them. She felt all powerful as she held the bird in her arms, the entity she had given life to and saved. Her magic was something intimate. Its true awakening and Breksta's ability to direct it was like unlocking some old memory inside Breksta. Something that she had forgotten but always knew was there. The raven cawed softly, bringing Breksta's attention back to the present. Although she was able to revive the bird, its injuries were still in dire need of medical assistance.

"He will be alright?" Breksta asked once again.

Aristotle sighed. "Yes, the raven will be *just fine*." Aristotle took a breath and turned to look at her with a hopeful expression. "You truly have the gift of Nyx."

Breksta's heart swelled, recognizing a feeling she hadn't experience since she was a small child. This was pure joy. She was now free from the Academy and free to make her own choices. Most of all, she felt the joy of discovering her gift. Her life would never be the same.

Breksta thought for a moment before speaking. "My gift from Nyx is extremely powerful, yes?"

"You're correct," Aristotle said smiling.

"So, if Nyx and Morpheus are all-powerful deities, why don't they stop the Academy from killing the Dreamers? Aren't the Dreamers their own descendants?"

Aristotle's face hardened. "It's not that simple. They are dead."

"Gods can die?" Breksta asked, scrunching her brows.

"They passed long before we came around. The dead remains of the gods receded to their natural elements. Nyx to the night, Morpheus to the dreams of humans. Humans were deemed too chaotic and thus were reduced to dealing with their own conflicts. Gods are only called upon in great times of trouble and sorrow."

"Why weren't they called upon when the Dreamer War began?" said Breksta after a pause.

"Please don't ask me any more questions about this," Aristotle said softly, his eyes pained.

Breksta nodded respectfully. Her questions still plagued her, but she would find another time or another way to have them answered.

"Do you have Dreamer magic?"

"My power is more of a burden than a gift. It's the power to foresee possible futures."

Breksta's eyes lit up. "You can see the future?"

Aristotle raised an eyebrow, like he had heard that reaction many times. "No, just the possibilities."

"Can you see mine?" she asked tentatively.

"I haven't used my power in years. And it shouldn't be done lightly. I have been a teacher of Dreamers for a long time now and have found that my responsibility is to be a teacher and guide only. Everyone must make their own choices, independent of my glimpses of the future," Aristotle added, as he pulled into the driveway of the house.

"Like you taught my mother?" Breksta asked cautiously. "And my father?"

Aristotle smiled as he shut off the ignition. "Yes, just like them."

Breksta wanted to ask Aristotle more questions. With the awakening of her magic, she yearned for a deeper understanding and connection with her past and her Dreamer magic, but she knew she had to proceed slowly. For the moment, they needed to tend to the bird in her arms.

The sun had already dipped below the horizon when they reached the house. The sky was still light, and the night chill had begun to set in. Breksta carefully maneuvered her way out of the truck as she held the raven.

"We need to remove the bullet and give it antibiotics," Aristotle said as he shut the car door. "Do you have medication in your plane?"

Breksta nodded, and they walked together to the plane. Breksta unlocked the plane, and they made their way to the lower level where the sleeping quarters and first aid were located. Aristotle tended to the raven's wounds when suddenly the electronic voice of the ship rang out.

"Incoming message from Academy Headquarters."

"Go, I'll deal with this," Aristotle said reassuringly.

Breksta raced up the ladder to the panel where a red blinking button flashed brightly. Breksta pressed it, and the recording of Hestia's crystal-clear voice rang through.

"Breksta? Are you there?"

"I'm here," Breksta said, preparing another message to send back as she listened to her friend. However, once she heard Hestia's entire message outlining the director's plan for war and mind control, Breksta's mind started to reel. Before she could formulate any clear thoughts, Hestia's voice was replaced by the director's. "Hestia, my dear. What could you possibly be doing here?" The sound ended abruptly.

Breksta slapped her fist against the panel. "No!" she screamed, utter dread searing through her blood.

"That was your friend, if I'm correct," Aristotle asked from behind her, his voice gentle.

"I must go help her. The director knows that she helped me, and she'll kill Hestia. The director is going to wipe out the remaining Dreamers, and my friend with them. I … I need to go," Breksta shouted, blinking back frustrated tears.

Aristotle put a gentle hand on Breksta's shoulder while the other one held the raven. "I can't let you do that," he said, his eyes sad but his voice stern and clear. "You must stay here to strengthen your magic. There is a—"

Breksta brushed off Aristotle's touch. "I promised to return, and now she needs my help. I have my magic now."

Breksta began to enter the coordinates of the Academy, but Aristotle turned her around to face him, his eyes blazing. "You cannot do this, Breksta Vilkas. You haven't even scratched the surface of your magic. And that magic is too rare and powerful for you to go in there and get yourself killed. You must understand. Your magic is the only way to restore the balance of the world. You're the only one," Aristotle emphasized. "I understand that now. You are the *only* one."

"Why must it be me? Why can't you do this? You're a Dreamer; why can't you help the world with your power?" Breksta retorted.

"It's not my destiny. It could've been your mother's, but now it's yours. Your mother would not have wanted you to abandon the world."

Breksta hesitated and considered Aristotle's words. His words brought back a rush of the promise she had made to her mother. She had promised her long ago to choose the world first. But it was only now that Breksta realized how difficult that choice was. Now she knew the consequence of leaving to help Hestia: it would lead to the destruction of the world, and it would be on her hands.

The director was already complicit in the murder of Dreamers, but Breksta would then be complicit in killing the entire world. So it wasn't actually a choice. She couldn't choose her friends over the world. Breksta knew that if Hestia were in Breksta's shoes, Hestia would, despite deep guilt, choose to save the world. Hestia had always held a deep sense of empathy for others; that was what drew Hestia to Breksta when Breksta first arrived at the Academy and made Hestia stay by Breksta's side throughout all her struggles. Breksta knew Hestia would hate her for it if Breksta chose to go back and save Hestia. Even if Breksta saved Hestia, there would be no life left for them to live.

However, Breksta wasn't yet ready to accept her helplessness at Hestia's fate. She gritted her teeth and squeezed her eyes shut. "Destiny doesn't have control over me. While I am still living and breathing, I can make my own choices. You don't know what she would have wanted," Breksta retorted.

"Do not taunt destiny, Breksta. She is unyielding and persistent. You can't outrun her. And I do know what your mother wanted. She wanted a safer world for you, and she thought that by choosing her friends and choosing to fight with the Dreamers she would restore peace to the world. She was wrong. She was one of the only people who could have used a failsafe to keep the world from destruction. If she hadn't chosen her friends, but rather the failsafe left by Nyx, this war would have ended. I know you care, Breksta. I see your great empathy for your friends and even for that raven when you ran to save it. The world needs your care and your help, Breksta, but your friends cannot live if you leave."

"What do you mean she chose her friends? You said earlier that my mom helped people," Breksta insisted.

Aristotle's eyes grew angry. "She left us, Breksta. She chose to save her closest friends instead of the Dreamers as a whole. She chose you, to take you away and leave the rest of us to die. She could have saved all humanity with the failsafe. But she lost faith—in herself, in the dead gods, and in magic. So, I beg of you, don't define yourself by your mother's actions. You can change this, once and for all."

Breksta felt tears threaten her eyes for the second time that day. Her heart was torn. She knew she couldn't choose her dearest friend, despite the pain Breksta knew Hestia would go through in the Academy. And she knew that Hestia, who lived to help others, wouldn't forgive Breksta if she chose to save her.

"What must I do? And what is the *failsafe* you keep mentioning?" Breksta finally said, her mind made up.

"You need training first. The failsafe, a flower, will need to be accessed by you when the time comes. I shall tell you the specifics tomorrow, and tomorrow we shall begin your training in earnest," Aristotle said. "Thank you, Breksta," he added.

Breksta swore she saw the twinkling of tears in his eyes, but she didn't say anything. She powered down the plane and went into the house with Aristotle. She gave the raven one of the pillows from the couch where the raven immediately curled its wings and fell asleep. Breksta collapsed on Aristotle's couch and closed her eyes, praying to dead gods for Hestia to stay alive.

CHAPTER 27

HESTIA AWOKE TO THE BRIGHTNESS of her mother's war room, tied to one of the chairs. She looked around the room frantically to gage the consequences of her actions. Unbeknownst to Hestia, a squad of twelve cadets stood at the ready behind her. In front of her was the Dreamer, Mr. Fukushima, who stood beside the director.

The director looked at Hestia with the utmost animosity. "You have committed treason against the Academy by contacting a fugitive, disobeying direct orders, and sharing top-secret information. Therefore, it has been decided that you are too dangerous to be sentenced to prison."

Hestia held her breath, almost certain that her death was approaching. It saddened her greatly that her own mother didn't only want to convict her daughter of treason but kill her. She felt immense grief for her friendship with Breksta, who she would never see again. How dearly she wished to see her friend one last time, to express all the thanks and goodbyes that she would never have a chance to say. Although her grief threatened her eyes with tears, she would die without giving her mother that satisfaction. She closed her eyes as she waited for her sentence.

"You will have the memories of your traitorous acts wiped, including the actions of your co-conspirators Olivia and the fugitive Breksta Vilkas," the director said apathetically.

Hestia's eyes snapped open. "What? You ... you can't do this. I would rather die!"

Cold dread washed over her at the thought of losing her best friend, the only real friendship she had ever had, and the only true human being she had ever known. Losing Breksta would be like losing a part of herself, a half of her soul. Their mutual dependency wasn't only how they stayed alive but why they stayed alive.

The director didn't flinch as Hestia protested and thrashed to get out of her bonds. "I can. Perhaps you should have valued our relationship more than the one with a traitor. Commence, Dreamer."

"Please," Hestia begged, her voice shaking as tears ran down her cheeks. She didn't care about saving face any longer.

"Please, I'm sorry. Don't do this! We can still find some way to make it work, Mom ... please."

To Hestia's relief, the director stopped in her tracks. Perhaps she had been swayed by Hestia's appeal to her as a mother. But to Hestia's dismay, the director responded, "You have made it clear that I'm no longer your mother. And you're no longer my daughter. Mercy doesn't look kindly upon those like you." Her eyes flaming with anger, she gestured to Mr. Fukushima to begin.

Hestia struggled in her bonds, the rope tearing and bruising her arms as she tried to break free. Mr. Fukushima looked sadly at Hestia. Even though he didn't know her, he could understand her terror and helplessness.

Hestia couldn't help her terror, and all thoughts of her dignity disappeared. She cried and tried to stand, only to have her chair held down by the cadets behind her. She attempted to scratch the cadets behind her with her nails, despite her bound hands. But her fighting was in vain as Mr. Fukushima touched Hestia's forehead with the tip of his finger and Hestia went limp.

Her mind was slowly overtaken by Mr. Fukushima's. She felt his mind tightening around hers like a snake, suppressing her thoughts even as she tried to put up walls. It was then, as she fought to keep every last part of her protected, when Mr. Fukushima spoke in her mind.

Be still, child.

No, Hestia growled.

Please listen before I alter your mind. It's of the utmost importance, and we don't have much time, Mr. Fukushima stated, his tone turning urgent.

Hestia stopped putting the walls around her mind and tried her best to relax, which proved to be difficult with another's conscience in her mind.

Good. In a few moments, I will remove the memories of the girl your director has compelled me to erase. However, I suspect, by your reaction, that she is close to your heart, Mr. Fukushima said, his voice kind and gentle.

She is, Hestia admitted, a wave of sadness hitting her, knowing she would never remember Breksta again.

I understand, child, and I'm truly sorry. But take solace in the fact that the director doesn't know the extent of my magic. It cannot truly remove memories, but rather it suppresses them, like one suppresses traumatic memories, Mr. Fukushima elaborated.

So, there might be a chance I could remember Breksta? Hestia asked hopefully.

A fraction of a chance. Understand that I shall be suppressing your memories of the girl, and consequently, you will begin to remember the love you once felt for your mother. Be aware that the suppression can cause some damage to your psyche and can also cause pain.

As long as there's a chance for me to remember Breksta, I will stay alive, Hestia stated, reaffirming to herself the memories of her long relationship with Breksta.

I will now begin, Mr. Fukushima said sadly. *Be strong, child.*

Hestia took a deep breath as she felt Mr. Fukushima search through her mind. It was a deeply intimate experience to have one search the mind of another. Hestia felt Mr. Fukushima take each and every memory of Breksta and put it in a place in her mind that she couldn't reach. With each memory, pain ricocheted through Hestia, as if Mr. Fukushima were taking the very bones from her body. The pain was excruciating as the memories flickered and were extinguished. Soon, the very last memory of Breksta, the one where Breksta had hugged Hestia tight and promised to come back for her, was gone. Hestia no longer even remembered the conversation with Mr. Fukushima. Hestia was numb, the only lingering thought was the unquestioning loyalty to her mother and the Academy.

Weakness followed immediately after she opened her eyes, and she slumped in her chair, her mind fading to black.

A deep fatigue resided in Hestia's mind as she awoke on her hard, military cot to the sound of Ms. Adams shouting at the cadets to awaken. Hestia sat up, shaking her head to rid the sleepiness from her mind, and turned to the cot on her right, expecting to find something or someone. However, she didn't remember who or what and felt a headache grow the more she tried to think. She stood and distanced herself from her strange thoughts.

Olivia mumbled quietly underneath her thin, gray blanket.

Hestia spoke in a level voice, "The director has commanded us to wake up, Olivia. You would do her and your country a disservice by not helping the war effort as much as you can."

Olivia tossed off her blankets immediately and stood, saluting Hestia for being her mother's second-in-command. "I'll get right to it, ma'am."

Ma'am, Hestia thought to herself. The word certainly had a nice ring to it after all the years in the Academy being disliked by the other cadets for her excellence in every subject. Perhaps there had been more reasons, but Hestia couldn't identify them in the cloud of sleepiness. Another headache followed. Whatever other reasons existed, she deemed them irrelevant.

Hestia made her way between the cots, waking the cadets. Once all the cadets were up, despite some groggy protesting, Hestia and Ms. Adams stood before them. The cadets looked to her with submissive expressions, the same expression they showed to the director, and Hestia smiled. This was who she was meant to be, beside her mother and beside Ms. Adams as she took up the mantle of the Academy and eventually led the cadets to secure an everlasting peace by ridding Dreamers from the world. This invasion was the beginning of it all, the beginning of victory, and Hestia never doubted it for a second. She smiled widely despite the small headache at the back of her skull.

"Today," Ms. Adams began with her hands held behind her back, "we continue our war preparations. Each of you will be put into divisions based on your regular training groups. Half of the seniors will conduct strategy sessions with the director, led by our esteemed second-in-command, Hestia." The cadets clapped with gusto, despite it being early in the morning, and smiled kindly at Hestia, who returned the smile. "The other half of the seniors will lead the lower classes in their preparations of weapons, aircrafts, and supplies."

"You are dismissed. Proceed to your stations," Hestia instructed.

She led the cadets down the stairs. They spoke to her in a friendly fashion, telling her about their excitement for the coming war and the good they will bring to the world. Hestia felt proud of the world her mother had built and the protection the Academy brought not only to her, but to hundreds of children and families dedicated to the Academy's cause of world peace. Humanity had enough of coexisting with Dreamers, these terrorists that destroyed lives and tore families like her own apart without remorse. This would be the end of centuries of conflict, and Hestia felt proud to be the one rewriting history at her mother's side.

Finally, Hestia reached the war room and led the cadets to where the director awaited. The director stood as Hestia entered the room. She smiled and Hestia returned a smile, but there was something lingering in the director's eyes—a distrust and some darker emotion that Hestia couldn't identify. Hestia was certain it was from the stress of preparing for the war, and perhaps from an escaped fugitive that Hestia had heard whispers about the night before as she fell asleep. Hestia shook herself; the thought of a fugitive worsened her headache, so she put it behind her.

"Mom!" Hestia exclaimed as she raced to embrace her mother.

The director embraced her daughter, though Hestia noticed that the director held her at a distance. Hestia didn't mind, though. She was glad to be in her mother's service, learning about leadership at the Academy to eventually become its leader.

"How was your sleep?" the director asked, a hint of suspicion in her tone.

Hestia paused. "I believe I had a dream … but I can't seem to remember it now."

The director smiled widely. "As dreams often are. Forgotten as figments of our active imagination. Let us begin our preparations."

The cadets sat, looking to the director with eager faces as she began outlining their plan. They would attack from the east, utilizing most of the hundred and fifty aircraft in an all-out assault. The cadets would be split into three groups, each attacking one of the three last strongholds of the Dreamers: San Francisco, Los Angeles, and Seattle. Each city would be attacked with large and small aircraft that would land just outside the city where the Dreamers were. The larger aircraft would carry ground troops and ground vehicles, including tanks, to the drop zones in the west. The smaller aircraft would provide aerial support, taking out the hideouts with missiles, and back up the ground troops. Together, the aircraft and ground troops would surround the Dreamers, cutting off their exits from the city, which would put an end to this long, drawn-out conflict.

Once the director finished the in-depth description of the attack, many of the cadets looked hopeless at the sheer scale of the attack. In their eyes, Hestia saw fear. These cadets needed inspiration, and Hestia would give it to them.

She stood, leaning close to her mother, and whispered, "May I speak a few words?"

The director hesitated but eventually nodded, eyeing Hestia slowly as she took a seat.

"Cadets of the Academy," Hestia began, feeling the full weight of responsibility and the attention of the cadets on her shoulders.

"I know you all have reservations about this attack—"

The director caught her hand. "Where are you going with this, my dear?" she hissed.

"Trust me," Hestia said gently, more like the Hestia Breksta knew, although Hestia did not know that. The director nodded slowly, releasing Hestia's hand.

"It won't be easy," Hestia continued. "It'll be the most difficult battle you have ever fought. These people, these … monsters, are forces of nature. They have dangerous abilities that are backed up by their unyielding faith in their gods. They are resilient, which is why they have survived for so long. But so have we. We have survived through hardship and death, bringing us to this moment where those hardships can become victories. My father and grandparents were murdered by Dreamers, and I know many of you have similar pain, but now is not a time for remembering the past. We must look to the future, the future we want for ourselves and the future for generations to come. The Academy has been our home for all our lives, and it's time to spread our home to the rest of this country, to share our values and reclaim the country that our ancestors once thrived in. We must strive for greatness, for if we wait, greatness will pass us by, and we *will* watch our enemies thrive. So, join me, in our pursuit of greatness and the end of tyranny!"

Hestia looked around at the cadets, feeling her cheeks flush from the power of her speech as well as from how well the words resonated with her soul. The cadets no longer looked afraid, and each stood, cheering and clapping for her. Hestia smiled widely, basking in the attention of the other cadets as she moved back to sit at her rightful place beside her mother. The director smiled at her as well, using one hand to tuck stray hairs behind Hestia's ear.

"You've made me so very proud, my love," the director said sincerely to Hestia.

Despite the lingering headache, Hestia smiled and felt at home.

CHAPTER 28

HAVING BEEN ON ANOTHER ASSIGNMENT from the director, Icarus didn't know about the capture of Hestia or what her fate had been. He felt a creeping sense of dread as he approached the security room where his mother had ordered him to meet her. The room held footage from various security cameras around the Academy and the bunker. Icarus had a suspicion about why his mother wanted to see him, although he still had hope it wasn't what he suspected. That hope quickly dissipated as he opened the door to his mother's terrifying gaze.

"Icarus Adams," she began, pointing to the seat for Icarus to sit in front of the fifty security monitors stuffed in the small room.

"Hello, Mother," Icarus said, forcing a cheery tone.

"Don't patronize me," Ms. Adams exclaimed.

Icarus kept a steady gaze on his mother. "Why did you call me here? You know I'm preparing for the coming war."

"Are you preparing for it? Or sabotaging it?" Ms. Adams spat. "Explain to me what in the world this is!" Ms. Adams shouted at Icarus as she pointed at one of the monitors.

The monitor showed a blurry image of Olivia and Icarus going into Ms. Adams's room to get the keys for Breksta. The image was incriminating, but Icarus was still relieved that the video was of the break-in and not of his conversation with Mr. Fukushima. Thankfully, Ms. Adams didn't know the full extent of Icarus's treachery.

"The girl lied to me," Icarus lied. "She said that the keys were for the director, and so I obliged. Aren't we taught to never disobey the director?"

Ms. Adams's eyes flared as she clenched her fists. But after a few deep breaths, the anger in her voice dissipated. "You made a grave mistake, Icarus."

Icarus hung his head, pretending for the sake of his mother. "I'm sorry. How can I make it up to you?"

Ms. Adams pondered his question before she replied, "The only way you can make up for this mistake is to catch the fugitive you let loose. That will count as your final mission to graduate."

Icarus snapped up his head to look at his mother. Perhaps this mission wasn't a way to make up for his mistake in his mother's eyes but to gain more knowledge of his father. Breksta's escape as well as the earthquake had been the catalyst for Icarus to learn more about his past. Now knowing his father's role in supporting the Dreamers, he could join Breksta in her freedom under the guise of capturing her and finally piece together his father's life. He was certain he'd also find answers for himself there. He nodded to his mother, smiling as he said, "Of course. I won't let you down."

His mother returned a stern glance. "No you won't, Icarus. For if you do, you'll have disgraced our family's name and destroy everything I have been working for."

Icarus clenched his fists, taking a deep breath to hide his true emotions as he always had and answered, "When have I ever failed?" he whispered, so tired and angry that everything he did was never enough.

"Excuse me?" his mother asked, putting a hand on Icarus's shoulder and forcing him to look at her.

"Nothing," Icarus said, twisting his shoulder away. "I'll inform the director of my mission."

With that, Icarus left his mother in the room, feeling his anger at his mother grow. A change was awakening within Icarus. He was no longer just his mother's perfect son. He was his own man, now beginning to model himself not after the Academy's perfect cadet, but after his father.

"Welcome, Icarus," the director said warmly in an out-of-character sort of way as she stood in front of her desk in the control room.

The cadets were clapping for Hestia, who was beaming in her seat. Something was different about Hestia. Her smile was brighter, and her shoulders were held farther back, as if she shouldered her new responsibility as her mother's second with ease. He couldn't understand Hestia's sudden change, so different from the Hestia who had just helped her friend Breksta escape. Perhaps it was *because of* Breksta's escape. Icarus wondered if this is who Hestia would have been if Breksta never set foot into the Academy. Icarus kept his awareness of Hestia's new personality in the back of his mind.

"Madam Director, I need to speak to you," Icarus clarified as he entered the room.

The director looked over at Icarus, the happiness in her eyes dimming slightly as she spoke. "Please give us the room. Hestia, you stay."

As the cadets filed out of the room, the director gestured to the seat opposite Hestia on her left.

"Take a seat," she said.

"Thank you," Icarus replied as he tried to relax. He needed to specifically outline the mission his mother wanted him to take, not to show any disobedience to the Academy.

"May I speak frankly, Madam Director?" Icarus asked, clasping his hands on the table.

The director nodded, leaning back in her chair as she listened.

"I know that the coming days will be filled with war preparations and training, but I have an idea that could ensure the success of this attack," Icarus said, looking between Hestia and the director as he paused intentionally.

"Proceed," Hestia cut in.

"As you both are aware, a fugitive Bre—"

"Yes, we are aware of the fugitive, and we are making it one of our priorities to take care of her," the director interrupted.

Icarus paused, looking to Hestia who touched her temples gently, wincing from some apparent pain. "Are … are you alright?" he asked.

Hestia nodded, shutting her eyes tightly. "Please, continue."

"Very well. As I was saying, this fugitive still poses a threat to the Academy's security. I propose a small, elite team track her down—"

"And end her," the director finished. "I have been considering possible candidates for such a mission."

"Well," Icarus said, feigning a smile, "I would be honored to be part of that team. I, along with Hestia, am at the top of the class, and I believe my skills in tracking as well as gun weaponry qualify me to be on this team."

The director nodded slowly. "I've been keeping track of your training in the past years, sometimes almost overtaking Hestia's … almost. I see your mother has been putting a lot of effort into your work."

Icarus smiled. "My mother enjoys perfecting my skills, and I have developed much patience and diligence in my training. Hestia has also been a good source of *friendly* competition."

The director's eyes darkened ever so slightly. "Yes, we do our best to push our cadets. I must be frank, Icarus. You *are* high on my list, but you aren't at the top. Why should I choose you instead of an already graduated senior with more experience in the field? For such a dangerous enemy, what assets do you bring to the table?"

Icarus swallowed under the director's razor-sharp gaze. "I believe that instinct is more important than experience. Yes, the graduated seniors may have more experience, but I have intuition and instinct when it comes to fighting. I'm observant, which proves to be a great strength for tracking, and have the determination to see the mission through. I won't fail you."

The director nodded slowly. "Instinct is an important asset. If I agree to this, I want the mission to be clean and efficient with no strings left untied. And you will need to be accompanied by two other cadets. I have cadets in mind, but is there anyone you want on this mission?"

Icarus paused, running a finger through his hair as he thought through the individual skills of each cadet. "Olivia, for her skill with electronics and her prolific flight training."

The director nodded slowly. "She's a bit young, but she could do."

Icarus nodded. "And … Hestia."

The director's eyes flashed with something that Icarus thought was worry or fear, something that he had never seen in the director's eyes before.

"But she is my second," the director spoke quickly. "She belongs by my side, preparing to lead the attack."

"She is the top cadet of our class," Icarus pushed. "I couldn't find a better partner for such a dangerous mission. Especially with her friendship—"

"No, it won't do," the director cut in. "She must stay here. With me."

"Mom," Hestia said gently, placing a calming hand on the director's hand. "You trust me to lead our army into war, right?"

The director nodded slowly, hesitant in her answer. "I do, my dear."

"Then this mission is nothing but a small excursion. We'll be done in a few days, and I'll be by your side during the attack. I promise," Hestia said with confidence.

The director took a shuddering breath before answering, "Icarus, because of your devotion to the Academy and your skills, I will agree to this … and to your chosen team. But if anything goes wrong, I will be notified immediately, and I will go myself to end this once and for all."

Hestia moved to hug her mother tightly. "Of course. It will only be a few days."

"A few days," the director mirrored her words emotionlessly. Yet, Icarus noticed from the small twinges in the director's face that she was merely suppressing her emotions.

"Hestia, go fetch Olivia. I will send Icarus over in a few moments," the director said, gesturing to the door. Hestia complied and exited the room.

Icarus turned back to the director who now wore a colder expression. He wasn't sure if it was because of his presence or her daughter's leave.

"We must set a few ground rules, Icarus," she spoke in a cool tone.

"Anything." He spoke curtly to speed up this process. Especially after Mr.

Fukushima's horrifying demonstration of power by taking away Olivia's memories, Icarus found that he grew more and more afraid of the Academy, especially the director. And he now understood that beyond Ms. Adams's pretense of being a kind and caring mother, she was a liar and a horrible woman. Even though his mission was a front for him to find out more about his father, he had begun to question the Academy's actions and wanted to get far away from its reaches. Small thoughts lingered in Icarus's head. How long would it be until the Academy turned on him as well? How long until his mother found out the truth? Would she also turn on him, leaving him to the wolves? He could now see that the Academy and its leadership posed a threat to not only him, but to the entire world.

Just as quickly as he considered his mother and her motivations, Icarus's mind turned on itself. His mother had always protected him. Were the mission and his escape a betrayal of the protection and the life she built for him? Perhaps, but he also remembered what he'd learned about his father, the kind-hearted man he never had the chance to know or mourn because his mother rarely spoke of him.

Icarus knew in his heart of hearts that his path, no matter where it led, had to be his decision. That was a compass he would never lose again. Listening to the director, he used this moral compass to find his way through her words.

"On this mission, don't mention the fugitive's name. Make sure that Olivia does the same. Hestia has already had such a hard time since the fugitive escaped, she feels betrayed and hurt. This is a chance for her to find balance in her life; make sure she gets that, Icarus."

The director's voice was seemingly sweet and caring, but Icarus detected a darker undertone present in her eyes.

"I understand, Madam Director. I won't let you down," Icarus stated firmly, as he rose from his seat, saluted, and left swiftly in pursuit of knowledge and his desire to make his father proud.

CHAPTER 29

BREKSTA SAT WITH HER LEGS CROSSED and her eyes shut tightly in concentration. She and Aristotle had continued their training on the second day since Breksta's arrival. She sat on the grassy area outside of a small church and faced the bay, its breeze teasing her hair. She pushed her hands through the spiky grass until she felt dirt. To her left was the church while a large cross loomed to her right. But Breksta wasn't here for the religious experiences one can feel in places of worship. She was here for the dozens of cremated ashes buried in the long rock boundary that faced the ocean behind the cross. In Aristotle's words, Breksta's objective was to try and resurrect at least one individual from the ashes. Despite worrying about Hestia's peril, Breksta still felt excited to use her magic.

"I will warn you, Breksta. Magic has a mind of its own. It's not a gift freely given, and there is always an exchange of energy. Each Dreamer discovers, in different ways, the toll magic takes on them. For some, it is quick aging, for others, they are more susceptible to disease. It's true that the fate of the world and the failsafe rests in your hands. But I also care about your wellbeing. So prepare yourself."

Breksta opened her eyes, looking at Aristotle cautiously. "What will be the toll on my magic, Aristotle?"

Aristotle sighed. "Necromancy is a very rare ability, Breksta. Know that to raise the dead, energy must be exchanged in one form or another. Life is temporarily given to the dead, so my best guess is that small parts of your life force will be exchanged with the dead."

Breksta breathed in a shaking breath. She thought that Dreamers had magic without consequence. That people like her mother were gifted with magic. But now Breksta understood the true tragedy of the Dreamers. They had fought the Academy, knowing that there would be some retribution from their own magic. Not only were they hunted like animals by the Academy, but they were slowly losing parts of themselves with each use of magic. There was no escape. Even if Dreamers used their magic in self-defense to push back the Academy, their magic would exact a payment for that self-protection.

But Breksta steeled her mind. She needed her inner strength now more than ever. She needed to do her best to protect all of humanity, even if it meant retribution to her life.

"I'm ready," she said, closing her eyes again.

"Concentrate on the energy of the people here," Aristotle said softly, standing behind her with his hands clasped behind his back.

She sunk her fingers deeper into the ground and slowly sent her mind out through her fingertips like underwater sonar. She felt so much around her: living things, Aristotle, the worms, herself. But she felt the dead, too, the people who rested, cremated and placed in small urns stored in perfect square cabinets that faced the bay. Suddenly, Breksta heard a sound that wasn't an actual voice. Even without speaking, Breksta knew it was a being that beckoned her to open her eyes.

To her surprise, when she opened them, she didn't see the lush surroundings of the island, nor did she feel Aristotle behind her any longer. She was in pitch darkness; it was like a space without stars or light. A vast empty space. Breksta suddenly remembered Erebus who said he had been in a place just like this, a starless space, before he was called to the land of the living by Breksta. This must be the same place, Breksta thought as she tried to move around and speak. She found her voice minuscule in the endless void.

And just like Erebus said, the being was all around Breksta. It was difficult for Breksta to comprehend what it was—something sentient, an entity with a mind but no body, free of all earthly tethers, a being unbound and endless. Soon, the vast silence became too much for Breksta to handle. She felt as if she were stretched thin, her mind and thoughts scattering. She could hear voices in the darkness, frantic rasps of the death that swirled everywhere, threatening to drown her. Breksta tried to concentrate on her consciousness, imagining in her mind that she was back on the island. She imagined her body sitting there; she imagined the grass and wind and salt of the ocean. She clung to those thoughts and images amid the whirling voices, and the black void folded in front of her. With a woosh, Breksta felt the grass beneath her fingers once again. She gasped, clutching her chest as if she had been resuscitated from drowning.

"Are you alright?" Aristotle asked, placing a calming hand on her back.

Breksta swallowed. She closed her eyes as a wave of nausea passed and nodded slowly.

"What did you see?" Aristotle asked.

"Emptiness. A void. But it was as if the darkness were alive. Erebus told me that he had been to a similar place before being summoned back by me," Breksta said, still trying to catch her breath.

"Good," Aristotle said softly. "You've done it, Breksta. You moved into the realm of night, the place where spirits go after death and where the goddess Nyx used to rule. Catch your breath, then I want you to focus on summoning one person, alright? Can you do that?"

"Yes," Breksta said, slowly bringing her hands back to the grass to begin again. She imagined the bustling life here in the small town. She imagined every Sunday when people came to worship and greeted each other with kind smiles, connected by an almost familial bond. Slowly, she felt a warm, gentle, old energy flow toward her. The energy was like the warmth of the sun on a windless day. She began to see spirits materialize in front of her in the dark realm.

Slowly, her vision shifted back into the shadow world where the spirit and energy from one of the people in an urn crawled up Breksta's arms and into the center of her being. As soon as the other peoples' energy touched hers, Breksta saw flashes of memories.

A young girl and her father singing in the church. The father growing old alone on the island while the daughter waved goodbye out of a plane's window as she went to explore the world. The father was buried here. Breksta felt a twinge of sadness but allowed the memories to flow and unfold in front of her mind's eye.

An old woman, whose siblings had all died, had found refuge on this beautiful little island. She had a jewelry business of her own. Sometimes, she gave out bits and pieces of precious jewels and silver to small children who stumbled upon her jewelry stand. She, too, had died here, after heart failure. Breksta winced but pushed through.

A young man who wished to start a church—in memory of his late father, who had been a minister and brought joy to many. The man succeeded and built the church beside where Breksta stood. He had even found a lovely woman to be his bride in the process. But she had a growing tumor in her body. She was buried here, and the man followed soon after, dying from heartbreak.

The flashes from the energy Breksta absorbed weren't merely memories. Their sadness and grief became her own, unearthing deep emotions that Breksta had buried after her mother's death. She opened her eyes to blink away the pooling tears, returning to the living.

"What's wrong?" Aristotle asked, looking quizzically at Breksta.

Breksta turned and cleared her throat before she answered. "I can remember their lives … like mine. And their pain. How can I not feel this pain?"

Aristotle mused over her words before answering. "Instead of raising the dead and bringing the person into your mind, practice exchanging your life force to form their body."

Breksta blinked and steeled her mind, trying to forget how the pain of those dead people reminded her of the pain Hestia was most likely going through. Their incomplete lives weren't so different from the broken lives she and Hestia had been forced to live by the Academy and the director.

Aristotle nodded. "Single out one person to put energy into, then form their body. Think of nothing else."

Breksta took another breath and set her hands into the dirt. She decided to focus on the first man whose daughter had left. She allowed the man's energy to flow through her once more. But this time, when she was hit with the man's memories, she offered hers as well, exchanging her memories and energy. The man's energy responded almost instantaneously. Once again, she was in the dark realm.

"Focus on forming the body of the person," Aristotle said gently. "Use the memories to conjure a perfect image."

Breksta nodded and called for the man's memories again. It was like dragging oneself out of bed, bone tired and wishing for sleep. But she persisted. She began shaping the man's energy, forming it in the dark realm and sending out her energy to keep the man grounded in the world. The man's energy and spirit moved from a bodiless being into a physical body. She sent her energy out through her fingers, which caused ripples of pain up her shoulders and toward her center, making her dig her fingers into the dirt and grit her teeth.

Aristotle put his hand on her shoulder. "You can stop if you need to. You can't force this."

"No," Breksta shouted, breathless as she struggled to speak in the real world while she balanced the man's energy in her mind. "I can do this."

Aristotle moved away from her, and Breksta continued. She called the man's energy from his vat of ashes inside the stone wall. She was his sculptor, copying the man from his memories. She sent pulses of energy through her fingertips, reviving the edges of his face and limbs. Breksta watched with awe as her own magic and life force strung this man back together. Purple light again streamed out from her hands like rivers of sand that combined with the white energy, the man's energy, streaming from the stone wall. Breksta stood and let loose her magic. The purple energy swirled in combination with the man's white energy, creating a tornado of beautiful light until Breksta knew it was finished and called back her magic. The light receded, and Breksta left the dark realm, returning to her world where a man stood, purple wisps of light lingering on his skin.

"Incredible, Breksta," Aristotle said as he rushed up to the man. Aristotle inspected the man, who looked confused and flinched at Aristotle's calculative glance. Aristotle ignored the man and turned to Breksta. "Ask him to move. See if you can control his movements."

Breksta shrugged, stood up, and raised her hands. "Jump up and down five times."

Purple whisps of magic, small compared to before, escaped her fingers and encircled the man as if creating puppet strings. The man jumped up and down five times. Breksta smiled at her power and then relaxed. She allowed her power to recede, and the man cocked his head before turning into white light and disappearing back into the stone wall.

Once all the magic had receded, Breksta didn't feel relief. Breksta felt the pain from the earlier exertion of her magic, but it was tenfold. Her knees buckled, and she cried out at the agony that pulsed through her body.

Aristotle rushed to her side, taking her arm, and spoke in a fearful voice, "What's wrong, child? Is it your magic?"

Breksta managed to mumble out a few words through the head-splitting pain, "I don't know. It's … everywhere."

"This must be your magic's toll," Aristotle observed. Offering support to help her walk, he added, "We need to get you back to the house."

Breksta nodded and shifted her feet slowly as they walked toward the truck. Aristotle shouldered most of Breksta's weight, keeping her arm looped around his shoulder. He curled his arm around her waist and practically pushed her into the front seat of the truck. Breksta curled inward immediately. The pain felt as if a part of her energy was being syphoned to an outside source, and she was growing weaker. Aristotle sped along the road, until they reached his house.

Breksta didn't care how fast he drove—all she cared about was for the pain to stop. In those moments of agony, Breksta didn't care to understand the world after death; rather, she wanted to avoid it at all costs. Perhaps she was dying a slow, agonizing death. At that thought, memories of Hestia and her kindness came to mind. Tears streamed down her face, both from her physical agony and the idea that she would never see Hestia again. Her dearest friend. As the pain increased, she focused on breathing, just as Hestia had taught her, and on staying alive.

"You need to get up," Aristotle said gently, swinging her arm around his shoulder to help her exit the truck. Breksta didn't nod this time; she merely complied. She shifted her feet, her breathing labored with each step she took. Finally, Aristotle allowed Breksta to collapse on the couch. Drenched in sweat, she gripped the edges of the couch as the agonizing pain stripped more of her energy. Aristotle returned quickly with a glass of orange-colored water. He brought the glass to Breksta's lips.

"Drink this, it's an immune booster," Aristotle said quickly.

Breksta gulped down the liquid and lay back, shivering on the couch. Aristotle brought a blanket and set an extra pillow behind Breksta's head.

She managed to croak out, "What's happening?"

Aristotle hesitated, pacing the floor before he stopped and looked at her sadly. "Like I said, this is your toll. But it's rare to see such a violent exchange."

He raced back to the table where the leather-bound book lay and flipped the flaking pages gently. "*The Book of Transcendent Beings* explains, 'Nyx's magic is a darker magic than that of Morpheus's, for she is the direct descendent of chaos. However, her magic is known for great transformation as well as destruction. Often, side effects to the magic-wielding individual are due to the energy transfer during necromancy or the raising of the dead. That energy is never returned. Effects of magical exertion include lingering pain, headaches, weakness, and...'"

Breksta felt an ominous tone in Aristotle's pause. "And?" she asked.

Aristotle locked her eyes with a grave, pale face. "Death."

Breksta closed her eyes tightly, both from the pain and frustration.

Aristotle noticed Breksta's frustration and added, "However, it seems that small amounts of exertion will only lead to short-term side effects. You'll get better, Breksta. I promise."

Breksta sighed with annoyance. "But it won't stop me from dying the next time I use my magic."

Aristotle began in a gentle voice, "I know how you feel. I—"

Breksta's eyes flashed open dangerously. "Do you? I have magic that got my mother killed, Dreamer magic that thousands have been murdered for. I have this power that is *key* to saving the world while I can't even save my friends or keep myself alive in the process. There's some dark realm that I can't even begin to explain, and you're supposed to be the one to train me. Now you tell me that my path will lead to my death. If Dreamers must pay something to use our magic, then do we truly even have power?"

Breksta sighed, a small tear escaping. Aristotle's expression hardened into sadness. "I'm sorry," Breksta said quietly, her eyes shut tightly in pain. "I didn't mean it. I'm just—"

"Frustrated," Aristotle finished. "Frustrated at the magnitude of your power and the restraints that counter that magnitude. I do understand, Breksta. My power takes its toll too."

Breksta nodded agonizingly.

"Rest for now. You will heal," Aristotle said softly, brushing a comforting hand over Breksta's forehead before pulling her blanket to her chin and moving away.

Breksta, despite her pain, smiled ever so slightly at the kind and almost fatherly gesture. "Thank you," she whispered and felt her consciousness fade.

CHAPTER 30

ICARUS FELT A CRAWLING HEADACHE in the back of his head from staring at the maps and screens. The three of them—Olivia, Hestia, and Icarus—had been looking for Breksta for hours, scouring the world for her plane. Hestia's face was ghost-pale with a sheen of sweat that glistened in the light of the room. Olivia glared at the map of the northern hemisphere, frantically typing away at her computer.

They had first started by trying to track Breksta's plane, but the signal of the plane couldn't be pinpointed. She had obviously turned on the anti-detection capability of the plane and left it on.

Hestia struggled through the process of finding Breksta, having to take a small tablet that Icarus could only guess was medication for the headache she tried to hide. But her winces and often clenched hands betrayed the true pain she was experiencing. Hestia declined Icarus's promptings to rest and focused her entire being upon the task of tracking the traitor.

"Here, drink," Icarus said, handing her a bottle of water.

"Thank you," she murmured.

Olivia continued to tend to Hestia while Icarus tried more methods to locate Breksta. Sometimes, Icarus glanced at Hestia. He couldn't fathom what was happening to her. She seemed different. It was like her soul had been emptied and she only retained the principles of the Academy, a physical manifestation of the world he was trapped in. A part of him wanted to help her escape what bound the two of them to the Academy: the connections both had with their mothers and their conflicting senses of duty. But the other part of him knew that he had to prioritize himself, to pursue what *he* wished for, rather than what anyone else wanted. He had lived only to serve his mother and the Academy for so long. Now he had to live for himself. So, he tried not to notice Hestia's strangeness. Instead, he threw himself into the last task he would ever do for the Academy: locate Breksta.

They worked deep into the night. Hestia was soon well enough to join their search again. They tried all different methods, including heat signatures and satellite pictures. Icarus's eyes were heavy, and his back ached from sitting in the chair. And despite the small hints Olivia gave him, saying things like, "I can't see it very clearly, my eyes are probably tired," or "we should get up and move around, we've been sitting for a while," Icarus ignored them and pressed on. The search for Breksta was, in a way, a metaphorical search for Icarus's own father. And as the clock neared four in the morning, Olivia's mind began slipping into a less controlled form of herself that allowed even the strangest of ideas to come forth.

"I might have something," Olivia said quietly, bringing her computer to the center of the table. Hestia and Icarus turned from where they had been staring at the maps and heat signatures on the wall.

"Do you remember the old math classes for polynomials and quadratics?" Olivia asked. Icarus and Hestia nodded, frowning at the mention of old methods. "Well, I think we're going about this in the wrong way, using only technology. I found a place along the western coast that has some sort of communications blackout. I can't track any type of signal over that area."

Icarus crossed his arms, looking at the same map he had been staring at for so long that the countries lingered even after he closed his eyes. "What does this have to do with old math?"

Olivia's eyes sparkled, the excitement a byproduct of her lack of sleep. "We know her first location was in the airplane's warehouse, here." Olivia dragged the interactive map to the Academy's location.

Icarus leaned closer to the map. "Continue."

"Let us imagine that after two days, the fugitive has stopped flying. Her next known location was a few feet out of the hangar. Then, her last known location by our sensors is about a mile to the northwest from the Academy."

Icarus knew where Olivia was going with this and pulled up a graph on his own computer. "So, if we plot the points and connect them in a parabolic curve…" Icarus trailed off as he traced the points into a curve. A quadratic equation sprung from the curved shape. Icarus transposed the wide curve of the parabola onto the map. The vertex was the Academy, and the parabola cut across the Midwest to Orcas Island, the western edges of Canada, and Alaska. The other side of the parabola went over Greenland and over the other side. Icarus raised a hand and gave Olivia a small high-five.

Hestia smiled slightly, leaning toward the screen and squinted.

"Look, the curve also intersects the blackout in the west," Hestia said, pointing at the small island in Washington.

Icarus grinned as he turned to Hestia. "And what are the chances that the fugitive went to the blackout spot?"

Hestia clutched her temple before zooming in on the map. "It's very likely."

Olivia jumped in. "I looked at the Dreamer strongholds, but none of them are on this path. Most of them are in the lower west coast, California, and Nevada. This path only crosses Oregon, Washington, and Alaska on the West Coast. Perhaps the fugitive isn't taking refuge with Dreamers. Or maybe there are strongholds we don't know about."

Icarus's heart raced. "I'll inform the director. It's time to ready the planes," Icarus commanded.

"Yes, sir," the girls replied in synchronization.

Icarus smiled. Breksta would lead him directly to a Dreamer, and perhaps, to his father's history. Deep down, he hoped his efforts would also allow Breksta to find the life she wanted for herself.

"The time is ten a.m. Approaching destination in T-minus ten minutes," the plane's electronic voice spoke.

Icarus and Olivia shook themselves awake as Hestia directed the plane down to a cruising altitude. Hestia's fingers twitched as they held the throttle and joystick, her eyes focused on the distant horizon. Rain barraged the windows.

After discovering the island, Hestia had volunteered to fly the plane and land it, insisting that she wasn't tired. Icarus could tell from the way her voice trembled slightly that her headache hadn't gone away. Icarus remained concerned about Hestia's welfare but saw that she wouldn't give in to the pain.

Taking the opportunity to rest, Icarus thought back to what happened before they departed. He'd exchanged a quick goodbye with his mother, who was perhaps more affected by the war than Icarus had previously realized.

Icarus opened his mother's door and found her sitting in her chair with her hair tied back in a messy bun, the black hairs mixed with gray ones that fell loosely at the nape of her neck. She was typing on her computer and looked up at Icarus with a tired smile.

"I heard you're leaving soon," she said, turning in her chair to look at him.

Icarus nodded. "Right now, in fact."

This, Icarus realized, this moment, might be the last time he saw his mother. If he were to find and pursue his father's past, that path would mark him as a traitor in his mother's eyes and the Academy's. If he couldn't find out more about his father, that path would leave him distanced from his mother since they could never speak about him. Although she'd said that one day she would tell him the whole story, she never had. After learning about his father from Mr. Fukushima, he understood why. If they did speak about him one day, he knew her version would paint his father as the one who betrayed them. Both paths, it seemed, led him away from his mother, but perhaps that was for the best.

Ms. Adams nodded. "So you have a plan."

Icarus nodded again. Despite it all, Icarus found himself still caring about his mother. He felt torn between the difficult training she had put him through and the times when she showed him her motherly love and caring. Unable to reconcile the two versions of her, he decided not to try and understand his feelings anymore. He moved to hug his mother for the first time in a long while, knowing he would need to let go soon.

"Whoa, Icarus," Ms. Adams exclaimed, patting his back. "Where's this coming from?"

Icarus spoke softly, "Just in case … this mission doesn't go successfully."

Ms. Adams pulled away from Icarus, gently cupping his face. "Now why would you think that? I've trained you well, so you have nothing to fear. You *will* return, that's guaranteed."

Icarus nodded, biting his lip to keep the truth from flying out of his mouth and to keep his emotions in. "Of course," he finally said. "I'm just being paranoid."

Ms. Adams pulled him close in another embrace, which surprised Icarus. "Despite your mistakes, you've made me so very proud, my son." Ms. Adams smiled, ruffling Icarus's short hair before she added, "Now go. Save the world."

Icarus turned quickly to leave, knowing he couldn't keep his true feelings in if he stayed any longer. He took a deep breath and paused. And though he couldn't admit it to himself at the time, Icarus was feeling the grief of losing someone who was still alive.

As he stood from his seat and approached the navigation panel where Hestia sat, Icarus tried to forget those emotions and his final moments with his mother. A communication link popped up from the panel, and Icarus pressed it.

The director's voice streamed through, making Hestia's fingers twitch. "Good morning, cadets."

"Good morning, Madam Director," they replied unanimously.

"Approach this mission with caution. Based on the possible motive behind the fugitive's disappearance, she could prove more dangerous than we anticipate. Gather information on the first run of the island and report any suspicious activity. Locate her and take her out quietly and swiftly. Good luck."

The communications link ended abruptly, and the cadets watched as Hestia lowered the plane closer to the ground. Icarus moved back to his seat and buckled himself in. A minute later, Hestia landed the plane in a large wheat field, its golden stalks crushed under the plane's hefty weight.

"Arrived at destination, Orcas Island," the electronic voice spewed out.

Icarus jumped up from his seat and began giving out orders. "Olivia, since you've had less experience in the field, I'm giving you the job of communications and tracking."

"Of course," she responded affirmatively.

"Hestia and I will track the fugitive in person. From the maps of this island, I believe there are a few towns and places where she could be hiding."

Hestia swiftly left her seat and prepared herself without saying a word. Icarus and Hestia armed themselves with various weapons. Icarus had always been built for gun warfare; he had always been a perfect shot. Hestia was as well, but her specialty was blades that matched her cunning precision. She slung a long, Claymore blade across her shoulder before tucking a silenced pistol and thin dagger into her belt. She nodded at Icarus to open the ramp. Together, they exited with their raincoats and began the hunt.

As they made their way along the black asphalt road, the rain pelted down on them. Neither spoke as they walked with single-minded purpose.

Hestia began to consider the purpose of this mission. She was both excited and disgusted. She longed to catch the fugitive, to prove to her mother that she was a great leader and a well-trained assassin dedicated to the Academy. Yet, she was disgusted by the idea that there was a fugitive of the Academy, someone who turned their back on its teachings and kindnesses, someone who would betray the one institution that existed to prevent the world from descending into primal chaos. Hestia would kill the fugitive and the dreams of anyone else who intended to betray the Academy.

She paused for a moment in her thoughts. She noticed that whenever her anger at the fugitive grew, she felt a lingering pain, but she couldn't remember who hurt her. The more she thought about it, the more the splitting headache grew.

They reached the first signs of human existence, a town with a white sign that read "Eastsound" and looked out toward an open bay. Together, Icarus and Hestia searched through the town, walking past banks and diners and markets and shops until they found a church. Suddenly, Olivia's crackling voice came through their microphone system.

"Hey, th-at place has l-arge surges of—"

Hestia touched the earpiece. "Large surges of what?"

"Energy," Olivia finished. "It seems to b-e com-ing from…"

They ran forward to inspect the area when suddenly their earpieces went quiet.

"Olivia? Do you copy?" Icarus asked.

He was met with silence. He sighed and knelt to inspect the grass outside the church. Part of the green grass had been singed and black. When Icarus touched it, the grass disintegrated into ash. Hestia strode toward a stone barrier, following ash along the way. On the other side of the barrier, she found multiple small cabinets lined up with urns inside. Hestia knelt to examine one overturned urn. Ash had spilled out from an urn with a picture of a man on the outside.

"Do you think she did this?" Icarus asked.

"She was definitely here," Hestia said, feeling her heart race and her mind throb with pain as she looked at the open cabinet.

"Why would she need this? What could she be planning?" Icarus asked.

Hestia shook her head angrily. "I don't know. But whatever it is, it's not aligned with the Academy's wishes."

They walked away from the church and continued through the town. After they'd traveled a distance away from the church, their earpieces lit back to life.

"Can you guys hear me?" Olivia repeated, screaming into the earpieces.

Icarus and Hestia winced. "Yes, yes we can," Icarus answered.

"I lost you both for a long time," Olivia said. "I think it was from the energy surge. It's particularly strong around the area where you were standing."

"We discovered an area near a church where people are buried. It seems something has gone on there recently. The grassy area was scorched, and we found an open urn with ashes spilled out onto the ground," Hestia explained. "You should update the director on the communications jam. Also, can you copy the energy signature and see if it shows up on any other part of this island?"

"On it."

Hestia kept walking. "We should keep looking. She can't hide from us forever."

Icarus followed, jogging to catch up with Hestia's quickened pace.

Hestia was agitated. As she thought more about the fugitive, she became angrier. She didn't understand why the world had to be in such a conflict, why the Dreamers wouldn't just surrender to their inevitable defeat. Deep inside, Hestia hated this mission because it demonstrated the Academy's weakness and inability to control others. All she wanted was for her and her mother to be able to live peacefully. Hestia's yearning for peace suddenly awoke something in her. Something flashed before her eyes.

A flash of short white hair. A warm smile. Bright laughter in a dark room that looked like the solitude boxes. A name lingered in Hestia's mind, but just as she tried to sound it out, it vanished. A wave of agony followed by nausea made her head throb. She squeezed her eyes shut, trying to stop the pain.

"Hey, what happened?" Icarus asked, shaking Hestia's shoulder.

Hestia opened her eyes and found that she was on the ground, the grass tickling her cheek as the rain seeped through her rain jacket. Icarus was in front of her, kneeling, a worried look plastered on his face.

"What's going on?" Olivia asked through the microphone.

Hestia pushed the wet strands of her hair out of her face as she sat up slowly with Icarus's help. "I … I don't know. The pain is getting worse," Hestia murmured.

"We should get indoors and wait out the storm," Icarus said, offering a hand to Hestia, who took it gratefully.

Together, they stumbled toward a small bakery across the street from the church. It was a quaint bakery with wooden furniture and still held trace scents of bread and pastries. But Hestia noticed none of those features as Icarus helped her into a chair, where she promptly collapsed from the effort and pain. She lay her head down on her folded arms, her eyes closed as the cold, fatigue, and pain consumed her. She shuddered in silence, her raincoat soaked through, and tried her best to keep the tears from falling.

She didn't understand what was happening. All she wanted was for the war to end and for her mother and her to be happy. But as she allowed in those thoughts, the pain intensified. Hestia hated herself for being so pitiful and weak. The director had taught her to be strong, and yet here she was, weak, vulnerable, and helpless. Not able to manage these emotions of self-loathing, she closed her eyes. She tried to picture happier times as Icarus busied himself by working with Olivia remotely to locate the fugitive.

Icarus was aware of Hestia's intensifying pain; he was becoming better at understanding and empathizing with others. "Here," he said, after rummaging through the bakery and finding a faded orange sweater. "Put this on."

Hestia accepted the gift with a nod, removing her wet raincoat to trade it for the warmer sweater. Icarus hung up Hestia's raincoat and continued to speak softly to Olivia as he worked with the small, phone-like device to expand the thermal sensor's search radius.

Hestia continued her half-slumber-like condition as Icarus continued to work with Olivia, who had notified the director about the strange ashes and communications blackout. It was around eleven thirty in the morning, approximately an hour and a half since Icarus and Hestia left the safety of their plane, when Icarus and Olivia finished their task regarding the heat sensor. Icarus gently shook Hestia awake.

"Can you focus now?"

Hestia nodded, sitting up and pointing to the water canteen Icarus was carrying. "Can I have that please?"

Icarus handed her the container and waited as she managed to swallow some of the water. As she started to hand the container back to him, Icarus prompted, "We need to talk."

Hestia nodded slowly, her eyes heavy from her body's exertion. To her relief, she found that the headache had decreased to a subtle throbbing in the back of her head.

"First, about the heat sensor Olivia and I sent up. We were able to connect the heat sensor to one of our satellites that is passing overhead as we speak. It will send us an image of the last known places where heat was recorded, then we can use those coordinates to track the fugitive."

"Very good," Hestia said as she tried to hide her lingering weakness.

"Second…" Icarus said, hesitating.

"What is it?"

"Well, I was going to ask you the same thing. What happened out there?" Icarus asked, looking through the window as the rain continued to fall.

Hestia paused. She honestly didn't know. As much as Hestia wanted to avoid another cycle of intense pain, she decided that she needed to risk it and confide in Icarus about what was happening to her. She wondered whose white hair she had seen, whose smile had made her feel whole, and whose laughter felt so familiar it was like a part of herself had been reborn.

"I saw something," Hestia began. "A flash of white hair, and a smile, and laughter."

Icarus's eyes widened. He was almost certain that the person Hestia had seen was Breksta. "Do ... do you know who it was?" Icarus asked hesitantly, remembering the director's warning about not mentioning Breksta.

Hestia's headache flared, but she persisted, "No. Yes? It was so familiar, Icarus. What does it mean?"

Icarus paused, wavering about what to say next. He didn't know what would happen if he told Hestia about Breksta, especially since Icarus now suspected that something had happened to Hestia. He was beginning to wonder if the director had forced Mr. Fukushima to wipe out her memories just as he'd been forced to do to Olivia. Although the director told him not to mention Breksta because it was too upsetting for Hestia, it seemed as if she remembered nothing about her dearest friend. If that was true, she might not know that they were here to kill her best friend. He knew it was cruel to lie, but perhaps it was for the best, at least for now. Lying was, and still is, mercy, he told himself.

"I'm sorry, Hestia," Icarus said, apologizing more for lying than for pretending to not know. "I don't know who it is."

Hestia's confusion and headache grew; her frustration teetered on the edge of rage. Her questioning thoughts brought more intensity to her pain and a profound sense of emptiness. A void existed within her, and she couldn't seem to find the reason why. Within the confines of her mind, she felt an immense blankness. Something was missing. But she didn't know where to start looking or how to find it. With that thought, she had a sudden knowing that she'd lost something essential to her life. That notion drove her to the precipice of madness.

Finally, her anger lashed out. "Then what use are you to me?" she shouted at Icarus.

CHAPTER 31

HESTIA LEFT THE BAKERY, slamming the door behind her. She could hear Icarus's persistent steps coming after her, but she didn't care. It was as if the world itself was lying to her, playing a game of cat and mouse. Even with Icarus running after her and calling out her name, she ran along the streets as the rain poured down. She didn't care where she went; she just needed to get away from the pain and the emptiness. She ran past the empty shops and felt the rain sink into her skin through the sweater. Neither the inner storm nor the outer one subsided. *Perhaps,* Hestia thought, *running away from the storm was better than staying in its eye.*

Hestia continued running without turning back. She finally reached the edge of the town where a downhill slope approached a long beach with a small yellow house beside it. Hestia was so blinded by her anger and helplessness that she ran past the house and onto the beach. She didn't notice the Academy's plane beside the house as she raced by. Finally, she felt as if she could run no more and sunk to the wet sand at the water's edge. She sat as her anger slithered viciously beneath the surface. Looking out to the vast bay, she wondered if perhaps running had been the wrong idea. Perhaps she should dive into the storm, into the depths of the sea, and surrender herself to the chaos of the universe.

Hestia stood unafraid, letting her anger show her the way. She smiled at the roaring ocean in front of her, for she knew, despite its power, that whatever happened next, this was her choice. This wasn't her mother's decision or the Academy's. Somehow, that knowledge was important. She waded into the ocean as the cold waves lapped at her feet. She didn't stop. She walked into the waves despite Icarus's shouts from behind. She focused on the roar of the ocean that matched the roar of anger within her. The waves reached her knees, then her thighs, then her waist. Hestia felt freedom in this choice as her anger gave way to the purest form of strength: defiance. In that moment, Hestia felt that her mother had somehow let her down. With each step deeper into the ocean, Hestia's thoughts became clearer. She could now see that she would never be good enough or strong enough for her mother. In the director's eyes, she would never *be* enough. But deep in her heart, Hestia knew that she was enough for herself, and that was what mattered most. Now she knew what she had to do. She wouldn't allow herself to be pushed off the cliff by her mother; rather, she would jump in of her own volition.

She dove into the water and fell into the darkness. Just as the darkness embraced her in its arms, Hestia heard a name, spoken softly in the black waves.

Breksta.

Icarus watched with horror as Hestia dove into the water. Standing on the road, battered by rain and the ocean wind, Icarus finally understood Hestia's sudden change and why she would throw herself into the ocean. Hestia was fighting a war within her mind, and the director had used Mr. Fukushima to wipe her own daughter's mind. Icarus didn't know when it was done, but he was now certain it had happened. That was why the director didn't want him to say Breksta's name.

A sudden crack of lightning brought Icarus back to his senses. He focused on the task at hand below the churning waves to save Hestia. He had seen where she entered and quickly cast aside his communication device on the beach before swimming in that direction. Opening his eyes and feeling the sharp sting of saltwater, he saw a shape in the water. He caught a glimpse of a red clump falling toward the ocean floor. It was Hestia. Icarus swam down with all his might against the strength of the ocean, reaching out until he gripped the edge of Hestia's sweater. Slowly, Icarus pulled her to the surface, gasping at the sweetness of air. But just as Icarus took a deep breath, another wave crashed on him, sending him and Hestia both back down. Icarus engaged in a battle with the ocean to save Hestia and himself.

Exhausted, Icarus crawled out of the water and onto the beach with Hestia. He set her down, noticing the stillness of her chest, her closed eyes, and her blue lips. Icarus's mind defaulted to the Academy's training. Realizing that Hestia wasn't breathing, he immediately began CPR, performing chest compressions as he'd been taught. He paused and checked her breathing. Nothing. Trying to stay calm, he began the compressions again. He wasn't about to let her die no matter how tired he was.

After what felt like an eternity, Hestia sputtered. He turned her on her side as water spouted out of her mouth. Finally, she opened her eyes.

"Brek-sta," she gasped, trying to sit up and clutching Icarus's arm for stability.

Surprised, Icarus blinked the rain from his eyes. "You remember?"

Hestia moved her mouth as she tried to speak but was wracked by coughs.

"We need to get warm, but you're in no shape to travel back to our plane right now. There is a plane just up the hill. We can go there."

Icarus procured his communication device before helping Hestia stand. They hobbled back toward the yellow house, making sure to stay out of sight. They entered the Academy plane, which was unlocked. Hestia didn't speak as they climbed down the ladder into the belly of the plane, and Icarus focused on helping her.

Soaked to the bone, they sat together on one of the mattresses. Icarus located blankets and wrapped himself and Hestia. He continued to tend to her, giving her some purified water to drink. They both settled in, doing their best to stay warm as they rested.

Icarus was the first to speak, although he was unsure whether speaking to

Hestia about Breksta would trigger another dangerous episode. Ultimately, he decided it was necessary.

"When I asked you on the beach if you remembered, you tried to say something. What was it?" Icarus asked.

Hestia was silent, her eyes dull.

"Hestia?" Icarus asked again, speaking softer.

"My mother," Hestia finally said, her eyes beginning to show signs of anger. "She ... isn't truly my mother. She's a dictator. She can't even see my suffering right in front of her. Couldn't she see how hard I was working to try to please her?"

Icarus paused. He had meant to ask Hestia about how she remembered Breksta's name, but considering the idea of the director's hold over Hestia that mirrored Icarus's relationship with his own mother, he had to stop.

"I'm sorry?" Icarus said, unsure of what Hestia needed to hear.

Hestia pursed her lips before speaking. "When will we ever be enough for them, Icarus?"

Icarus was taken aback by the depth of Hestia's pain, like his in a way, and it took a while for him to regain his words.

"It's not about them, our mothers, Hestia. At the end of it all, they ... aren't enough for us either. They aren't the perfect mothers we wanted them to be," Icarus said sadly, recalling their training. "It's the striving for potential and greatness that defines us as worthy and powerful people—not perfection."

Hestia looked to Icarus, her eyes fragile. "Icarus, aren't we enough by existing? Why must there be a bar we have to reach?"

Icarus studied Hestia momentarily. Wiping Hestia's memory seemed to have broken something inside her. It was as if Breksta was the only thing that had held Hestia together, and Icarus both envied and pitied Hestia for the relationship she'd had with Breksta.

Breksta was someone who was there for Hestia, to pick her back up when the darkness overtook. Sadly, Icarus had no one other than himself to rely on. Yet, for Hestia to have the person she'd depended on taken away was a pain he couldn't imagine. Hestia had been with Breksta for so long that they'd become inseparable. And for the director to separate the two dear friends was unforgivable. Having the director as a mother was perhaps one of the worst things anyone could live with.

Hestia cleared her throat and spoke. "I remember a name. It belongs to someone I can't seem to remember."

"What was the name?" Icarus asked.

Hestia took a deep breath. "Breksta," she breathed and smiled. "Yes, that is the name. I remember it so fondly," Hestia continued. "Do you know whose it is?"

Icarus didn't know what telling Hestia about her lost friend would to do to her, considering her current state of mind. He was at the same crossroads again. Was it merciful to keep Hestia in the dark about Breksta, whose life had been marked for death? Deep in his heart, Icarus felt compassion for Hestia. She and Breksta had a kind of inseparable bond that even magic couldn't erase—the type of bond that the heart remembered, even without the mind. In honor of that bond that Icarus wished he'd had in his life, he told the truth, but only a fraction of it. He attempted to embody the compassion Mr. Fukushima told him his father had shown.

"Breksta is the girl you saw," Icarus began. "The one with white hair and a warm smile and laughter. She is your friend, and you are hers, but your mind was erased."

Icarus was certain that the director had wiped her own daughter's mind, but he couldn't include that detail and cause Hestia more pain by telling her. He focused on Hestia's reaction about Breksta.

"But ... how can I not remember? I must be able to," she exclaimed, jumping up from her seat. "How could I just forget a person but still feel the fondness of her name and the warmth of her friendship? How is that possible, Icarus? And what do you mean that my mind was erased? How can a mind be erased? Who could do such a thing?"

Icarus realized that more than her memories of Breksta been erased. The scene they'd all watched as the director forced Mr. Fukushima to erase the memories of Olivia was missing as well. He wanted to tell Hestia everything that had transpired, but he feared that if he told her the truth about her mother's actions, Hestia's fragile mental state would worsen.

"I ... don't know, Hestia," Icarus said. "But we do know where the fugitive is. So, we need to focus on regaining your strength. Once this mission is over, we can figure this out together. Can you do that for me?"

Hestia nodded slowly. Icarus broke a small smile before reaching into his pocket for his communication device to check on any new developments. To his dismay, a dozen missed calls lined the screen. He clicked open the call link between Olivia and the director and waited.

"Good afternoon, Madam Director, Olivia," Icarus answered in a monotone voice when they picked up.

"Icarus, you're alright!" Olivia exclaimed. "Is Hestia there?"

"Silence, cadet," the director cut in before Hestia could say a word. "For the last half hour, we lost communications as well as visuals on both of you. Would you care to explain yourselves?"

Icarus swallowed nervously. "We were trying to locate the fugitive and the Dreamer but thought the loud communications would disturb the hunt."

"Well, that doesn't explain why Hestia's breathing stopped," the director said. Icarus swore he could hear a quiver in her voice. "Did you let something happen to her, cadet?"

"No, ma'am," Icarus spoke, avoiding Hestia's angry and surprised gaze.

"Lies!" the director exclaimed. "I have both your vital charts right in front of me. Heart rate increase, increase in sweat, all signs of the liar you are, Icarus Adams. I'll be taking charge of your mission; I will be on the island promptly with a team of elite cadets. Keep a watch on the fugitive, but do not engage, I repeat, do not engage. This is an order from your commander."

The communication cut off, and Icarus sat there stunned as he was met with Hestia's angry expression.

"That was my mother, wasn't it?" Hestia asked, letting the blanket fall to the ground as she stood.

"It was," Icarus sighed, frustrated at himself for allowing this mission to go sideways and decreasing his chances of ever learning about his father or saving Breksta. "The director is taking over this mission and will arrive on this island in a few hours. Our job is to keep an eye on the target and wait for the director's orders."

"What's the point, Icarus?" Hestia snapped. "We're her puppets, left to dance on her strings without any care from her about our thoughts, our emotions, or our lives. Why don't you ever fight? Don't you have anything you care about enough to fight?"

Icarus tried not to show his anger at Hestia's resistance. Of course, he had things he cared about: his father's past and how that would shape his future. But not everything could be acted upon with brute force like Hestia was suggesting. Icarus needed time to consider what to do next.

"Please, Hestia. If we carefully strategize our actions, we can finally have lives of our own, away from our parents," Icarus suggested.

Hestia's eyes were icy when she spoke. "My mother shaped my life. Is it not fair for me to reshape mine to the way I wish for it to be? And the only way for me to do that is to push against her wishes. I'm not you, Icarus. I'm not a coward."

Icarus was slighted by Hestia's words. The director had torn his family apart, killed his father, and perhaps altered his mother to become the manipulator she was. What right did Hestia have to call him a traitor? He was merely trying to be strategic. And although Hestia's method was sometimes tempting to Icarus—who was taught to suppress everything—he knew that his tight control of his emotions and actions would finally come in handy. He just needed to be patient.

In the end, he vowed to be his father's son. Icarus had to believe that the wait would lead to success. Hestia was right about one thing: Icarus wasn't her, and he would not give in to revenge and darkness.

CHAPTER 32

BREKSTA AWOKE TO THE SMELL of coffee and rain. She moved her hand to brush away the hair from her face. To her surprise, the movement brought no pain. She moved her feet to untangle them from the blankets and pulled the ends of her blanket around her shoulders, creating a cloak fit for a regal queen despite the blanket's ugly brown colors. Aristotle looked up from where he sat at the table, coffee in one hand and the well-worn book in the other. He moved to help her, but Breksta brushed off his help.

"I'm fine, really. It doesn't hurt now," Breksta insisted with a slight smile.

The pain was gone, but her body still felt weak. The effects of her magic had left its internal scars.

"It's around five, and I made you some eggs," Aristotle said, pointing at the table. "It's the only professional meal I can make."

Breksta smiled despite her weakness. Eggs were a part of her fond memories of her mother and Hestia, so she welcomed them. She dove into her food and pointed to Aristotle's book.

"Did you find a cure for me?" she asked between bites.

A dark expression crossed Aristotle's face; his eyes no longer bright. "I have scoured every edge of Nyx's magic and Morpheus's as well. Healing was a property belonging to some Dreamers. But Nyx is a different being. Because her magic draws from darkness and night, the powers are transformational, residing in necromancy, death, or sorcery. Simply put, Breksta, you have dark magic that cannot heal or be healed by any mortals. Not even other Dreamers can heal you."

Breksta dropped her smile and put down her fork, her hands twitching nervously. It was as if Breksta's fate was tied to pain and death. So Breksta decided that if she couldn't escape such pain and agony, she might as well devote her suffering to a good cause.

"How do I unlock the failsafe then?"

"It'll be difficult."

"Do I need to remind you of all I've sacrificed to be here," Breksta said darkly, the thoughts of Hestia at the hands of the director resurfacing.

Aristotle nodded and turned the book so Breksta could see. In the center of the page was a drooping pink flower with three buds all shaped like upside-down bells. Surrounding the flower were letters in a language that Breksta guessed was Greek. The flower was held in the hands of a woman with flawless white skin, wearing a black cloak that descended into the stars of the night sky behind her.

"Nyx?" Breksta guessed.

Aristotle smiled slightly. "Yes. But we're interested in the flower in her hands."

Breksta leaned closer, trying to get a closer look.

"That flower is the key to reviving Nyx."

Breksta's hand shot up to the table in surprise. "Revive a goddess?"

Aristotle looked her square in the eye. "Yes, Breksta. The same failsafe your mother might have accessed to save us from this wretched war."

Breksta moved her hands back to her lap and spoke with hesitation, "I ... I don't understand."

Aristotle continued, "Let me explain. Your goal is to retrieve the flower in the next few days. It lies under the lake on this island."

Breksta's mind whirled. "That's why you have lived here so long! You're protecting the failsafe."

"Yes, part of my job here is to protect the failsafe, with my life if necessary.

But I have also waited for you. Long ago, I foresaw that a girl possessing strong magic would set foot on these shores, in the darkest time of the world. I thought it was your mother, and perhaps it could have been her. Prophecies are interesting that way—there are many ways for the world to come to the same conclusion. I only confirmed your part in it yesterday when you awoke your power."

The implications of his words sunk into Breksta. Death had lingered in her mind, especially after seeing the place after death and experiencing unexplainable agony the previous day. But she would save the world and keep her promise to her mother despite the pain and loss, especially to Hestia.

"How do I get it?" Breksta urged.

"The failsafe is guarded faithfully by guardians to the goddess. I've never allowed Dreamers in, except one, Erebus, the boy you said you revived in the Academy."

"Erebus? Why did you let him in?" Breksta asked.

"His power was that of shadows. Like yours, it was closely related to Nyx. Although Erebus wasn't blessed with the power of Nyx like you, his imaginative use of magic and training made me think that he could be a good candidate. However, he … was badly wounded after entering. It wasn't his destiny. We never knew what the guardians did to him, but they spat him out half dead. When he healed, he left and never returned. Little more is known about the guardians themselves. But I'll take you to the lake and find a way for you to enter the temple beneath the water to take the flower *without* hurting the guardians. The one condition you must remember is that you *can't* use magic while you are retrieving the failsafe."

"Why not?"

"You must save all your strength and magic for the resurrection. That's why I had you practice on the raven and the man back near the church. Your necromancy is the key to reviving Nyx so she can restore the balance of magic in our world."

Breksta swallowed nervously. "Where do I perform the resurrection?"

"I'll prepare the portal to Nyx's dimension while you get the failsafe. The failsafe can unlock a passage to her dimension where you shall revive her," Aristotle said in absolute seriousness.

Breksta felt her breath grow shallow at the scale of Aristotle's plan. It was only days ago when she left the Academy, thinking that freedom would finally be hers. But now, the lives of Hestia and everyone else on earth weighed heavily in her hands. Doubt began to plague Breksta. Was her magic strong enough for the resurrection? Would she be strong enough? And if the resurrection succeeded, would Hestia still be alive to live in the world Breksta was trying to bring about? And most of all, could Breksta herself survive the resurrection?

Blood pulsed loudly in Breksta's ears as the thoughts swirled violently in her head. She closed her eyes, wishing the weight of her decisions could fall away into the background of the thrumming rain. She knew what Hestia would do. Hestia would do what was necessary and finish the plan. And so Breksta vowed with new vigor that she would complete the plan, no matter the cost: for her mother, for Hestia, for everyone else trapped in the Academy.

"Alright," Breksta said curtly, opening her eyes.

Aristotle noticed her new determination and smiled. "You'll need a sufficient weapon." He stood quickly and approached his bed beside the window.

Breksta followed, feeling a small glimmer of excitement as she sat beside Aristotle on his bed. Aristotle rummaged underneath his bed until he came up with a brown cardboard box. He handed it to Breksta.

"It's from your mother," he said with a soft, sad sigh.

Breksta took the box with shaking hands. She hadn't encountered her mother's possessions since her mother's death. She opened the box and found a few soft-edged photos and a wrapped object. She picked up the photos and examined them one by one. The first was the same photo Aristotle had on his fireplace.

Aristotle touched the edge of the photo with a shaking hand. "That was the day when we first began training the Dreamers to use their magic. She was so excited and proud, seeing everyone's gifts." He hesitated before continuing, "She would be proud of you too."

Breksta nodded, not trusting herself to succumb to tears if she spoke. She retrieved another photo with a tan-skinned man standing beside Asteria, his arm around her waist and a bundle in Asteria's arms.

"Is that?"

"Yes," Aristotle said, smiling widely now. "That's you ... and your father."

Aristotle's smile grew solemn. "They were both happy then. With you, how could they not be?"

Breksta blinked away a tear and tucked the photo away. Her life had come off its hinges in so many ways, and she wished for one good thing to come out of this. She couldn't fall apart before she revived the goddess. Afterward, she could grieve all she wanted.

The last photo was of a slightly older Breksta who must have been one or two years old. Her white hair was just as disheveled as it was now, and her small hand clung to Asteria's tightly while the other hand was in her mouth. Breksta laughed brightly, feeling a bit of the weight she had carried all these years lift at the young and gentle photo. This was who she could have been, who her mother should have been. *No*, she reminded herself. She could muse all about that later, when this mission was done and the world rebalanced. Breksta allowed herself to feel an intuitive feeling of happiness and joy. Perhaps Breksta could find this happy life with Hestia after her mission and the Academy's end.

"I like this one the best." Aristotle grinned, gesturing at the photo.

Breksta nodded and placed the photos on the bed. She pulled out the wrapped object and ripped off its paper wrapping. Underneath the wrapping was a dagger in a leather sheath.

"It was your mother's," Aristotle commented with a bittersweet smile.

She pulled off the sheath to reveal the shining blade that reflected her determined eyes back at her. The handle held a beautiful purple stone and brown leather, smoothed by years of wear, wrapped around it. The dagger's body was onyx with a wide hilt that thinned to a razor's edge at the tip. It was light in Breksta's hand and felt like a perfectly balanced blade.

"I trust this will be sufficient protection in the hands of a trained professional," Aristotle said, grinning.

Breksta nodded and smiled in return. "More than sufficient."

"Good. Because in the meantime, while you heal, I'll teach you about the revival. We shall go tonight."

Breksta spent the rest of the evening with Aristotle, her blankets bunched around her shoulders as she listened to him speak. The failsafe, or flower, was the key to the revival. It was the key to Nyx's realm, just beyond the borders of Orcas Island's reality. Nyx's realm was a realm anchored to earth that Nyx created as the failsafe before her death. She had done it for the Dreamers and humanity, in case either unbalanced the world. The key to the realm could only be accessed through the goddess's own descendants, keeping it safe from outsiders. Breksta listened to Aristotle outline the history until her ears grew dull to the sounds of human speech. The weight of the world rested on her tired and weakened shoulders.

Breksta wondered if this was what her mother felt during her time raising the Dreamer resistance. She felt closer to her mother than ever, and that closeness motivated her to complete this mission. She only hoped that Hestia and the others who had paid a price for her could survive until she could restore balance to the world and finally end the Academy's totalitarian grip over the world. Failure wasn't an option. Failure meant the destruction of the world and those she cherished dearly. She couldn't fail, under *any* circumstances.

The rain hadn't stopped at around five in the afternoon as Hestia and Icarus sat in the plane in dead silence. It was Hestia's prompting that made them leave the warmth of the plane to scout the surroundings, especially the lone house next to the plane.

"Olivia, we'll do some reconnaissance of the house. Keep an eye out for us," Icarus whispered, touching his earpiece to activate it.

"Alright, the director is arriving around ten tonight," Olivia spoke calmly into the earpiece.

Icarus sighed loudly; his hands clenched tightly until the whites of his bones showed. The director's arrival to the island irked Icarus, for his plans to question the Dreamer that Breksta said she was trying to find were almost demolished. Most of all, though, Icarus kept thinking of the director. After being raised in the Academy, he expected her coldness, but her new anger, clear and vicious, perplexed him. Why *now* did the director begin to show her anger and frustration?

The logical explanation was that the coming war induced the director's anxiety. But Icarus sensed a deeper fracturing and long-held fears rising to the surface. This fracturing, accompanied with Hestia's sudden outburst, made Icarus conclude that the two circumstances were somehow connected, perhaps due to Breksta. Wiping Hestia's mind had somehow destabilized both women, driving them toward a dark precipice that concerned Icarus. He would watch Hestia and the director when she came.

"Icarus?" Olivia spoke into his ear and jolted him from his thoughts.

"Right, we're going," Icarus commanded.

"I have an update on the energy signatures you asked about at the church."

"Yes?"

"There are three signatures on the island. One at the church, where you were. The other on the top of one of the island's mountains. And the final one on a lake."

"Good work, update the director on that. Keep us posted," Icarus added.

"I will." The earpieces buzzed and went silent.

"Quiet. We're close," Hestia hissed as they neared the fence surrounding the house.

Both ducked behind the fence, allowing their dark clothing to merge with the dark colors of the bushes. The rain obscured their view of the house from the fence so Icarus pulled out a small pair of binoculars from his pocket and adjusted them until the inside of the house became clear. A silvery, white-haired man sat in a chair with a dark book in front of him. *This must be the Dreamer Breksta came to meet*, Icarus thought.

"Let me see," Hestia said, grabbing the binoculars before Icarus could answer.

Another person moved and sat at the table alongside the man, a large blanket pulled around the person's shoulders. Hestia gasped; it was Breksta.

"It's her," Hestia said, her mouth agape. "The girl I saw ... Breksta?"

Icarus took the binoculars and looked. He slowly put them down, speaking in a cold voice, "That's the fugitive. You stay here and do some surveillance; I'll go and listen in."

"Icarus," Hestia said slowly. "Why..."

Hestia wanted to ask Icarus why they were hunting this fugitive who was supposed to be Hestia's friend ... or at least she had been. But he disappeared before she had a chance to say another word. She was left to wonder what she was doing and why.

Hestia sat, pulling her knees to her chest and wrapping her hands around them. Her mother was coming. There was no denying that. All because she had failed and because her mother didn't trust her to complete the mission. Hestia felt a brooding anger grow as the rain fell, cool against her skin. She tipped back her hood and allowed the cool rain to soak into her face, momentarily feeling the most human she had felt in a while.

In her mind, though, she screamed and banged her hands on imaginary walls, wishing that she didn't feel torn, wishing for her pain to end. But her face conveyed nothing. Only a small tear trailed down her face and mixed with the rainwater so that no one could see her torment.

With the knowledge of Breksta, she began to feel overwhelming fatigue and familiar thoughts flow into her mind from a pit of dark pain within her. Hestia was so tired. She was tired of fighting someone else's war. She was tired of striving for perfection. She was tired of her life, even without trying to find out who her friend was, why her mind was empty, and why they were hunting her friend. The worst of it all was having a monster for a mother.

Distance had grown between her and her mother. She remembered sitting on her mother's lap in her office and her mother's silver tears as she recalled the attack. Her mother never cried, and she never showed Hestia any emotions. So Hestia had convinced herself that her mother's cold exterior was also the interior. The cold commander to the cadets had grown into her mother's soul, latching onto her heart, and syphoning all the warmth that may have existed in the past. She wanted her mother's unconditional love, with no strings attached. But she would never have it, no matter how hard she tried. It was these ideas that broke Hestia. *Nothing matters*, she thought, *not promises or laws or threats, nothing*. That idea almost made her laugh—the simple truth that none of it mattered. Why had she never thought of this before?

Slowly, with the rain's constant drumming and after years of struggle, Hestia stopped fighting. She stopped trying to find the truth. She wasn't being defiant; rather, she felt indifferent and subdued. Her mother had won. She finally gave in because it was easier than swimming. She let herself be washed away by the droplets of rain and allowed one more tear to fall. Wiping it away, she began her surveillance of the house.

CHAPTER 33

IT WAS ALMOST ELEVEN THIRTY when the director arrived on the island. Hestia and Icarus continued to monitor the house, awaiting the director's arrival to continue their mission.

"She's here," Olivia spoke into the microphone, jolting Icarus and Hestia out of their silent watch.

"Does she want us to return to your plane?" Icarus asked.

"Go to the one behind the house. We can establish an intercom link there," Olivia replied.

"We're on our way," Icarus confirmed.

He stood up and began to walk toward the plane when he noticed that Hestia hadn't moved. He turned and found her still crouching on the ground, her hood covering her head.

"Hestia," he whispered.

She said nothing. Her gaze was fixated on the house, as if she hadn't heard him or Olivia.

"Hestia," he hissed.

She still did nothing, her back hunched with her forearms resting on her knees. Icarus walked over and gently tapped her on the shoulder.

"We need to go," he said quietly.

She turned to him, her eyes hollow. It shocked Icarus to see how much she had changed in the past days. The girl who ran to Breksta when Breksta escaped the collapsed buildings was gone. The girl who was angry and scared when Icarus asked if he could help with Breksta's mission was forlorn. It was like she had been hollowed out. He wondered if the mention of her mother would draw emotion, any emotion.

"Your mother's coming, Hestia," he murmured, offering his hand to her.

To Icarus's relief, he saw a flicker of acknowledgment in Hestia's eyes. She stood, batting away his hand. She walked toward the plane silently as Icarus followed. Soon they reached the ramp to the plane and opened it. Hestia quickly turned on the control panel, and an intercom link appeared. She clicked it, and the director and Olivia's face appeared on the screen.

"Hello, cadets," the director said.

"Good evening, Madam Director," Icarus said out of habit, awaiting orders as he studied the director and Hestia's demeanors.

"Hello," Hestia said coldly, her eyes unwavering from her mother on the screen.

The director nodded at Hestia, her lips tightened to a thin razor's line. "I've arrived, cadets, with an extra battalion because you aren't capable enough for this mission. You have betrayed my trust. If this mission weren't so important and dire, I would have you all sent home and thrown into the solitude boxes," the director commanded, her voice rising in anger.

Icarus opened his mouth to apologize. "I'm—"

"Quiet, Icarus Adams. You've done enough to endanger my second and this mission. Olivia and I will fly close to the house along with the other senior cadets. We will bring the long-distance sniping rifles, land the plane as close to the house as we can to avoid being heard, and walk on foot to back you up. Hestia, Olivia, and I will wait outside the house with half the battalion in case the snipers fail. Icarus, you and the other half of the battalion will snipe our intended target and the Dreamer from a distance. If there is any resistance, the rest of the battalion will quickly snuff it out. We shall arrive soon."

Icarus nodded in response. He felt a roaring anger grow within him. The director had broken so many families, so many Dreamers who his father had protected, like Breksta's family. And he was certain that the director had broken his family too. Although he didn't have proof, he was convinced the director had killed his father in retaliation for his father's part in the Dreamer attack. Maybe even his mother was a victim of the director's cruelty.

Icarus began to consider that his mother's strictness and cruelty wasn't to hurt him. Maybe her actions had always been to keep the two of them safe from the director's wrath. With a father who betrayed the director, it would've been easy to label the Adams family as traitors and treasonous people. So perhaps all her strictness and her avoidance of maternal interactions with Icarus were a shield of protection from the director. By teaching him to fend for himself and be quiet in the face of authority, she kept Icarus and herself safe from the director's suspicion.

Suddenly, he saw the director for who she was. A cruel woman who would destroy all Dreamers, and even her own daughter, to satisfy her need for revenge. In that moment, he decided that he would no longer be a mindless slave to this Academy and the director. He promised that he would save his mother, despite all her shortcomings and not let her be destroyed. In the meantime, though, he would have to do as commanded and bide his time until he could make his move.

Breksta lay in bed, practicing the techniques Aristotle had taught her in preparation for her coming trials. Without using her powers, she went through the motions of searching for the dead and feeling the energies around her as if she were about to perform a resurrection.

Breksta took a deep breath and gazed outside at the drumming rain. She wanted to stay in this quiet space for a little longer, hearing the ocean and watching the flames flicker in the fireplace. Her mind was at ease as she watched the colorful embers rise and fall and knew what she had to do as the clock ticked to midnight.

She took one last look around Aristotle's house, hoping that she would soon return to the comforts of this small house. Steeling her mind, she told herself she was ready. She would be valiant and persistent through it all. She moved to wake Aristotle, shaking him from his slumber.

He turned over and tried to focus as he looked at her. "Is it time?"

"Almost," Breksta replied. "I can't sleep; we might as well get going."

He was already dressed as he grabbed a jacket lying on the table. "You have your dagger?"

Breksta nodded. As Aristotle collected his keys and his rifle, she asked, "Do you have what you need for the portal?"

"Yes," Aristotle said as he grabbed a large bucket filled with white sand. He opened the door slightly to keep the rain out. "Let's go," he instructed as they raced to the car, trying not to slip in the downpour.

As Breksta opened the door to enter the car, she gasped. Something unexpected caught her attention: the fiery red hair of her best friend.

"They're escaping! What are your orders, Madam Director?" Hestia shouted with the director behind her, opening fire on the truck. Her green eyes locked coldly on Breksta's as Breksta jumped into the truck and slammed her door shut.

Breksta and Aristotle ducked as the bullets hit and shattered the window behind them. Aristotle gunned the engine and took off toward the failsafe in Mountain Lake. As they sped away, Breksta heard the director's shouts.

"Did you see her?" Breksta asked, her old fears pumping adrenaline through her veins.

"Who?" Aristotle asked, his eyes glancing to the rearview mirror.

"The director," Breksta breathed.

Aristotle cursed under his breath. "How did she find us?"

Breksta shook her head. She didn't know. Fearful tears threatened her eyes, but she tried to calm herself with the breathing exercises Hestia taught her. She couldn't break down now. But as she thought of Hestia, a wave of fear and grief washed over her. Why was Hestia trying to kill her? What had happened after she escaped? She shook her head, telling herself there was no time to think about anything but her mission. It would all end well—it had to.

The director, Olivia, and a group of cadets ran toward the house as Aristotle's truck sped into the distance.

"Back to the plane," the director commanded, turning back to the plane they had just landed.

Icarus and Hestia raced behind her to the plane and rushed in. Olivia had already powered on the systems as the director's entourage flooded into the plane.

"Go! Go! Go!" the director yelled, materializing beside the control panel with Olivia at her side. With Olivia taking control of the flight, they were soon hovering above the bushes. Olivia pushed the thrusters and shot the plane off into the sky, trailing the truck.

The director's anger was seething. She had no idea where the two Dreamers were going, but she would stop them. She had already caught one Vilkas and wouldn't let another destroy her plans for the world she had carefully built. Asteria had taken her family, and Breksta had taken Hestia. Vengeance was an angel the director knew well. And this angel would kill Breksta Vilkas.

"How long were they there? Do you think they overheard our plan?" Breksta asked, looking out the window behind her as she unsheathed her dagger.

"I don't know. But we must assume that they're here to kill us. Do you know those cadets from the Academy?"

"Yes," Breksta said slowly. "Two of the cadets are in my class, but I don't know why they now want to harm me."

"There's no time to consider why. You can't let anything interfere with the mission, Breksta. If it comes down to it, you may need to kill your comrades."

"No," Breksta exclaimed, her fear coming out as anger. "It ... can't come down to that. I won't let it!" Even though Breksta knew that her sacrifice might be necessary, she was still afraid of the possibility of death and the possibility of leaving this world.

"Just focus on getting the failsafe. Remember, you need to place the flower in the ground before saying the incantation," Aristotle instructed, accelerating the truck up the hill.

Breksta's fingers twitched as she ran them along the blade's handle. They sped under the arch marking the entrance to the national park and their closeness to the lake.

"Prepare yourself for the guardians. No matter the insanity of the world outside, the most important thing is that flower and you. If you are killed by the guardians, the world loses its only chance at survival," Aristotle continued.

Breksta barely heard his words. Deep down, although Breksta didn't wish to admit it, she was afraid. She was afraid of the resurrection and of the pain of her magic to resurrect Nyx. But she bit her lip and closed her eyes tightly and practiced her breathing once again. Aristotle put a comforting hand on Breksta's shoulder, turning from the road to look her in the eye.

"I believe in you, Breksta Vilkas. You have the power and will to save our world, with or without your magic."

Breksta murmured the next words in fear of what she would hear. "Did you see that in your predictions?"

Aristotle smiled with an inexplicable sadness. "I don't need to foresee the future to know that you are powerful, Breksta. In more ways than you can imagine."

Breksta allowed those words to linger in her mind as they sped on, knowing the director's plane was somewhere nearby. Soon, Aristotle pulled the car into a gravel parking lot. He hopped out, and he and Breksta raced down stone stairs to the water's edge. They stood on the dock that rocked from the waves of the lake caused by the wind.

Aristotle had to shout over the wind gusts. "I'll set up the portal and keep it safe until your return."

Breksta nodded and looked at the dark waters apprehensively. She poised herself to dive when Aristotle called her name. She turned and, with rain-soaked arms, he enveloped her in a hug. "Even though the dead are gone, they still watch over you. Your mother watches over you, Breksta Vilkas. The gods do too. They await your help as do we all."

When Breksta pulled away, Aristotle's eyes were filled with tears.

"Goodbye, Aristotle," she said, trying not to let her tears show.

She turned and dove deep into the waters, not knowing if she'd ever resurface again.

CHAPTER 34

"THE FUGITIVE JUST DOVE into the water," Olivia exclaimed, pointing through the plane window at the splash at the end of the dock.

The silver-haired man raced from the edge of the dock toward his truck and rummaged around. Hestia swore she saw fire in his hand.

"We'll split up," the director commanded. "Hestia, Icarus, you take half the cadets to go after the fugitive. The rest of you, come with Olivia and me. We're going after the Dreamer. We cannot let the fugitive divert the Academy's plans."

Once the plane hovered low enough over the lake, Hestia, Icarus, and their group of cadets dropped out of the end of the plane's ramp and straight into the water below. Olivia and the director landed the plane next to a grove of trees. Olivia and the other cadets moved through the trees in search of the man.

The water was freezing even at the surface. Breksta could see the bare shapes of fallen trees, their long trunks pointing toward the ground. But the rest of the underwater world was filled with shadows. A piercing purple light drew her attention at the center of the lake. The purple light illuminated a temple of granite stone at the very depths of the water. She surfaced one last time, taking quick, shallow breaths followed by a deep one before plunging into the frigid depths.

She pumped her arms, frantic to reach the temple as her air slowly left her. Just as the last bubbles of air left Breksta's lungs and she felt the painful hollowness of her chest, her fingers touched the mossy stone. It glowed brightly and allowed her in along with the water before slamming shut. The water receded into the gutters at the base of the walls.

The temple was made of pure white granite on the inside walls while the ceiling comprised of black stone with precious gems that twinkled to create a perfect constellation of the night sky. The temple didn't look large on the outside, but on the inside, the majestic, milk-white, Greco-Roman pillars lifted the ceiling high.

Breksta walked from the first room, sucking in air that had replaced the water. She continued into the next room that appeared to be a shrine. On the walls, past the pillars, the same milk-white stone had been used to carve statues of howling wolves. At their feet, bowls with open purple flames lit the room and burned so hot that Breksta could feel the heat even ten feet away. An apprehensive feeling crept up her neck, paired with strange echoes that bounced off the ceiling and made her whirl around. Icarus and Hestia stood together, a group of cadets behind them. Their weapons were raised toward her. Breksta bared her teeth and prepared herself.

"Don't resist, and we won't have to hurt you," one of the senior cadets said calmly.

"Never," Breksta growled, pulling out her dagger.

"What odds do you have, Breksta," Hestia spoke coldly. "Just give in. The Academy always wins in the end. Nothing you do here will possibly matter."

This Hestia was different from the one Breksta knew. She was cold and distant. But no matter how much it hurt Breksta to see her friend so coldhearted and unlike the Hestia she had known, she wouldn't give in. Suddenly, a dozen howls pierced the air. Breksta turned and saw that the sounds emanated from the statues.

Hestia frowned but unsheathed and turned her blades to the wolves. Purple light shone through the wolves' eyes, and the twelve marble figures leapt to life, facing the three of them. The wolves bared their teeth and stood at the feet of the large statue at the end of the temple. The statue towered over Breksta's head ten-fold. It was of a woman holding a black staff in her hands. Her long, flowing black hair led into a long black cape the color of the galaxy. Breksta knew it was Nyx. And these wolves were the guardians, protecting their goddess.

"What are those?" Icarus exclaimed, looking through the barrel of his assault rifle at the teeth of one of the wolves.

"Breksta, call off your dogs," Hestia said coldly, gripping her daggers tighter.

"They're not mine. They belong to the goddess," Breksta said, admiring the beauty of the animals and remembering her days in the forest.

She addressed the wolves in a loud, booming voice. "Guardians of Nyx, I am Breksta Vilkas. I've come to retrieve the failsafe."

The wolf at the head growled and then did something surprising. He spoke. "A handful have come to prove their worth to the goddess. All have failed. And so will you."

The wolves charged, and Breksta took a deep breath as she prepared her dagger—to do what she had to do, even to fight her friend.

"Breksta, surrender and we can stop this madness," Icarus shouted.

Hestia sighed and brandished her daggers. "The madness has already begun."

The head wolf charged at Breksta with snapping jaws. Breksta leapt out of the way nimbly, only for another wolf to jump toward her. She dove quickly and hit the floor. A wolf leapt on top of her, and Breksta raised her dagger instinctively. She held the handle with both hands so that the blade protected her from the wolf's snapping jaws. The wolf's weight pressed the blade toward her face, drawing a line of blood from the side of her cheek. Enraged, Breksta wriggled underneath, shoving the wolf off her. The wolf growled and whimpered as a bullet struck its body and blood spurted.

"Stop!" Breksta screamed. "We just need to defeat them, not kill them."

"You caused this," another cadet shouted as he let loose a spray of bullets at the incoming wolves.

Two wolves were circling Hestia, growling and snapping their jaws. Breksta raced over to help, but not before Hestia sunk twin daggers into the wolves' skulls.

Her eyes flamed as she pulled the daggers out and glared at Breksta. "Stop your tricks, Breksta."

"I'm not tricking you," Breksta pleaded. "You need to stop killing the wolves."

Hestia managed one more hateful look before another wolf jumped up and knocked her over. Breksta moved to help her when she was suddenly faced with the wolf leader. The male's pelt was a dark, flowing black just like the goddess he served. He bared his teeth as he and Breksta stood at the base of the goddess's statue.

"I sensed your intentions when you entered," the wolf's deep voice echoed through the chamber. "And though they are noble, it does not change the fact that we have our orders and you have violated the sanctuary of our goddess."

The wolf leapt at Breksta. She slid out of the way, but not before the wolf's claws sunk into her leg. Breksta screamed and twisted, trying to dislodge the wolf's claw. She fell, her back slamming against the marble floor. She gritted her teeth, bending her knee before she thrust the blade into the wolf's underbelly. Growling, the wolf leapt away as the tip of the blade dagger cut a line across its chest.

"I'm trying to help people," Breksta said through gritted teeth. "She's dead, and you are doing her no service withholding the failsafe from the only person who has the power to use it."

The wolf hesitated and pondered her words. Its dark eyes blinked intelligently. "Perhaps you're right. But perhaps you're wrong. We have protected this temple for eons, against even her descendants centuries ago who had malevolent intentions."

The wolf pounced, and Breksta steadied herself to meet it. The knife met muscle, then bone, embedding itself in the wolf's shoulder, making the wolf howl with pain. Breksta pulled out the dagger. "I don't want to fight you," she pleaded. "I just want to help the Dreamers and the world. Just tell me how to do that."

The wolf's eyes flashed with rage. "Your words may be eloquent and compelling. But your violent actions speak otherwise."

Then the wolf and Breksta began their dance. The wolf lunged and Breksta defended, sustaining small wounds until she saw the chance and dealt a strong blow to the wolf, weakening it. During their skirmish, Breksta lost track of Icarus and Hestia's movements, but she trusted they could take care of themselves. The fight with the wolf had given her barely any time to think, but the wolf's last words gave her a thought. Perhaps her words were not convincing enough, but her actions could be.

She raised her hands in surrender. "I understand now. The failsafe requires something."

The wolf spoke again, "The failsafe comes at a price. For the power to change all lives, you must be prepared to surrender your own. To unlock her magic, you must give your own."

Although the wolf's words scared her, with a reminder of the sacrifice she might have to make, she swallowed her fears and persisted. She knew her purpose now, and she had promised her mother she wouldn't fail.

"I'm ready to pay it."

The wolf stopped in its paces.

"Approach the goddess's statue," the wolf's deep voice spoke.

Breksta let her dagger clatter to the floor as she approached the statue of the goddess. She stood unmovable in front of the empty bowl at the foot of the goddess. She uttered a quiet prayer to her mother and Nyx as she placed her hands on the bowl, leaving bloody handprints. She knew she had promised Aristotle not to use her magic, but there was no other way. She remembered Aristotle's training and concentrated on her center. She allowed a small fraction of her life force through her heart, her shoulders, and her arms. As intense pain set it, she gripped the bowl tightly and steadied herself. She pushed the energy out of her hands and opened her eyes. The bowl was no longer empty. Inside, was a small, flickering purple flame. From certain angles, Breksta could see her own memories flicker before disappearing.

"The goddess thanks you for your sacrifice," the wolf said, pulling its lips back in what Breksta thought was a smile.

Breksta felt weaker, but she smiled. She turned away from the statue and looked at the wolves. To her surprise, the wolves, including the injured ones, had formed a protective ring around her, baring their teeth at Hestia, Icarus, and the other cadets.

"What did you do?" Hestia asked with bitter hatred.

"Please, just trust me. I'm going to save everyone." Breksta said gently, "J—"

But before Breksta could finish, a purple glow began to emanate from the wolves and engulfed every corner of the temple. Breksta shielded her eyes from the brightness. Once the light dimmed, Hestia, Icarus, and the cadets were gone.

"What did you do to them?" Breksta exclaimed.

The head wolf turned to her. "They've been banished from the temple to the surface world. I sensed you didn't wish to kill them. As the sole passer of our trials, we now serve your will as well as the goddess's."

The wolf approached Breksta's side and nodded toward the stone bowl. "Your sacrifice is rewarded by the goddess."

Breksta found that instead of her energy, a small, pink, bell-shaped plant stuck out of a pile of dirt inside the bowl. Breksta pulled out the entire plant, including its roots, and cupped it in her hands. She smiled, and the wolf bowed its head to her.

"It was an honor serving you. I trust you shall bring great change upon the world."

With that, the wolves walked back to their places and turned to stone. Purple light whirled around Breksta as she grabbed her dagger, then it became so bright that she shielded her eyes once again. When she opened them, she was in the woods alone. She gasped as she looked around. Olivia lay against a neighboring tree, her head bloodied, and her eyes closed. The Academy plane was aflame. Breksta guessed it was Aristotle's doing, but he was nowhere to be seen. The cadets too were gone. She spotted the white sand on the ground, intertwined like serpents that formed a mandala.

"Aristotle?" she shouted. "I got it! I got the failsafe."

"I don't think he will be able to congratulate you on whatever silly failsafe you have," a cold and familiar voice spoke from behind her.

Breksta knew who it was before she turned around. The director stood with a gun placed on Aristotle's temple while a gag covered his mouth.

Breksta said through clenched teeth, "Let him go. This isn't a fight you can win."

The director didn't smile and spoke coldly. "On the contrary, I think that our odds are just fine."

The cadets stepped out from behind the trees. Hestia and Icarus bore disgruntled looks, most likely not too happy about where the wolves dropped them off. Although some cadets appeared to be injured, most were in good condition to fight Breksta.

"You don't understand the forces you are meddling with," Breksta said, leveling her dagger at the director in warning.

"You're in no position to make demands here," the director spat out.

Aristotle used his teeth to pull off the gag enough to speak. "Do it, Breksta. Plant it—"

The director bore the butt end of her pistol into Aristotle's spine, and he went limp to the ground.

"Stop this, and I won't have to use my magic on you," Breksta said.

"If you do, Breksta," the director replied, "he dies, then you."

The director gestured for another cadet to force Aristotle's unconscious form to his feet. "Your family has taken everything from me. I want you to watch him die. Just like your mother," she said with mania in her eyes.

Breksta held back her raging anger. The director was the one who had taken everything from her, and Breksta was the one who had to suffer. Because of what the director had done, she now had to endure the pain of the failsafe, the resurrection, and the toll it would take on her magic. She hated the director and wished for her destruction. Breksta walked backward slowly with her hands raised above her head until her foot met a hole in the ground. A ghost of a smile lingered on the director's lips, and the rest of the cadets stepped toward her into Breksta's trap.

"His death will be on your hands," the director said calmly.

Breksta glanced down and found that everyone, including Aristotle, stood on the white sand of the portal. She had no time to waste. In the blink of an eye, Breksta knelt and pushed the flower's roots into the hole.

"Nyx, I bid you. Rise," she whispered under her breath as the flower glowed a deep purple until a black mist surrounded them all and they fell into darkness.

CHAPTER 35

BREKSTA PEERED UP at the peach-colored sky adorned with marshmallow clouds. A luscious green field spread out in all directions behind her, while a snow-colored cliff above the sea lay in front. This place was like the fjords of Ireland that Breksta had dreamed of seeing one day. Her eyes pooled with tears, knowing her fate had sealed itself just as the portal behind them did.

"Where are we?" Hestia exclaimed behind her.

Breksta ignored her. She felt Nyx's power all around her. The energy and magic that Breksta possessed within seemed to be mirrored in the air.

The director looked at Breksta, for the first time with fear. "What have you done?"

Breksta turned and looked without any remorse at the director. "This is the end, Madam Director. You can't fight this any longer."

Breksta walked slowly toward the edge of the cliff, leaving a trail of blood from her injuries behind her. She sat on the ground and closed her eyes. This was the moment she had waited for. She blocked out her worldly problems, her past grief, and her memories. She focused solely on the energy around her that hummed in the air. She called the magic in her veins to finish what her mother started.

"You're a monster," Hestia screamed, making Breksta snap open her eyes. "You just wanted more power. You're a fugitive, but you were a part of the Academy once. How can you betray us?"

Hestia, Icarus, and the director prepared their weapons and faced Breksta. Breksta stood and turned with a tired slowness. She noticed a slight hesitation in Icarus, but her eyes were drawn to Hestia. She didn't want to fight her friend, but she would: for the world, for the Dreamers, and for the life she could possibly live after the resurrection. She sheathed her dagger and allowed the intuitive flow of magic to flow out of her fingertips. Her energy came from her center mixed with Nyx's energy around her. She dug her fingers into the dirt, summoning the dead that she felt around her. The ground erupted with glowing skeletons made of pure purple energy that clasped their bony hands around the cadets. Breksta already felt the toll of the power—the pain that drew life from her veins—but she continued. She was stronger now.

Afraid, Hestia and Icarus struggled and kicked against the skeletons whose cold, dead fingers pulled them down to their knees. The director seemed the most fearful and kept her eyes trained on Breksta. They had traded places. Now Breksta was the one who controlled the director. The only difference between the two was that Breksta had a greater mission in mind: the greater good of the world, which stopped her from wasting her energy.

"You see me as a monster now," Breksta said sadly to Hestia. "But I promise, I'm trying to help everyone. Just wait, Hestia. It will be over soon."

"You must stop this, t-this *madness*," the director said shakily, her eyes frantic and pleading. "Your mother killed my family, and you have twisted Hestia. If you don't stop this, I will kill everyone you have ever loved. I'm giving you a choice now, child. Stop this madness."

Breksta's eyes glowed purple with anger as she stared down her old fears in the form of the director. "I choose this, my destiny. Everyone I've ever loved has already been taken and twisted by you. I'm going to save what little I have left: my friends. *I* am going to make sure you can't hurt anyone again and that the world doesn't destroy itself at your hands."

With her back to the cadets, Breksta raised her hands to the sky to begin the resurrection. She directed all her energy toward the sky, releasing the magic she'd used to hold down the cadets, and directed it to call in the bits of consciousness that belonged to Nyx. Across the sky, Breksta felt the scattered, fractured pieces of Nyx coming to her. Nyx's fragmented consciousness was a tangle of intangible thoughts, whirling in Breksta's mind. Breksta could've drowned under the power of Nyx's consciousness, but instead, she called it to her like she called her own magic. Giving the goddess a direction to flow, Breksta began building the goddess's form. She opened her eyes as she watched the glowing figure solidify in front of her. The long cape the color of night became clear, and Breksta could almost see the goddess's face. But as the goddess's life took form, Breksta's life began to dissipate. Pain sprouted from her center and spread like a cancer to her limbs. She gritted her teeth to hold steady.

At that moment, Hestia rushed toward her, now free from Breksta's grasp, and tackled her to the ground, severing Breksta's magic from the sky. The figure disintegrated, fading back into the sky. To Breksta's surprise, Hestia pulled her pistol from her belt and pointed it at Breksta's chest. Breksta blocked Hestia's hand, pushing it to the left and sending the pistol flying over the cliffside. Hestia aimed a punch at Breksta's face while Breksta quickly kicked her friend in the stomach. Breksta took the chance to roll away to the side and faced Hestia, who now stood on the edge of the cliff. Breksta unsheathed her dagger and bit her lip against the agonizing pain. Hestia turned back with more anger in her expression than pain.

"Please, Hestia, why can't you see that I'm trying to save you?" Breksta said, wincing as she felt the weakness and pain of her magic in her limbs.

"I don't know who you are," Hestia retorted coldly with rage-fueled eyes, no longer the kind girl who welcomed Breksta to the Academy so long ago. "You escaped the home the Academy built for you; Icarus told me. You're a monster who needs to be rid from this earth."

Hestia's words cut deep and Breksta hesitated, doubting herself. Breksta knew the importance of this mission, to save the world and her friends on this earth. But seeing Hestia in such turmoil, with such anger, she felt it was her fault for not going back for Hestia. Breksta wished she could save the world and save her friend from her pain and anger. Such a life would be her wish for Hestia, and perhaps for herself if she survived. The thought of Hestia's happiness fueled Breksta to keep standing.

However, with Breksta's hesitation, Hestia took the opportunity to unsheathe her dagger, approaching Breksta with a hunter's gaze. "I won't let you destroy the world because of your anger, or your cowardice, or whatever it is you feel in your empty heart." Hestia paused, her eyes softening ever so slightly as she spoke in a quieter tone. "I ... I can give you another chance. I mean, the Academy can perhaps give you one. Then you can know friendship or any of the good things the Academy has to offer."

Hestia's eyes were angry, but her anger had lessened and revealed the kind Hestia that Breksta knew so well. Breksta relaxed slightly, seeing that the real Hestia was still there, even if it seemed that the current Hestia did not remember.

"I'm not giving up on you, Hestia," Breksta said with a gentle smile. "Don't you remember? You comforted me every time I cried after my mother died; you told me that we would be friends, and that we would always be there for each other. So now I'm telling you it's okay, Hestia. You don't have to fight for the Academy or the director anymore."

Something flashed in Hestia's eyes, perhaps realization or acknowledgment of the truth in Breksta's words. But just as quickly, it disappeared, and the anger returned. "You're right. I serve her," Hestia said bitterly, lunging at Breksta.

Hestia's and Breksta's daggers met each other with a hollow metallic clang. Hestia's strength overpowered Breksta, but because Breksta had trained with her friend for years, she knew how she fought. Breksta shifted her feet to the left and pulled back her knife to her side, making Hestia stumble from her own force. Hestia whipped around just as Icarus moved to Hestia's side.

"No," Hestia said, holding her hand up behind her. "This is my fight."

Icarus touched Hestia's shoulder and spoke, "Hestia, I think she is right—"

"No!" Hestia said harshly, pushing Icarus to the ground. "I won't allow anyone to follow her. Neither will I allow her to take another step. She's weak and won't be able to survive for long."

Breksta momentarily noted Icarus's change of heart. She couldn't believe that he was siding with her now, after his previous devotion to the Academy. She hoped that perhaps he could help with the resurrection in some way ... Before she could give another thought to Icarus, Hestia rushed toward Breksta and charged her.

Hestia struck first and swung her dagger horizontally toward Breksta's face. Breksta ducked and pushed her body into Hestia, knocking her friend off balance. Breksta knew that she couldn't survive this fight, injured and drained from the first failed resurrection. She would fight on the defensive until she could talk Hestia down from the fight. Hestia stumbled back and circled Breksta again, her eyes holding a calculated gaze at Breksta.

"Stop," she yelled, raising her hands in a sign of surrender with her back to the cadets. "Stop this."

Hestia cocked her head cautiously. "What game are you playing?" she asked.

Breksta shook her head, wincing. "This isn't a game. You're my friend, Hestia. I ... I couldn't hurt you. So please, stop fighting. We still have time to fix this."

Hestia laughed a cold, dark laugh. "A friend? Ha, I wouldn't dare be friends with the enemy," Hestia exclaimed.

Tears threatened Breksta's eyes. "Hestia, please—"

"No! Explain this to me. If we were friends, then why was I in the Academy, alone, and you, here, a fugitive? Why did you leave me?" Hestia shouted, brandishing her weapon at Breksta.

"I'm so sorry, Hestia," Breksta said, as a tear trailed down her cheek. "But ... this is the only way, best for everyone. God, I wish you could remember ..."

"Well, I remember nothing. Only that you have brought me great pain and anguish. But don't worry. I'll end the pain, right here and now."

"Hestia, I *promise*, I'm doing this for you, for Olivia, for all of us, and for the lives we deserved," Breksta said, shaking from weakness and pain. "Please, let me do this."

Breksta took a deep breath and dropped the dagger, holding out her hands to her one true friend. She trusted that the real Hestia still remembered. She had to. Breksta had known Hestia long enough to see that her friend had fought a valiant battle in her mind, resisting her mother and the Academy's control. Hestia merely needed to be reminded of their friendship, which was the one thing no one could take away.

Hestia stood an arm's length from Breksta, and the conflict in Hestia's eyes showed clearly. Where the girls held eye contact, Breksta saw a sliver of the real Hestia. The dagger that Hestia held in front of her chest quivered, as did Hestia's hands.

"You can stop fighting now, Hestia," Breksta said softly, reaching out to cup Hestia's cheek. Hestia shivered at the touch and kept the knife at Breksta's chest. But the dagger didn't move closer, and Breksta took that as a good sign.

"You are worthy. You are loved, even in your darkness, even in your pain. So please, you can put this down. Let me help you," Breksta whispered, using the other hand to push the dagger down by its hilt. Hestia didn't resist the action. Breksta smiled, knowing this was the beginning of peace and salvation for the world.

But the good signs were for naught, as the director sensed Hestia's coming betrayal and commanded, "What do you think you're doing? Finish her."

Hestia's eyes flashed, and all the remnants of gentle Hestia receded. Hestia plunged the dagger into Breksta's abdomen.

The dagger didn't hurt at first. It was the coldness of the blade that surprised her. Breksta stumbled back and clasped her hands around the dagger's hilt. Pain erupted from her center, shortening her breath. She felt an intense burning sensation, white-hot pain that spread through her body. Breksta's feet wavered as they tried to keep her upright. She looked at Hestia and was met with shock and coldness in Hestia's eyes, the two sides battling within her. Breksta realized this was the end. Her destiny was completing itself. She had no more time. The world was broken and divided, and even if Breksta saved it, it would remain so; this was humanity's nature. Breksta accepted her death with open arms, and she released her grip on the dagger, letting her arms hang loose as she sank to the ground.

Suddenly, from behind Breksta, two pistol shots rang out. Breksta turned her head to see Icarus hold a smoking pistol in his hand as the director and Hestia fell. Breksta screamed despite herself, kneeling at Hestia's side. But she realized that Icarus hadn't killed both. Icarus had shot Hestia's lower calf, while the director had a seeping red hole in her forehead, just like Breksta's mother.

Icarus looked to Breksta with a pleading expression. "That's for my parents. Now my mother and I can be free of her, Breksta. Use your magic. Save us."

Breksta nodded, whispering a soft goodbye to her friend as she summoned her magic. She knew she couldn't complete the ritual, but she would do what she could. She was weak, and her energy was drained. She raised her hands shakily to the sky. This time, she didn't call the goddess to the ground to form her body;

she called the goddess to herself, to her body. She felt the strong magic and the goddess's mind course through her, causing her to scream in agony. But Breksta didn't stop. She called more and more of the magic, until every inch of her body was filled with Nyx's energy and all she could feel was pain. Her eyes were closed tightly, and she allowed herself to finally collapse to the ground.

The goddess's consciousness formed crystal-clear thoughts that echoed in Breksta's mind. *My child,* the goddess spoke in her mind.

"Nyx," Breksta whispered with relief. She lay with her back on the grass with the dagger still in her stomach.

You have done well, the goddess spoke kindly, her voice rich and musical.

"Can you bring the magic back?" Breksta urged, coughing in response to the exertion.

Yes, I shall do it now. Do not resist my magic in your veins. Let it flow.

Breksta nodded and shifted so her eyes cast up to the sky. She felt the goddess move her hand toward the sky and through her fingers as the goddess shot a mix of purple and galaxy-colored light. The stream of magic continued, and Breksta felt her energy drifting away. As her magic left, her agony grew, bringing tears to Breksta's eyes. But Breksta was too exhausted to even cry out. She lay there, writhing in pain, until finally the stream of magic ended, traveling through the sky to the ends of the earth.

It is done, my child. You have succeeded … at a cost, the goddess said softly.

"My friend…" Breksta murmured.

She is here. I have healed her mind, and the little one's, too, but you have little time. I will leave her a gift. Just tell me what it shall be.

Breksta swallowed, small tears trickling from her eyelids as she thought of everything she couldn't say, the promises she could not keep. She knew what Hestia needed, and Nyx sensed her thoughts.

I understand, the goddess whispered, and Breksta knew the goddess was smiling from within. *It shall be done. I thank you for your service, child,* the goddess said before disappearing from Breksta's mind.

Hestia knelt beside Breksta, turning Breksta to face her. Tears traced down Hestia's cheeks as she gazed at her friend, finally free of her bonds.

"I'm so sorry," Hestia murmured, her voice shattering.

Breksta smiled weakly but stopped quickly as the pain intensified.

Hestia slung her arm under Breksta and slowly brought her to a reclined position, making Breksta tremble in pain.

"I can get the knife out. Icarus, give me your jacket," Hestia ordered, opening her hand to Icarus expectantly.

"No," Breksta whispered as she looked up at her best friend. "I don't have much time."

Hestia shook her head, smiling a smile of denial. "You're going to be okay, Breksta. We can heal this."

Breksta grabbed Hestia's hand. "No. I allowed the goddess to use my body as a vessel," she said between winces. "This is the end, Hestia."

Tears streamed down Hestia's face as she chided Breksta, "Stop this! We-we'll save you."

"No, you can't. You've seen my wounds."

Hestia clasped Breksta's left hand and murmured in a broken voice, "Why did you do this? Why?"

"It's my destiny. And I would do it a million times again. I'm only sorry that I hurt you and Olivia and perhaps Icarus as well," Breksta said weakly.

Hestia's tears fell and sank into the ground. "What about you? What about *your* life?"

"My life was flawed and beautiful, especially with you, and my mother, and Aristotle … I-I'm not afraid, Hestia. I think that deep down, I knew this would happen," Breksta added.

Breksta raised her right hand to touch Hestia's cheek but watched as her skin began to glow transparently with purple light. The tips of her fingers had already begun to fade.

"I'm sorry, I'm sorry," Hestia sobbed, repeating the words like vows, as if each would bring Breksta back and keep her alive.

Tears dripped down the sides of Breksta's face. "You'll be alright. And you'll take care of everyone."

Hestia shook her head. "I don't … think I can."

Breksta thread her fingers through Hestia's tightly, her last bits of energy used to sear a new promise. "Please."

Hestia took in a shuddered breath before answering, "I promise."

Breksta lay back, her white hair splayed against the grass, and smiled. Her arms had begun to fade.

"Thank you … for being my friend, Hestia," Breksta said, her eyes bright despite the pain.

"And you, mine," Hestia answered in kind, matching Breksta's bittersweet smile.

Breksta's legs faded and turned into purple light that fled to the heavens. Icarus knelt beside Breksta as well, managing to thank her. Soon, Breksta's torso had faded and only bits of her face remained. Her last words left her lips in whispers, the final remnant of her life, "I … love you, Hestia."

Hestia's tears fell fiercely as she answered, "I love you too."

But it was too late. Breksta was gone, faded into the wind as purple light. The kind, brave soul was no longer at Hestia's side. Hestia let herself fall into the grass, crying out as her heart broke into small, fractured pieces that fled into the void of the ocean with Breksta.

CHAPTER 36

HESTIA WAS INCONSOLABLE from the moment they were spit out of Nyx's realm back to the forest, the plane behind them destroyed and still burning. Icarus still clutched his pistol in his hands, unable to let it go and properly process what he had done, what Hestia had done, and what Breksta had done. But at the sight of Hestia's trembling, writhed form curled on the ground, with tears streaming down her face, Icarus dropped his pistol and ran to her side. As he knelt by her side, she turned to him, her red hair plastered to her cheeks from the rain and tears as her bloodshot eyes stared into Icarus's. She paused, as if trying to hold the last bits of herself together before relaxing into his arms, silent tears continuing to fall. Icarus held her as she cried, trying to find words to soothe her grief, but found none. Around them, the cadets who had been left in the forest came out from behind the trees, confusion on their faces.

"She's gone," Icarus told them. "The director too."

Icarus felt Hestia tense at the mention of her mother. She seemed as if she wanted to say something but instead moved out of Icarus's arms. She stood and began backing away, her eyes a mixture of grief and disbelief as she bumped into Aristotle's unconscious form on the ground. At the touch, Aristotle awoke.

Icarus moved to help him up, the rest of the cadets tensing around him, some drawing weapons.

"It's alright," Icarus said to the cadets. Turning to Aristotle, he announced, "It's over now."

"Breksta?" Aristotle whispered hoarsely.

Icarus shook his head, gesturing with his head at Hestia's grief-stricken form.

Aristotle lowered his head. Icarus saw the twinkle of tears in his eyes as Aristotle whispered, "Poor child." Icarus didn't know if he meant Hestia or Breksta, but either way, Icarus agreed. He watched as silent tears fell from Aristotle's eyes. Aristotle didn't move to wipe them away.

Finally, Aristotle reached out and gently grabbed Hestia's hand. "I'm sorry," he murmured. Hestia did not speak but shook her head, as if trying to deny their deaths.

"Icarus," one of the cadets said. "What … what do we do now?"

Icarus remembered his mother in the Academy, who awaited his return. He remembered their goodbye, which Icarus had thought might be the last. But now he saw his mother's protection clearly, and he needed her to know that he understood and that he would protect her from now on.

He also recognized that with the director gone and the magic Breksta had done, the war was over—there was no reason to fight any longer. The Dreamers were just like the Academy—people who needed healing and peace and time.

"We need to return to the Academy," Icarus said.

The same cadet, with dark, tightly curled hair, retorted, "To do what? The director is gone. Her second is in shambles, and now we're—"

"We need to stop the war. I'll explain later, but the director was wrong. The Dreamers were never our enemy."

The cadets looked at each other frantically. The one with curly hair spoke again. "What are you talking about? They've been the ones who initiated violence and conflict, and endangered regular people. Now you want us to just let them go?"

"Yes!" Icarus commanded, his anger rising. "We'll make our way to the planes back down the mountain and go back to the Academy. If you want to go back to the Academy, you'll follow exactly as I say."

The cadets grumbled but were quiet. They had learned long ago to be mindless servants.

Icarus squeezed the injured, including Olivia and Hestia, into Aristotle's truck. They made their way down the mountain to the planes. He bade farewell to Aristotle, who made him promise to ensure the end of the war with Dreamers. Together, the cadets returned to the Academy.

Icarus, followed by a despondent Hestia, was greeted by his mother. Her innocent smile let Icarus know that she thought he had succeeded. Yet, as the cadets streamed out of the planes, Ms. Adams looked for the director. Icarus shook his head as he neared.

"Hello, Mother," he said, meeting her confused gaze.

She narrowed her eyes. "Where's the director, Icarus? And what of the mission?"

"She's gone, out of our lives finally. And the mission failed," he said. He wouldn't hide his truth any longer.

Her eyes fumed with anger. "Icarus Adams! How—"

"Our fight is over, Mom," Icarus said. The words of peace in his mouth felt nice, ringing with his father's memories.

Ms. Adams was stunned; she opened her mouth to speak, but Icarus silenced her with an embrace.

"I'm so sorry," Icarus murmured. "I'm sorry that you had to protect me, alone, without Dad. I understand now that you truly did it all to protect me."

His mother wrapped her arms around him tightly, his ribs crushing under her strength.

She didn't say anything for a long time. But when she did, she whispered, "Thank you."

Change wasn't easy in the Academy. It took months of lessons with Aristotle—who was willing to teach in the Academy and tell his stories for the cadets—to begin to break down the walls they had placed around their minds and hearts. Before they began, though, Icarus and his mother had to convince the other teachers of the necessary change, bringing Aristotle and a healed Mr. Fukushima to unveil the truth of the lives of Dreamers as well as Breksta's resurrection of Nyx and the consequences.

Some teachers caught on quickly and were set loose to teach the cadets the truth. It was during that time when Icarus noticed a change in the teachers. One evening, after spending hours in an old classroom breaking apart the causes of the attack on the White House, Icarus made his way to his mother's room in the hangar to eat. In one of the adjacent rooms, a bright green light flashed underneath the door, followed by a shout and a crash. Ms. Adams poked her head out of her room, and she and Icarus rushed to open the door.

The teacher was on the floor, his chair knocked over and his glasses crooked on his nose. Breathless, he looked at Icarus and then at the plant on his desk. Ms. Adams gasped. The once small cactus was now overgrown, possibly six feet in size and touching the ceiling. The edges of the cactus touched the bookshelf, preventing the shelf from falling.

Icarus moved to help the teacher up. "What happened?" Icarus asked.

"Well ... I was grabbing a book from my shelf. As you can see, it is over-stuffed, and I was trying to get out a book when I heard the nail on the wall give way. I reached out my hand to try and stop it, and there ... there was this green light! It came from my hands, and suddenly, this plant grew out to keep the shelf upright. I fell back in surprise ...What ... what is this, Icarus?"

"I ... I don't know," Icarus replied, obviously perplexed.

"Go get Aristotle," Ms. Adams said.

Icarus nodded. When Icarus told Aristotle what had happened, Aristotle smiled. He explained to Icarus that the resurrection had truly worked, and magic was returning to half the population.

After this first incident, many more followed, cadets and teachers came into possession of their magic. Aristotle's job then changed, and he became not just the teacher of the history of Dreamers but also a teacher of magic, like he had been to Breksta and Asteria and all his students before. And slowly, life began to thrive in the Academy. Soon, when Icarus, his mother, and Aristotle deemed it safe enough, they began to welcome Dreamers into the Academy.

Most were hesitant. Many were glad that the war was over and continued their lives far away from the Academy. But some, who were curious or wanted food and resources, eventually accepted the Academy's invitations.

Ultimately, the Academy became a haven for all, a place of life for students and teachers, children and parents alike. Icarus was satisfied. He was still curious about his father, and after asking Mr. Fukushima all he could, he asked Dreamers and Aristotle if they knew anything more about the senator. Some did, and Icarus carefully recorded their stories to form an image of the man his father had been. Gradually, as the year went on, he found that he was satisfied with what he'd learned. He learned, too, that he couldn't be his father and should focus on shaping the Academy into the future they were creating rather than dwell on his father's past. His mother noticed this and was pleased. He and his mother grew closer, in part from her sharing her memories of his father. They formed a strong bond and healed through their teachings at the new Academy. Although he was happier than he'd ever been, he was aware of Hestia's sadness and grief that lingered.

Her grief, once loud and raw, hadn't gone away with time, but she learned to control it. In the first months after returning to the Academy, her eyes were permanently red. Either Icarus or his mother got her up twice a day to shower, eat, and move around. In those early days, Icarus or his mother watched her as she ate, making sure she finished her food. They gave Hestia her mother's old room, hoping it would give her privacy in her grief. And sometimes, when Olivia and Sitara weren't in their new classes, Icarus would bring them to visit Hestia, hoping their presence would help. But at the sight of them, she burst into tears, reminded of Breksta's connection to the two girls.

His mother once brought in a doctor to check on Hestia. She concluded that Hestia needed help to process her grief. And so, three times a week, the doctor visited Hestia, speaking to her in gentle tones and asking questions, as she worked to help Hestia find her way back to the living.

In the beginning, Hestia was unresponsive. She didn't speak to anyone and would only nod or shake her head to answer. It was as if Hestia didn't want to stop herself from drowning, as if she wanted death to take her.

As the months passed, Hestia began to talk with Icarus when he visited her in the afternoons. One afternoon, after more than six months had passed, he posed a question, "What if you took that trip yourself? I think it would be good for you," Icarus suggested. During their conversation that day, they had talked about Breksta's plans to travel the world.

"Never," she whispered, pulling her blanket tightly around herself.

"Hestia…," he began. "Hestia … it wasn't your fault. She understood what happened to you. And she had her own mission … to fulfill her destiny, which I now know from Aristotle meant that she might not survive. She knew she was the one to restore balance, that it might cost her life. That was the price she was willing to pay. She didn't want to die, but she was willing to so the world could go on. She wanted a better life for you, and all of us."

He saw her face begin to relax, as if his words had thawed a frozen part of her.

"Do you think she wanted you to drown yourself in grief and not go on and live?" he added.

"No, she wouldn't have wanted this," Hestia murmured.

Icarus nodded. "You have to forgive yourself. Promise me."

Her eyes flickered with recognition at the word *promise*. And that was when Icarus knew she would find her way forward.

"I promise," she said.

"Now let's go see Olivia and Sitara. They've ended school already," Icarus said, offering her a hand.

Tentatively, she took it. He led her to the edge of the forest where the students were playing tag. Olivia and Sitara ran to her when they saw Hestia. And as they hugged her, he saw the first ghost of a smile on Hestia's face. She was healing, and so was he.

EPILOGUE

HESTIA STOOD AT THE FOOT of her plane, getting ready to leave the Academy a year after Breksta's death. It had been a year since her mother's death at Icarus's hand as well, and it had been the most painful year of her life. Olivia and Sitara were by her side, begging her to stay as Icarus laughed. Ms. Adams, Aristotle, and Mr. Fukushima stood to the side, watching her with smiles on their faces. Deep down, they knew that Hestia wouldn't return to the Academy, not after everything that had happened.

Once Sitara and Olivia had finished saying their tearful goodbyes, wrapping their arms around her waist tightly, Icarus walked toward her. His eyes twinkled with understanding.

"You deserve this," he said. "Just let me know if you need anything, ever."

Hestia nodded and wrapped her arms tightly around his neck. His hands found her waist as he returned the embrace.

"Thank you," she whispered, "for saving me … from drowning."

"You would've done the same for me," Icarus murmured.

Hestia pulled away, picking up her duffel from the ground and throwing it over her shoulder.

"Take care," he said, touching her shoulder gently.

She nodded in thanks. "You too," she said as she boarded the plane.

The group who'd helped her find her way back to life waved as she left, watching as the plane became smaller and smaller in the blue sky until it disappeared.

To her surprise, Hestia felt sad leaving the Academy. Yet she also felt freed.

It took a few hours before she landed her small plane beside Aristotle's house. Until now, she hadn't returned to Orcas Island. They had conducted a funeral in the Academy seven months after Breksta's death, beside the forest where they had built a new gate into the Academy. Hestia and Icarus had made a new sign for the Academy.

"Breksta's Academy," it read. And underneath the name was a small carving of Breksta with the words, "For Dreamers and non-Dreamers alike. For safety in our world, and for a place to dream."

Hestia had planned the start of her trip so that she would visit the island on the first anniversary of Breksta's death. She stepped off her plane, finding her way to the edge of the familiar road. She made her way along the beach and soon reached the end where she was met with a rock wall. She sat at the water's edge, taking off her shoes with her back against the cool stone and her feet pointed toward the ocean.

She gazed out at the horizon as an empty feeling settled in her chest. Breksta had brought back the magic, and once again half the population had magic, restoring balance to the world. Icarus, his mother, and Aristotle had grown the Academy, and it was now a place of life and a haven for all, Dreamers included. Hestia had begun to heal. She should feel proud and relieved, she thought. But she felt nothing, her emotions spent and tired.

Suddenly, the rock wall quivered beside her. She backed away quickly, watching as a small hole materialized in the wall. She peered in, and to her surprise found a crisp white envelope. She took the envelope, looking around quickly to find the source of the strange wall opening.

On the back, written in loopy letters, it read: "To Hestia."

Hestia ripped open the seal with shaky hands.

My Dearest Hestia,

If you are reading this, then you have found my last gift to you. Nyx ensured that you would get this when the time is right, and I hope it is. I told Nyx what I wanted to say as I am lying on this cliff. I don't doubt that I will die, my destiny fulfilled in the process. But I know that won't be a condolence to you.

When we fought, you were so angry and bitter and alone. I promised I would never let you feel that way. And I promised that I would go back for you. But I broke that promise. I have now completed my new mission, to save humanity, you included.

I don't know how you will feel when reading this. But I want you to understand that I accepted this mission with my whole heart and hope that the world will be there to thank me. Mostly, I feel that despite my mother's death affecting me greatly, I never did truly appreciate your presence in my life that helped me heal. I couldn't see past my pain in the Academy to truly cherish the laughter and memories we had, my dearest Hestia.

I certainly wasn't the best at friendship, leading you to trouble with your mother. But you have shown me that being kind and loving is true strength. That is why I love you the most. If I become a legend, then you are the one who taught me how to become one.

Before the resurrection, I hoped that I could still change my destiny, save the world, and live so you would never have to read this letter. I hoped that once this was all over, we could go and explore the world together, just like we always dreamed. Camping in the forests and lakes of Europe sounds especially incredible now. Such ethereal and sensory and simple pleasures derived from simply being in nature, breathing the fresh air, lying in the leaves of a forest; I miss those things dearly. And it's my hope that you get that chance to feel those things, for you deserve better, Hestia, and you deserve to be happy.

I know I will miss your birthday, so here is to your nineteenth birthday! I asked Nyx to create this gift for you so you will always have a small piece of me, a fragment of my soul, to remember me by.

This is for the promise I broke to come back to you, to stay by your side through thick and thin, and to protect you; alas, I have done none of those

*things. But now you will always have a piece of me, so I never break those
promises again.*

Love,
Breksta Vilkas

Tears fell from Hestia's eyes. She looked inside the envelope and found a
silver-black ring. On the inside, the small and lopsided words, "I Promised,"
were engraved. She slipped the ring onto her pinky, allowing the metal to warm
her finger. Within the curves of the metal, she thought she saw the whispers of
Breksta's purple magic.

"It's beautiful," Hestia whispered, to herself and perhaps to Breksta's spirit.

Hestia sealed the letter again and wiped away her tears, looking out to the
vast ocean of possibilities before her. She stayed there for quite some time, sitting
as the cold water that she had plunged into a year ago lapped at her feet. Hestia
touched the ring, twisting the small band of metal as she allowed herself to feel
her sadness. It was the growing darkness that eventually brought her back to
reality. The sun would be setting soon. She took in the ocean's air and the spray
of water against her legs. She would remember this—she would remember
this fondly.

As she stood up, she spoke to the world around her, and to Breksta's spirit,
if she was there. Looking down at her ring, remembering the echoes of Breksta's
words, she declared, "I … I'll go explore." Hestia nodded, sucking back tears. "I'll
explore the world, just like you wanted to. I think I deserve that. And I won't be
back … for quite some time."

A small part of her laughed inside at the irony. A year ago, Breksta wouldn't
have imagined that this was Hestia's life now. *No, Hestia thought to herself,
Breksta really did predict many things.*

Hestia knew that people couldn't offer to her what she needed now. She
needed solace and closure and peace, and she needed to find them on her own.
Hestia turned and walked to her plane, leaving the beach behind her.

"Goodbye," Hestia murmured, to the island and to Breksta, and finally to
her mother.

She had never truly mourned her mother's death, which was intertwined with Breksta's. But now, she needed to let it go, sending her grief into the sea with the foam and seaweed.

As Hestia departed and directed her small, sleek plane toward the rosy horizon, she marveled at its beauty. She touched her ring, a reminder that Breksta, in some form, was here with her. Hestia smiled finally. She was in no way healed of her wounds, for they hurt with every reminder of Breksta. Hestia wasn't sure her heart would ever be whole again. At times, the sadness was so overwhelming that Hestia wished she had drowned in the bay beside Aristotle's house or that Icarus had killed her too. But on other days, she knew that her life was Breksta's final gift to her and to take away that gift would be the worst disrespect to her dear friend.

As Hestia flew away, a simple pleasurable thought came into her mind. Wearing Breksta's ring, in a small way, meant that Hestia was taking the adventure they both deserved.

ACKNOWLEDGMENTS

I WANT TO THANK THE MANY PEOPLE who have offered little words of encouragement and shown excitement about my writing and my story. I appreciate each of you.

Most importantly, I want to thank my parents and my sister who kept me motivated about telling my story and listened to my long monologues about plot and character development.

I also want to thank my editor, Donna Mazzitelli, for guiding me through the completion of my very first novel and for the support she has offered to help me find the core of my story.

ABOUT THE AUTHOR

NATASHA QUAY is a high school student and writer. Along with her parents, she divides her time between Taipei and Seattle. Natasha has played violin since she was four years old and now performs with her school orchestra. She is also an avid reader, and some of her favorite books include *Little Women*, *The Plague*, and *If We Were Villains*.

Natasha began writing in middle school and plans to continue studying the craft and literature in the future. She hopes her book will inspire others to become more interested in the arts, literature, and the world of writing.

www.ingramcontent.com/pod-product-compliance
Lightning Source LLC
Chambersburg PA
CBHW031429240626
47154CB00001B/263